INTO DARKNESS

Anton Gill

IN MEMORIAM

Nicci Crowther (1950 - 2008)
Kunigunda Messerschmitt (1910 - 2007)
Arthur Nebe (1894 - ?1945)
Hartmut Schickert (1950 - 2008)
Anthony Vivis (1943 - 2013)

1

The staff car sped through the dull countryside on the short drive to the Wolf's Lair. Colonel von Stauffenberg braced himself. This had to go without a hitch. He dabbed sweat from his brow with a handkerchief. He mustn't appear nervous.

He was Chief of Staff to General Fromm. Fromm wasn't the strongest card in the deck, but his role - as head of the Home Army, with its bases in Prague, Paris and Vienna - was vital. Without it, they hadn't a hope of succeeding.

Fromm was with the other conspirators in Berlin. They should be able to contain him if he showed any sign of wavering.

Stauffenberg glanced at his watch. The flight from Berlin had been held up - it often happened now, there weren't enough planes and those that remained were worked too hard. Though they still had time to make the meeting, he needed enough breathing space to prime both packages.

He put his anxiety aside. His standing as a war-hero and trusted executive officer - now that his wounds had removed him from active service - placed him above suspicion - as long as he trod carefully; as they lurched from one disaster to another, paranoia was rife in the High Command. The enemy had launched their D-Day offensive a month earlier, and the American troops were fresh, well-fed, and well-armed.

As the car swept over a low hill, the young colonel saw the outer gates of the compound ahead. The muscles in his face tightened. He'd have given his eye teeth for one last cigarette...

He scanned the area as they approached. The amount of building work going on no longer surprised him - he was no stranger to the Wolf's Lair - but it flew in the face of reason. The war was lost, and they were still expanding the Führer's secret HQ in the Masurian countryside. Hitler's dreams of the divine intervention which would confirm his ultimate victory overrode any other consideration.

2

There were delays at both the outer and inner checkpoints. The SS corporals pored over his papers with needle eyes, though his face was well known to most of them. Then at last they were in the central compound.

A knot of officers awaited him. Stauffenberg climbed out of the car and exchanged salutes, shook hands.

Field-Marshal Keitel looked up as Stauffenberg entered his office. 'You're going to have to hurry...'

'I know I'm late, sir, but -'

Keitel was flustered. 'The Führer's brought the meeting forward half-an-hour. And there's been another change. They're still working on the bunker. It's not ready. We're using one of the conference huts instead.'

'That can't please the Führer.' *Christ*, thought Stauffenberg - *a wooden hut*!

'Of course not. He values his safety. But he puts the Fatherland first.'

Stauffenberg was barely listening. His mind raced. Another half-hour off his dangerously tight schedule, and a wooden hut. It wouldn't contain the blast. Without the aftershock of the explosion rebounding off the solid concrete walls of the bunker, how could he be sure of success?

He kept his voice as level as possible. 'Has my ADC arrived? He flew with me from Berlin but he had... some business to attend to at the airfield here.'

Keitel glanced at him sharply. 'How should I know? Ask my adjutant.'

The adjutant directed a sergeant to escort Stauffenberg to a cramped office, where his ADC, Werner von Haeften, was already waiting for him. Stauffenberg breathed more easily when he saw the briefcase, which the lieutenant placed carefully on a table as soon as they were alone.

He opened it and took out a freshly pressed shirt.

'More wasted time,' Stauffenberg muttered as Haeften helped him shrug it on.

'We need an excuse to be here; they have to see you've changed.'

It wasn't a bad excuse. Out of respect for the Führer, Stauffenberg needed to freshen up for the meeting; but the manoeuvre ate into the scant fifteen minutes they had left.

Haeften dug into the briefcase again and carefully removed out the fuses, and the two precious one-kilogramme packages of hexogen explosive.

They worked as calmly as they could, but nevertheless fumbled in their haste - Stauffenberg thought that he knew more about the charges than Haeften, but his crippled left hand didn't allow him to work quickly enough.

They had one bomb primed and ready, but still out in the open, when there was a knock at the door.

The orderly sergeant put his head round it. 'It's time, Colonel.'

He disappeared again, noticing nothing, but leaving the door ajar. They could sense him waiting just beyond it to escort Stauffenberg to the meeting. They looked at one another. Both men were beginning to sweat. That was no good. It was a hot day, but there is always something distinctive about the smell of fear.

3

Haeften picked up the device, and slipped it into Stauffenberg's own briefcase. 'Once you've set the fuse you have ten minutes.'

'Sir?' They heard the orderly sergeant shifting anxiously from one foot to the other.

'What about this?' Haeften indicated the other package of hexogen.

'No time. Back in your briefcase. Shit!'

'Will one be enough?'

'Damn all we can do about it now. Just make sure the car's ready.'

'Anything wrong?' The orderly sergeant pushed the door wide.

'Bloody tie,' said Stauffenberg, trying to straighten the knot. 'Done now.'

'Sorry to rush you, sir, but you know what the Führer is like for punctuality.'

God had to be with them, Stauffenberg told himself, saluting Haeften and following the orderly sergeant out into the compound. How deeply he had prayed at Mass early that morning. It was in God's hands now.

As soon as he reached the crowded antechamber of the conference room he took off of his cap and belt, and, whilst fussing with some papers, he reached into his briefcase and squeezed the glass acid capsule of the fuse with a set of pliers, specially adapted for his crippled hand. The fuse made a tiny popping sound which stopped his breath for a moment, but only he heard it - the noise was drowned by the conversation of the men already there. One or two nodded a greeting.

He waited until the others had filed through into the conference room.

One final check. Then he followed them. Two guards took up their positions in the antechamber as he left it.

The meeting began just after 12.33pm.

4

The place was dominated by a huge map table with heavy oak supports, and surrounded by twenty-four senior members of Hitler's entourage. Only Heinrich Himmler, the head of the SS, and the head of the Luftwaffe, Hermann Göring, were absent. The Führer stood in their midst, sweating slightly. He looked up as Stauffenberg entered and gave a brusque nod. 'You're late,' he said, but there was no anger in his voice.

Forcing himself to breathe evenly, Stauffenberg looked round. The walls were of plain wooden planking. Sunlight found its way through the occasional chink, picking out motes of dust, which sparkled like tiny diamonds.

He made his way towards Hitler, found his place, opened his briefcase and drew his papers from it. He was about to place it on the floor, as close to the Führer as possible, when a keen young SS officer whom Stauffenberg did not know eased it out of his battered hand. 'Let me help you, sir...'

He could see sympathy and admiration shining in the aide's face. A man of perhaps twenty-five, looking at one of the heroes of the war. He watched as the young officer reverentially set the case down by the table support, on the side *away* from Hitler. The support was solid wood. How much would it cushion the blast? Well, there was nothing Stauffenberg could do about it now.

'I'd consider it an honour, sir, if you could find time to let me buy you a drink when the meeting's over,' the young man whispered. 'Our families knew each other before the war.'

'I have to get back immediately.' Stauffenberg looked regretful. 'There's a plane waiting.'

'Of course, sir.'

The young man took up a position about a metre behind his chair. When the bomb went off, he would be directly in the line of the blast.

Stauffenberg shook off the thought, glanced at his watch, thought of the fuse burning through. In this heat, it might do so faster. Ten minutes was a guideline. Too cold and they wouldn't work at all, too hot, and -

'Are we ready, gentlemen?' Keitel asked.

Stauffenberg was aware of Hitler's eyes on him. Had he seen the look at the watch? Had his ultra-suspicious mind gone into overdrive? But the Führer was preoccupied. There was a new battalion of Home Guard to discuss. They were raking every man who could stand on two legs into the Wehrmacht now.

'I'm sorry,' he said. 'I have to make a phone call first. To Staff. I'd have done it before, but the meeting was brought forward...'

'Get on with it,' Hitler said. 'Make it quick. I want you to report every detail of this to your dear boss General Fromm and his gang of penpushers in Berlin.' The Führer paused. 'Bloody shame, what happened to you. Need more men of your calibre at the Front.'

Feeling sweat run down his back, Stauffenberg slipped away from the meeting, leaving his papers on the table and his cap and belt in the antechamber as a sign of his imminent return. He prayed that Haeften had got the car, and sighed with relief when he saw it parked nearby.

Stauffenberg quickened his pace. 'It's done,' he said quietly.

'Get in,' Haeften said. 'Quick!'

'Any trouble with the car?'

'Nick of time. There wasn't one standing by for you. Had to throw my weight around to get this one.'

'Thank God you can perform miracles sometimes, Werner!' But he thought, it's a pity we have to have a driver. Couldn't Haeften have taken that duty himself? Or would that have looked suspicious?

The two men drove off at exactly 12.42.

***

They heard the explosion as they sped through the gates of the outer compound. The driver slowed for a moment as both his passengers started in their seats. 'Don't worry, sir,' he said. 'Didn't sound like much - animals blunder into the minefield around the compound all the time. Even a small deer can set one off...'

The two officers looked at each other. Even though the hut was a large one, near the centre of the inner compound, there were very few people about at this time of day, and if enough people shared the driver's assumption, it might be a minute or two before anyone responded. In any event, Stauffenberg thought, there'd be a few moments' confusion before the truth sank in. And the main thing was that they were out of the place.

He looked through the narrow rear window as the complex vanished round a corner. Haeften opened his briefcase and extracted the unused bomb. He opened his window, and, keeping an eye on the driver, threw the second package - about the size of a small book - into the dense undergrowth. No time to destroy the evidence, or conceal it more efficiently. But that wouldn't matter if they succeeded, or even if they didn't.

Either way, the die was cast.

There was a Heinkel 111 waiting to fly them from Rastenburg to Berlin. They took off, unchallenged, at 12.50.

Stauffenberg faced three hours without contact, without knowing whether his attempt had been successful.

'Please God,' he said quietly to himself. 'Please God...'

5

This was their last chance, thought Hoffmann. The war was hurrying towards its end and the Gestapo were at their most dangerous now. This would fuel their anger. There'd be a purge. Few would escape.

It was over. He stood in the middle of the room, collecting his thoughts. As soon as the call had come in, he'd raced across Berlin to the Bendlerblock, hardly believing that it could be true. So well planned. And by the best men - the General Staff, for God's sake; and yet it had failed. The key players had been arrested before he'd arrived, so that was out of his hands. Hadn't they read their Clausewitz? 'Better rashness than inertia; better a mistake than hesitation'? The question now was, what to do?

General Fromm, a stocky man, normally used to throwing his weight about, now sat nervously at his desk, fiddling with a pencil. He said,

'What the hell do we do?'

Max Hoffmann turned away from him to the window. In the high ceiling, a fan turned, but the room remained hot and stuffy. Hoffmann wiped his face. Through a gap between the blackout blinds, he could see parts of the other two sides of the enormous grey building, which, with the wing he was in, embraced a long, rectangular courtyard.

The night would be a long one.

All the windows were covered, though a few spilled yellow traces into the gloom. The lights were dim in the office where Hoffmann stood.

The whole building wasn't generating enough light to guide the bombers. Not that it mattered. They'd taken to raiding in daylight. With sod-all to oppose them, the enemy had grown confident. A few outmoded Messerschmitts and Heinkels are all we have now, Hoffmann thought. He remembered the worn-out anti-Semitic joke of Göring's – "if the Tommies and the Ammis ever manage to fly over Berlin, you can call me Meyer." The *Reichsmarschall* was addicted to hunting. Berliners were calling the air-raid sirens Meyer's hunting horn, these days.

Several cars and a couple of vans were neatly parked at the far end of the courtyard. At its centre was a mountain of sand and a stack of scaffolding. God only knew what work they were doing here. General Staff Headquarters. You'd have thought it was big enough already. Especially now.

'What do you think, Commissioner?' the General insisted.

'It's a delicate situation,' Hoffmann said, not turning back. The courtyard was busier than it would usually have been at this time of night. Men, some in uniform, others in dark suits, emerged from the entrances which punctuated the building and darted across black cobblestones to dive into other doorways. Most carried briefcases, but there was also a handful of SS soldiers with guns. As Hoffmann watched, three men in raincoats hustled a fourth, who wore the uniform of the General Staff, into one of the cars, and drove off through the big gateway leading out of the complex to the city.

If you listened hard, you could hear the distant rumble of tanks.

Hoffmann turned back to the room, loosening his tie. He had to say something to the General. The man was losing his grip. Not just any general, either, which made it trickier. No-one in the High Command was in the habit of asking the opinion of a mere policeman, even one as elevated as Hoffmann. It was a question of etiquette.

It was high summer, and the weather had leant heavily on everyone all day. At dusk, a light breeze had brought relief, but that was gone, and everyone was uncomfortable in the stillness. Fromm's tunic, undone at the throat, revealed a leathery neck.

'Well?' asked General Fromm. His fingers were slippery with sweat. He put the pencil down, and lit a cigarette. Hoffmann knew that the General was thinking of his future. He'd been in the building the whole time, with the conspirators. Who could tell whether or not suspicion might fall on him? Would they see him as a prisoner or a fellow-conspirator? He needed an ally.

The office was well furnished. The General's desk and chair were mahogany. There were two leather armchairs, a boxwood filing cabinet, and an elm coffee table. Along one wall was a sideboard containing glasses and, Hoffmann guessed, looking at the General's florid face, a solid supply of drink. Above it, a rectangle of wallpaper was paler than the rest. The picture that had hung there leant against the sideboard, its back to the room. Hitler's portrait. No-one had thought of putting it back up yet.

By the sideboard stood a thin man of sixty, the General's orderly, in a crisp waiter's jacket with golden epaulettes. He was staring into space, but he was alert. Hoffmann wondered what he thought of it all. Probably just wanted to keep his head down until it was over, like most people. Beyond the desk, a doorway led to the corridor.

The office was connected to a larger room, a boardroom, by high double doors, now open. The windows of this adjacent room gave a restricted view of the river. Hoffmann leaned against the door-jamb and looked in. The General stood up and joined him, not standing too close. Hoffmann was a head taller. The General didn't like it.

Near them in the boardroom, either side of the doors, were two small desks where two women clerks sat at typewriters, over which reading-lamps hunched, offering the only illumination. The women sat ready to type any possible interrogation. They were too scared to be bored. At one end of the large shining table in the centre sat a small group of men, guarded by an edgy trio of teenaged soldiers commanded by a corporal, all in black uniforms that didn't fit too well. Most of the prisoners wore the uniform of the General Staff. The red trouser-stripes looked grey in the dull light.

One of them, a colonel, an aristocratic man in his mid-thirties, bearing old injuries that could only have been sustained in action, sat slightly apart. His right hand was gone, his left badly crippled, and he wore an eye-patch. He looked up sharply as he sensed Hoffmann watching him. Hoffmann looked away. He wanted no eye contact, for Hoffmann knew him: Colonel Claus Philipp Maria Graf Shenk von Stauffenberg. The war hero. The man upon whom the whole success of the enterprise had hung, he knew; the others had, he supposed, not dared act without him. They'd lost hours waiting for him to get back to Berlin after the bomb to kill Hitler had been set.

In a corner, beyond the table and under the windows, a body lay, covered by an army blanket. Hoffmann wondered why it had not been removed. Blood had seeped through the blanket, leaving three oval stains, which had ceased to spread some time ago. Four flies buzzed around the body, one or other of them continually settling briefly on one or other of the stains.

6

Hoffmann looked at his watch: 23.00. 'What time did you place them under arrest?'

'I've told you already, and I can't be more precise than I have been. As soon as someone managed to get a call through to the outside and the first SS reinforcements arrived, with a unit of Gestapo in tow of course. Damn it man, they had *me* under arrest themselves until then.'

'So you say.' Hoffmann's tone remained polite.

The General didn't like this cop, with his big nose and his heavy moustache. Knew him slightly. Nodding acquaintance. Cocktail parties. Looked like a night-club bouncer. How he had got as far as he had, was beyond Fromm, though the General wished now that he had cultivated the bugger more.

'I was outnumbered. No-one had any idea what was going on. It was a farce. Buggers running around like headless chickens, even the SS, until they finally managed to gain the upper hand with that awful little Major. What could I have done?'

'How well do you know these officers?' Hoffmann asked, lighting a cigarette.

Fromm knew exactly what was behind the question; it was insolent: the man suspected him of collusion.

'Hardly at all.' He angled his head in the direction of the body under the blanket. 'Knew General Beck in the old days, of course.'

Hoffmann turned away, and walked back to the window. The activity in the courtyard had subsided. Groups of SS stood about, shuffling their feet, as before, but now only a handful of officials scuttled to and fro. Hoffmann wondered how much time he had. He was tense and tired. It wouldn't be long before someone would arrive with direct orders from the Führer and take command. Some SS bigwig like Skorzeny. He'd have to act before then.

This General was scared. That was to Hoffmann's advantage.

He slowed his breathing, drawing on his cigarette.

Fromm followed him to the window, needing to know what to do. Hoffmann knew the signs from a thousand interrogations. But there could always be that last moment of stubbornness, or a panicky bid for freedom, that kept the sheep from the pen, the fish from the net, just when the fight seemed to be over.

'I find it hard to believe that General Beck was involved,' said Hoffmann

'He was their leader.'

'How do you know?' asked Hoffmann. 'He retired years ago. Thought his main interest was gardening, these days.'

The General spread his hands: 'I caught them red-handed. The coup was staged from here! They were only waiting for Stauffenberg to get back from planting the bomb.'

'I've read the report.' Hoffmann looked over the General's shoulder at the battered figure of the young staff colonel, his face in profile. He might have been sitting for his portrait. 'Couldn't carry off the coup without him here, could they? I'm sorry, General, but I find that hard to believe.'

'He ran the coup, yes. Beck was the planner. Beck's been involved for years.' The General babbled this like a confession. 'Stauffenberg was their front man. The one with charisma. The one the others followed, more than Beck. Beck's an old man. Was.'

'You are well-informed.'

'You haven't spent the whole day with them.' The General collected himself, needing to dissociate himself from the men in the other room. 'I may have been too lenient,' he conceded. 'I should perhaps not have permitted him to take his own life.'

Hoffmann looked at him. 'But you were old comrades. As you say, you knew each other in the old days, before the Führer came to power.'

'The same is true of many of us, Commissioner Hoffmann; but most of us are loyal.'

Hoffmann said nothing. He looked through the open doors at the body, no more than a vague shape in the dim light. He remembered Beck too, but he could not think about that now.

He lit a new cigarette from the stub of his old one, ran a finger round his collar to loosen it some more, and turned back to the General.

'It's a pity he couldn't have shot himself without help,' he said. 'No-one could then connect you with a spontaneous suicide.'

'I know,' muttered the General. 'But could I do? An old man. Someone we'd all looked up to for years. A former Chief of Staff, for God's sake. Surely the least I could do was let him take his own way out. Let him have some dignity.'

And escape the Gestapo, thought Hoffmann. He closed his eyes for a moment, taking refuge in himself, gathering strength. 'Three bullets,' he said. 'From three different pistols.'

'Beck used his own. A Parabellum. The muzzle slid off his temple. He was sweating.'

'And the Mauser? Who fired that?'

16

'One of my officers. A reliable man. He was nervous. General Beck, after all -
'

Hoffmann thought about the old soldier lying on the ground beneath the blanket, his head matted with blood and brain At peace after ten years of swimming against the tide.

He envied him. Where was this tiredness coming from? He had to shake it off. He looked at his watch again. The phone lines out of Berlin would be restored soon. How long had he been here? An hour? Longer. Before the call came which had summoned him here, he'd had a long, tense day himself, topped off with a frantic briefing before the drive to the Bendlerblock. At least his own police sources still worked.

'Then?' he asked.

General Fromm was unwilling to go over all the details again, but he said, 'My staff sergeant shot him in the neck. Used his service Walther. Severed the spinal cord. It was the only merciful thing to do.'

'Was that the soldier I saw with Beck's overcoat?'

The General was defiant. 'Fine leather. It's a tradition. It's what General Beck would have wanted.'

'What steps have you taken?'

'We brought the others here,' the General said sullenly. 'I organised a court-martial.'

'Indeed?'

'This is a military matter!'

'What was the verdict?'

The General looked at him, but said nothing.

'Must have reached it quickly.'

7

Hoffmann knew all about General Fromm. Head of the Reserve Army. A Berliner like himself. Professional soldier. Pragmatist. The plot had failed so he'd fall neatly back into Hitler's camp. If he could. Like most of them here. And now he was rattled. Good.

Hoffmann wondered if the General believed the Third Reich had a future. The enemy was swarming into France from its bridgeheads. Italy had crumbled. 'You're still the officer responsible for this mess,' he said. 'You have a lot to explain.'

'I believe we are still permitted to behave like officers,' General Fromm replied angrily.

But Hoffmann knew the General was unsure of his ground, because of his own senior SS rank. The Criminal Police had long since been swept up into Heinrich Himmler's enormous security organisation, which was why, when he was in uniform, Hoffmann wore that of an SS-*Brigadeführer*. No-one, not even generals, would stand up to the SS after what had just happened.

'Our Führer has just survived an attempt on his life,' Hoffmann said. 'The most serious to date.' He cleared his throat. 'The Fatherland stands at the crossroads of destiny. Our Führer would be distressed to learn that any of his officers felt they could not behave as such, at any time, let alone now.'

The General, outmanoeuvred, said nothing. Hoffmann knew Fromm was thinking: was the policeman going to report him for allowing Beck to shoot himself? Had he then compounded the error by appearing to criticise Hitler? But he was still a general, damn it, and loyal, thank God, and *he'd* made the arrests, so he should be in the clear. If only he could be *sure*.

As Hoffmann watched him, the General lit a cigarette and went back to his desk.

Hoffmann was content to let the matter drop. He didn't want to make an enemy of this man, who could be useful to him before the big guns arrived. He had to mask his impatience though, play the fish slowly, gamble with the time.

Hitler had survived Stauffenberg's bomb against all the odds. When order was restored, Germany could expect a whirlwind.

'There still remains the question,' said the General, recovering himself, 'of what we do with them.'

'What do you suggest?'

The General bit his lip. 'The SS have everything under control.'

'But you are still the senior officer.'

'I'm aware of that,' replied the General.

'We must move forwards,' Hoffmann motioned towards the men in the other room. 'Or would you prefer to wait until the Gestapo bigwigs get here and hand them over?'

The General had an idea. 'You said I was wrong to allow Beck to shoot himself.'

Hoffmann looked at him.

'But at the same time you say the Führer would not wish officers to behave other than *as* officers in a moment of crisis?'

Hoffmann inclined his head.

'So please tell me,' said the General. 'What would the Führer *want* me to do with my prisoners?'

Hoffmann considered, 'You've had your court-martial. Too late to change that.'

'Exactly.'

'And this is a military matter.'

'Yes!'

Hoffmann looked at his watch again. 'The Gestapo are going to cast their net wide,' he said. 'Many, many more than these men will be caught in it.' He looked over again at the staff officers seated at the end of the table. They could smell the cigarettes and were looking across hungrily; even Stauffenberg was finding it hard not to unbend. Hoffmann drew an unopened packet from his jacket pocket and walked over to them. He placed the cigarettes, and a box of matches, on the table. 'Please,' he said. Turning back, he suggested: 'Give them some brandy, too.'

The General hesitated before nodding at his orderly, who opened the sideboard and from it produced a full bottle and glasses, which he placed on a tray with two ashtrays - fastidious fellow, this orderly - and carried them to the prisoners.

One of them stood up, drew himself to attention, and saluted in the old manner, hand to forehead; there was enough light to see genuine gratitude under the irony. Another officer slumped further into his chair.

'Cigarettes and cognac,' murmured the General, feeling himself cornered. 'You realise what they will expect from this?'

Hoffmann looked at him. 'The decision is yours,' he said. 'You may be right about officers being permitted to make a dignified exit. And what else is left for them?'

The General drew himself up. 'Where is the senior Gestapo officer?'

'You don't need to consult him.'

'Forgive me, Commissioner; but of course we must. We'll need to use SS-men for the firing squad in any case. There aren't any real soldiers here, only pen-pushers.'

'I'll have him sent for.'

'Do you know him?' asked Fromm, a tiny suspicion glimmering in his mind.

'I trained him.' Hoffmann noticed the General's reaction. 'It's a pure coincidence that he's here; but I do know who he is. Do you imagine I would have come here without being briefed?'

He opened the door which connected the office to the corridor and admitted a younger policeman, maybe thirty years old. Bespectacled and shabby, he looked more like a schoolmaster than a cop. The General could see at a glance that he was too intelligent to be trusted.

'This is Dr. Kessler,' said Hoffmann. The General nodded distantly. The young man's dark eyes looked at him appraisingly, and he didn't like it. Kessler himself didn't like what he saw.

'Where is Major Schiffer?' asked Hoffmann.

'In the radio room, sir. I'll get him.' Kessler was gone in a moment.

'Are we going to drink your health, or what?' came a voice from among the officers at the boardroom table. The orderly, having deposited his tray, had been hovering, awaiting orders. The men had helped themselves to cigarettes, and the smoke curled towards the ceiling. Some were smoking in a leisurely manner, others urgently. Hoffmann looked at them. He knew they were afraid of using up the comfort too soon. The fast smokers looked jealously at the cigarettes remaining in the pack. Hoffmann wished he had another, and put what was left of his own on the table.

He looked at the General, who jerked his head at his batman. He in turn uncorked the bottle and, in a gesture of solidarity, filled the glasses to the rim. There wasn't much left in the bottle at the end of the round.

Kessler returned, accompanied by a man a couple of years his senior, dressed in a dark grey suit, immaculate, white shirt and dark blue tie. He was like a matinee idol, complete with a little brown moustache. He nodded soberly at the General. Kessler stayed by the door. The three others moved to the window and talked in low voices. The officers at the table smoked and drank, watching. The orderly stood near his tray. The women clerks and the soldiers fidgeted. Tension filled the room like gas.

It took barely a minute. Schiffer left the room, and in the silence those remaining listened to his footsteps recede. The General returned to his desk, but did not sit down. He took a cigarette from the box on his desk but left it unlit.

Hoffmann remained by the window, looking out. He watched Schiffer emerge into the courtyard with an SS officer. A unit of six soldiers formed up near the pile of sand, while three other men ran across to the parked cars, started three up, and drove them round to where the soldiers were, positioning them so that their headlamps illuminated the sandbank, like theatre lights on a stage.

Hoffmann crossed to the boardroom. Some of the officers were already on their feet. They finished their drinks and put out their cigarettes after taking long, last pulls on them. Their guards looked at one another. Their corporal nudged them to attention.

Hoffmann glanced at Fromm, but the General didn't look up. He stood by his desk, staring at something there. A scratch? A speck of dust?

Hoffmann spoke to the SS corporal: 'Take the prisoners to the courtyard.'

He looked nobody in the eye as the officers walked past him. But one of them whispered, so softly that he might have dreamt it, 'Thank you.'

8

One hour after the executions, Hoffmann sat at his desk at Police Headquarters in the Werderscher Markt. His head felt light, but the weariness which had dogged him most of the evening and night had left him. On the desk, among the stacked papers, stood a half-empty bottle of *Fürst Bismarck* in an ice-bucket, and an overflowing ashtray. Christ, what high stakes they had played for. What would he do now? He opened the drawer and looked at the pistol in it. Should he use it?

Not that. Not yet. But for the moment, nothing seemed real. Time to take stock, keep calm.

Once the firing squad had done its job, the sergeant-in-charge had picked his way between the bodies delivering the *coup de grâce* to each with an automatic. There was no need for this ritual, everyone could see that. It was done for the SS photographer. The dead men didn't look dignified. The bodies were shoved into a van and driven away for burial in a nearby churchyard. By the time the main body of SS reinforcements, led by a gaggle of panicky top brass, arrived to establish a military presence on behalf of the Führer, it was all over. The SS strutted, threw their weight around, but there was little for them to do. Hoffmann stayed long enough to make his report and to watch the General driven away under escort.

Opposite Hoffmann in his office, watching him think, sat a man in a tailored English suit, a discreet enamel Party badge in the buttonhole of its jacket. He was thin, neither tall nor short; balding, and stooped, as a person who spends a lot of time bent over books often becomes. He looked fresher than Hoffmann, though he, too, had been on his feet for most of the last eighteen hours. He'd probably taken time to shave and change, however quickly, before coming here. That would have been typical of Hans Brandau.

He'd barely sat down and accepted a schnapps before his questions started. Hoffmann took him through the details, his professionalism overcoming his own hammering heart: fear mixed with excitement, but useful to fuel alertness.

'Where did it go wrong?' asked Brandau. 'Did the SS - ?'

'No, they weren't there. Nobody knew.'

'Then how?'

Hoffmann spread his hands. 'They destroyed their own chances. I got a call - when? - mid-evening.' He rearranged some papers on his desk, and pulled a blue dossier from the top of a pile. 'Here it is. Thin enough, but there's not much to say. They cabled Berlin the news that the bomb had gone off, but it took three hours for Stauffenberg to fly back here.' He moved his shoulders around to get some of the stiffness out of them. 'Seems the people in Berlin couldn't do a thing without him. He pushed the file across the desk.

'Nobody here did *anything*?' Brandau asked.

'No. Panic? I don't know. Good news for Hitler.' Hoffmann looked at the man. He didn't need to tell him his thoughts. In those three hours the conspirators could have taken the initiative, whether Hitler was dead or not. 'General Fromm just sat on the fence, jumped back into the fold when it was clear the jig was up. Not that it'll help him.'

Brandau smiled sourly. 'Especially when Hitler finds out he had them executed.'

Hoffmann said nothing.

'It was on his orders?'

'Oh, yes.'

Brandau twitched briefly at the badge in his lapel. 'What about my people?'

'The Gestapo? You were represented. Major Schiffer was there before me. Fromm consulted him.'

'Where did he spring from?'

'I don't know. He doesn't work for me anymore. He must have been the duty officer.'

'I'll look into it.'

'Do we have time for that?'

'If he was detailed to be there on purpose, he's more important than we thought.'

They sat, for a moment, in silence.

Brandau looked at the bottle on the desk. 'Another?'

Hoffmann shrugged. 'Not me.'

Brandau looked at the policeman. 'How long have we known each other?'

'Ten years.'

'And still you don't trust me.'

'You're a lawyer.'

'We're both Party members. Show some solidarity!'

'You joined in '26 - you're a bloody newcomer!'

'And you're the bigger fool!' Brandau laughed, poured himself another schnapps after all.

'We're both fools. We expected great things.'

23

Trust wasn't a prime commodity in either of their professions, certainly not now; but they had learnt that a moment would arise sooner or later when it would become indispensable.

Brandau's lean face was cast into shadow by the light from the desk lamp. He couldn't settle, and shifted in his chair.

'The place isn't bugged,' said Hoffmann.

Brandau pulled out a leather case and waved it at Hoffmann, who said no. The lawyer drew out a bent black cigar from it, a *Krummer Hund*, and lit it. 'I am nervous,' he said.

Knowing what the lawyer's work involved, Hoffmann understood why.

'I don't like the idea of waiting,' said Brandau.

'They've blocked the main roads.'

'A man in your position - '

Hoffmann shrugged. 'No good. I'm waiting for a phone call.'

'Then *when*?'

'To move now would be madness. We're trusted.'

'Do you think so?' Brandau looked at his cigar, and dropped it in the ashtray.

Hoffmann reassured him. 'They'll put me in charge of the investigation. If there's anything left to investigate.'

'You personally? You're head of the Criminal Investigation Division.'

'None better, then.'

Brandau reached for the bottle again, but changed his mind. 'How many did Stauffenberg get?' he asked.

'A handful of senior officers. No-one vital. A lot more badly injured. Loss of hands, limbs. We're only getting preliminary reports.' He looked across the desk. 'Not your boss. Not Himmler. None of the top brass. They weren't there.'

'Well, the objective was to remove the head... '

'Hitler's fine. The blast blew his trousers off, I gather, but otherwise...'

Brandau laughed, stood up, walked to the window, looked down without seeing anything. 'All for nothing then.'

'Yes.'

The lawyer hesitated before asking his next question: 'What about Hagen?'

9

Hoffmann was suddenly quiet. 'Hagen?'

'He's there, isn't he? At the Wolf's Lair, with the Führer. I'm sorry, Max, but you must have asked yourself the same question.'

'It's likely,' Hoffmann agreed. He didn't want to think about Hagen now, but he couldn't avoid it. He tried to concentrate on Hitler's headquarters, deep in the East Prussian countryside. *The Wolf's Lair.* Who thought these names up? *The Eagle's Nest* - for God's sake!

Of course Hoffmann knew that Hagen would be there. Where else would he be? Not in Berlin, where the enemy's bombers were making it harder to survive every day. Bit of a wonder he wasn't in Paraguay already. But if there was still money to be made, why should he leave?

Hagen.

'He'll have covered his back,' said Brandau.

'He's a loyal servant.'

'Long time since I saw Hagen. Still look like you, does he?'

'Just the same' said Hoffmann. 'Mirror image.'

'I'm surprised he hasn't got out already,' said Brandau. 'He must know what's coming.'

'He'll have plans.'

'Do you know what they are?' Brandau sat down again.

Hoffmann looked at him. 'I can get good intelligence; but Hagen's inaccessible.'

'D'you think he might make for Paris?'

'Why would he do that?'

'Routes to Spain from there.' Brandau leant forward. 'The Boeselager brothers even got their bloody horse to Longchamps. And with the fucking Tommies already in France! If the Boeselagers could do that ... ' he trailed off, then added: 'It's something to consider.'

'That was ten days ago. I arranged the travel permits.' Hoffmann said.

'Took a chance.'

'They didn't carry my signature. Lifetime ago, anyway.'

Brandau, thinking of Paris, was on the point of asking another question, but changed his mind. 'I can't bear this waiting.'

'Everything's in place. Keep calm. We'll choose the moment.'

'I admire your faith. Personally, I doubt if the moment will be ours to choose after tonight,' snapped the lawyer.

In the outer office, the phone rang brassily. It rang a couple of times before Hoffmann's secretary picked it up. Had the young lieutenant not been at his desk? Had he been at the door?

They heard his voice, muffled, as he spoke. A moment later he came in, a slip of paper in his hand, which he gave to Hoffmann. Hoffmann dismissed him, glanced at it, and handed it to Brandau. 'What I was expecting,' he said.

***

It was a short drive from Werderscher Markt to Gestapo Headquarters in Prinz-Albrecht-Strasse. The night had become fresher with the approach of dawn. Hoffmann, in the back of the staff Mercedes, opened the window, and tried to stop his mind from racing. He wished the journey could go on forever, from nowhere to nowhere, always in transit, no stopping, no responsibility. Might it be like that after death?

The cobbled streets were clear of traffic. The first pencil-lines of dawn were in the sky. A handful of women, shapeless in battered overcoats and headscarves, carrying pickaxes and shovels and marching in a gang, were the only people he passed in the scant kilometre that separated the two official buildings. The women going to clear debris at some bomb-site. Hoffmann looked at them and the ache within him pulled at his body like a torn muscle.

Hoffmann knew how little he was liked among the people he dealt with. The Gestapo resented anything the Criminal Police had under its jurisdiction, and to keep his department independent and non-political, as far as that was possible, had been a losing battle until recently, when the Third Reich began to look a little less invincible than everyone had thought. He thought of the other departmental heads, in their black uniforms or dark suits. All younger, all with higher ranks, all filled with mistrust and envy.

One thing they held against him was that he came from Berlin. Born there. The rest of them were provincials. As for the Führer, he hated the capital, and its people, who'd never turned out to cheer him. That was one of the reasons he planned to bulldoze the place as soon as he could, to make way for the wedding-cake-buildings and grandiose boulevards of his pet architect, Speer. One of the Führer's first acts had been to tear up the lime trees from *Unter den Linden* to make a broader avenue for his processions. Hitler had always hated Berlin, and one of his first acts was to rob its greatest street of the meaning of its name.

26

To begin with, though, Hoffmann had swallowed it all. Well at least the Socialist part of the National Socialist German Worker's Party - that seemed to make sense at the time.

10

Hoffmann pondered this as they drove through the hammered streets. He had lived too long since Kara had died. He had lived too long with the two-sided life he'd been doomed to, or chosen. Many had shot themselves rather than go along with the demands of the regime. Few had decided to fight it. Was he a traitor, or was he still trying to be a saviour? It was too late to be the latter, and, unlike many, he'd never seen himself as the former; but there was still unfinished business.

His car drew up in front of the ornate façade of Number Eight. A well-scrubbed young man, with dark blond hair so heavily slicked with brilliantine that, in the light, it looked black, in a uniform so close-fitting he might have been costumed for a ballet, was standing in the main hall. Greeting him with a brisk salute, this adjutant led Hoffmann along familiar corridors to a massive oak door, on which he knocked, before opening it immediately and standing aside.

Heinrich Müller's office was a dusty mausoleum of nineteenth-century grandeur, a big as an apartment and far too large for the scattering of furniture it contained, though every effort had been made to make the contents seem imposing. The man himself was, as usual, securely buttoned into his own tight-fitting black uniform. The huge desk was clear except for a blotter and two telephones, but tables surrounding it bore towers of files. At a smaller desk in a corner the inevitable clerk sat in the island of light provided by his desk lamp.

Müller and Hoffmann faced each other across the room. Both heads of department, but only notionally equals. Hoffmann may have led the Criminal Division, but Müller ran the Gestapo's Anti-Insurgency Group, and, effectively, the whole shooting-match these days. This was a show Müller would be running.

Hoffmann looked at his opposite number, his face expressionless. Müller, an ex-cop, a bullying little man of vast ambition and fussy, aggressive manners, had always stuck in his craw.

Today, the Gestapo chief was less sure of himself than usual. He stood up at Hoffmann's entrance, for one thing, and came round the desk with his hand outstretched. 'Max,' he said.

'Heinrich,' replied Hoffmann, noticing that the little toad had scarcely sketched the Hitler-Salute in the air. Things were bad. Müller waved at an armchair embroidered with hunting scenes in red and green. Müller was always swarthy, but Hoffmann could smell cologne on him and saw that his shirt was clean and his uniform neat. The emergency hadn't interrupted his usual shit-shower-shave routine.

'No sleep at all,' grumbled Müller, 'Same for you?'

'Yes.'

'Cock-up. Fucking idiot Fromm. Schiffer should have stopped it. Did you speak to Schiffer?'

'Schiffer's not my man any more. And Fromm was the senior officer present.'

Müller wasn't listening. 'The Führer wanted them kept alive for questioning.' He gave Hoffmann a sidelong look. 'I won't be held responsible.'

'I don't see how you could be.'

'It was out of my hands. And yours. Can't blame Schiffer either. Useful man. As you say, Fromm, that fucking shit, was in charge.'

'Where is he now?'

Müller looked up sharply. 'In custody.'

Hoffmann knew how little Müller liked him. They'd co-existed somehow, all these years, colleagues and rivals. Not for very much longer.

Müller turned his back, and shuffled papers. Then he barked at his clerk, who came over and shuffled some more, while Müller paced in front of his desk. All this was clearly a pantomime, for Hoffmann could see that the document the clerk handed to his boss had stayed on the top of the first pile from the word go. Self-importantly, Müller ruffled it in his hands. Small, pale hands, covered in coarse black hair. 'This is a direct Hitler-Order,' he said, thrusting the grey sheet of paper at Hoffmann. He lowered his voice in theatrical reverence, but he couldn't keep out an edge of jealousy. 'He wants you at the Wolf's Lair at 09.00. Your plane leaves at 05.50. They'll send a car to pick you up.'

'For a meeting?'

'What?'

'Am I coming back immediately?'

'Of course not! The Führer expects you to carry out a thorough investigation.'

Hoffmann resisted the temptation to ask what purpose that would serve. Why was he being ordered out of Berlin? Berlin was where any investigation should take place. Or was this another of Hitler's whims?

'I'll take Kessler with me.'

Müller smiled unpleasantly. 'I thought you might. It'll be a reunion then. I'm sending Schiffer along too. As an observer for my department.'

Hoffmann wasn't sure that was good news.

11

Things moved quickly then. Hoffmann returned to his office to fill a briefcase with the reports Kessler had put together, before making his way home to pack his own bag (he'd never used a batman), shower (hot, for once, a miracle these days) and change into uniform.

He stopped the car at an Imbiss to snatch a vile acorn coffee and an even viler Knackwurst sandwich (made of what, for God's sake?), which, hungry as he was, he could barely eat.

He picked up Kessler and they drove to Rangsdorf aerodrome. There were things to discuss which Hoffmann preferred not to be overheard, and he would still keep some of the essentials from his Number Two. He had never felt that Kessler's loyalty was in question, but at such a time it was better to be discreet, and there was another consideration: he had no desire to hand over any information which could be tortured out of him. Moreover, he knew that Kessler was simply too intelligent to be trusted completely.

***

Kessler looked at his boss.

The crime was about as significant as you could get. He knew that even with Hoffmann's record as an investigator it would be unlikely that they would find any stones unturned by the SS. They had jumped to it, Kessler had to give them that. Stauffenberg's bomb had gone off, but as the colonel had feared, its effect had been muted. The hut had been wrecked and there was total chaos for some time afterwards, but Hitler and most of the top brass had escaped with their lives. A handful dead, some badly wounded. The Führer was shaken, but, physically, had suffered no more than minor burns and cuts.

According to the reports, one of the conspirators had managed to relay a message to the Berlin Staff officers involved in the coup by half-past one in the afternoon, but they had just waited another two hours for Stauffenberg to return. By then it was too late. Stauffenberg had done his best to rescue what was rapidly turning into a fiasco, but his efforts to keep the coup alive were in vain.

All that time, Hoffmann had remained calm and distant. Kessler wondered about that. He knew that his boss hadn't given up whatever battle he was fighting - he scarcely dared give it a name - yet. He knew how tenacious Hoffmann was, but wondered how much longer he could go on. Kessler knew better than to try to get any closer to him, in normal circumstances, than the unspoken limits set between them allowed. He was hungry to ask a multitude of questions, but realised that to do so would drive Hoffmann deeper into himself. Well, experience had taught him that Hoffmann would tell him what he needed to know as and when it became necessary.

They were all tired. More than tired. Despite his excitement, Kessler felt his mind drift, though when it did, he pulled it sharply back to the here-and-now. There was nothing he could do but wait and see, he told himself, though he could not suppress his impatience. And there was Emma to think about...

They arrived at Rangsdorf in good time, but the plane had technical problems. The aircrew and the ground-crew were shouting at each other on the tarmac, but no back-up craft was available. The passengers were obliged to sit in a canteen which had nothing to offer them except dry rolls and more ersatz coffee. Kessler's stomach would never get used to the muck. News of the delay had been telegraphed to their destination, but everyone was aware of the kind of temper the Führer would be in when he learned that his schedule would be thrown, today of all days. And Hitler disliked early rising.

Apart from Hoffmann, Schiffer and himself, there were half a dozen other men on the flight, all in uniform. Kessler was the only one in a suit. He had changed and showered since the previous night, but he was aware that he looked as rumpled as ever.

***

The repairs took half an hour. Hoffmann leaned back in his seat as the JU-52 taxied onto the runway. He glanced across at Kessler. He had been with him for a decade and was now twenty-nine. He had a brilliant mind, and the Führer still recognised the value of such things, especially where they concerned his own security. For all his efforts to shelter him, Hoffmann knew that the young man's life wouldn't have been worth a prayer otherwise.

As it was, Kessler had made Inspector without ever joining the Party. Interesting man. Straight into the police from school, bypassing university, disgusting his father, a features writer on the left-wing Berliner-Zeitung. Herr Kessler was gone now, of course, long gone. The news of his death had reached Hoffmann in a letter from the chief of police in Wuppertal, where a concentration camp for political dissidents had been established in a disused factory. Hoffmann only learned the truth much later, and kept it to himself.

At that time, Hoffmann hadn't been able to believe that the State could keep a prisoner for four days in a dog-kennel, and then, when he was released, barely able to stand, feed him on salt-herring smeared with axle-grease; and when he vomited, make him eat the vomit. Kessler still believed he had died of a straightforward heart-attack.

His father's arrest had, curiously enough, fired Kessler's zeal: a cynic might have thought that the son had buckled down to work because he knew he'd be watched, and didn't want to disappear into one of the camps they were setting up for people who tried to make things difficult for the Party in the early days. Hoffmann had kept him away from political work, and detailed him to the homicide and drugs unit; but Hoffmann had noticed that politics was a subject Kessler kept quiet about.

***

It was the first flight Kessler had ever made. He looked through the window, his tiredness dispelled by anticipation. The Junkers roared and shuddered. Most of the men on board had made this journey before, but there was apprehension in the cabin: would the thing shake itself to pieces?

The young inspector took off his glasses and wiped them on his tie. The chocks were pulled away. The plane jolted along the runway and pulled abruptly into the air. Kessler gasped. It amazed him that after all he had seen in the past ten years he could still lose himself in a new experience.

He watched Berlin recede beneath him, but his mind irresistibly returned to the work the next few days held, and, because she was never truly absent from it, especially now, to Emma. Whatever else happened, she had to be protected. At all costs. Kessler admired Hoffmann, but latterly he'd admitted to himself that that admiration wasn't unqualified; and these days one had to qualify loyalty with a sense of survival. Hoffmann was… what? Roughly twenty years his senior - in fact he knew exactly, he'd seen the files.

He looked out of the window again. Nothing but clouds below them now. They reminded him of the gentle winter hills down in the Allgäu his father and mother had walked him over during their Christmas holidays.

But he didn't have time for all that now.

12

Everyone on the flight was fighting sleep. Across the aisle, facing an elderly, clerkish SS-captain (the flight was full of desk-soldiers), sat Ernst Schiffer, hot in his uniform, his neck bulging over the collar. He fiddled with papers on his lap.

Hoffmann knew Schiffer wasn't concentrating. He tried to avoid catching the man's eye, failed to, and nodded, glad the noise of the plane prevented conversation. He remembered the day his former protégé had told him he was transferring to the Gestapo. What could he do but congratulate him? Fast-lane promotion, staff car, Party brothels, Scotch whisky, all the other perks. He wondered what Schiffer was thinking now. Did the man still believe it had all been worth it?

Hoffmann looked out of the window at his city, at the swathes of rubble the enemy bombers had already cut, at the ruined towers and crumbled walls. The Lancasters and the B-17s were doing Hitler's demolition job for him, but Hoffmann doubted if Albert Speer's mighty buildings would ever rise from the ashes now. Columns of smoke and dust moved like ghosts over the rooftops.

He tried to concentrate. He would sift through the evidence, but as the guilty men, the principals at least, had been arrested or killed, he could not see the point of this exercise. He'd have been more useful in Berlin. Which begged the question of how much Hitler still trusted him.

He thought about Berlin, disappearing now as the plane climbed through cloud. He thought about how it had changed in a decade, though the changes were easy enough to map after the short, hopeful, unstable 1920s. As a young policeman then, he'd known an open city. The world had beaten a path to its door, bringing dollars and pounds and francs with it, attracted by a downward-spiralling currency which made a foreign beggar a king there.

Too many memories to contain.

Hoffmann gave way to them. He had done well; he'd married, had a daughter, and learned how useful cocaine was when you were working twenty-hour shifts. He thought of the early years of the Reich, and of how Berlin, stripped within a year or two of its inner life and its most interesting citizens, had bowed under the yoke.

It all seemed to have happened to someone else, even to another city. The Berlin of 1944 and the Berlin of 1933. A blink of Time's eye.

The Junkers reached cruising height, and its engines settled to an even rumble. Cradled by the rhythm, Kessler's hands once or twice loosened on the papers in his lap and he started to give way to the sleep they all needed.

Hoffmann, looking around, wondered how many of his colleagues were seriously concerned about the attempted coup, except insofar as it might affect them personally. No-one with any intelligence, and these administrators were all bright, could think that the Führer had a future. But he was still to be feared, still had his loyal dogs. Everyone had his own interests at stake; no-one knew what would happen to him if the top man fell, and so the bastard survived. But that had always been how dictators managed it.

He thought of Brandau. His missions to Switzerland had started a year earlier. Hitler knew nothing about them, and, like Brandau, Hoffmann was counting on the mounting confusion to provide a forest for him to hide in. But he was getting tired of the game. He hadn't slept for twenty-four hours, and his eyelids drooped. He dreaded sleep, for it might betray him - he couldn't remember when he had last slept a whole night through - but now he fell into a flickering half-slumber.

His daughter's face came into his mind. Emma. He knew all about putting pressure on people through their families. They'd do it to him without hesitation. The fear woke him for a moment, but he was too tired: he subsided again. It wouldn't help to worry, and he had laid what plans he could.

His sleep grew deeper, the plane's engines faded to a murmur, and then ceased. He saw his wife. He seemed to be awake, and he saw her with absolute clarity, but her face was still. He knew he was looking at a picture of her, a photo he had taken on their honeymoon in Perthshire. She'd bought him a tartan tie: Hunting Fraser. Where was that tie now?

Ursula had been dead fourteen years. He remembered the face of a woman of thirty. The dead do not change. He had not even forgotten her voice, and they say that's the first thing you forget. Her smell clung to her clothes and for months after she had gone he would plunge his face into them, bringing her back; but it faded, blending with the lavender that scented her wardrobe and outlived her. He carried one of her handkerchiefs in his breast pocket, dabbing it with her perfume when everything else, everything personal, had gone; but then he smelt the same perfume on a woman he passed in the street and it became just another scent. He let go without forgetting. Grief is the price you pay for love.

She would have been be forty-four now. Even in sleep, still, the thought prompted him that if he'd done more for the marriage, they would have been closer. But he'd had a career to forge, and he was a selfish man.

Her face stayed a long time.

13

Hoffmann awoke. The elderly SS-captain was dozing. Schiffer glanced up dully from his papers. What was he reading? He had loosened his collar, and his right hand loosely clasped a damp handkerchief. Fighting sleep, thought Hoffmann. Two middle-aged colonels were conferring. One of them wore hair-dye, which was running a little in the heat.

What was going on in all those minds?

Suddenly he heard laughter, close to his ear, but it wasn't coming from anyone in the plane. He started; it had sounded so real. Though he fought it, he was falling asleep again without realising it.

Another face appeared, the face of the woman who had laughed a moment ago. The face was strong and in movement, a vivid memory, a colour film. Not looking at him, as Ursula's had, as if drowned, through a veil of water.

He could hear her laughter. He could feel her breath. But then all faded as quickly as it had appeared. He had scarcely had time to grasp it, none to savour it. In his dream he found himself complaining that it was unfair, that she should have stayed longer. Another voice told him that she was still there, and always would be.

He had no photo of her. But he would never forget her face or her voice.

He had mourned Ursula. Ursula too had died young, but at least she had died in peace.

Kara had died in pain.

There were more images, but now they were confused, coming from nowhere. Kessler chasing a leveret. A little boy running towards him through a garden. The almond-white body of a sixteen-year-old heroin addict, pulled out of the river Spree, lying on the bank next to the glittering water. Long dead, but still vulnerable. What he'd thought at the time. His first case. Never found anyone who knew anything about the girl. Then a mountainside, a dark green forest, a lake deep within it. Then nothing.

He plunged into other dreams.

The moon, a searchlight, lit the earth. No escaping it.

A copper star on fire in the sky, leaning over hundreds of people running across a compound. Dogs: dark, low shadows thrusting and darting amongst the crowd. From the crowd, a little boy breaks free and runs, fear in his eyes.

The eyes of the dogs.

Hoffmann was looking at a flock of geese. A flock of geese had replaced the people. The noise they made was deafening, but behind it you could hear the jagged roar of an engine, and a boy screaming as dogs chase him down as they would a hare.

Hoffmann woke up. He wondered how he'd been able to sleep, though sleep had brought no relief.

The plane's engines throbbed.

He was sweating. How long had he been asleep? Minutes? He couldn't have cried out, he hoped, for all was quiet around him. Kessler was hunched in his seat, his eyes closed, but his body somehow not relaxed enough for sleep. Around him, men worked at their papers, as Schiffer continued to do, or they talked quietly, smoked, drank schnapps, or slept. But what were they thinking? He had always been perplexed by the idea that you couldn't guess the thoughts even of the person lying next to you in bed, the person you'd just made love to, the old friend you were having a drink with. Experience had taught him how to sniff out lies when questioning a criminal, someone under stress; but how did you deal with the secrets of those you were supposed to trust, your intimates?

He knew how to veil his thoughts, keep them secret.

There had been other attempts on the Führer's life, and some had come very close to succeeding. He had been in charge of the investigations. This time, this last time, there had been a better chance than ever. People in power had wanted the assassination to succeed. The war, already lost, would have ended immediately, with some chance of negotiation with an unbeatable enemy, and no more deaths in the concentration camps.

Hoffmann thought of the enemy. American troops and tanks pouring through the breach in France. He thought of the food they must have. How fat the *Ammis* were. He thought of the artificial starvation in the concentration camps. Oh, God, he thought, if we had only killed him.

But they hadn't, they hadn't even had the balls to press home the little advantage they had, and it wasn't as if there was anything to lose. Now, people continued to go through the motions. He tried not to think of the long trains in the east, in Hungary, still rolling, taking the Jews to their deaths; and the pale officers issuing orders, unstoppable. His right hand rested on his service Walther. Why not end it now? But he knew he couldn't. He had too much to take care of.

He looked at his watch. 0730. He stooped for his attaché case, rested it on his knee, and drew some papers from it. He hated mornings. Always, for him, these days, they were a reconfirmation of hell, though sleep and the night brought him cruel dreams.

He would not sleep again now.

14

The wheels of the Junkers hit the sand of Rastenburg aerodrome an hour later. Hoffmann, ushered down a long corridor, underground, felt his throat wear dry, as it always did when he met Hitler. The man's temper had worsened with time, and, as he wasn't mad enough to believe his own propaganda, his ascending desperation made him more capricious. This time it would be worse than ever.

But he was mistaken.

The Chancellor, though greyer and more shrivelled - and his uniform, though well-cut, sat as always like a sack on the unhealthy, bent body it clothed - was in an expansive mood. He was jumpy, but euphoric. He was fifty-five years old. He'd cheated death for the forty-second time.

Adolf was still taking no chances. They met in the deepest of the underground offices, those built to withstand the most powerful enemy bombs, if the bombers ever got this far. Hoffmann realised that even if the conspirators' single bomb had gone off in any one of these ninth-circle conference rooms, no-one would have survived the blast. The solid walls would have contained the shock-waves and bounced them back on the Nazi High Command.

Hitler knew it too. 'The cunts would have got me if we'd held the meeting here.' He waved an arm at the concrete walls that encircled them. He spoke more loudly than usual on account of temporary deafness.

Hoffmann wondered if he had in fact damaged an eardrum. His voice was hoarse, but measured. The experience had evidently knocked the stuffing out of him, and the unusual bonhomie was a reaction to it. Hitler was still in shock. They had never got this close to succeeding before. The man's hair was singed, and one side of his face was bright, shiny orange. Some kind of ointment. He smelled of 4711 cologne, though that didn't disguise his stale breath. And Brilliantine. An interesting cocktail, good scents covering bad. It was unfortunate that he chose always to stand too close. Hoffmann, watching him, and resistant, after long exposure, to the famous charisma, could see nothing but triumph dancing behind the eyes.

'It was Providence,' the Führer continued. 'Providence that we had the conference in one of the huts. We had the builders in to reinforce the bunker.' He giggled at the workaday phrase he had used. 'Don't you think?' He didn't wait for an answer. 'Of course, they were cowards,' he plunged on. Cunting cowards! Or they would have stayed and gone up with me, seen the job done properly.'

Hoffmann remained silent. The idiotic political monologue had yet to be endured.

'And talking of cowards - ' Hitler had begun to pace. His back was bent, his wounded right hand clasped his left wrist behind his back. His left hand twitched, dancing in the air, as if trying to escape. It was cool down here but sweat had begun to darken the Führer's shirt as he hit his stride. Hoffmann wondered where the blow was going to fall. He wished he could sit down. He wished he had a cold schnapps in his hand. He waited.

'Fromm,' spat Hitler. 'He was there all the time. He had command. What did he do?' He waited, turning a burning eye on Hoffmann.

Why did everyone tremble at this fucking maniac? Why did Hoffmann himself tremble? He could reach out and break his neck, this minute. They were alone. Hitler trusted him. But Hoffmann failed himself. Why, after so long, and with so little to lose? Was it simply the fear of the torture?

'Well? You were there! Well?'

'They had General Fromm under arrest -'

'Don't make excuses for him!' Hitler hit the table in the centre of the room with the flat of his hand. 'He did nothing! He allowed them to take over! And then, after you'd arrived, he had them *shot*!'

'Yes -'

'And compounded cowardice with treachery.'

Hoffmann waited.

'He had them *shot*! He took it upon himself to give them a court-martial and then shot them! Without consultation!' Another pause. Then: 'What is the punishment for high treason?'

'Hanging.'

'Hanging! He should have held them until he'd got an order for their formal interrogation. He should have handed them over to the SS!'

Hoffmann knew what the hangings were like. He'd attended them often enough, in the nave-like execution chamber at Plötzensee, the guillotine - seldom used because it was too quick - to one side, like a stage property, the iron girder with its many hooks stretching from wall to wall three metres above the floor. He thought of the workmen who'd installed it. What had they thought when they were doing the job?

It lasted twenty minutes on the one centimetre diameter wire, if you were lucky. Naked men twisting in front of the cameras. Who were the film-makers? Who operated those cameras? What made this whole operation work?

'The SS were present,' Hoffmann said. Was he not one of them himself?

'Yes, some shitty little junior officers. Except you, of course, my dear Max. But in those circumstances it was Fromm's command. No-one, not even you, with the power to countermand him!'

'General Fromm was loyal.'

'Then why did he order the executions? Christ, I'm surrounded by fools!' Hitler had been making a bad-tempered tour of the room. Now he came close again. Under the cologne, close to, he smelt like an unventilated room. His skin was sallow, and two deep furrows ran from the corners of his eyes. A creamy gobbet of spittle clung to the centre of his lips.

'We are setting up an Investigative Commission. I'm giving it to Kiessel and Stawizki. I want to see how they make the rest of the traitors sing.'

Hitler interrupted himself, changed tack. 'I want you to go over the ground here. Pick up what evidence you can. The SS collected the remains of the bomb and the briefcase it was in, but questions remain. I want this documented. How they got it in, how they primed it. I want security recommendations. Some shitfuckers around here will wish they'd never been born. Questions?'

'I'll do as you say, Führer; but wouldn't I be of more use to you in Berlin?'

'I'll decide where you're of use. I think Berlin's in safe enough hands. And we don't need your techniques there. We don't need scalpels there, we need bludgeons!'

'Sir.'

Hitler paused, closing his eyes. When he opened them again, it was as if a cloud had passed. 'Don't worry, Maxie,' he smiled. 'I'm still in one piece, and once we've got the Persian oil we'll kick the Russians in the arse - I hear dogs are more intelligent. All we have to do is hold the Americans in the west...' He trailed off. 'And we'll have you back in Berlin in a couple of days, don't worry.' He shook himself, and patted Hoffmann's arm stiffly, smiling that tight smile again, his lips thin black lines. 'You're one of my best men. Clear up here as fast as you can. I need to see how they did it. Then go back and deal with Fromm. They've arrested him. Build a case. Not too complicated, there isn't time. Just fucking throw him to the People's Court!'

Footsteps outside, and a rap at the door. Hitler grimaced, tapping the air with a finger near his ear, and yelped an order. A pale SS officer entered - did any of them ever see daylight? - clicked his heels and saluted. Hoffmann's interview was at an end. He was aware of how seldom the Führer saw anyone alone any more, and was unsure how to interpret the honour; but after he had saluted and prepared to go, Hitler called him back, the sly look on his face again. 'Hagen will brief you further,' he said.

15

Hoffmann screwed up his eyes against the sunlight, but breathed the air hungrily. It was cooler here than in Berlin, but his uniform was too warm, and after the airless chill of the bunker, he started to sweat.

He thought about the Commission Hitler had mentioned. Kiessel was a glacial functionary whom you couldn't imagine ever having been a child. Stawizki had built a reputation over the past two years for his ability to extract information from a suspect within twenty-four hours, while still leaving them sufficiently intact to die slowly on the gallows for the benefit of the Führer's home movies. Neither was known for his investigative experience. There'd be mass arrests and many deaths.

And Hoffmann wasn't in Berlin. Two days now was an eternity. Why had he been sidelined? He wondered if he could risk ringing Brandau. Better not. He rejoined Kessler in the temporary office that had been consigned to them in a hut near the centre of the main compound. Kessler was reading the contents of a red file.

'This has arrived for us.'

'What is it?'

Kessler handed it over. 'Update of their preliminary report on their investigation here. The SS security unit did it.'

'Give us anything?'

Kessler shrugged. 'They've done a good job. I'd say we were scarcely needed.' He paused. 'The would-be assassins used a plastic explosive. One packet, just under a kilo. In a briefcase. They used two tetryl detonators and there was a time-pencil with a ten-minute delay. Completely silent. Interesting to know where they got that from.'

'We'd better find out, said Hoffmann. 'What else?'

'They found another, similar bomb - without a fuse - in the undergrowth just beyond the compound. The conspirators must have chucked it out of the car as they drove away. I guess they intended to use it too, but they were interrupted before they could prime it.'

'Two bombs would have done some real damage.'

Kessler pushed his glasses back up his nose. 'Two bombs that size would have done the job, even if the meeting had been in the open air.'

There was a pause. Hoffmann thought: why hadn't they just stuck the second bomb in with the first and prayed that one fuse would trigger both?

Kessler looked at him. 'How is he?'

Hoffmann remembered that Kessler had never met the man. 'He's making a remarkable recovery. Where's Schiffer?'

'He said he'd meet us here, sir. Had to go to a meeting.'

Must have been important, thought Hoffmann, as Schiffer was supposed to be keeping an eye on them. But it was perfectly possible that he had other agendas.

It was hot in the wooden block though the windows were open and a breeze was sweeping the compound from the woods. There was a table, around which stood three chairs. On the table, a telephone, a typewriter and a pile of paper in a tray. A calendar on the wall. 21 July 1944. Its only adornment was a quotation from Mein Kampf. There'd be one for every day of the year. Today's was: Thus did I now believe that I must act in the sense of the Almighty Creator: by defending myself against the Jews I am doing the Lord's work.

'What do we do, sir?'

'Get a list of the people who were in the hut when the bomb exploded, and find out who can be interviewed. Talk to them. And talk to the people in Communications. Who was working in the radio room at the time, if there are any left who haven't already been arrested. And get a list of all the men who have been. Where are they? We must interrogate them as well.' Hoffmann made for the door.

'What about Schiffer?'

'He can catch up with us. I want to know who's been arrested here.' A thought struck him: 'They should have given us the lists already. Off you go. And throw your weight around; we've got the boss's mandate.'

Kessler hesitated.

'What is it?'

The younger man looked at him and smiled. 'This isn't the time.'

'What is it?'

'I wondered how Emma was.'

'She's fine. You know that.'

'So -' Kessler obviously didn't know how to go on '- Nothing's changed?'

'Nothing.'

Kessler hesitated again. His eyes were dark. 'Sir … '

'What?'

'I'm on your side. I have to tell you that. Whatever happens.'

'I don't know what you're talking about. And you're right, this isn't the time. Now get on.'

Kessler nodded and walked off quickly. 'You fool,' he told himself angrily. 'You picked the mother of all wrong moments. You should have known.' But he also knew that he couldn't keep his personal anxiety bottled up any longer. Now he'd have to bide his time and let Hoffmann make his own approach. If he ever did.

Extra guards had been posted, and there was a cordon round the bombed building, which squatted, broken-backed, twenty metres away. The communications people would be busy, making sure everyone in the remains of Greater Germany knew nothing had changed. The war hadn't stopped; the fight went on.

16

Hoffmann watched Kessler make his way to the Commandant's offices. He looked around the scattering of buildings moored in the sand, between which men were hurrying with papers and briefcases under their arms. The wind brought a scent of cigar smoke. The scent of a good cigar in the open air. Hoffmann was reminded for a moment of the business quarter of Berlin in the old days.

The door of a hut near the innermost barbed-wire fence opened. Two men emerged. One was Schiffer. The other, in a dark suit, was tall, Hoffmann's height, and solidly built. He moved lightly. He carried himself like someone used to power. Schiffer had noticed Hoffmann immediately. He spoke briefly to the other man and hurried over to him, his boots kicking up sand. The other man stayed where he was. He rocked on his heels, and looked about him idly.

'Check the route from here to the aerodrome,' Hoffmann told him, brushing his apologies aside. 'And find the car that took the conspirators there, and the driver. Go over the car, and question him. Get him to drive you along the route. Slowly.'

'I think that's already been done, sir...'

'Do it again.'

'I'm here as an observer.'

'This is an emergency. You are a good investigator - at least you used to be. You're probably rusty, but you were one of my best men and there's -' He chose his words carefully, since he was well aware whom Schiffer might report them to: '- likely to be material the people here haven't picked up. It's our job to find it.'

Much as all his own police instincts were aroused, Hoffmann knew how improbable this actually was. The ground would have been stamped over by hundreds of feet, crucial evidence destroyed. And in any case the less they found the better. Not that anything they did find would change much now. He knew that matters had gone too far for any formal investigation to be worth shit. At best, Hitler wanted more material, more paperwork, to justify his actions to himself. The man still clung to the illusion that he was running a legitimate state, an attitude which all his close associates except perhaps Goebbels had long since abandoned. If police work was to be done, however, he'd see that it was, however futile its effect.

He squared his shoulders and walked towards the hut where the civilian stood. It had been years since their paths had last crossed. Hoffmann was trembling. He dug his nails into his palms as he walked. The other man's face was bland, agreeable.

Hoffmann found himself able to salute and shake hands. 'Hagen.'

'Commissioner. It's been a long time.'

The two men entered the hut together. Hagen closed the door behind them and waved at one of two wicker armchairs. Hoffmann's eyes sought out the stump of his enemy's left ring finger. The top two joints had been shot away, Hagen had explained, in a dogfight in 1916. In fact they had been sliced off by a flick-knife in a club brawl in 1921. The heavy signet ring he wore sat next to the stump, on the little finger. Hagen had never flown a plane in his life, and was no more a fighter ace than the cabarettist, Paul Linke.

The chairs stood either side of a low table on which was a bottle of champagne in an ice bucket. Two glasses shone in the sunlight. An electric fan cooled the room.

In a corner was a desk on which were an intercom, two telephones, a pen set and a blotter. A large photograph of Hitler on one wall glared across at a Werner Peiner landscape depicting robust, half-clad peasant girls gathering apples.

'Champagne? Or is it too early for you?'

Hagen's tone was exactly as Hoffmann remembered it. Bantering, confident, and faintly patronising. He wondered what Hagen and Schiffer had been discussing. Maybe Kessler would be able to coax something out of Schiffer. They were old colleagues too, though scarcely friends. Co-stars of the so-called Hoffmann Academy, the bunch of young cops taught by the master a handful of years ago. A few were still around.

'Dom Perignon,' Hoffmann said.

'1933,' replied Hagen in his plump voice. 'Not the best ever, but good enough to mark the occasion.'

'Which is?'

Hagen looked surprised. 'Our reunion, my dear Max.' He picked up a napkin and folded it round the shoulder of the bottle. 'Will you?' Without waiting for a reply, his tongue pushed between wet lips in concentration, he drew the bottle from its icy bath and wrung its neck expertly, at the professional barman's forty-five degree angle, so that the cork yielded with a gracious clop, and no wine was split. He filled the crystal flutes with all the élan of the Adlon's sommelier, and held one of them so close to Hoffmann's hand that he had to take it. Hoffmann looked at him.

Hagen suspected nothing, Hoffmann decided. Hoffmann must be a better actor than he'd thought. Unless of course it was Hagen who was the better actor.

'If we don't drink to our reunion, then we certainly must to the miraculous delivery of our dear Führer from the jaws of death.' Hagen's meaty but manicured hand grasped the stalk of his flute, raised it, and tilted it, ready to clink glasses.

'Why not to both?'

They drank, and sat down. They looked at each other. Hoffmann could read nothing but cameraderie in Hagen's sky-blue eyes. The face was rounder than it had been, well-shaved, and the golden hair and even the golden eyebrows were well groomed. He wore a lightweight suit of dark-blue English wool, a pale blue shirt and a burgundy tie with a paisley motif. His shirt-cuffs, projecting an even centimetre from his jacket sleeves, discreetly displayed thin gold links. The backs of his hands were covered in soft golden hair.

Hoffmann was used to taking in detail. Hagen's feet were sheathed in burgundy socks and highly-polished black brogues. There was not a speck of dust or a drop of sweat on the man. He was covered with a patina of wealth. He was an elegant, softer reproduction of Hoffmann himself.

The champagne was too cold, but Hoffmann couldn't taste it anyway.

'Cigar?'

'Wasted on me.' Hoffmann lit a cigarette and watched Hagen perform a fussy little ritual with a big Cohiba. Few people smoked in the compound. It was said the Führer could smell tobacco at fifty metres.

Hagen was untouchable, a man who believed in his own myth. Unless it was just that all these expensive props in some way served to justify the man's existence to himself. Hoffmann could scarcely believe that he was really there, opposite this creature, drinking good champagne. He wanted to take out his gun and blow the man's head off.

'And how did you find dear Adolf?' Hagen pulled at his Lancero and let the smoke out slowly through his mouth and nostrils.

'He told me you'd fill me in on the background details.'

'Is that so?' Hagen raised an eyebrow. 'Quite the joker, our Führer, isn't he? He told me that you were to interrogate me and that I should hold myself in readiness - his very words. But really just a piece of whimsy, wouldn't you say? To bring us together again?' He paused, enjoying his cigar, too strong for the subtle wine.

Hoffmann knew the man was buying time.

'How long has it been?' said Hagen.

'Nearly ten years,' said Hoffmann.

'Oh dear. And so much has happened since.' He raised his glass again. 'To the success of your investigation. We'll crush these General Staff bastards as surely as we'll crush the enemy.'

Hoffmann raised his own glass.

17

The apartment was small, neat, impersonal, and, above all, undisturbed. Hoffmann had checked for microphones, as he always did, before unpacking his case. Nothing. And no-one had been there during his absence.

The walls of the L-shaped living-room were covered with an unassuming collection of Dutch land-and- seascapes, all except the longest, which was hidden by bookshelves, untidily crammed with legal works, art books, and a handful of novels, plays and poetry. A copy of Shakespeare's Complete Works, in English, was sandwiched between Volume II of Schiller, and a copy of Goethe's *Elective Affinities*. There was also a number of permitted foreign works, by men like Steinbeck, Caldwell, Robert Graves and Thomas Wolfe, all pushed well back on the shelves, along with Voltaire, Calderón and Machiavelli.

The bookshelves dominated the room, which contained a fairly new sofa and armchair, and a cabinet containing bottles and glasses. There was a telephone on a small table near the door. In the foot of the 'L' was a small dining table, seldom used, piled with books and papers, and two chairs. The window revealed the apartment block opposite, beyond a row of sycamores, but if you leaned out and looked to your left, you had a distant view of Pariser Platz and a corner of the Hotel Adlon. So, not a bad address. The block Hoffmann lived in had one other advantage for anyone who valued their privacy: there was no porter. Porters were informers.

Apart from a small kitchen, in which nothing much more serious than coffee had really ever been made, and a slightly larger bathroom, there were two further rooms. A single bedroom, and a double - which Hoffmann used as an office. The office contained a desk and chair, and another bookcase which held dictionaries, a handful of religious works, an encyclopaedia, and several banker's boxes, each marked with a number referring to old cases, pre-1933, which Hoffmann had been involved in. A typewriter on the desk was covered with dust. The room had once contained a double bed, but some years earlier Hoffmann had ceased to have any use for it. In the single room was a wardrobe and a chest-of-drawers, each only half-full, and beside the bed a table bore another untidy load of books, together with a brass alarm clock, a bottle of aspirin, a soda syphon, a tumbler, and a small automatic pistol. A reading light with a green glass shade bowed over this collection.

His apartment. Not far from the office, and comfortingly impersonal. The kind of place you could lose yourself in, hide in, and at the same time close the door on behind you when leaving forever, without a trace of regret, though he would miss the books.

This place had never felt like a real home. Hoffmann had moved here after his wife's death, inheriting some of the previous tenant's furniture. These days he spent little time here, other than to sleep, read, and, occasionally, eat; but the eating was always done standing up, walking about, and the food was always brought in, cold snacks, bread and cheese, Knackwurst, a glass of beer. Coffee was a luxury now. He rationed himself ever more strictly as his precious hoard of the real stuff dwindled. Colleagues, he knew, laughed at him behind his back, called him 'the monk'. In his position he could have done as they did, for there was no lack of French champagne and Russian caviar, American cigarettes and English shoes if you had the money and the influence to acquire them. But Hoffmann couldn't take that advantage any more.

It wasn't the thought of the frozen men on the East Front, dressed in uniforms made of wood-pulp, drinking acorn coffee and eating their own dead horses, that stopped him. It was his life that stopped him. He had lost his appetite. There was only the game left.

Ten years. It had lasted too long for all of them. He remembered the first disillusionment. Then, struggling with the mental shackles of his upbringing, education and professional training, and not always succeeding, he had, with others, put on what his friend General von Tresckow had called the Shirt of Nessus. Something that seared your skin and would kill you in the end.

Hoffmann had received the message while he was still at the Wolf's Lair, from the East Front, encoded and sent on via his Berlin office, but still an insane security risk, given its contents, though no doubt his subordinates there thought it was something to do with the investigation. The news was that General Tresckow had killed himself.

Tresckow had tried to kill Hitler a year or so earlier. The bomb had been planted on the Führer's plane. It had failed to go off because at high altitude the cold had prevented the detonator from working.

Hoffmann thought of his friend, fighting a losing battle with the Russians on the East Front, probably guessing that he'd be a marked man now - he wasn't known for his uncritical devotion to the Führer in the Reich's darkest hour.

The officer who'd sent Hoffmann the news hadn't been discreet. The coding had been hasty. Only the chaos had permitted Hoffmann to read and destroy it before anyone else cottoned on.

Tresckow, according to the message, had taken the news of the Wolf's Lair attempt calmly. 'As God once told Abraham that he would spare Sodom if he could show Him ten just men there, so let us hope God will not destroy our country, because we stood firm for it. Not one of us can complain that we must die. Everyone who joined us put on the Shirt of Nessus.' Tresckow had gone out into No-Man's -Land, carrying two grenades. He knew that by ending his life in that fashion, he'd be reported killed in action.

Hoffmann had to go on living. He had business to attend to, and, not being an officer trained in the traditional Prussian school, he had no desire to die. Tresckow was scared of being tortured, and he was enough of a realist to guess that he'd crack. The toughest lasted twenty-four hours. That was the limit. Hoffmann knew that from his own experience. At least it'd been within his power to give the Staff Officers a clean exit. But that was the least he could do. They'd shared a common goal, a common - what? Guilt? Hardly that, it wasn't treachery to try to save your own country from evil.

He swept an eye over his bleak domain. He'd only been gone two days, but the air was already musty. He had to beat down sadness.

18

It was late. He switched on lights, unbuttoning his uniform tunic as he did so. Beyond the heavily-curtained windows Berlin, once a kaleidoscope of light, lay in darkness, hunched against another air-raid. And not only was the city dark, it was silent. No buses, no trams, no taxis, and, at night, no people. If you listened, you wouldn't even hear a telephone ring. This was a city on its deathbed, and the people on its streets in daylight walked like a people already defeated. The radio bulletins, with news of tactical retreats, victories in places no-one had ever heard of, and promises of ultimate victory based on such insanities as Persian oil, did nothing to change that.

Everyone knew the Russians were closing in, and the daytime air-raids were increasingly frequent and audacious. The Luftwaffe was a spent force, and the enemy knew it.

Hoffmann had called at the office on his way back and brought home with him a bundle of files. He put them on the coffee table, checked that the curtains were well drawn, switched on a reading-light over the armchair, and poured himself a brandy. Then he took the lid off a tobacco-jar which stood on the cabinet, and from it took a small twist of brown paper, one of many, and rubbed the white powder it contained onto his gums.

He paced the room, thinking about the reports Schiffer and Kessler had presented him with. There'd be typed copies for the record on his desk by mid-morning, but there was no sense in them other than the observation of protocol, because, as he'd expected, they'd discovered nothing new. Most of the officers at the Wolf's Lair implicated in the coup had been arrested. One or two had shot themselves. One or two were on the run. Hoffmann would have to cobble the reports together into something flattering to Hitler's ego. Well, he'd done it before. Perhaps that was the only reason he'd been called in. Perhaps the Führer genuinely still trusted him. But in that case, why had he removed him from Berlin at such a crucial time? He couldn't be implicated in the coup; he'd only arrived at HQ after the tables had been turned.

And the meeting with Hagen, difficult as it had been for Hoffmann to endure, had borne no fruit either, though Hoffmann found it profitable to discover that Schiffer and Hagen knew each other and made no secret of the fact. Hagen was what he had always been, a man who slipped through every net and climbed every ladder with ease. A moment would come when Hagen would jump off the Party train as it rushed to its destruction. Hagen was a survivor. But where would he run? Had he made plans, prepared his ground? Of course he had. And he'd been right about one thing: it had been one of Hitler's sadistic little whims to reunite two men between whom such hatred existed.

He sat in the armchair and pulled the files towards him. The slim dossiers of those who had disappeared during the two days of his absence. Hoffmann drank some more brandy. How many of these people would he know? Each file contained no more than a couple of pages, prepared in a hurry, but each represented a life. Hoffmann had brought home fifty-two. All these people had been at their desks forty-eight hours ago. Now they were dead.

The Gestapo had been busier than he'd expected. He worked methodically through the paperwork, the official reports replicating each other to such an extent that before long he was barely aware of any difference between the people who had been shot, strangled, found in the River Spree, who had fallen from high windows or rooftops, or who had 'committed suicide rather than face their crimes'. The majority of the files had their owner's deaths entered officially as 'natural causes' - fatal strokes and heart-attacks: cover-ups so well-known that their use was an open secret and even a joke. Many private citizens: a bar-owner, an archaeologist - who had been arrested because the Gestapo had confused his title with 'anarchist', as if he'd advertise such a thing - three doctors and five nurses from the Charité hospital, a bus-conductor, an undertaker. A number of civil servants and army officers too, as well as clerks to the General Staff and several secretaries.

There was no pattern, nothing to link these people either to each other or the coup. It was simply a purge.

He rose, lit a cigarette, poured himself another brandy, filling the glass. He took a long swallow and was refilling when the doorbell rang, once, briefly.

He looked at his watch: half-past midnight. Putting down his glass, he crossed the tiny hall. He knew who it was.

'Any company?' he asked immediately.

'No.' Kessler sounded surprised.

'Sure?'

'Yes.'

Hoffmann told himself that there was no reason why his subordinate should have been tailed. He was still a trusted senior official. No-one had bugged his apartment or his office. He was one of the men who authorised such things!

'Come in.'

Kessler took off his coat and bunched it on the rack.

'What have you got?'

The detective took off his glasses and rubbed his eyes. 'Two things. Hagen first.'

'Yes?'

'What he was discussing with Schiffer.'

'Yes?'

Kessler opened his palms. 'It was to do with technical supplies to the camps in Poland.'

'The labour camps, yes?' Hoffmann felt a familiar tightening of the stomach.

'They're expecting a big new intake. Hungarian Jews. Mainly at Auschwitz-Birkenau. Hagen is organising a trainload of disinfectant for the showers, to be sent there from Hamburg. It's for delousing the new labourers. The firm that makes it is called Tesch and Stabenow. It's a kind of gas. Hagen has an interest and collects a fee from the State as well. Schiffer was bringing him his orders.'

'I see.' Hoffmann knew all about the gas, and wished he didn't know what the news meant. How far away was the enemy? Could they not advance any faster? He looked at Kessler's face. Kessler was too intelligent not to know what was going on in Poland. 'And here?' he asked. 'What is happening here?'

'That's the second thing. They're preparing another round-up,' Kessler replied. 'But they're cutting us out as far as they can. This is to be a Gestapo operation.'

'How did you find out?'

'My assistant, Sergeant Kleinschmidt.'

'Trust him?'

'I think so. They're going to co-opt some ordinary police, just constables, to flesh out the numbers. They've already started.'

'Who are they after?'

Kessler shrugged. 'Big fish.' He took two sheets of paper from his pocket. 'Here's the list. Not complete.'

'Where did you get this?'

'One of the secretaries in Müller's office works for us.'

'And I didn't know?' said Hoffmann, angrily.

'No-one wanted you to be compromised.'

'You stuck your neck out. How did you find this secretary? Man or woman?'

'Woman, sir. She was in our department before. Doesn't like it over there. Says you can hear them in the cells at night.'

Hoffmann looked down the list. He closed his eyes. This was bad. 'Get yourself a drink,' he said.

'Thank you.'

'Everyone's on this list,' he said. 'How did they find out so fast?'

'They took a lot of people down to Prinz-Albrecht-Strasse for questioning. There's been a lot of singing.'

Hoffmann looked at the list again. People would be using the purge to settle old scores. It always happened. Everyone would be terrified now. Everyone would be yelping to save their own skins. But there were plenty of names that counted.

'There's a Commission,' said Kessler.

'I heard.'

'No courts-martial. People's Court.'

Hoffmann was silent. No-one was ever acquitted there. His thoughts turned back to Kiessel and Stawizki. Kiessel would gain a man's confidence, play father confessor. You always want to think the best of the guy who's got power over you, especially if his uniform's like yours, we're all on the same side, aren't we? And what a relief to talk to someone man-to-man, to unburden oneself, anything to get out of this room and back in the open air. And if they were stubborn, there was Stawizki. Hoffmann knew him, had had drinks with him, knew that his favourite dish was *boeuf stroganoff*, that he did a bit of market gardening, that he told jokes brilliantly. He'd visited him and his family - two boys, two girls - in their villa in Dahlem. But he was under no illusion about what Stawizki did. He had been obliged to attend one of his lectures. Stawizki had demonstrated the thimbles - his own invention - sheaths like miniature iron maidens that fitted over the fingertips and, when tightened, crushed them. There was a similar apparatus for the legs, and a metal hood for the head, which, when heated... Then there were the traditional methods, which Stawizki had refined: the rack fitted with wire, not rope, which was just thick enough not to sever the wrists and ankles.

'Sometimes you only have to show the subject the equipment,' Stawizki had said, as the slides clicked on and off the screen. 'You don't have to use it. But you must always leave traces to show that it *has* been used. Sometimes you don't even have to do that. Just arrest the family, parents, children, especially little ones, spouse, and threaten them. Nothing to it.'

Relatives. Emma.

19

'Are they going after relatives yet?' Hoffmann asked.

'I don't know. They will, I think.' The two men exchanged a look, thinking the same thought.

All means are justified when it is a question of national security, thought Hoffmann bitterly, remembering a note from one of his own lectures. And all that Himmler shit about bad blood running in families and having to be extirpated, so if the son is a criminal, the parents and the sister must also be judged and punished - hadn't he himself had to work along those lines?

He had been thinking about his daughter since the coup had misfired. Would Emma remain safe where she was? She wasn't the least of his worries, but she was young enough to pick up the pieces if she survived. Hoffmann hadn't seen her for months, but her letters, one a fortnight, never failed. Still studying the violin and still wanting to play professionally; but a year or so ago a new note had crept into the letters, and her manner when he got out to Nikolassee to see her had become, if not distant, then at least reserved.

He knew that doubts had formed in Emma's mind. She had grown up in a purely Nazi, purely Germanic world. She hadn't travelled, she had had to endure schools which taught hatred of Jews, mistrust of outsiders, and the essential superiority of her race. But she had kept her integrity. The aunt she lived with in Nikolassee, Ursula's sister, had seen to that, with the help of hidden books and music. A great risk, because children were encouraged to speak out if they suspected that anything didn't fit; but Emma from an early age had kept quiet.

Would it be best to leave her where she was? To move her risked drawing attention to her, at a time when the best advice to anyone remotely near the centre of the web would be to keep one's head down, and pray. Was it worth taking that risk? If he arranged for her to go to the country, might that not just be viewed in the same way as other privileged departures were being viewed? Unofficially, behind the Führer's back, a lot of serious money was finding its way into Switzerland, and people with influence were beginning to look to the great expanses of South America as - so the joke went - the new *Lebensraum*. Hoffmann had no such ambition for his daughter, yet; but he was a prominent officer of the regime and would have no problem with travel permits. One of his own sub-departments issued them.

It was far from certain that the Gestapo didn't already know where she was. The daughter of a high-ranking official, and close to Berlin; she'd be on the files somewhere.

A decision had to be made now. There wasn't much time left, and there was no-one better able to help him than Kessler. Kessler had known Emma since he was twenty, and she was eleven. He knew where she was, one of the few who did, and the only policeman, and he had not betrayed that trust. He had to believe that what Kessler had said to him at Hitler's headquarters was the truth.

Hoffmann refilled their glasses. 'I want you to do something for me.'

'Yes?'

'It's about Emma.'

Kessler looked up.

The problem was that sooner or later you had to trust someone. You had to take the risk, or you could do nothing at all. He knew how Kessler felt about Emma. He'd seen love grow between them over two years. Didn't some kind of future lie with them? Shouldn't he give that a chance? But was there a choice anyway? *He* would have to get away. He couldn't look after her any more. He knew the Gestapo would be on her track once he'd gone. He had to move her somewhere safer, out of Berlin.

He should have prepared for this better. He should have organised an escape. To Sweden. To Switzerland. To Spain; and from one of those countries to the United States. But he hadn't. He'd resisted. He'd staked too much on the success of the coup, and he hadn't wanted to lose her. He'd dreamt of a time when they'd be able to play music together again, his amateur clarinet chasing after her agile violin. He knew now what a selfish and sentimental vision that had been. He'd left this decision late. His last hope was Kessler. But he was trading on emotions. Risky.

'What do you want me to do?'

It was still hard to take the step. 'I may have to go away soon. I need to be sure that Emma will be in good hands.'

Did Kessler really love his daughter? Love her enough?

'What do you want me to do?' said Kessler again.

20

Hoffmann looked at one of the landscapes, one by Aelbert Cuyp, on the wall. A field with two cows near a gate, a city by the sea in the background. Ships leaving. How he envied their passengers.

'I think I can trust you.'

Kessler couldn't be deep-cover Gestapo, he told himself again. No-one could be that clever. No-one could get that far past his defences. Surely. He'd protected Kessler from what at the very least would have been a dead-end career, given his father's background and his own refusal to join the Party.

Hoffmann was aware of the depth of Kessler's devotion to him. But he was unaware that Kessler knew all about him. Kessler knew his most carefully-hidden secret, since Emma had told him, and Kessler was good at asking questions in the right kind of way. Hoffmann was a good policeman; but he was a good trainer too. He'd taught Kessler and many others, but Kessler had been the best. Hoffmann had been too busy to realise that a time would come when the chicks would be able to teach the hen.

'I'm worried about Emma,' he said stiffly, for this was hard for him. 'Many people who have nothing to do with the conspiracy are going to be sent to the camps or killed. I want you to make sure she's safe.'

'Whatever it takes, I'll do that,' Kessler said. He hesitated, and pushed his glasses back up his nose.

'What is it?'

'It may not be important, but there's something else you must know. There's a rumour that Hagen's disappeared.'

21

Kessler had not stayed long. After he'd gone, Hoffmann looked through the files, but finally given in to sleep. When he awoke, he drew the curtains and opened the window. It was still night. Rain was falling and the streets were slick, but the air was clearer than it had been and Hoffmann breathed it in gratefully. He had slept more than an hour, deeply and without dreams, waking to find himself better rested than he'd hoped. He washed in cold water, shaved, and changed into uniform again, since a day of official meetings lay before him. By the time he had drunk two small cups of his precious coffee, he felt ready to face the next round.

He was filling his briefcase with dossiers when he heard a gentle tapping on the door. An unexpected visitor, this time. Things were moving fast.

Hoffmann knew that the Gestapo would not knock like that. They would jam their fingers on the doorbell, they would hammer; and above all, they would have turned up earlier, between two and three in the morning, when people are at their most disorientated and vulnerable.

The rapping came again, quiet, but urgent. Now he recognised a pattern: two - three - two. Hastily, he went to the door.

Brandau pushed past him into the living room. Hoffmann could smell tobacco, alcohol and sweat. Brandau usually smelled of nothing but cologne, and his tie-knot was always perfectly centred in its snow-white collar. But he wasn't drunk, not in the least: his eyes were clear.

Hoffmann followed the lawyer. Brandau sat briefly on one of the dining chairs but, unable to rest, stood up again and paced the room.

'What's happened?'

'It's over.'

Hoffmann was ready for it. He hardly dared to think that he had got away with it for so long. If he felt anything immediately, it was relief. But his mind was racing. It had to be betrayal; he'd covered his tracks too well for anything else.

'Have you any idea how much time we have?'

Brandau poured himself a brandy. 'It'll take a while for the paperwork to go through. I misrouted it to Department Six. It'll take time to send it back from Overseas Investigations to Department Four.' He sketched a smile. 'It's just as well that our beloved State Security uses Roman numerals for its departments.'

'How long does that give us?'

'Four or five hours?'

'Good.' Hoffmann took a book from the shelves, Hölderlin's *Collected Poems*, and leafed through it hastily.

'When I was a boy...

...a god would rescue me

From the yells and blows of me...'

The photograph fell to the floor. He rescued it, glancing swiftly across at Brandau. He looked hard at the picture, then made his way to the kitchen, where he took out his lighter and set fire to it, crushing it into a bowl, and afterwards washing the black ashes down the sink.

'You shouldn't have kept that anyway,' said Brandau, not without sympathy.

'Gone now.'

'Last trace?'

'Last. Of all of them.'

'Photographs aren't people. Anyway, they're a luxury. Who has photos? '

'How else can you hold their faces in your mind when they are dead?'

'He isn't dead.'

Hoffmann said, 'I hear Hagen's buggered off.'

Brandau did not seem surprised. 'Where?'

Hoffman shrugged, but Brandau read the anxiety in his face, and read his thoughts. 'In his shoes, I'd be heading for Rio, not Bamberg,' he said.

'Not if he thinks he got unfinished business.'

Brandau paused briefly. 'And Emma?'

Hoffmann glanced at him. 'She'll be all right.'

'Got someone to look after her?'

'I think so.'

Hoffmann moved around his flat, gathering what he needed quickly and without hesitation, and packing it all into a small leather bag secured with two leather straps. This was a moment they'd imagined for a long time. The next step was to get back to the Werderscher Markt and pick up the car.

There were other things that they'd had to leave to chance - a motorbike patrol passing at the wrong moment, a phone lifted at the wrong moment - but, failing that, they knew what to do.

Hoffmann went to the bedroom and collected the little automatic from the table.

'How did they get to us?' Returning, he was buttoning his tunic, checking quickly round the flat. He scooped the contents of the tobacco-jar into his pockets, and swung his coat over his shoulders.

59

'They arrested our Communications Officer. He'd only been given all the names at the last minute, but they were all the key names. Obviously he had to have them; but he was a weak link, a bad mistake, young, only a captain, nice apartment, dependants, wife and five kids, one more coming, wife had got the Mother's Cross for breeding, everything to live for. They turned him over to Stawizki, who gave him a couple of turns on the rack, just enough to let him know how easy it'd be to separate his gut from his prick, and he caved in.' Brandau went to the window. 'They killed him anyway of course. And they've arrested the family.'

Hoffmann picked up his case, took a look round the apartment. He'd have to abandon the bundle of case-files he'd brought from the office. Not that that mattered. Nothing could help the people they concerned now, anyway.

'Come on,' he said.

22

The sky was overcast, you'd have thought it was autumn, and the silence was almost complete. They walked fast to Unter den Linden and turned east, making their way towards the Police Praesidium. There was no-one about, but guards, dulled by boredom and fatigue outside government buildings, pulled themselves to attention as they passed, seeing the tall man in the black uniform and the smaller man in the suit, who, they could smell, was Gestapo.

The road shone after the rain. A car hissed past them going westwards towards Pariser Platz. It glistened. Against the sky ruined buildings rose like dead trees.

'What about you?' asked Brandau.

Hoffmann looked at him.

'Where will you go?'

'Nothing fixed.'

'Why not come with me?' Brandau said.

'What would I do when we got to the frontier? Share your papers?'

'We could arrange things, once we're in the south.' Brandau spoke more softly. 'There are agents in place already.'

'Of course there are,' said Hoffmann. 'Even the Gestapo admits that. In Lörrach, in Freiburg. Two English, three American - ' He broke off, looked into the other man's eyes. 'You know why I can't go,' he said.

'Of course,' said Brandau. 'But look after yourself.'

It was too late, Hoffmann thought as they walked on in silence. No-one could oppose Hitler now. It was over; it wouldn't be Germans now who brought the Third Reich down. Perhaps it had always been too late. One thing was certain: the country would have to accept whatever shit was handed it when defeat came.

He looked at Brandau, who had rebuttoned his collar and adjusted his tie. The shirt was not as clean as the lawyer might have wished, but he'd managed somehow to regain his poise.

He was the one who really had to get out. The Americans in Bern trusted him, and believed his story.

How long had Hans been running errands to them from Himmler now? A year? Hoffmann thought of the bullying little head of the SS, a self-important jack-in-office invested with pseudo-mystical leanings and a sadistic streak. All that Nordic shit. It was a pantomime, little pricks dressed up in their minds like Odin and Thor. What masters they had served!

But not stupid. Himmler had seen the end coming long before the others, a good year ago, and sent feelers out to the enemy secret service almost immediately. Brandau had told Hoffmann the plan: Himmler would succeed Hitler - who was mad anyway, everyone knew that - negotiate a peace, save his skin, and sweep all the horror under the carpet. He'd even fatten up the people in the Camps, give them decent clothes, and then, but not until then, hand them over.

What Himmler hadn't known was that his go-between was offering secrets to the Yanks on his own account. Brandau, used to double-work by now, was putting it to good use to ensure his own future. And so far, so good. There were papers waiting for him at the frontier town of Lörrach. They'd get him over the border to Basel. From there all he had to do was ring Bern, and they'd come and fetch him.

He envied the lawyer. He was the clever one. He had no family. Lived alone in a smart apartment on the Königstrasse. Saw a classy whore - Helga - in a five-star joyhouse opposite the Hotel Esplanade on the rare occasions when the need took him. Only shared her with two other clients, both *Brigadeführers*. Had a tight circle of close friends, none of whom knew anything about him.

Thinking of Brandau's whore brought to Hoffmann's mind one of his own close friends - if friend was the right word. That old crook Veit Adamov, whom Hoffmann had got to know when he was on political surveillance, tracking communist agitators. Veit had changed his spots and survived the new regime by making pornographic films for the SS middle ranks.

They were good films with proper narratives, some of them based on the more earthy folk-tales collected by the Brothers Grimm, which was just like Veit, and not a bad idea at all, plenty of scope there for all sorts of diversion, you could even throw in torture and death; and he cast genuinely attractive stars. Veit enjoyed powerful protection, some said from Göring himself, and made his films right under the Führer's nose. Gone the Marxist documentaries he'd made in the Weimar days, when you could actually say something, even if nobody did anything.

When the change came, the famous Seizing of Power, Veit the Survivor took over from Veit the Idealist. Russia didn't appeal, so he hid his Marxism under his cloak, and protected himself by providing the men who sat around the conference tables and restaurants in Berlin, sending blood-soaked orders to the men operating on the bleak wooded plains of Poland, with just the distraction they needed. Escape. Drink and porn. But had Adamov got out? They'd lost touch in recent years and Hoffmann couldn't be sure that the man hadn't sold out completely. He couldn't quite believe that he would, but he knew Adamov would do almost anything to ensure that his own neck remained unbroken. Pity, he could have done with someone that resourceful now.

But now, Brandau was Hoffmann's only hope. Even if Hoffmann did get out, after his work was finished, he couldn't prove to anyone outside that he'd been anything other than a loyal servant of the Party. Only if they'd succeeded in killing the Führer would they have been able to drop the disguises they'd worn so long; but they had failed. Hoffmann had led seven investigations into attempts on the Führer's life. He'd fudged them, but he'd always been a passable actor. The Gestapo had been taken in. But why should the Allies believe him? And even if the truth came out, it would still look to the enemy as if he and the others had just been trying to hedge their bets, once they knew the jig was up.

There wasn't much to be proud of. But there was still just enough time left to create some good out of it. Some form of redemption. Until he had at least tried to achieve that, Hoffmann would not take either the cognac-and-bullet route, or try to save his skin.

A block from Werderscher Markt, on a quiet corner, they parted company.

'I'll pick you up by the river. Be ready.'

'I know where. And if you don't show?'

'Then that's it. I don't doubt you have a backup arrangement.'

Brandau almost smiled. 'How long?'

'Twenty minutes.'

23

Hoffmann walked through the courtyard of the Police Praesidium and climbed the familiar main staircase to the first floor. There were hordes of staff about already, more than usual, quickening their pace when they saw Hoffmann striding past. Christ, thought Hoffmann, Brandau had better be right about that misdirected report. He'd expected more warning than this.

He reached his office, where he dismissed the night-secretary immediately. On leaving, the secretary reported that *Gruppenführer* Müller had authorisation to requisition whatever *Kriminalpolizei* resources he needed. It was hardly surprising.

He unlocked his desk and, from the back of a drawer, took two cyanide phials. He checked the contents of the desk, and arranged a little disorder in the papers. Just to keep the bastards busy later on. There were few personal addresses. Those there were, he placed in the big ashtray and set fire to them.

Finished with his desk, he moved to the filing cabinets, and did the same thing there, creating disorder, and destroying the handful which he thought remotely likely to incriminate others. Then he pummelled the ashes to dust and threw them into the stove in the corner which was used for heating the office in winter.

He picked up the telephone. He looked up at the huge city map which dominated one wall. The switchboards would be incredibly busy. It was unlikely that calls would be monitored at a time like this. Crime never sleeps, and this was a golden opportunity. Who's going to worry about crooks when everyone's chasing traitors? No-one's going to trace calls from the poor old Crime Squad now. Or so he reasoned. Time should be on his side for another few hours. At least until mid-morning.

As he looked at the map he thought of the old days, when things had been simpler, just matters of murder and drugs to deal with. All the old gangs had gone to Frankfurt or Munich now, anywhere away from the east, because they'd known for months that the Americans would get Munich and the Russians would get Berlin.

Point is, calling from here is safe, and as far as people here are concerned, I'm still the boss.

He thought of Hagen, too, but there were more immediate things to concern him. There would be a car at his disposal. There was one standing by for him twenty-four hours a day. He often drove himself, a habit he'd established years ago in anticipation of just such a moment as this.

He placed his call and now the phone was ringing.

'Pick up,' he said to himself, looking at his watch.

Then he heard Tilli Cassirer answer, sleepy, irritable and defensive, until she heard his voice.

'Fais très attention au champagne,' said Hoffmann. 'Ça éclate ici. Je te joins dès que possible pour m'en charger.'

He listened to her voice for a moment, then hung up.

He went to get the car.

24

Though they'd changed details in the plan with changing circumstances, essentially it remained the same as it had always been. There'd been some question about whether or not to leave Berlin together, but together they would, in case of need, make an impressive-looking team, which would doubly secure their passage. On the road, away from Berlin, they should be able to pass themselves off as two Nazi officials sharing the burden of an onerous investigation, and their cover was aided by Brandau's independence of Müller's direct control. The police arm of the Gestapo didn't quite control the Legislature, and in any case later, by the end of that day, the day of their escape, when the truth would be out, it wouldn't matter anymore.

The Mercedes at their disposal was a hard-topped grey 770 with, as the garage sergeant proudly pointed out, a full tank. The sergeant was a small, oil-stained man who smelled of axle-grease and pipe tobacco. He looked like a miner. He could have been anything between forty and sixty. Hoffmann had known him over a decade, during which time he had not changed one iota. He was unaffectedly unctuous, and hoped to run a coach company once the war was over. He dreamt of taking tours to Scotland.

'Where's my usual car?' asked Hoffmann.

'Service,' said the sergeant apologetically. 'We did send a message.'

'Very well,' snapped Hoffmann.

'You'll find this one as good,' continued the sergeant. 'It's new.'

'Run in?' This was a stroke of luck. A new car, not his usual one. He hadn't banked on that.

'Of course. No snags. Don't worry, sir. It won't let you down.'

'Good.' And just that little bit harder to trace back to him, if he knew how the paperwork went.

'Be needing it long?' the sergeant asked as he filled in forms in his greenhouse-like office in the underground parking lot.

'Can't say.' Hoffmann signed four times, took the keys, and crossed the concrete to the car. It still smelt of leather. Hoffmann put gloves on, turned the key, pressed the ignition, and the big engine rumbled into life. He drove out of the garage and headed south, taking the road alongside the Kupfergraben to the point where it turns east to rejoin the Spree. There, under an old elm tree, he drew up, and looked around. Brandau was sitting beside him within ten seconds.

He smiled. 'Nice car. Congratulations.'

'Enjoy it while you can.'

'When this is over, I'm never leaving a book-lined study again, ever.'

'See anyone?'

'No.'

Hoffmann reached into his pocket and proffered one of the cyanide capsules.

'Do you really think I haven't got my own?' said Brandau, 'Kind of you, of course, but do save what you have for yourself.' He lit a cigarette and gazed at the dreary street they were passing.

'One should be enough,' said Hoffmann.

'It never hurts to be sure,' said Brandau, 'As my governess used to say.'

They drove over the Spittelmarkt and down Seydelstrasse, along Kottbusdamm and through the battered suburb of Neukölln. In all that distance they encountered only a handful of other vehicles, two small black cars, almost certainly Gestapo, a police motorcycle-and-sidecar, and an empty troop-carrier whose half-tracks clattered deafeningly on the cobbles as it roared past them.

They were beyond the outskirts of Berlin when they heard the sirens. The bombers had come. A dawn raid.

'That'll help us,' said Brandau. Hoffmann looked at him, and wondered if his own face was as grey as his colleague's.

They couldn't hear the distant hum of the Lancasters, or whatever the fuck they were this time, over the sound of the car's engine. But they could hear the crump of the bombs as they hit.

Hoffmann drove on, across the flat plain. The city stayed in view. He could see flames flare as he watched in the mirror.

They reached the edge of the marshes. He pulled over.

'What are you doing?'

'Want to see what's happening. A minute, no more.'

Even at that distance they could see the city burning in the gathering light. The flames devoured the sky. Hoffmann could almost think he could see individual tongues of orange, yellow and red, dancing among the carcasses of the buildings that together had once been home.

This was a big raid. The bombers hung black in the sky like insects, moving in slow motion. There was little to resist them. A few anti-aircraft units had opened fire, and tinier specks, Messerschmitt 110s, dived and weaved among the bombers, but there were only three of them. When two had been shot down, the third wheeled away.

'We must go,' said Hoffmann.

Brandau got back into the passenger seat. Hoffmann paused a moment to rub the contents of one of his brown twists of paper onto his gums, then got in without another look back.

Behind them the city burned. The Opera, the Bode Museum, the Palace, the Cathedral, all were hit, and with them the tinderbox districts of the poor, the shops and the hotels of the Ku'damm, the newspaper offices, the cinemas, the schools, the zoo.

Near the Tiergarten, Hoffmann knew, there were stables. He remembered fighting in the trenches in the last war, and the horses which had been hit by incendiary bombs, escaping, their manes on fire, galloping and stumbling, screaming across the broken land, unable to escape the death they carried on their backs. He wrenched his mind back to the present.

Further down the road there was a setback, an unforeseen obstacle: a tree fallen across their path meant a detour.

They drove on through a ghost landscape, finally taking a road which led through lakeland. Away to the left a ragged line of woods was roughly etched on the horizon. Ahead of them and to the right, a grey plain punctuated by clumps of stubborn coppice and reeds crouched under a sky which might have belonged to a gloomy mezzotint.

Hoffmann pushed the heavy car on, cursing when it skidded on the wet road, fearful of sleep, of losing concentration, for the lakes came close to the edge of the tarmac. Hoffmann had planned this route weeks ago, covering the territory, insuring himself, but this road hadn't figured in his plans. They weren't running late, but before too many people were up they needed to reach the deep lake surrounded by dense woodland which he had selected.

Country people usually rose early. Now, peering through the dismal half-light, he wasn't sure he hadn't lost his way. But the air-raid had helped them. They had seen no country patrols; they all had their heads down. The enemy was known to dump unused bombs randomly on the countryside before turning for home. That knowledge might keep the farmers indoors longer too. And if the worst came to the worst the big official car and his uniform would impress a local police unit. The worst part of the journey for unwanted encounters had been the *Autobahn* just south of the city, and that had been empty. Perhaps their luck would hold. He concentrated on the road, but there were some thoughts he couldn't keep back.

Whom would they send after him, once they'd found out?

And Emma? Would he ever know if Kessler had succeeded? If they got her, and thought she might know where he was ...

He couldn't think about that. Kessler would get her away. He would get her away. No doubt of that.

He shook his head to clear it. Even so, unbidden, Kara's face appeared in his mind.

He hadn't been able to give himself time to think about Kara since dreaming of her on the flight to the Wolf's Lair.

Now he spoke to her quietly, reassuring her that he hadn't forgotten, that she ought to know that he hadn't forgotten.

Kara. Kara. I love you.

He thought of the call he'd made to Tilli Cassirer. Had he been rash? What if they'd logged it? Had it been foolish to speak in French, and use such a clumsy code? The people he was up against weren't all fools.

But he'd needed to take some action. If there was the slightest chance that Hagen knew, it would mean the end, and no chance of saving what remained of his self-respect, let alone anything else.

The car banged violently as he hit a pothole. Brandau, who had been staring silently ahead, lost in his own thoughts, looked across at him sharply. No damage, but a lesson. Concentrate.

'Got a gun with you?'

'Yes,' said Brandau.

'Size?'

'Standard 7.65.'

Hoffmann nodded. He hoped they wouldn't need to use guns. If it came to it, he had his service automatic, his own 7.65, and the little Walther Model 9 which his grandfather had given him in 1921 when he'd graduated from police college. Not much bigger than a cigarette case and about the weight of a glass of wine, it was powerful enough to keep him out of trouble, and it was the gun he'd hang onto until the end. And of course the third pistol for the fake suicide, if they had time to set it up.

The Gestapo investigators wouldn't buy it for long; but it'd give them perhaps three days.

25

They came to a junction, and looking to the left, Hoffmann recognised a landmark, a battered and neglected roadside crucifix, half life-size. Beyond it he should be able to rejoin his original route. Luck was smiling on them. He looked at his watch, and accelerated. Back on the right road.

Rose grey light in the sky now. Are those storm clouds to the south? Where is the wind coming from?

The engine purred. Nice and quiet. Farmland beginning. Empty.

What might have once been potato fields. Or beet. Balance the time between having enough light to find the right spot, and the time when the farmers got up and started moving about, chasing the last bony cattle out into the fields, casting an eye around their territories.

Beside him Brandau had begun to doze, lulled by the rhythm of the car, but jerking himself awake every time his head fell forward.

***

They used to shoot looters, Hoffmann remembered, thinking of the farmers, about twenty years ago, when times were hard. As a young homicide cop he'd arrested a farmer who'd shot an entire family, father, mother, and three children, all starving, for trying to steal potatoes from him. That was a bad case. The farmer had shot the man first, then the woman as she knelt over her husband. The kids had just stood around, too hungry and cold and bewildered to do anything else, and he'd picked them off one by one; a girl of eight, and two boys, ten and five.

Hoffmann had seen the man hanged. Jaw set, eyes front. Open until the moment when they put the sack over his head, and open under the hood, no doubt, until the end.

It was then that Hoffmann started to take an interest in the Party. It was the only thing that seemed to offer a way out of the tottering Republic, which had never got under way, never got out from under the shadow of the last war, which he himself had lived through as a teenager, just in time to enlist for the last year, seen his father go away to it, a quiet maths teacher, come back even quieter, spend every hour he could in his study, hardly ever speaking; his mother always pale, the house later sold, the money worthless in days because of the inflation then. And the Left was a house divided against itself, leaving a gap for the Party. So he joined. Some kind of structure and what looked like a solid socialist plan that might work.

So it goes.

In the end there was nothing particularly socialist about the National Socialists. Political plans that look big always boil down to the same thing, Hoffmann supposed. But you survive, if you're lucky, and you bury your principles, and you learn to turn a blind eye. You do your job and you keep your head down. Unless in the end you can't live with yourself without doing something about it.

Brandau was staring ahead, eyes dead. Hoffmann tried to think of something to say, but couldn't. Hardly a friendship, but they depended on one another. Apart from that, and the battle, what had they had in common?

Hoffmann dug in the breast pocket of his tunic and pulled out his packet of cigarettes, offering it to Brandau, who shook his head. Hoffmann lit one, felt better. The snow he'd rubbed onto his gums had kicked in. He glared into the coming day. The road ran straight ahead now. Another half an hour, maybe less. They'd have to start looking soon. For the moment, they might have been alone on the planet.

Was it only two years since he'd first had to listen, over cigars and cognac, to the big fish discuss the best way of getting rid of the Jews? The Chancellor had hoped to get control of Madagascar and send them all there. Then there'd been a plan to send them into exile anywhere, but only the Danes would take any, and they couldn't take them all. In the end there had been a conference at Wannsee, and what began experimentally in the backwoods of Poland later became a major, formal operation.

Hoffmann knew all about that. He'd been part of it.

From the beginning of 1941, plenty of those who were detached to the east to do the dirty work began to drink. A simple escape, unless you were one of the ones who were actually mad, who thought the killing was ideologically sound, or you were one of those who couldn't afford to lose control, like Hoffmann himself. For most of the rest, there was the bottle.

Hoffmann thought again of the dead family in the potato field. Twenty years ago. But in those days, dark though they were, the city stood, the hospitals functioned, the nation was one among fellow nations. It was a pariah now, and amidst the wreckage, the farmers' fields yielded little or nothing.

Why had so few risen up against the Party? After the first euphoria, when it became clear to anyone with eyes to see that the angel of salvation had black wings, and talons that dripped blood?

71

There were abandoned cows in distant fields in Poland and he had seen them wandering, their udders distended, moaning in pain. There was no-one to milk them. The noise they'd made was the most desolate of all the desolate sounds which haunted his memory.

26

He felt a hand on his arm.

'The car's veering,' said Brandau. 'Let me drive.'

'I'm all right. We'll be there soon.'

Brandau peered off to his right. 'There's open water over there,' he said. 'And a sand-bar.'

Hoffmann pulled over and looked past the lawyer into the gathering light. The sun was above the horizon now, and the clouds to the south has disappeared. A sand-bar didn't sound good. No, it had to be the place he had chosen. There was still time to find it. He put the car into gear and drove on.

The road narrowed. Tall clumps of reeds grew at the very edge of shallow lakes. Some of these lakes, you could walk out hundreds of metres and still only be up to your knees, though you had to beware of quicksand. The lake they needed shelved sharply, and was deep enough to drown a man in, for a corpse to be lost in.

Brandau swivelled in his seat, reaching for the leather case they had brought with them.

'What are you doing?'

Brandau looked at him. 'I thought, a little of the brandy ... '

'No.'

'A centimetre or so won't make any difference.'

'No. Have a drink after we've got rid of the car. When we get to the village. This has got to look convincing, at least to the people who find it.'

'They'll loot it anyway. All this good stuff.'

'As long as it convinces them.'

The track to the lake would appear any minute now. Then perhaps thirty minutes' walk to the priest's house. Hoffmann pulled the car round a corner, sweating in his uniform as he changed gear to cope with a sudden abrupt slope which took them up onto a brown plain, dotted with copses and, black against the skyline, the wood they'd been looking for, the branches of the wind-twisted trees like a madman's hair at this distance.

'There!'

Heavy as it was, the car lurched as the wind gripped it. They were out of the lee now. The country road was stony, so they could move fast across the plain, the Mercedes sending pebbles flying but leaving no other trace. Hoffmann drove fast, racing the rising sun. As they reached the wood, which the road skirted, they could see low houses half a kilometre away. They seemed part of the earth.

'Look for a track on the right.'

Brandau looked at his companion, hunched over the wheel. He peered into the black trees.

'There!'

Hoffmann stopped on the road and climbed out, walking round the car, gently kicking stray leaves and twigs over the verge, and frowning at the impression the Mercedes' wheels had left. The lane that led into the wood was firm enough to support the weight of the car. They were still in the game.

He'd left the engine running, but though it scarcely made any noise above a purr, he squinted over to the distant houses, looking for any sign of movement. There were dim lights in one or two windows, but otherwise nothing, and no dog barked.

He climbed into the car again and they nosed down the track. Two, three hundred metres. Then a cave-like opening appeared between arching trees to one side. A smaller lane. Hoffmann turned the car more cautiously this time, and he felt the tyres crunch on the ground beneath. The new lane was surfaced with crushed seashells from a time when this part of Germany had been under an ocean. He slowed to walking speed, barely able to prevent the car from stalling, his leg muscles straining with the tension of balancing clutch and accelerator. He was smiling now. Let the bastards from Gestapo HQ in Fürstenberg sort *this* out, he thought. He was pleased to feel the old excitement rise in him again. This might work.

The track - it was so narrow, and so crowded with trees, damp all year round, that it might have been in a tunnel - led down to a narrow strip of beach at the edge of the lake - his lake. The sun was up now, but here it remained dark, and secret. They pushed on for another hundred metres or so, following the track as it wound through the trees. Both men strained their ears, listening to the sound the tyres made. Sooner or later they'd hit sand. They'd have to stop then.

Hoffmann hit the brake and disengaged the gear the moment he felt the wheels slip.

'Here.'

He reversed gently, back along the shell path for about five metres. On the left, there was another track, even narrower, sloping off into the undergrowth. there was a kind of man-made gulley, ancient, some kind of prehistoric quarry perhaps, down there. Hoffmann edged the car towards it until the track gave out. He pulled over into the crowded wood, crushing saplings. Other young trees arched their branches over the 770 like protecting arms.

He killed the engine and the lights.

'Stay where you are for a moment,' he told Brandau, who nodded, lighting a cigarette. The leaves rustled like tissue paper in what little wind could reach this spot. He climbed out, placing his feet carefully on the ground, which was covered with moss and loose stone. They'd leave no traces here, and what disturbance they made would quickly be obscured by the wind and the light summer rain which once again had begun to fall. The only clues Hoffmann intended to leave were ones which would convince his pursuers that he'd come here alone. If all went according to plan, Brandau would be drinking hock in Bern before the Gestapo picked up his trail, and they'd drag the lake for Hoffmann's body. After all, suicide would be the logical way out. Not even unusual. But he knew that whoever was sent after him would be able to second-guess his every move. After all, they'd be people he'd trained himself. He couldn't count on anything else. Her made a shortlist in his mind.

'Pass me the car papers.'

Brandau took them from the glove compartment.

'Thank you. Now, edge over here and get out this side. Try not to disturb anything.' Hoffmann knew he was being over-cautious, but he could no more change his own habits than he would underestimate whoever was sent to track him. Brandau climbed over the driver's seat to join Hoffmann. Without the engine's hum and the car's comfort to buffer them, the wind and the trees were alien and wild. Near at hand, some water-bird shrieked, and something scurried in the undergrowth.

Hoffmann had opened one of the rear doors. On the back seat was his black leather greatcoat. He leant in and pulled the small brown suitcase out from behind the driver's seat. He opened it and checked its contents with care. Brandau knew what treasures there were: a half kilo of real coffee, a bar of Hershey chocolate, a bottle, three-quarters full, of Napoleon cognac, a silver hip-flask of Irish whiskey, two packets of Player's, one open, a Walther service pistol, and a packet of American condoms. Also, a change of underclothes, a green shirt, a box of birdshot, and a towel stolen from the Hotel Kaiserhof.

The essentials that Göring or any other high-up would take on a shooting party. Hoffmann hoped the trail he was laying would be suitably confusing. They'd link it to him in the end, but that would take them time. Then, with luck, they'd think he'd set it up to disguise his own suicide. They'd think he'd deliberately wanted to tie them up for a day or two so that his associates and family could get away.

If they bought it. Hoffmann couldn't count on Gestapo numbskulls being set on his track. Everyone knew how his mind worked.

All he took from the case was three packets of oval Muratti cigarettes, which Brandau had brought him some time ago from Switzerland.

Around them, the wild duck were stirring. Brandau watched through the trees as a trio of them scampered across the lake, scattering the water with their wings and their feet as they took off, hurting his eyes with their freedom.

Hoffmann placed the birdshot on the back seat. He stowed the case back behind the driver's seat, leaving one of its straps trailing onto the passenger seat to betray its presence, but discreetly. Removing the anonymous greatcoat, he closed the doors quietly and went round to the boot. Then he locked the car and, motioning Brandau to precede him, moved away from it, kicking the ground and the grass into some kind of shape, leaving only his footprints visible where they made any impression at all. He didn't imagine they would last, but he couldn't guarantee how long it would be before the car was found. The locals would know these woods as well as he did. Nothing could be left to chance.

They made their way to the point where they had turned off.

'Follow the path back to the edge of the wood. Tread carefully. Keep to the verge. When you get there, stay just inside the trees.'

Hoffmann watched Brandau disappear up the track, and took stock. He wondered again how much time the set-up would buy them. Some forester would find the car within a day or two. The longer the better. If their luck went the other way, a farmworker would stumble across it later that morning, but he doubted if that would happen. Either way, there'd be hesitation and delay before anyone reported it to the local police. More fear, hesitation and delay then, but finally the cops would open the car and see what was in it. They wouldn't touch it at first, wouldn't do anything. No-one at first would dare to assume that it had actually been abandoned.

They might think *Reichsmarschall* Göring had gone duck shooting to take his mind off things. Stranger things had happened.

They'd keep the car under observation, but they'd inform the Gestapo, who would run a check on the registration number and solve the mystery. But that would take a while. The bureaucracy was like tangled undergrowth. Then, the Gestapo would raise the alarm. Then, they would start to look for Hoffmann's body.

27

It wasn't by any means perfect, but once they'd finally traced the car to him, and they knew he was part of the conspiracy, they might just think for a minute that he'd killed himself.

He didn't have much time to set up his suicide. He rolled his shoulders, relaxing the tension, put on the greatcoat, and walked down to the lake.

He skated his feet across the ground to leave as little mark of his passage as possible, just to make things more confusing; but when he came to the sandy beach he no longer bothered. No footprints here would last more than half-an-hour - there was enough tidal flow in the lake to ensure that.

He reached the water in two minutes. He took out the spare Walther service pistol, checked it, and fired one shot. No-one would hear it at this distance, and the noise was whipped away by the breeze. Then he threw the automatic a few metres into the lake, to ensure they'd find it with just enough difficulty. He hurled his holster and gunbelt after it. Then he took out the car papers and threw them into the wind. No suicide note, nothing too clever - a man who's about to kill himself isn't going to care what traces he leaves; but a man who's faking his suicide needs to organise them.

He took off the gloves at the shore and washed his hands. A relief. He threw the gloves into the shallows. Another clue for them to play with.

He re-joined Brandau. On the way, he flung the car-keys into the undergrowth, on the other side of the path from the car.

The rain still fell, no more than a light drizzle, but the sun was hazy and the storm clouds were back. The wind began to gust again. The farmers, hopefully, would stay indoors.

They walked fast, going back along the road for a kilometre before turning off onto a lane, rutted by cartwheels. Now and then there was a gate, which allowed a view of meadows, which, in any normal year, would have been planted with wheat or rye.

In one or two, there were turnip patches. Brandau and Hoffmann passed these quickly, as they were likely to be guarded. Any farm boy, running back unseen to report their presence, would be a danger; but if they showed no interest in the food, there'd be no reason for the guard to move.

They gave farms a wide berth because of the dogs.

28

They reached Teudorf, the large village – almost a town – which was their destination, later than they'd hoped. Fortunately the church and vicarage stood at its edge, since there were a few people about by now. Hoffmann's uniform might draw unwelcome attention in a biggish place like this. It was time to shed that skin.

They moved through the outskirts cautiously, and met no-one.

The vicarage was a grey two-storey building with a red roof and rectangular windows, which were blocked by net-curtains, and set at regular intervals. It stood in a large garden surrounded by a yew hedge which separated it, *via* two gates, from the church and the road.

Once inside the road gate they breathed more easily.

They didn't have to knock. The door opened as they approached it.

It revealed a man in his mid-forties, balding, greying, unshaven, his dark shirt stretched over a jutting beer-belly; but when he moved, light on his feet. Black trousers, brown carpet slippers. An intelligent but, at the same time, rather loose face. A drinker, but not one who'd lost all control.

The man ushered them in.

They stood in a large stone vestibule, lit by one high window. An ancient oak table flanked one wall, piled with tattered prayer books and pamphlets, among which two heavy brass candlesticks stood like towers. Above the table an *Ecce Homo* and an *Ascension of the Virgin*, both nineteenth-century copies of Renaissance originals, hung lopsidedly in gilded frames.

'Hello, Franz,' Hoffmann said.

The priest grinned at them. He gave Hoffmann a bear hug.

'Maxie, you bloody old rogue. I've been expecting you for a week. Couldn't you have called? No, I suppose not.' He looked at Brandau. 'You must be Hans. Maxie's mentioned you.'

Brandau looked at Hoffmann in alarm. He would have expected a stranger to address him as Dr Brandau, and he wasn't happy that this untidy and erratic country parson knew who he was. He extended his hand cautiously, and the priest seized it in both of his and pumped it up and down, before clapping him on the shoulder. 'You must be knackered. And starving. You certainly look like shit. Come in. Monika's in the kitchen. She's looking forward to seeing you.'

He led the way down a broad corridor, off which several rooms led. Their doors were open, and Hoffmann could see as he passed that only one or two were occupied. The others were more or less empty, their only contents ancient church detritus: battered angels, a noseless armoured martyr; paint peeling from an large baroque St Denis, his mournful head clasped in an attenuated left hand, the right raised in blessing, though the index and middle fingers were broken off at the first and second joints. Catholic stuff, pre-Reformation. How long had it been here? There was a smell of damp wood; but ahead came the promise of a warm kitchen.

A gaunt, once beautiful woman with tired eyes stood in the door, leaning against the frame, her long arms folded across her chest.

She was thin, dressed in a green cotton smock and an old blue skirt, both of which hung too loosely on her. She gave them a tired welcome before turning to quieten a small terrier which, unsure of itself, made a sound between a growl and a snuffle. Given a biscuit, it subsided, and took the booty to its lair under the dresser, from where it made an occasional, half-hearted threatening noise. She nodded the men into the room but didn't shake hands. She seemed too weary to make the effort. She smiled though, a smile as thin as her body.

29

Hoffmann glanced around. He'd been here a few months earlier, delivering the equipment they needed for the next phase of their escape, but Monika had been away then. He'd chosen the moment because of that. There was no reason to doubt either of them – Monika or Franz – though he knew the extent of the risk they were taking, and what would happen if the trail led here.

How familiar that kitchen was. He'd known it twenty years or so.

Franz Galen had come here as curate as soon as his seminary year as a missionary in China was over, and had stayed ever since, succeeding to the post when Pastor Bönig had died in – when was it? '29 or '30? He'd married Monika the same year, whichever it was, but the marriage wasn't a success.

They had given up hope of children early, and even called a halt to sex, as Galen had confided to Hoffmann over a bottle one evening, five years later. A pity, but something which went some way towards explaining Galen's relentless bonhomie, and his wife's *mal du siècle*.

Hoffmann hadn't seen Monika since the war started. In those five years they had both aged fifteen. In a different time he and Franz had been students together. He'd read Hebrew with her husband, before he stopped studying for the priesthood and his life had taken a different direction. Seemed like a dream to him, but, for all that, more real than what was happening now, in that oversized kitchen, dreary despite the warmth and the residual smell of cooking, with its empty ham-hooks on the ceiling. Maybe it was just that it needed a fresh coat of paint.

This was the room they lived in. There was a parlour for formal visits, Franz had an office, and, somewhere, there must be a bedroom; but they were places for work and sleep only. Outside the kitchen, the house was cold, even in summer. There was no life in it.

He shook his head to dispel his tiredness as he sat down. He mustn't drift. He wondered when he could allow himself another dose of snow. If all went well, he'd be able to sleep that night. He'd have to. He looked at Brandau. He was just as exhausted. How did he manage? Would he fall asleep on the train? Would he talk in his sleep?

Breakfast was on the table. Black bread, yogurt, cheese, hot milk, watered; acorn coffee. Galen fussed about in a larder beyond the stone sink and emerged with a shrivelled salami, which he placed on the table with a flourish.

'Such as we have, we give thee,' said Monika, with just enough irony to reach Hoffmann, as she put a saucepan of water on the hob to boil. Franz appeared not to hear this, but continued to busy about, producing knives, mugs and plates for his guests.

'Eat,' said Franz, joining them at the table and pouring out coffee. At least it was strong. Monika had added chicory to mitigate the taste. They drank it as if it were nectar.

'You look worse than he does,' the priest told Brandau. 'There's just time for you to take a bath. I'll give you a fresh shirt and socks and pants, so you don't have to use the spares in your case.'

'Thank you,' said Brandau. 'We'd better make it an exchange, because I don't suppose I'll ever be in a position to give them back.' He was wearing a Swiss cotton shirt, and silk socks and underwear. He doubted if the exchange would be to his advantage, and hoped he wouldn't swim about in the huge clergyman's clothes, but any clean clothes were better than what he was wearing. His undergarments were beginning to stick to him, and he could smell himself. He couldn't recall ever having been able to do that before.

'Don't worry, Hansi,' said Franz, catching his expression. 'I've got some old stuff that's a bit smaller than what I wear now - from before I went on the beer!'

How long it had been, Hoffmann thought, watching Monika as she added hot water to the coffee, catching her blue-grey eyes for a moment, but failing to hold them. He had hesitated before taking them into his confidence, but he knew they had sheltered people before, without fuss and without fear, as a straightforward Christian duty. Until recently they'd kept a Jewish student in the house; she stayed for eighteen months. In the end they'd managed to get papers for her, passing her off as their niece; and Hoffmann had provided her with travel permits as far as Elsaß-Lohringen. With luck she would have made it over the border into France and lost herself there in the mass of people whom the Occupiers and the Vichy collaborators spent so much time trying to control.

If she got past the police. Police, Hoffmann thought. He thought of the zealous Jewish police in the Warsaw Ghetto. Of the French police turning their Jewish fellow-citizens over to the Germans. Only too happy to please their new masters.

The Galens had guarded the girl until late last year. No-one in Teudorf had blown the whistle on them, which meant either there were no informers here or the Galens were very good at keeping secrets. They enjoyed Hoffmann's discreet protection, without knowing about it - not that it was worth much; but the local district police chief was an old friend, who owed favours, and who kept an eye on things.

They breakfasted hastily, Hoffmann surprised at how hungry he was, and noticing the same reaction in Brandau, though both men tried to eat as little as possible. They didn't want to cut too deeply into their hosts' food supply. The dog remembered Hoffmann now, and emerged from under the sideboard to lie on the floor at his feet, placing its head on his boot. Under the table, he scratched its nose with his other foot, and it wheezed contentedly.

'What's his name?' he asked Monika, wanting in some way to break her silence.

'Her name. Spitzi.' She looked at him ironically. 'Don't say you'd forgotten.'

Franz was looking at his watch. 'Well, gentlemen, if you've had enough... ' Under the jollity he was keen to see the back of them. Hoffmann was aware too that Galen had noticed him looking at Monika. But that was so long ago it should hardly have registered now. Still, if he hadn't been so tired he wouldn't have stared so long.

30

They left the table. Franz led them through the apparently endless house to a large drawing room. It was clearly never used and had the melancholy, oppressive atmosphere rooms long uninhabited always have. A clock on the cracked marble chimney-piece had long since stopped, and in one corner by the ceiling a massive black damp patch had established a menacing presence. The room was dim, its narrow windows, with their yellowing net curtains, shaded by a section of the yew hedge, so that the crepuscular light within was probably as bright as it ever got. On the floor by the hearth were two cheap suitcases, their lids open. How had Galen known, or had he done this every morning in anticipation of their arrival?

Brandau's was the smaller of the two. It contained pyjamas and slippers, a change of shirt, socks and underwear, a razor, a spongebag and - bizarre touch - a New Testament.

'There's a bathroom across the hall. You can wash and shave there.' Franz told Brandau. 'Monika will bring you those clothes of mine, and don't worry, she'll knock on the door and leave the stuff outside. Wouldn't want her getting too much excitement at this time of day!' He grinned broadly. Brandau put a polite expression on his face and left.

'Want to take a bath yourself?' Franz asked.

'I have to shave off my moustache. To go with the photos in the new documents.'

'But you've always had a moustache!'

'Only since I was eighteen, and the photos were shaved specially, by a very expert artist.'

Galen laughed. 'I wish I could ask you to stay here and rest for a night, but you're going to be red hot before you know it. You're going to want to put as much space between you and Berlin as you can while they're still running round in circles.'

Hoffmann nodded as he stripped off his uniform and dumped it on the floor with his service cap and the papers that went with his old life. From the larger suitcase he took a set of civilian clothes and put them on. A good blue suit, crumpled - why had the Galens not hung it up, it needed to look impressive, but it was too late for that - Party badge in the buttonhole, a blue shirt, dark enough not to show dirt for days, a grey tie, an old tweed overcoat. A pair of his own shoes. Otherwise the contents were the same as Brandau's, except that there were two changes of shirt, and so on. Hoffmann would be on the road longer than his friend.

Meanwhile Franz had unlocked an ebony sideboard carved with wild men whose faces were composed of leaves. From a concealed compartment at the back of one of its cupboards, built into the original piece of furniture two hundred years ago, he drew an envelope which he placed on the console table between the windows. It contained a Swedish passport for Hoffmann, and papers for two Party officials authorising travel in any part of what was still called Greater Germany, though large tracts of that territory were inaccessible now, having been occupied by the Russians. The papers were duly signed and stamped and otherwise accredited. There were identity documents to go with them, and one single railway ticket for Munich.

'Where are you going, Max?' asked Franz.

Hoffmann pocketed his documents, and replaced the others in the envelope for Brandau. 'You know better than to ask me that.'

'Who would I tell?'

'Better you don't know. You know why.'

Franz spread his hands. 'They'll never come here.'

'I hope not.'

'Are you going to Sweden? I mean, the passport ... '

'Not yet.'

'I'd like to know. I want to pray for you.'

'You can do that anyway.'

'Fuck you, Max.'

With the toe of his shoe, Hoffmann nudged the SS uniform and the rest of the stuff he'd shed. 'Will you burn these? Immediately we're gone.'

'I kept some petrol back.'

'You'd better bury the greatcoat.'

Franz thought for a moment, then said, 'Why don't you take it? It might help. Looks the part.'

It was a good suggestion. 'Will you be all right, Franz?' asked Hoffmann, slipping the coat over his shoulders. The thoughtful expression hadn't left the priest's face.

'Of course.' Franz looked at his watch.

'Take care when you burn that stuff. Use wood and straw too, and leaves if you can. It'll smell like a bonfire then. People can smell petrol.'

Franz grinned. Hoffmann was relieved to see it; but he didn't have time to think about whatever cloud had passed across his old friend's mind just then.

'Teudorf's a pretty tight town,' said the priest. 'Only the mayor and the deputy chief of police are real Nazis, oh, and the brewer, but they're a half-hearted bunch, especially now. So don't worry. Just get out of here, fast.'

'Yes.'

'One other thing. You could do with a hat. You can have one of mine. Black trilby. No-one will recognise you then.'

Both men laughed a little. Once he'd put it on, with the greatcoat, Hoffmann looked like a copybook government official. 'This is good,' he said. 'I should have thought of it.' His mind was too full - he had to keep a clear line. He knew he was in danger of making mistakes.

Soon afterwards, they returned to the kitchen, Hoffmann now touching his tender upper lip. Brandau, wearing a clean shirt from which his neck protruded like a tortoise's, was waiting, drinking a schnapps. He smelled of cologne.

'Home-made,' he said. 'Potato schnapps. Very good.' He raised his glass in a toast to Monika, who stood at the far end of the large table. The dog came tottering up to Hoffmann and tried to launch itself at him, succeeding only in pushing itself onto its hind-legs for a moment before collapsing back again, though not without scrabbling at him for a foothold. It looked up at him with expectant, kindly eyes, and wheezed with pleasure again.

'And I toast your bare forelip. You look ten, well, five, years younger!' said Brandau; but humour was fighting a losing battle against nerves.

'We've packed you some food.' Monika placed two grey paper bags on the table.

'Thank you,' said Brandau, without enthusiasm.

'Black bread, some cheese. Not much, I'm afraid. And a flask of water each.'

It wasn't until he saw those sorry little bags that Hoffmann began truly to feel like a refugee; or until then that the width of the river he'd crossed became really clear to him. Brandau wanted to put his food in his pockets, but the pockets were too small.

'There's a basket on the front of the bike,' said Franz. 'You can put them there.'

'We'd better get on,' said Hoffmann. From the window, Franz was watching the road beyond the church gate. 'Everything ready?'

'Yes. Come with me.'

Franz opened the back door, which led from the kitchen, and they followed him across a small courtyard, Brandau first, murmuring his thanks and his farewell. Hoffmann did the same, but as he looked back from the other side of the courtyard, he saw that Monika had turned away. Her hair was as rich and long as he remembered it. He remembered its smell. She closed the door.

He thought of the seminary in Würzburg where he'd studied with Franz. He thought of a doctor's daughter in the town. A serious-minded girl, but one who, in those days, was still capable of laughter.

Rivalry? Nothing was ever said.

And then his gradual falling out of faith, the appalling doubts, the desperate need to accept separation, and his leaving. Berlin was a long way north. He hadn't written, nor had she.

He remembered his father's relief, and then his horror when his son announced that he intended to join the police.

The long haul of life. Some plusses. Occasionally, real daylight. Those were things to be remembered as well.

Spitzi followed them to the high double doors of an outhouse whose walls abutted the courtyard, and then abruptly returned to the parsonage, to scrabble at the closed door.

Franz unlocked the outhouse doors and swung them open. Inside was the black Volkswagen Hoffmann had left here in May. It had civilian plates and its tank was full. There were two extra cans of petrol in the boot. It had taken Hoffmann all his clout and all his charm to get them.

'Kept her warm?'

Franz looked at him. 'Little beauty. Tempted to take her out for a spin.'

'Glad you didn't. Tyres?'

'Fine.'

'Thank you, Franz.' Hoffmann looked around. The outhouse was high, barn-like, and dim. It smelt of straw. There was a workbench in one corner. The place was warmer than the house. 'And the bike?'

'Over here.'

Brandau and Hoffmann followed Galen to where a green bike leant against a bale of hay. Brandau dropped his provisions into the basket, where he found a pair of cycle clips. Galen really had thought of everything.

'Long time since I've ridden one of these,' said the lawyer.

'It'll get you to the station. Not far.'

'What do I do with it when I get there?'

'Leave it outside. You'll see a bicycle rack. Its owner will come and collect it before you've settled in your compartment.'

Hoffmann looked around again, breathing the comforting smell. It was all so secure here, so natural, you wouldn't think anything out of the ordinary was happening anywhere.

Hoffmann turned to Franz and shook his hand. 'Thank you, old friend.'

'Christian duty.'

'More than that.'

'If we meet afterwards,' Franz said, addressing them both, 'I've still got a bottle or two of *Eiswein*. Really good stuff. Better than champagne, and it's good until 1955, which gives us plenty of time. I won't drink it until then. After that, if you still haven't shown up, well, it'd be a pity to waste it.'

He shut up then, as they could hear the noise of a farm cart labouring along the road, so slowly that they thought it would stop. But the heavy tread of the mule drawing it didn't change rhythm, and it passed.

'Let's go,' said Hoffmann, briskly. He got into the car and started it. The motor hummed into life at the first pull of the button.

He reached a hand out to Brandau. 'Goodbye, Hans.'

'We'll keep an eye on you from Bern.'

'Just make sure you get there.'

'Good luck.' Brandau spread his hands. They ought to have had a more formal leave-taking than this, thought Hoffmann, after what they'd been through.

A gravel drive led to the church gate, already open, beyond which the drive curved to the left and down to the road. Galen walked to the road and looked carefully left and right. Then he waved his hand.

Hoffmann pushed the VW into gear, grinding the box as he did so, and flinching; but it was all right. He pulled away slowly, turning right onto the road and out of Teudorf, heading south. He didn't look back.

31

Hoffmann drove hard for two hours along roads deserted except for the occasional ox-cart or small military convoy. He drove through huddled villages that looked deserted, and past grey farms whose yards were morasses. He found a stretch of road by a pretty little beech-wood and pulled over into its edge. He climbed out and stretched - his frame was better suited to a Mercedes than a VW - relieved himself, walked up and down, shaking his limbs. He felt better alone.

Just one case to close.

It would be a gamble, but what wasn't? Would he have time to finish his work before they caught up with him? In the few days before the young communications officer had denounced him under torture, he'd seen the size of the operation Hitler had mounted against the conspirators. Now that the Führer had recovered sufficiently from his shock not to shit himself every time a shadow moved, and convinced as he was that some kind of divine hand held itself protectively over him, he had unleashed a whirlwind.

Much as he wanted a future beyond this mire, Hoffmann was under no illusions.

The little Walther automatic dug into his hip. He took it out and checked it. He had two clips of ammunition, and one more in the gun. And his service pistol. Plenty. Stawizki wouldn't get to play tunes on him.

He lit one of his Murattis. Good cigarettes. Even tasted good in the fresh air. He'd give himself time for one quick smoke. He thought of his father, nicotine-stained fingers like his own, always smelling of tobacco, always in a tweed jacket, always sad that his son had never shared his enthusiasm for mathematics, which he'd taught for thirty years in the same school in Dahlem. His horror in 1919 when Hoffmann, fresh from the trenches, had announced that he was going to study to be a pastor.

'Are you quite mad?'

'No.'

'But how can you have reached such a decision?'

'I want to help people.'

'Then be a doctor.'

'I want to help them spiritually.'

'Then be a psychiatrist. Go to Vienna. I'm sure I - '

'I can't help it, father.'

'There's no reason in religion. No rationale.'

'I think there is.'

But he'd been wrong.

The sun was well up now. It wasn't a particularly hot day. There was still a haze which hadn't dispersed.

Along the road came a man tending a gaggle of geese, maybe fifteen of them. Hoffmann leant against the car, watching.

As they came up, the geese became uneasy, chattering nervously. Hoffmann didn't like geese.

'Smells like a good cigarette,' said the man. About sixty, weatherbeaten face, short white hair, countryman's clothes, carried a long stick. Where had he come from? A hamlet off the road? Hoffmann hadn't passed anywhere for several kilometres.

'Have one,' said Hoffmann.

'Swiss,' said the man, accepting. He didn't look like the kind of person who'd know.

'Black market,' said Hoffmann. He didn't want any conversations. The cigarettes were a mistake. He looked at the man's eyes. Intelligent. Who might he tell?

'I must be going.'

The man inhaled, ignoring this. The geese tutted, uneasy at having their trek interrupted. 'A very luxurious smoke, best I've had in years. Don't worry about the geese. Except Otto,' he pointed to the gander, an elderly, bad-tempered looking bird, which despite some aggressive posturing was nevertheless keeping its distance. 'But even Otto is beginning to see sense.'

'I know about geese,' said Hoffmann.

'Do you?' The man looked thoughtful. 'Really.' He paused for a moment. 'I'm still learning about them.'

'Really?'

'Yes. Used to do something else.'

'I must be going,' Hoffmann said again.

The man shrugged. 'Of course. You look like a busy man.'

Something made Hoffmann relent. 'Have another cigarette.'

The man looked at the proffered packet, but shook his head. 'You probably don't have many, and you'll need them more than I do. But thank you.'

Hoffmann watched him go, the geese following him eagerly, like a bunch of children. The man didn't look up or wave when Hoffmann overtook him a few moments later.

32

The brown plain had taken on colour; the green of trees and the blue-black of lakes, poppies in the hedgerow and the scattered blues and yellows of wildflowers. The sky was full of swallows. Still not much traffic. Every so often, he passed a wooden cart, laden with hay or manure, always accompanied by a bent figure alongside a gaunt horse or mule. There was more active and even prosperous farming here than around Teudorf - look at that flock of geese, how had they survived so long? - but not much sign of life in the handful of villages and hamlets he drove through.

He'd covered fifteen kilometres after his meeting with the gooseherd when he saw the roadblock.

He looked at his watch. Nine. Better time than he'd thought. Mühlersheim already. On a hill in the middle distance he could see the modest Gothic cathedral and the grey-and-beige buildings spilling down the slopes from it to the river, and the tanning factory, the road ahead running towards them.

A pretty sorry sight, this roadblock. A tractor trailer hauled across his path, yoked to a bored-looking ass, accompanied by a more bored-looking countryman in shirtsleeves, and a waistcoat made from a potato sack. Two Home Guard types, fourteen or fifteen years old, thin necks sticking out of heavy collars. As he drew up Hoffmann could see that their necks were rubbed raw by their uniforms. Shifty eyes. Their rifles - old Type 98s - were too big for them. But their fingers were on the triggers, and they were levelling the guns at him. Don't underestimate fear; that can kill you. Don't show fear either. He gave them no more than a glance, and shifted his attention to their boss.

The man in charge was a plump SS *Rottenführer*, about thirty, could be older, didn't matter, whose black uniform was shiny with wear. He was shiny himself, sweating. His cap was too small for him. Little film-star-type black moustache. He held up a meaty hand and approached the car. Hoffmann sensed his uncertainty. The car was modest, but new, and these days any car was a luxury - who had petrol? - and was to be treated equally with suspicion and respect.

He lowered the window and waited. The corporal waddled over and leant towards him. Hoffmann smelled a cocktail of odours: beer, schnapps, BO, boiled cabbage, sausage, tobacco; the smell that haunted a thousand offices and a thousand torture chambers and a thousand prisons. The smell of the poor.

Only in the east, in Poland, had it been different. Acrid there, the smell, the smell of starving women. Everything was grey there. And there was another smell, the smell of burnt meat.

'Out,' said the SS man, but hesitantly. Perfect specimen. Bully. As ready to cringe as to hit. He scratched his left upper arm. Was his service tattoo irritating him?

Hoffmann uncoiled himself from the small car and draped the leather greatcoat over his shoulders. He towered over the other man. He placed Galen's black trilby on his head. He saw the man's eyes go small and clever. The boys had lowered their rifles. They were already looking respectful.

'Papers,' said the corporal, with fading conviction.

Hoffmann wasn't going to overplay his hand. People were touchy these days. Too much arrogance or too little confidence could tip the balance. He allowed himself the ghost of a sigh, dealing with an underling, and produced his wallet, letting the silver eagle-and-swastika motif embossed on it catch the sun. He snapped out the travel authority and the identity card and held them for the corporal to take. He wouldn't give them to him.

Have they got my description out already? If they know, surely they'll be concentrating on the northern ports, and the Swiss border? Had keeping the greatcoat been a mistake, after all?

The corporal screwed his eyes up and looked at the papers. Hoffmann stood erect, drew in his breath impatiently, but not too impatiently. He could see that the corporal was just going through the motions. He wasn't reading the documents. He was seeing the symbols and the rubber stamps and the important signatures. After a minute he handed them back and saluted.

'Thank you, sir.'

'Doing your job.' Hoffmann briskly returned the salute. The boys stood to attention, and saluted too, muttering uneven Heil Hitlers at him. He nodded his approval and they looked almost as pleased as if he'd given them a kilo of coffee for their mothers.

He got back into the VW, waited until the ass had trundled the trailer off the road, and drove on.

It won't be long, Kara, he said to himself. It won't be long.

33

He drove south-west through the rest of the morning across the unforgiving plain, blinking his eyes against the sun, which had at last dispelled the haze. This part of Germany would have a perfect summer's afternoon.

Ten years, he thought. A long time for two people to occupy the same mind. *Two souls live, alas, within my breast.* Hoffmann grinned. Could Goethe have imagined this situation? He tried to suppress the memories that came to him, and failed.

His was a situation he could *control*. He knew which the true man was, and which the false. But the strain of maintaining the balance was great, and that of auditing the moral profit-and-loss account, greater still. That was a job he didn't dare address, because it would call into question which of the two men he'd made himself into had been the more effective, and he couldn't face the answer, any more than he could stop someone in a room at the end of a half-forgotten corridor in his mind working on the problem.

The last year had brought many things to a head. There had been a problem in the spring, deciding who should live and who die of among the seventy-six recaptured air force prisoners-of-war who'd escaped en masse from a camp in Poland, Stalag-Luft III. They were mostly officers, valuable men, pilots and navigators and bomb-aimers: the same sort of men, in fact, who were pounding Berlin - and Leipzig and Frankfurt and Dresden - to pieces now.

Plans for the assassination attempt on the Führer were already well advanced then, so there was no question of his compromising his position. The job had to be done, and it wasn't the worst he'd had to face. As usual, he'd approached it with the aim of mitigating its effect as far as possible. He'd done his best to select, as humanely as possible, the fifty men to be slaughtered by the Gestapo acting on a direct Führer-Order (the Führer had gone into one of his rare, carpet-chewing fits over this). Filing cards with the men's details had been piled up on his desk. From them he was able to sort categories of married and unmarried, those who were fathers and those who weren't; and able to sort the young from the old, as far as that was possible within an age range of nineteen to thirty. All the information came of course from conversations between prisoners and guards, who were airforcemen themselves. Friendships were struck up. Some of these people had been in camps for three or even four years. Name, rank and number only? Forget it. And some of them had been sending information on German morale back to their own secret service in coded letters home.

But shooting fifty of them in cold blood? No.

Fifty out of a total of seventy-six.

Filing cards on his desk.

Names, ranks, dates of birth. So many married; so many married with children; so many engaged to be married; so many single.

Fifty lives. A difficult choice.

He remembered the discussions over lunch with Kaltenbrunner of the Central Security Office, and with Müller of course. Those endless business lunches to talk about the measures to be taken, and how they could be covered up. Everybody hated bomber crews, everybody hated Allied airmen in general, but killing prisoners out of hand wouldn't do Germany's reputation a lot of good if the Allies found out and made propaganda capital out of it.

The lunches in Berlin generally took place at the Adlon, over Dover sole and Pouilly Fumé. And, inevitably, Hennessy XO and Monte Cristo cigars afterwards. As for the subject, they might as well have been discussing commodities, and the tendency to use euphemistic language - 'product' when they meant 'people' - muddied everyone's thinking. Something else he had to be aware of.

If he got out of this, he'd live on black bread and water for the rest of his life. He owed that to the ghosts, who would in any case never go away.

Latterly, the two other men, both younger and more powerful than him, had passed remarks about his being the only Berliner in the High Command; and once or twice he'd caught up with a comment from behind his back - especially from Kaltenbrunner - about the size and shape of his nose. At the time he'd been confident of Hitler's support, and as for his looks, his Ancestry Certificate showed an impeccable Aryan line: his family went back a century in Berlin, and three hundred and fifty years before that in Kiel. He was a good deal 'purer' than most, and as for physical appearance, it was a common joke in Berlin, though still whispered, that as far as all that was concerned, Hitler, Himmler, Göring and Goebbels were hardly paragons of any Master Race.

He'd put matters off for as long as he could, which was to say, no more than a week. Then he'd sat down at his desk and drawn up the death list in an hour. Balancing so many fates that quickly. Seeming to know these people, but not knowing them at all; only really knowing that his judgements, though based on what he hoped and prayed were the most humane principles he could evoke, were nevertheless mere guesswork. How did he know *this* wife wasn't pregnant? How did he know that *that* marriage was a success? He balanced youth against responsibility: he put all the men under twenty in one pile; some of the older fathers went into the other.

The next job was sending the telexes authorising the murders to regional secret police cadres scattered from Hamburg to the Saarland to Krakow, wherever the escapers had been picked up and were now being held in ordinary police station cells.

Which meant his own men would have to hand the prisoners over to the Gestapo.

There was no way out. None. He went through the motions with disgust, but it had to be done. There were big things at stake now. In a few months, perhaps, the Nazis would be swept aside. The sacrifice had to be made. But then there had almost been a hitch at the end. It might have ruined everything, as he then had thought. But to what good end, after all, had he kept his cruel word?

The sun was beginning to beat through the windows of the Volkswagen. His senses had been fully alert to get him through the roadblock, but the involuntary recollection of the enemy officers from Stalag-Luft III and their fate had lowered his spirits, and the tiredness which he continued to battle would not be defeated. His head felt light, objects seen through the windscreen seemed far away, as if he were looking at them through the wrong end of a telescope. His mouth and nostrils were dry, his eyes prickled, and his new suit rubbed uncomfortably against his thigh. The car was too small for him. He felt cramped.

He was tempted to stop in Mühlersheim, find a hotel, see if they had anything decent to eat and a room he could use for a few hours. He hesitated right up to where the road leading to the centre of the town diverged from the one he was on, which bypassed it.

He drove on. It was too soon. He'd find somewhere quiet where he could pull over and sleep for an hour, two if he was lucky. That night he'd find somewhere with a bath or shower that worked. Maybe he'd get the suit pressed, even have them launder the things he was wearing. The hotel staff would remember that, but it was important to look as good as possible for as long as possible. He should be able to manage that for a week. More than enough time, God willing, to get the job done. How long he'd be able to keep the car was another question - with luck, until it ran out of petrol - and he couldn't guess how long his forged identity papers would last, though there was no way that his pursuers could possibly know what they were, or under what name and cover he was travelling.

He had no material problems: there were plenty of banknotes in the lining of the back-seat of the VW, as well as hotel and travel warrants.

What he needed most, though, was time, and nothing could buy him that.

34

Hoffmann reached Althof at six in the evening. It'd been slow going for the last hour. A long column of prisoners in an assortment of old clothes, guarded by weary, teenaged SS-men, were marching west, five abreast, perhaps two thousand of them. They had all but blocked the road before turning north at last. Some were dressed in striped-pyjama concentration camp issue, most in anything from the remains of Russian army uniforms to battered suits and even cocktail dresses. Some of the women wore makeup. What bizarre order had permitted that? An attempt to make it look as if they'd been treated like human beings?

He hunched over the wheel, and tried to meet no eyes as the prisoners were beaten off the road to let the car squeeze past. Some fell, and did not rise; but the ranks, unbidden, machine-like, reformed: five abreast.

His own eyes ached. He would have to stop. He could see, as he passed the town's name on a metal plate nailed to a post by the side of the road, one hundred metres before the scruffy outskirts began, another sign, battered, hanging awry, and half obliterated by filth and rain: *Juden Unerwünscht* - Jews, Keep Out. The worst horror committed by the Party seemed like a distant memory, though it was still going on, more fiercely than ever, even now all was lost. The wrecked sign was like a ghost of itself. People had other things to think about these days.

The officials at the road-block here all but waved him through. Galen had been right after all: the trilby and the leather coat were a good combination, though he could have done without them in July.

There was enough cloud on the horizon to guarantee a glorious sunset, but nothing could lend much charm to Althof. It was a new town. Built thirty years earlier on the back of a now-obliterated farming village to house workers, it had spread since then and now sprawled beyond the low hill at its centre, where the great grey factory squatted like a grotesque cathedral over the surrounding, unlovely countryside.

The straggling wind blew up dust and last year's leaves. The place smelled of hot oil. The oldest buildings, shed-like, were made of wood; later constructions were of glossy brick - dark red and black. Even at the end of a perfect day they seemed to be hunched against rain, their slate roofs slick, sloping steeply. The most recent edifices were concrete rectangles, punctuated evenly by square windows, placed in ranks divided by unmade roads caked with dried mud. Here and there a spindly silver birch or a dusty, obstinate buddleia, dead-and-alive, stuck out of a gutter or clung to a crack in a building. Dry ivy scattered across walls without disguising or adorning them. It was hard to distinguish the blocks of workers' flats from the factory - smaller than it, they looked like its spawn. They manufactured ball bearings and tank tracks there. Before the war, the product had been tinned sausage.

Until recently, when the money had run out, Althof had been busy enough to lose oneself in, and there was still enough activity to suit Hoffmann's purposes. He could see the black hulk of a church on a small rise some way off, and wove a way through the streets towards it. Soon, he reached the main street, where a handful of shops still had goods in them, mainly canned and bottled food from the north, herring and sauerkraut. From one window a cracked mannequin in a pinstripe suit leered at him. Another offered a sparse selection of wooden and metal toys: battleships and tanks.

He checked the fuel gauge. With the extra petrol he'd loaded, he could get to Leipzig. He thought of the Swedish passport but shook off the temptation. He had promises to keep before he could look after himself. So pressing were those promises that he was amazed that he could even for a moment have allowed himself to be tempted. He eased his hands on the steering wheel.

He needed one good night's sleep. He could be across the river Elbe by midday tomorrow. Or he could dump the car and risk a train. He thought about Emma. Had Kessler managed to get her away? Would she have the sense to bury herself deeper - he knew the Gestapo would discover the Nikolassee address, however well it was buried. At least Emma was grown up and had a protector. Maybe she and Paul Kessler would get away together? Brandau might even help from Switzerland. And now there were also American and English agents in Munich and Konstanz.

His heart raced.

A policeman's whistle, warning, not aggressive, thank God, brought him back to the present. He braked hard as a woman in a beige headscarf with an old pram full of kindling crossed the road in front of him. Her head was bowed, her body bent as if under rain. He himself didn't look at anyone, didn't look for the cop; looked straight ahead, easing his hands on the wheel again. They ached. His shirt stuck to his armpits.

He drove along the main street, which was long and straight, like the main street in a Western - some of the frontages even had verandas. As he passed them, he looked down the side roads. He needed a medium-sized hotel or pension, the kind commercial travellers used. Though they had served him well so far, and he could trade on the impression they made in the prevailing confusion, the trilby and the coat would soon have to go; it wouldn't be long before he met some real policemen and he didn't want to stand out too much, quite apart from needing to be a chameleon in order to stay ahead of the game. How he'd achieve that was another question, but it didn't worry him too much. He knew how to handle himself. Again the thought came to him that if only he had no-one else to worry about...

There was a certain amount of traffic even at this time of day - ox and horse-drawn carts, a few small lorries, some running on coal, and the occasional car. The dusty VW wouldn't draw undue attention.

He noticed an inn sign - *Zum Alten Wirt* - not far down a street to the right. He turned and glanced at the street's name-plate. A new name hammered lopsidedly over the old told him that this was now *Göringstraße*, but you could easily see that formerly it had been *Goethestraße*. He drove past the hotel slowly. There was a sign in the door - Vacancies. It looked about right, probably twenty rooms, maybe not that big. Halfway between a hotel and a pension, really. Well, he'd risk it. He couldn't sleep rough, couldn't afford to look too battered yet. Later it would be less important; later, it might even be an advantage; but not yet.

Twenty metres past the inn there was another right turn, which opened almost immediately into a square where several cars were, including a big, official-looking Maybach, and an equally impressive Horch. This seemed a good place to leave the VW. He'd be moving on at dawn in any case. He parked away from the two big cars and switched off. Immediately the indeterminate noises of the town replaced the VW's buzz. As he climbed out, stretching his limbs, a gust of wind caught his coat, and trouser bottoms, and blew grit into his eyes.

He looked around carefully, determining first that, coming back to the car in the morning, he could see it and anyone watching it, before he approached. The buildings surrounding the square had ten windows between them, half of which were smallish, and glazed with frosted glass. A light shone from one of the larger windows - it was still too early for the blackout - and none of them had curtains that he could see, not even the ubiquitous net curtains of his country - or shutters. Offices, then. The shadows on the rear wall, which were visible, were cast by angular furniture. There were no plants in evidence. As Hoffmann watched, a man in a suit moved into view, but he passed the window without looking out, and soon afterwards the light was extinguished.

Hoffmann stood for a minute, then opened the boot and from it took a leather bag, into which he swiftly stacked all the money and papers concealed in the VW's back seat. He took out his suitcase, locked the car, and paused again. He was alone. He made his way to the inn.

35

The room wasn't bad. He'd eaten in the restaurant, Bratwurst and fried potatoes, Bauernbrot and some decent cold beer, all miraculous in these hard times, though he'd scarcely tasted anything.

He hadn't expected to fall asleep easily, but in fact he'd faded into unconsciousness within minutes of getting into bed. But, as so often, there was little refuge in sleep:

He was in a field, on a parade-ground of some kind. It wasn't long before he recognised it. He knew where he was. It was close to dawn. He could feel the frozen air. He was in uniform, muffled up, but still the cold had penetrated his bones.

He could see the moon, very bright, and beneath it, to the east, a silver horizon. The grey earth of the compound gave its grey light back to the sky. The compound looked like the surface of a craterless moon. Sandy soil, where nothing moved, nothing lived, nothing was real; and the utilitarian buildings that edged it seemed to belong to a forgotten city.

Or - no more than this - to a light-industrial plant. Something prosaic, transformed by the moonlight into a stage set.

And now there was activity.

A vast copper star with six points hung in the sky and streamed blood. Under it, people flowed into a building, which was like the others, but set apart. There was a sign on the building which Hoffmann could not read, though he knew he'd seen it before. The *something* Foundation. The roar of an engine, coughing, trying to ignite, failing, trying again. Catching. Then, thirty-four minutes. He knew that they had timed it exactly.

Then silence.

The star caught fire and the light blinded him.

Then darkness.

But there was not a moment's peace. The darkness gave way to light: a summer's day in woodland; pale yellow sunshine dappled the leaves.

He could see now that the darkness was that of a pit, a big one, four metres deep. He had flown out of the pit into the light and now hovered unseen in the air above it. Around its sides stood the diggers, their shovels already returned to the others, the ones in uniform. The diggers' heads bowed. The diggers in rags, here and there the trace of a ruined city suit. Out here in the countryside. Standing now round the edges of the pit, facing it. Beneath them, more than the depth of a grave. A grave deep enough for many. Hoffmann tried to turn his head away but something clamped it to the view.

The cackling sound of machine guns.

Falling.

A different scene:

Why had he no power over what he saw? Naked women running through woodland. Ordinary women, buttocks grainy like in film, old buttocks, breasts up and down, labouring; young buttocks, young breasts, some of the women not women at all but kids, young girls, no breasts at all. Harsh light and deep shade. Running, running.

The trees - uncompromising columns, out of a forest painted by Klimt. Hiding one woman for an instant, revealing another the next. No-one protected for more than a moment.

Birch trees. Straight, cool, silver birches. Dark, healthy soil beneath them. Last autumn's leaves still there. Nice surface to run on, but slow, and the all-but ordered ranks of trees quizzing the sight as the trunks shattered the light before the eyes of the women.

What time of day? The women were running towards the light. Dawn or dusk. Sun low in the sky anyway.

Hard light though. Dawn then.

And then the insistent sound, duller than you'd expect. Gunfire.

He flew into the sky, as if a titan had picked him up by the shoulders, and saw a mottled field beneath him; mottled with women's clothes at the edge of a wood.

What time of year? The trees were in leaf, and the leaves were thick; and each leaf was a hand, and each hand was stabbed, and bled; and the blood was like rain. There was so much rain you might as well be in the tropics.

But it was cold. Every drop an icicle.

And the women who hadn't been cut down still ran, naked back and muscle exposed to the light.

All the sound dull, and no smell at all.

But the sight - would he ever forget the sight?

Or who had ordered this?

Words, unconnected, unconnected letters even, on a page. But a report, to judge from its grey card binding and blue ribbon. A list? On a large orderly desk in an office overlooking an avenue of lime trees. Now, it was early in the year. Buds on branches, but nothing else.

Then the trees were gone. Uprooted, dead. Nothing but processions after that, the whole width of the boulevard.

Birches. Limes.

Then something heavy and brutal was bearing down on him, pushing hard on his chest. It was fleshy and formless, but strong. Its skin was rough. So much of it pushed against his face, like a fat woman, that he couldn't breathe or see.

A choking sense of hatred and disgust brought him out of the dark. But even as he opened his eyes, released from one fear, he was delivered immediately to another. And, rescued from the dream though he was, he could still smell the cordite and the blood.

The hotel room was unfamiliar and threatening. For a moment it was still part of the dream.

But it became real with the dingy light that insinuated itself through the thin green gingham curtains. There was no way of guessing the time from it. Wiping grime from his eyes, Hoffmann lifted his wrist and peered at his watch. He could not see the dial.

He lay back and breathed quietly for several seconds before he could summon the energy to pull himself up and swing into a sitting position on the bed. He looked again. Four o'clock.

He remembered an old man, a communist he'd interrogated a few years ago. He'd said, 'Once I was afraid when I fell asleep. Now I'm afraid when I wake. The nightmare has changed places.'

He pulled himself together. This, he told himself, was nothing that a cold shower and a change of clothes couldn't cure. And a cup of real coffee. But there was no shower and there was only one change of clothes which he couldn't afford to use yet, as there was no laundry here. As for coffee ...

He stood. The room, dowdy in the half light, menaced him. He walked around it, listening to the creaking floorboards. He tried to tread lightly. The whole thing, his life, was like a ghastly dream.

Time to think. Get away with using the car at least one more day. Maybe get to Leipzig in it. Don't panic.

Too early to go down the corridor to the bathroom to see if there was a chance that the water was running. He wanted to be on his way. On the road he'd be free again. How much time had he got? Two days? It depended on whom they'd put on his tracks. He'd trained the best; they'd think like him.

He shook his head to clear it. He reached for the cocaine packets in his jacket pocket but then resisted. Later perhaps, when he left.

He reached for the tumbler of water by the bed and drank.

He looked at his suit on the chair. It'd be fine for a few more days, though already it was creased from the cramped car.

He sensed the beginning of autumn in the air. September and October. The best months of the year, for him.

Long before those months came, he'd be dead, or his business would be done. Perhaps both. Perhaps this was a room he'd relinquished the right to leave. He took out the Swedish passport and looked at it hard.

36

Paul Kessler put his arm around her. He was shy and clumsy about it but she nestled to him. The bus was nearly empty and they felt private and even - briefly - secure in their seats near the back as the bus rolled down an endless country road south-west out of Potsdam, in the direction of Magdeburg. Kessler wanted the journey to go on forever, for the bus to travel past the town, and go on through Germany to Belgium and France, and so on to the coast, where he and Emma would find a boat waiting for them to take them further away still, to the ends of the earth, to some island, quiet and peaceful, untouched by this war and by this regime. But the closest he could get to safety for her was his parents' old summer house in the country. He used it from time to time, and he knew most of the villagers. With luck, Emma's presence wouldn't raise too much comment. The address was probably on file somewhere, but his father was dead and his mother had left for America soon afterwards, so Emma might be safe here for a time. Until he could arrange something better. He steadied the bag of food between his feet.

None of the handful of other passengers paid any attention to the pale, donnish-looking young man wearing thick glasses, or the dark, slight girl next to him. The day had been overcast, but now, in the late afternoon, the sun had emerged to bathe the landscape in a rather melancholy light.

Kessler had a lot to think about. He knew he could tell Emma very little, which wasn't easy as she was curious and bright - would he have been so much in love with her if it had been otherwise? He'd have to count on her realising that the less she knew, the better. He wished he knew more himself, but appreciated why Hoffmann hadn't taken him into his confidence more than was necessary. He was hurt in a way, he would have liked to go with his boss, but he knew where he'd be most useful, and where his duty was. These were dark times. He would have enough to do, making sure he and Emma got through this. That was his first and overriding priority. He had spent a long time since his last meeting with Hoffmann trying to assess what the next few days would bring him, and how he would react to whatever next crossed his path. For the moment, though, he needed to concentrate on this job.

He looked at Emma, nuzzled her head, smelling her hair, luxuriating in it, in being in love with her, but part of his mind stayed detached, professional. The only chance of escape lay in being careful. He took his arm away as the bus turned right at a crossroad.

'Nearly there.'

'Yes.'

'I'll have to get back fast today, you know. You'll have to look after yourself. Don't stay here long if I don't return soon. They'll find out where you are, given time. The only question is when.' He couldn't bear to leave her alone like this, but what else could he do? Run away with her? No. The best chance of keeping her safe was to stay where he was, close to the centre of things, and keep his ear to the ground.

'Yes.' She smiled.

'I'll help you, of course.'

She looked at him. 'I have 3000 Marks, my violin, my mother's wedding ring, and a bundle of food vouchers. How far do you think I can go on them?'

Kessler said, 'I'll give you money, but it'll take a little time to get it.'

She looked at him. 'Whom can I trust?'

'You can trust me.' He squeezed her shoulder, but he still felt inadequate.

The bus slowed and stopped at a corner by a thicket near which an old highway crucifix stood. The cross was rusty and bent, and the wooden figure of Christ so weatherworn that the doleful features of his face weren't recognisable anymore; but someone had placed flowers there which, to judge by their freshness, were not more than a day or two old. Kessler and Emma were the only ones to alight. The bus rumbled away.

Kessler picked up Emma's case and led her down a lane which ran behind an untidy copse towards the village where the house was. God knows it was an obscure enough place, but it was still close to Berlin, and vulnerable. As a staging-post, this was fine, but for no more than a week or so. He would have to move fast.

'Where do you think my father is now?' asked Emma.

Kessler hesitated. 'He meant to head south.'

She looked at him again. 'Do you think he's still alive?'

'He isn't the type to give up. You know that.'

'They might have already got him.'

'If they had, I'd know. He'll be in deep cover by now.' Kessler tried to sound confident, but he wasn't at all sure. That Hoffmann had an agenda to fulfil was certain; that he wouldn't leave the country until he'd done his work would be typical of him. Kessler also had a good idea of what was occupying his ex-boss's mind at this moment.

He looked at Emma as she walked. How much had Hoffmann told her?

The less she knew the better. Everywhere, the Gestapo was on the tracks of conspirators' relatives. Emma, and her aunt, and her aunt's family, would be targeted. At least her aunt, back in Nikolassee, was resourceful and had some powerful contacts herself.

They reached the house and he hugged her tight. She responded less warmly, unsure of herself now, at the moment of parting.

'You're hurting me.'

He looked at her. 'I may never see you again. Do you realise that?'

She smiled again. 'Don't be silly. In a year this will all be over. We'll have the rest of our lives together then.'

He held her hands. 'If I'm not back within a week, leave. Go wherever you can. Don't stay here long.'

'Where shall I go?'

'Just get on the road.' He hadn't meant to sound so brutal. 'There are people moving west and south already.' He took what money he had on him and gave it to her. 'Take this. I'll bring more. But, believe me, the road will be better than arrest. If you get the slightest hint that they're looking for you, go.'

He had never told her he loved her. Now, he felt he had to, in case there was never another chance; but he could not bring himself to, because he might be saying goodbye forever. Why say such a thing at such a time?

If they were going to part, they had better get it over with. He took her into the house, lit the lamps, and showed her the rooms. It was a small place, not much to it. He wanted to stay with her. He left. Small shy kiss, not enough to express anything. He waited half-an-hour by the crucifix for the bus.

It started to rain. That penetrating drizzle which got through everything. He hadn't brought a raincoat. He kept wiping his glasses. He'd be drenched before he was home.

37

It was dark by the time he got back to his flat, wet through and cold after sitting on the bus in soaking clothes, to find a middle-aged man in the usual trenchcoat and trilby leaning wearily against the door-jamb. He pushed himself upright as Kessler approached and tilted his hat back. Kessler recognised him as one of Heinrich Müller's minions from the Prinz-Albrecht-Straße.

'Where the hell have you been?' said the man.

'Working.'

'You weren't in your office.'

Kessler just looked at him.

'Come on,' the man said, with all the authority he could muster.

'Where to?'

'Where do you think? The *Gruppenführer* wants you.'

'Lucky me.' Kessler let himself into his flat.

'Where do you think you're going?' But Kessler outranked the Gestapo errand-boy. 'I've been waiting an hour,' said the man, plaintively, as Kessler closed the door in his face, saying, 'Then you can wait a couple of minutes longer while I take a leak and get changed - you're not the only one who's had a hard day.'

Once alone, inside, he went and dashed cold water on his face. Something big had happened. No point in asking the stooge; he wouldn't know.

At least he had got Emma out - perhaps only just in time - the problem now would be letting her know what was going on, and telling her how she should react to it. He prayed she'd take his advice.

He took as long as he dared, changing into a fresh shirt, before rejoining the Gestapo officer, who set off angrily down the corridor as soon as Kessler emerged.

***

'Where did they find the car, sir?' Kessler asked.

'In a clearing down by the Kantersee - it's a small lake near Storkow.' Heinrich Müller shunted papers around on his desk, didn't look up. His balding head looked grey in the lamplight. Kessler had not been asked to sit down. The atmosphere was, Kessler thought, par for the course these days: a mixture of self-importance and panic.

'Is he dead, sir?'

'Who knows? Certainly looks like it. Enough of the shitholes have bumped themselves off in the last few days. Why should he be an exception?' Müller belched lightly, and Kessler smelled schnapps and sausage. He himself hadn't eaten since breakfast, and his stomach rumbled - he hoped Müller wouldn't hear. A cup of ersatz coffee he'd drunk had left its usual unpleasant aftertaste of acorns. He felt mildly sick, which didn't stop him wondering if he dared light a cigarette; he decided not to.

'Clever though,' Müller continued. 'Local cops thought it was Göring or someone on a hunting expedition and didn't report it to us for forty-eight hours.' A new thought seemed to strike the Gruppenführer. 'But if he shot himself, why bother to try to buy time?'

'I don't know, sir,' said Kessler, after a pause to ensure that the question was not rhetorical, and to give himself a moment, since the same question had occurred to him. 'Double bluff?'

'That's what I want you to find out. You were trained by the bastard, you should know how he thinks.'

Kessler knew Müller couldn't possibly really want him on the case. Surely he'd rather have handled it with men from his own department. Unless Müller thought that in times like these, Kessler would want to cover his own back. No, Kessler thought, he couldn't count on being trusted by these people.

'You're giving the case to me, sir?'

Müller riffled through papers on his desk. Kessler continued to stand, more or less at attention, among the packing cases that littered the room. The clerk who was filling them caught his eye for a moment.

'Yes.' Müller looked up, his irritation clear. 'You should be honoured. It's a direct order from the Führer.'

Kessler was silent.

'You know your boss better than anyone. Don't think we haven't had an eye on you.'

'Thank you, sir.'

'What?'

'Who actually found the car, sir?'

'A farmer, probably out trying a bag a duck. Reported it to the foresters. They told the local cops.' Müller fidgeted with his pen. Then he picked up a folder and pushed it across his desk. 'It's all in the fucking report.' He added, 'This is a big sweep, Kessler, and this is a big chance for you. Bring him down and you're made.'

Kessler drew himself up, his mind racing.

'So don't drag your fucking feet,' Müller went on. 'This is a personal betrayal, not just treachery to the Reich. It's a bitter disappointment. Can you imagine what a blow this is to the Führer?' He relaxed slightly. 'Look, he wants Hoffmann alive, so he can talk to him, try to understand what made him do this. They were close. He's had a personal copy of that report sent to him. That's how important it is.'

'Sir.'

'You're one of the few people Hoffmann trusts. No-one's in a better position to reel him in in one piece. I'm sure you'll think of a way. And if you do, you won't be the loser. Think about it.' Müller looked at him. 'All right. Go.'

Kessler was halfway across the mausoleum of an office before he recalled the new edict that everyone, even regular army and criminal police, now had to give the Hitler salute. Against his will, he turned and gave it now, as briskly as he could. It occurred to him that on entering the office he'd forgotten to do so, and Müller had not commented.

'I was wondering if you'd remember,' growled the *Gruppenführer*. 'Report every twenty-four hours.'

'Thank you, sir.'

'One moment. You'll need backup.'

'Sir?'

'Someone you can trust. '

'My sergeant?'

Müller looked at him. 'Why not? Kleinschmidt! Certainly. We know all about him. Dim but loyal. Been with you nearly two years, hasn't he? But remember, this is a highly confidential matter. Slightest sign of trouble, get rid of him.'

As he left, Kessler sensed rather than saw Müller reach for his telephone.

38

It would be impossible to leave before dawn, when the blackout was over, so Kessler went to his office before going home, rang to order a car, called the duty office to tell them to alert Sergeant Kleinschmidt that he'd need him ready at six, and then sat at his desk for an hour reading the file, which told him little more than Müller already had. Hoffmann's betrayer, he read, had been a certain Major Reichmann, an adjutant to one of the conspirators, who'd been easy to pump since he had a wife, children and parents, all within easy reach in the capital. Nevertheless they'd had to break three of his fingers and give him an hour on the rack before they broke him. (The report noted that Reichmann had died of a heart attack while in custody. His family had been arrested.) As far as the abandoned car was concerned, Police Sergeant Otto Strauss had stated that Hoffmann picked up the Mercedes and left alone from the Werderscher Markt depot. Scraps of what looked like official papers had been found on the lake shore and sent for analysis, but so far had yielded nothing. They hadn't found either the car keys or a body, but a frogman had recovered a service pistol believed to have belonged to the deceased (presumed), in the shallows. One shot had been discharged, but no bullet had been found.

Kessler went home, finding time for a beer and a fish-paste sandwich, increasing the stomach pains which had been plaguing him since the interview with Müller. He decided against making any calls, tried to sleep for a couple of hours, and at five returned to his office where he got through in three cases out of four. There was no way of contacting Emma. Maybe he'd be able to close this investigation fast and get her out by tomorrow evening. If not, and his heart ached at the thought, she'd be on her own.

Arno Kleinschmidt, 30 years old, unmarried, arrived at 05.45. He weighed 120 kilos, his suit stretched painfully over his back, and his hat was too small for his head. He might once have been good-looking, but his face had spread with the weight and he had the hamster pouches and red palms of a man too fond of his drink. He was the secretary of the Fat Fellows Club, a group which until recently had held regular and perilous boating trips on the Spree, which Arno used as an excuse to fraternise with certain of the other clubs that did the same; but those clubs had begun to dissolve, their members, once the doyens of Berlin's underworld, having started to leave to seek new burrows in cities likely to be taken by the Western Allies, preferably by the *Ammis*, who were rich, not played out, like the British.

Kleinschmidt was fresh and alert. He smelled of *4711* and freshly-smoked, real tobacco. His dark hair was brilliantined and his moustache neatly combed. His eyes were small, and seemed candid; but in fact you could read very little in them. His belly was what qualified him for membership of the Fat Fellows Club, whose criterion for membership was that you should not have seen your penis, except in a mirror, for at least five years.

'What's up, sir?'

'Hope you've had breakfast.'

'Well... '

'We're going to Storkow,' Kessler was pulling on his jacket as he made for the door.

'Is it far?' Kleinschmidt was a local man, and panicked at the thought of being separated from food, drink, and the city for more than two hours at a stretch. Berliners always had a Stulle in their briefcases, the joke went - sometimes a sandwich was the only thing in them.

'You can always pick up a Hackepeter somewhere, man; now get on.' Kessler was still hungry himself, and frankly he could have done with a schnapps after that interview.

'I should be so fucking lucky,' muttered Kleinschmidt.

39

The roads were jammed with military traffic, and they made bad time reaching the Kantersee. A wretched cop stood at the edge of the road by the track which led down through the trees. Rain dripped from his leather helmet.

The rain was fine, and irritating. Their mackintoshes were a poor defence against it and Kessler resigned himself to getting wet through for the second time in twenty-four hours. Soon they felt it reach and chill the bone despite the season. It fell with a soft, relentless patter on the boughs that sheltered the path. The rain was likely, despite the protection of the trees, to have wiped out most clues.

They took care to walk along the edge of the track, but there was no trace of anything that might have been of interest. A few low-growing shrubs had been clearly swept aside by the car as it had driven past them, and the fact that they had not yet recovered showed that the car's passage had been recent; but that merely confirmed what they already knew. As they approached the Mercedes, looming ahead like some large dead animal, Kessler hoped, fairly vainly, he knew, that any clues around it hadn't been ploughed under the boots of foresters and police since they'd known about it. Forensic detective work was newish; Hoffmann had been a pioneer. Ordinary rankers would still have no idea that they should tread on eggs around a crime scene.

Wet bushes snatching at his trouser-ends, Kessler took his time, ignoring Kleinschmidt's continuous grumbling behind him, picking his way until he reached the car. He'd seen nothing on the track, and it was no wonder. Rain dripped from every leaf, and nothing else around them moved except for a stag beetle which lumbered through the undergrowth and across the toe of his shoe as he paused to let it pass.

'See that big bugger?' said Kleinschmidt behind him, and Kessler without turning heard his sergeant trying to stamp on the insect; but the ground was too soft, and the beetle too heavily armoured. Kleinschmidt slipped and nearly fell, grasping a branch for support and cursing. 'Fucking countryside.'

Kessler reached the car knowing that the rain had dispelled any trace of earlier disruption or movement he might have been able to find.

The Mercedes itself was guarded by an even more miserable policeman than the first, who had shrunk into his cape and merged with the trees and stumps around him. He pulled himself sluggishly to attention as Kessler approached, and levelled his rifle at him. Kessler produced his ID, and the man lapsed into sodden indifference, rolling his shoulders to ease the pain in his back. They might as well have let the poor sod sit in the car, Kessler thought, but of course that would have been against all protocol. These days the usual method was to beat the truth - or at least something - out of any suspect; but in this case obviously the propriety of a formal investigation was going to be observed - more-or-less - to the letter. It was ironic, given the general atmosphere in which it was taking place.

He ordered Kleinschmidt, who was beginning to wonder aloud, though under his breath, why he had been brought along at all, to search the area surrounding the car to a distance of five metres, then changed his mind and made it seven. Where were the car keys? Had Hoffmann taken them with him? If so, why? Unlike him to forget them. Had he thrown them into the undergrowth to slow things up further - extra keys, if they existed, would have had to be fetched from Berlin? But you couldn't throw anything very far in this dense wood.

Kleinschmidt blundered off, pausing to put a cigarette in his mouth, swearing as it turned soggy and collapsed before he could even try to light it.

The car had sunk slightly into the ground. Kessler could see around the door-handles greasy traces where the rain had not fallen uniformly. There might be fingerprints, possibly, though he doubted it. The local cops had forced the lock, and since then too many people would have meddled.

He opened the driver's door and looked inside. Everything seemed to accord with the report. Kessler found an empty packet of British cigarettes - Player's Navy Cut - and an empty bottle of Hennessy XO; a Hershey bar wrapper, and a crumpled, empty bird-shot box. Nothing else at all.

Kessler poked around the interior of the car for some time more, as much to keep out of the rain as anything, so he was a little shamefaced when Kleinschmidt returned, streaming, to say that he had found the sharp end of fuck-all and if he didn't get a hot grog inside him soon he'd be a dead man.

Kessler indicated the contents of the car. 'Put this stuff in your bag - keep your gloves on - and get it back to the car.'

'Is this all?'

'Yes.'

Kleinschmidt almost grinned. 'Didn't leave much did they?'

As he spoke the rain suddenly hesitated, then ceased as if a heavenly hand had turned a tap off; soon afterwards the sun started to beat down through the still-dripping leaves. It quickly became unpleasantly hot.

Kessler told the policeman, who was shaking himself like a dog, that he'd soon be relieved, and, with Kleinschmidt bringing up the rear, made his way back to the road. He walked slowly again, but for a different reason this time. Things didn't add up. Despite the obvious looting of the car, why leave all that expensive stuff in the first place? There could only be one answer, to delay pursuers, and it had worked. But, as Müller had suggested, why would a suicide do that? Or *was* it a kind of insurance? No body had been found. He tried to read Hoffmann's thoughts. It could still be a double bluff, but without a body, what had he to go on? And why play for time, unless to keep the Gestapo occupied and keep their attention away from Emma and - the other child? Barely anyone knew about the other child's existence, though, and Kessler knew he wasn't supposed to. One of the many things, he suspected, that Hoffmann had kept from him, or thought he had. But buying time for them made a kind of desperate sense.

The question was, what kind of report should he make to Müller? Could he get away with saying that he believed Hoffmann had killed himself, that the Mercedes should be retrieved, that there was nothing more to be done? But wasn't that too obvious? If *he'd* seen through it, why not someone else - Müller was on the scent; someone closer, like his former colleague, Ernst Schiffer, for example, would be even more likely to. And Kleinschmidt, too, had probably, if he could be bothered, formed some opinion of his own. And where was the body? The shore shelved off steeply. Was Hoffmann's corpse by now in the depths of the water, where it would take frogmen weeks to find it, if at all? Could Kessler set them on that kind of goose-chase? Would he dare to?

They might as well get the car back to the pool before it rusted: whatever happened, there was nothing more to be gleaned from these woods. He thought, too, that if he could persuade Müller to give him some time in Berlin, he'd be able - if they hadn't put a tail on him - to see Emma again and get her to a place of real safety. If Hoffmann was still alive, and Kessler imagined he was, he was pretty sure he knew where his old boss would go. The others would assume that he'd make for Sweden or Switzerland, where, with his contacts in their police forces formed over twenty years and more, he'd have no trouble at all getting in and to safety. But the others didn't know what Kessler knew.

So the problem was, how to pull as much wool as possible over Müller's eyes, without making himself look less sharp than an SS dagger, and without compromising himself? And he had only a few hours to get a copper-bottomed solution together. He also had his own problems. He'd never been a Party member himself, but he'd been closely associated with someone the enemy would see as a Nazi bigwig. Kessler knew that the curtain would fall in a matter of months, and certainly no more than a year. He had to be sure that when the time came, everything was covered; and he knew what his priorities were.

Waiting by their car, they found the policeman guarding the entrance to the track in conversation with an SS motorcycle courier. Both men doused their cigarettes and stood to attention as Kessler approached.

'To what do I owe this pleasure?' Kessler asked the SS-man as Kleinschmidt heaved his bag of not-too-promising evidence into the back of their car, himself lighting up as soon as he'd done so.

'Message from Department Four, sir.' The SS man produced a grey envelope from his saddlebag. What the hell did Müller want now? Kessler took the envelope and slit it with his finger.

The note wasn't from Müller but from Ernst Schiffer:

Sturmbannführer SCHIFFER, E., i.A.: Gruppenführer MÜLLER

Berlin, RSHA, Amt IV

to: Kriminalrat KESSLER, P.

Strictly confidential state material!

Heil Hitler!

You are commanded to return in order to make your report in person to the Head of Department IV immediately on receipt of this Order, and to receive further instructions. This Order applies equally to Detective-Sergeant KLEINSCHMIDT, A.

You are to proceed directly to Department IV under motorcycle escort.

I am further instructed to inform you that a parallel investigation into the whereabouts of the suspect HOFFMANN's daughter has been today instigated under my personal command.

Heil Hitler!

(signed) SCHIFFER

Kessler folded the order carefully and put it in his pocket.

'Anything wrong?' Kleinschmidt asked, at his elbow.

Kessler looked at the sunshine on the raindrops, as it turned them into drops of gold.

'Nothing at all,' he said, and, turning to the SS-man: 'We'd better get going.'

40

Enough time had passed. Hoffmann had managed to dip in and out of sleep for another hour, though it was a painful experience, for every time he began to drift, fear of the dream jolted him awake. Now there was no longer any point in trying.

He rose and made his way down the still-silent corridor to the narrow bathroom, where he took a cold shower - at least there was water. Shaving, he looked at himself in the stained mirror. His reflection stared back expressionlessly through a storm of brown mottling. The face was flabby with tiredness, the grey eyes dull. Peeling colour print around the edges of the glass celebrated the joys of weekends at Wörthersee, and how affordable they were. The advert made him think back to what now seemed like an age of innocence, though of course it had been nothing of the sort, and many Berliners had been ashamed of their city's reputation for sex and sleaze. But it had been vibrant, too, and free, and the world had been there, the British, French, Italians, Russians, Americans, spending their hard currency like water and living like kings on a dollar when a wheelbarrow-load of Reichsmarks wouldn't buy you a cup of coffee. And how the city had opened its legs to them.

Working in the drugs squad, then vice, then homicide, climbing fast through the ranks, married more to his work than his wife, Hoffmann had thought himself in a kind of inside-out paradise; but he knew that the train all these revellers were on was racing towards a cliff.

He thought about the twists of snow hidden in the lining of his jacket. He wouldn't take one now. Better to leave it until he really needed it. Now, he was only relatively tired.

Back in his room, he dressed carefully, checking that yesterday's shirt wouldn't give him away today. It felt stale as he put it on, but he'd have to make things last until he got to Tilli's country house. No way of getting things laundered here in the time.

He bit his lip, thinking again of the clumsy code he'd used when calling her from his office. But it was done now, and for all his anxiety he couldn't believe they'd find a trail there. He needed to get *on*. He would keep the car. He packed his bags and made his way downstairs. The staff were up, and the coffee, which smelled almost real, was made, but as far as Hoffmann could see, no other guest was stirring. He'd heard no noise from the surrounding rooms in the night. It could be that he was the only guest. He took a cup of coffee and a glass of water in the restaurant. The coffee even tasted almost real.

The elderly man who had checked him in the night before had been replaced at the desk by a large, comfortable-looking woman. She leaned forward as he approached and looked at him with dark, sardonic eyes.

'Going far?' she asked.

'Business, you know ... '

'Early start. Usually means a long journey.'

'No peace for the wicked,' he said lamely. She looked at him darkly, and then gave an easy and lazy laugh; she pushed her body back from the desk, put out her arms and stretched luxuriously, looking at him all the time. Hoffmann smiled. It'd been a long time since anyone had come on to him like that, and he was surprised to find himself aroused. But there was something else. She seemed familiar. Did he know her? In which case, was he familiar to her, despite the change in his appearance, which wouldn't fool any former acquaintance. No point in taking risks. He'd have to get out fast.

'I know what you mean,' she said, and laughed again. He hadn't heard such a laugh for years, so confident and cheerful.

No. There was no way their paths had crossed before. He'd know. he'd see through it. He would have liked to know what she thought of all this mess, but her wide, lovely face seemed untrammelled by thought; and maybe that was why she seemed so carefree. She was perhaps in her late thirties. She'd run this hotel before the destruction had started, he guessed, and she'd be running it when it was over.

As he paid his bill, filling in the usual official forms quickly, she lowered her voice to say, 'Come back and see us again one day, when you're not so busy.' But then she was distracted by the telephone and turned away to answer it. She would have reported his stay to the local police. The papers he was using identified him as an official of the Ministry of Aviation. Would she make any comment, would they ask her any questions, when she rang to report his departure? *Did* she know him?

He left quickly, while she was talking. Three or four people were in the small outer lobby and he had to brush past them. Their eyes followed him. Hoffmann tried to look impressive, a man on a mission, on official business, the man he had always been until a handful of days ago, and still was, he supposed, in a different way. Of course the business wasn't official, now. He thought of his route. He would have to zigzag across country. Once they'd discovered the car, and discovered the suicide ruse, they'd send people north and south, towards the

Baltic ports, Kiel and Lübeck for sure, and towards the Swiss border. But if they picked up any other trail, he'd have to be ready for it.

He got back to the car having passed no-one on the street but a road-sweeper. Tucking himself into a doorway, he watched the VW and the windows of the buildings around it for two minutes before crossing the open space to reach it. None of the other vehicles from the night before had moved. If a cop had been keeping an eye on the cars overnight, he wasn't there now; but the Maybach and the Horch were cars for higher-ups, no-one would dare tamper with them, or even come near. There was no-one about, no movement behind the windows, and although he could hear a dog barking furiously not far away, the sound was muffled, and got no closer. The animal must be behind a wall, probably chained.

No-one had filtered away his petrol. Breathing more easily, Hoffmann stowed his bags quickly, and threw his coat onto the back seat. He pushed the starter button and the engine fired immediately, quelling another knot of anxiety. He put the car into gear, slipped back to the street and then down it, out of town, accelerating as he picked up the main road. He was surprised by the degree of relief he felt at his departure.

His thoughts turned to Emma. His anxiety for his daughter overwhelmed him, the more so because he could do nothing more for her himself. He didn't even know for sure where she was now. He prayed that Kessler had managed to get her away in time, and kept her safe, but prayers can seem very impotent things. He hoped her own good sense and resourcefulness would protect her, and that she wouldn't come to harm because of what he'd done, because in that case all the resourcefulness in the world wouldn't save her.

He'd find out, he told himself, but he had to accept that it'd be a long time before he did.

Thinking of Emma made him think of Tilli, and the responsibility he'd given her - or she had undertaken. God help him if anything happened to her. And yet the thought of Tilli was comforting. His oldest friend.

41

He'd known Tilli since they were adolescents - their parents had been friends. There'd been some experimental knee-fondling and kissing on backstairs and in corridors, but no closeness until much later, when they were adults, and then there'd never been any question of anything more than friendship. By then she'd become a star. He'd been to one or two of the plays she was in, and had finally steeled himself to re-introduce himself to her backstage.

They'd become close almost immediately, but she was married by then, and, apart from her career, she cultivated a salon at the centre of artistic and literary circles in Berlin.

The world she moved in barely overlapped with Hoffmann's, but the Nazis brought them together again. Tilli's husband, Hartmut Cassirer, well aware of what would sooner or later happen to him as a half-Jew, left for Buenos Aires as soon as he could, managing to take most of his banking empire with him, and leaving Tilli to look after their property in Germany, transferring it to her name. Hoffmann had been able to smooth Cassirer's way as far as travel documents were concerned, and Brandau, for a percentage, had tidied his business affairs. Tilli had returned to acting for a while, and, obedient to the new anti-Jewish legislation, had divorced her spouse in 1936. The marriage, she told Hoffmann, had been in trouble anyway.

Hoffmann knew that Tilli wasn't a convinced National Socialist; she had never been interested in politics. What she was interested in, at least at the beginning, was keeping her career alive: if she'd been a musician or a painter, she might have joined the American exodus herself, but she was no Dietrich, she told Hoffmann, and she lacked the confidence, with her stumbling English, for Hollywood. She had the same kind of statuesque body as Zarah Leander, whose most ardent fan was Hitler himself; but in time she grew disillusioned with the crap she was forced to perform, and with the disillusionment came a lack of conviction and interest in her work. She didn't need the money, and she hated the increasing censorship and paranoia that ruled the city. She closed the huge flat in Charlottenburg, and, resisting attempts by both Göring and Goebbels to persuade her to stay, moved to her estate in the south. The loss of celebrity and attention hadn't bothered her in the least; she'd seemed to welcome it.

Hoffmann hadn't seen her now for several months, unwilling to put her in any unnecessary danger as the last storm gathered; but now risks had to be taken; and Tilli had taken the biggest risk of all, on his behalf, already.

Risks. He thought of himself as a boy, skiing with his father in the Bavarian Alps - down from the top of the Ochsenkopf through the dark trees, and of his eight-year-old's fear and exhilaration as the wooden skis sliced through the snow and screeched on the patches of ice, juddering over clumps of earth and rock which the snow hadn't covered.

'You've got to get down the slope, Max; off the mountain, back to the valley. You can't think of anything else until you've done that. You can't go back, and you can't walk it; there is only one way to get home, and that's by going on.'

He had never learned how to control the speed properly; and when he panicked, he fell. But he still had to get down the mountain, and he knew that even now he would only be able to reach home once the work was done.

42

At a crossroads whose roadsigns had been removed, he turned in what he hoped was the direction of Neuenstein, along a country road which had been rutted by caterpillar tracks a few months earlier. The rising sun in his rear-view mirror blinded him for a moment. Ahead there was a small, dark fir-wood which formed a crescent around a sweep of sloping grassland on which three fallow deer were grazing. Three the hunters hadn't got yet, incredibly. As the sound of the car reached them, they bolted into the trees.

There was no traffic at all. There was not even a labourer toiling along the verge. He lit another cigarette. He couldn't shake off the dream of last night, but harder to bear than the screaming in his skull, which he'd almost got used to, as far as you can accustom yourself to a kind of moral tinnitus, was the thought of Kara, who, though he had spent years trying to lose her, had never gone away, and who, now at the end, had returned to haunt him again. It was as if she had become the representative of all the ghosts.

He gave in to thoughts of her. A long, oval face, straight nose, and dark lips, the lower fuller than the upper; and large, serious brown eyes, so dark they were almost black. A long neck, smooth brown skin, straight, fine black hair. Keenly intelligent , defensive, difficult, and independent. He'd never thought he'd have a hope.

They'd met in 1932, at Tilli and Hartmut's annual beginning-of-season party - the last one ever, as things turned out, for just before Christmas Hartmut had left. Kara was wearing a white silk dress. She was talking to a man of about Hoffmann's size and build, dressed in a dinner jacket. A trendsetter, thought Hoffmann. Most of the male guests not in uniform were still wearing, as he was, evening dress.

'Nice, isn't she?' said a man at his elbow, whose voice he recognised. He turned to see the glittering eyes, broken nose, and sauroid face of his occasional friend and occasional enemy, Veit Adamov.

'Do you know her?'

Adamov's short arms spread out to embrace the throng. 'I know everybody.'

'She doesn't look like one of your starlets.'

'Far too intelligent for that. But we used to share political sympathies. Seriously, that's how we know each other. We were comrades. I don't believe she's quite given up the cause, either. We still meet from time to time, for a drink, or when I'm short of money.' Veit looked at him. 'You think I'm lying.'

'I haven't seen you for a while,' said Hoffmann.

'Not since this time last year.'

'Been busy?'

Adamov shrugged. 'Nobody wants the films I make any more. Well, only the lighter stuff. I think it's all part of this New Dawn business.' He smiled and drew on his cigar. 'Time to think of a change of career.'

'Or a change of scene?'

Adamov shook his head. 'Not quite yet, I think. It's too interesting here.'

Their paths had crossed from time to time over the past decade, but usually only when the lightweight sex movies Adamov made went too far and attracted the attention of the Vice Squad. The director usually managed to get off any serious punishment by trading snippets of information about those underworld elements his work brought him into contact with, and, as vice was so often linked with drugs, the authorities found him more useful to them as a free man than banged up. The political units took the other films Adamov made, pro-communist documentaries, which his pornography subsidised, more seriously. Recently, fighting between communists and Brownshirts had escalated. There'd been many deaths. Adamov had joined the street battles at first, but lately he'd been keeping his head down. He wasn't working, either.

'Watch your step. We'd hate to lose you.'

Adamov took a generous swallow from his tumblerful of brandy-and-champagne. 'They can't catch me.'

'If they get into power, they will.'

'They'll get into power all right, but they won't last. This country would never accept shit like that - they even dress in the colour of shit, and not even very healthy shit either. Who could possibly take them seriously? Present company excepted, of course,' he smiled again.

Hoffmann didn't reply, responding to a wave from Hans Brandau, a lawyer he'd recently met through mutual dealings with Hartmut Cassirer. He noticed the young woman again; she was trying to extricate herself from the company of the man in the dinner jacket, who was leaning over her insistently.

'I doubt if she'll have anything to do with him,' said Adamov, brushing cigar-ash from his lapel. He was wearing a check suit, shiny with wear, almost the only man not in formal dress. Tilli, who, Hoffmann knew, generally invited a sprinkling of bohemians to shake up her stiffer-lipped guests, would have accepted this as part of her plan. And Adamov seldom drank enough to lose control. In the past, he'd faced the consequences when he had.

'Who is he?'

'Man called Hagen. Wolf Hagen. Quite close to Hitler, they say.'

The name rang a bell. A colleague in the Excise Department had mentioned it the other day in a general briefing - something to do with importing Swedish steel and pig iron on an unofficial level. Hagen was a businessman, good at under-the-counter deals; there were dozens like him.

'Got an honorary rank. Wears the old brown uniform sometimes. Doesn't suit him.'

'You should be working for us,' said Hoffmann.

'He's a *Standartenführer*. Likes to go out the streets too, and beat up a few of us wicked Lefties.'

'Sounds pleasant.'

'You don't believe me. I've seen him. Does it because he enjoys it. Bloody southerner.'

'Then what's he doing here?'

Adamov tapped his nose. 'Lip-service. He's also a snob, and these days you need to be in with the snobs who are in with the Nazis. Unfortunately. Not that he's a bigwig yet, but you never know.' The woman was beginning to look around a little desperately. 'Shall we go and rescue her?'

Before Hoffmann could react, Adamov was crossing the floor, his arms spread wide. 'Kara! Kara von Wildenbruch! My dear, it's been so long! And you mustn't monopolise poor *Freiherr* von Hagen - ' he threw in the aristocrat tag with a generous wave of one arm, scooping her by the waist with the other, and guiding her towards Hoffmann. 'Besides, there's someone else I'd like you to meet: *Frau Doktor* von Wildenstein, *Herr Professor Doktor* von Hoffmann!'

Hagen, almost drunk, made a poor attempt to hide his irritation, but his attention was diverted by his hostess, who'd also been watching. Adamov steered his two charges away to a table, covered with a white linen cloth, which served as the bar. It was laden with a battery of bottles, from humble beer to majestic champagne. Ignoring the disapproving steward, Adamov helped himself to a large glass, into which he poured a liberal amount of Cristal, topping it up, to the steward's horror, with an equal amount of Asbach-Uralt. With this he toasted Hoffmann and the girl, and disappeared in the direction of the buffet.

'Dr von Wildenstein?' Hoffmann smiled slightly.

'Professor von Hoffmann?' She wasn't at ease.

'I'm afraid my *von* is a figment of Veit's imagination. As is the professorship.'

'Mine's only inherited. I haven't done anything to deserve it.' She spread her hands, unbending fractionally. 'Thank you for saving me. I was beginning to think I'd have to faint, or something.'

'You should thank Veit.'

'Veit always has an ulterior motive.'

They both smiled at that, and talked of other things, finding out why they were both there, and how they knew the Cassirers. Kara's mother was a friend of Hartmut - 'But then the Cassirers know everybody.'

Tilli's guests were lawyers, actors, journalists, doctors and academics. Hoffmann remembered looking round the ballroom. Almost every man was wearing at least one gong, even if only campaign medals. A year ago, only professional soldiers, or those with the highest decorations, would have bothered to trot them out for Tilli's party. Across the room, Ernst Udet wore his Blue Max at his neck, but he was one of the few with anything serious to show off.

Kara had followed his gaze. 'You seem to be the only man here without some tin on his chest,' she said drily, and he wondered if she'd been able to sense his thoughts. His hand went up to his own throat. He'd considered wearing his medal, an Iron Cross Second Class, earned by getting a wounded captain back to the safety of the trenches, about two days before the Armistice. At the time he hadn't thought he had done anything particularly brave, and now only wore the decoration with his formal uniform. But for Tilli's party he'd seen no reason for it, and the space just below his white tie was empty.

'Did you miss the war?' she continued.

He started slightly at such a direct question, but replied, 'I was only in it for the last eighteen months. Acting Lieutenant in the Engineers.'

'Things are getting very military again,' she said.

'Is that a bad thing?'

'People have short memories.'

43

They had dinner together three days later. He knew she was wary of him, didn't like the idea of policemen at all, but he persisted. Small confidences emerged. He told her a few snatches of his life, like a kid, spilling out his story, about his father, his mother and sister, who'd gone back to Kiel after his father's death; and the bakery they ran there. She was interested that he had once intended to become a priest, and impressed at his knowledge of Hebrew, some of which he remembered, though it was rusty. Cautiously, with time, he became happy, and she grew more relaxed.

It hadn't been a profound affair to begin with; rather, one of occasional comfort and friendship. He hadn't slept with anyone since his wife's death two years earlier. Kara herself was a children's specialist at the Charité Hospital. She had graduated between the communist uprising that followed the war, and the financial free-fall of the early Twenties, deciding to become a paediatrician after working as a volunteer at an orphanage in Pankow during the hard summer of 1919. She still dreamed about the children's matchstick arms and legs, their swollen knees and their dark eyes, empty of anything, and old.

She was unattached, but wouldn't go into details. Hoffmann, resisting his instinct, didn't ask many questions. She didn't like them. It was pleasanter to let Kara tell him things when she was ready to, and so, beyond establishing their basic backgrounds, they didn't talk much about themselves at first. They both knew how important it was to be cautious with strangers, even if you were sleeping with them, and especially, he knew, because of his job, which she referred to with resentment. Hoffmann didn't tell her about his involvement with the Party. Already uneasy about the path the Party had begun to take, he guessed she disapproved of it. But his political beliefs were his own business, and in those days he was still telling himself that, after all, the Party was a vital force, and had a vigorous leader, who was presenting strong policies which would help the economy and reduce unemployment if he came to power, as seemed increasingly likely.

The sabre-rattling he was used to; but in 1932 he preferred to turn a blind eye to the dark side of the organisation he'd joined. Membership was doing his career no harm. Even when the beatings and the arrests started, when the big boys of the city's organised crime clubs were taking sides in the political skirmishing, and when some people were already starting to pack their bags, he kept his head down.

They'd met in October 1932. Six months later, in Spring 1933, the world had changed. The Nazis were running the country by then. And it was then she discovered that he belonged to the Party.

He hadn't so much hidden his membership from her, he told himself, as kept silent about it. He might have been forgiven for assuming she would have guessed. After all, he was a senior policeman. No-one got to positions like that - or retained them - unless they were either very astute, or with the Leader. It was getting close to Easter. People in the capital were making jokes about how the Easter Hare would be turning up in a brown uniform this year, and how the Party would only permit people to colour white eggs. The streets were gunmetal, slick with rain, glinting under the lamps. The traffic was heavier than usual. Over everything hung a greater anticipation than usual of the approaching holidays. You couldn't put your finger on it, but it was as tangible as if it had taken shape in the alleys and boulevards; and in one way it had: Brownshirts were everywhere.

They had even been accepted as auxiliary police.

44

One evening, Hoffmann was late arriving at her apartment. He hadn't seen her for days. He was hurrying. He'd only managed to find a small silver brooch to give her, and he was rather ashamed of it.

As soon as she opened the door, he knew something was seriously wrong. Kara barely spoke, didn't kiss him, avoided his eyes.

'How long have we known each other?'

'You know how long.'

'And how long have you been quite so close to them?' She held up a copy of the main Party newspaper. It was opened to a middle page, where an article halfway down reported his promotion to deputy head of the *Kripo*. There was no photograph, but there was his name, Maximilian Martin Georg Anton Hoffmann, and his Party number.

His throat dried and his blood pounded. 'Where did you find that?' he asked.

'In the hospital. Open at this page. By chance. Do you think I'd sift through this filth?'

He watched her.

'By chance!' she repeated.

Unless, he thought, it'd been left there for her to find. In which case, who could possibly know about them? Of the few that knew, he could think of none that wished them harm. They would not have been let into the secret otherwise. Perhaps this really was a coincidence, little as Hoffmann believed in them. Most lies are exposed; most buried things are dug up.

She wasn't a Party member, and had no belief in Hitler's values. But why had he skated over something he had nothing, as he still felt, to be ashamed of?

The answer had been skirting the back of his mind for a long time - since the previous summer at least, he now realised with a shock. He also realised that the reason he'd been unwilling to confront it was because then it would lead him away from a successful career, and into a forest of uncertainty and risk. Simple cowardice? No.

He knew that things were no longer going the way that he'd hoped. The socialist element of the National Socialist German Workers' Party had gone, and there was plenty to suggest that huge amounts would be invested in rearmament.

There remained national pride, freedom, and reconstruction - all these things he believed in. These he clung to, but he knew that questions would remain too.

'Look, I'm a cop,' he said, on his dignity. 'You know that. I have to jump through certain hoops.'

'I don't believe it.'

'Then why did you ever accept me as your lover?'

He regretted the words even before the look of withering scorn appeared on her face. He looked at her. It hardly seemed possible that only thirty-six hours earlier they had been wrapped around each other, eating and drinking each other. Another shock hit him, and he wondered if it had hit her too. Except at the outset, they hadn't exchanged too many ideas or personal intimacies because their real intimacy was so intensely physical. The time to talk would come later, but until this moment each had believed they'd found their Socratic matching halves, and that was enough. They'd both been lonely and they'd cleaved to each other. Sex rushes you into a closeness you sometimes want to think spiritual as well; but when it isn't you find that you haven't come home after all, but only moved to another hotel, and there's a bill to pay when you leave.

Did they both feel that now? He didn't want to believe it. Her expression had grown less angry. Perhaps, like him, she wanted this hurdle behind them. But his attempt at an explanation was lame. 'It's simply climbing rungs on a ladder. My work isn't political - '

'How can it not be, when you're part of this kind of establishment?'

Hoffmann knew he was lying again, to her, and, worse, to himself. He still believed that Hitler had found a way out of the thick dense maze the country was in, but his manner of doing so was something Hoffmann was finding increasingly difficult to justify. You can't just hack down the hedges, because that leaves simple destruction in its wake. He had opened the gates of his mind and there was no closing them again. He believed in justice, but he didn't believe in absolutism. Political disagreement had been a disaster for the country for years, but look at what else had happened that was good. Now an exodus of people had begun, artists, scientists, teachers, whose departure would make Germany a darker, poorer place. Berlin didn't like Hitler; but Berlin had a lot to lose; elsewhere, most people flocked to him.

Hoffmann didn't want this to come between them. He wanted to take her in his arms, and cut all this nonsense out. He could sense that she, too, wanted to get inside the safety of an embrace; but she crossed the room away from him. At least it was to pour them both a glass of wine.

'My work isn't -' he began.

'Have you looked at what's going on?'

The room was familiar. He felt at home here, more than he had done in two years or more. The furniture was modern, tubular steel and leather. Breuer, Mies The rugs were bright, Bauhaus designs. She handed him his wine and put on a record: *Solvejg's Song*.

'Sit down,' she said.

Through the windows, the city shimmered in the darkness. You could see the Pariser Platz and the Victory Arch, with the bulk of the Adlon Hotel in one corner, and, further south, the department stores on Leipziger and Potsdamer Plätze. Unter den Linden drove east under its old limes, and in the other direction he could see the dimmer lights of the Kurfürstendamm. Tall whores there, braving the April chill. He could see them in his mind's eye, he could see their steel-blue eyes.

Kara sat down opposite him, lit a cigarette and sipped her wine. 'You're not the only one to have secrets.'

'Are you going to tell me yours?'

'I don't see why I should. Especially now.'

'No harm will come to you from me,' he said.

'Can't know that.'

'No-one in a better position to help.' He kept his voice light.

'At what cost?' She looked at him. 'You kept silent. Why? Were you ashamed?'

'I haven't lied to you.'

'You kept silent.'

'It's not important.'

'It is.'

He spread his hands. 'What do you want me to do?'

Her eyes flared. 'Resign!'

'Impossible.'

'Why?'

'I'd lose everything.'

'You wouldn't lose me.'

He watched her as she refilled their glasses and sat on the sofa. A Moroccan rug hung over its cream back. She collected African art, and shelves along one wall held rows of wooden masks.

She could have been North African herself. She looked exotic in the room, in her black dress, high at the neck, and long-sleeved; unlike the efficient, neutral image she presented at the hospital. He wondered sadly if he'd ever know her better than he did now.

'We are living in strange times,' she said.

'That's been true since 1914.'

'They are getting worse.'

'No.'

'So you agree with what's coming?'

He shrugged.

'You know perfectly well what will happen. With your contacts, you probably know better than anyone.' She paused. 'What are you going to do?'

'I'll carry on. There'll always be crooks.'

She looked at him coolly. He didn't even know exactly how old she was, though he guessed she was about four years younger than he, which made her somewhere at the end of her twenties.

'What will you do?' he asked.

'I don't know.'

'Will you leave?' That was the last thing he wanted her to do.

'I have my work too.' But she didn't sound convinced.

45

Hoffmann drove on. Fields and forests. Once he passed a convoy of army lorries going the other way, five of them, lumbering east. They were covered in field-grey tarpaulins. He caught the eye of the officer in the staff car which led them, a tired colonel with grey hair, whose look was expressionless. Hoffmann slowed down, just in case he'd be challenged, but nothing happened. The convoy drove on. He couldn't see what or whom they were carrying. The drivers' faces were haggard.

He reckoned he would have this one last day before they picked up his trail, unless he was extraordinarily lucky. It was still unpleasantly warm. How he hated summer, that clammy, overblown season. He flexed his hands on the steering-wheel. They were red, and ached from driving. His thoughts turned back again.

He had joined Kara on the sofa. He took her hand and she had let him hold it. He wanted to kiss her. She pulled away slightly, but without withdrawing her hand.

'Are you going to tell me your secrets?' she asked.

'I don't know.'

He felt like an intruder. He had been complacent. He didn't like the unexpected. He liked things to be orderly; but he had also been too quick to take for granted the happiness he thought had fallen into his lap. He certainly hadn't questioned it.

It had grown dark in the apartment and Kara rose to turn the lights on, shutting out the night as she drew the pale curtains. She always managed to have fresh flowers in a vase. He was reluctant to leave, but he doubted if they would be spending this night together, if they ever did again. She switched on the lamps, and he watched as the light caressed her skin, making soft shadows on her neck, and across the backs of her hands.

They sat in silence, finishing the bottle and smoking. He knew he would have to go, but he couldn't bring himself to get up. He didn't want to leave this unresolved.

'When I read that, I was appalled. The paper is two weeks old.'

'How long have you had it?' he asked.

She glared at him. 'Since a few days ago. I couldn't call you. I didn't want to believe it. You've been promoted by the Party. Tell me you don't believe in them.'

'I still think I can do some good,' he said.

'And how much freedom will they give you for that?'

He wondered if he should tell her about the case he was working on, a fourteen-year-old prostitute, full of heroin, fished out of the Spree. Starving, but that wasn't what had killed her. It was really nothing unusual; and trying to catch the dealers was like trying to catch flies with your hands. They were too quick. You just had to go on trying. Sometimes there was a betrayal, sometimes a lucky stroke - then they got the bastards.

He caught the expression on Kara's face, saw that she was looking into herself, and desisted. This was something he recognised: it happened when a confession was about to break. It was just a question of waiting for it. His mind switched to its professional habit. He hoped to find brief refuge in the detachment that brought him. He fumbled with the little silver brooch, still in its gift wrapping in his pocket.

'Something I saw today,' she said. 'They brought him into Accident and Emergency, but he was a kid really, nine or ten, so they called me after they'd set his legs.' She was trembling. He didn't know if she wanted him to hold her or not. He made no move.

'What was it? Tram?'

She looked at him. 'No. It was your precious Brownshirts. Your Party men.'

The Storm Division had for years been Hitler's private force, but that was nothing. The Party wasn't the only one to have had a uniformed section, and there'd been bloody fights with the Communists and the Social Democrats every day, right up until the February elections, when the matter was closed.

'They beat him up because it's Easter.'

He paused before replying. 'I'll look into it.'

She shook her head. 'You'd never find the men who did it, and anyway they're just part of the machine.'

'Because it's *Easter*?'

'They were drunk, and they were hanging around the synagogue on Oranienburgerstraße, looking for trouble I guess. This kid was with some friends and he cheeked them, he gave them a mock-salute. Well, they chased him, and they finally cornered him in a cul-de-sac.'

Hoffmann looked at the pattern on the carpet. It had always seemed to be an abstract, but now he saw that it depicted something formal: the shapes of a river, a ploughed field and a bridge could be traced. He had never noticed them before.

'They beat him up, of course,' she continued. He'll probably lose his left eye. Then they started to leave. But they came back. They said, next week's the sacrifice of our god, the one you crucified. We think you ought to have a taste of what he suffered. And there was a loose kerbstone, and they levered it up and used it to break his legs.'

'He told you all this?'

'Yes, but not quite so calmly.'

'And you believe him?' He regretted the words as they left his mouth. Her eyes grew dark and she recoiled from him.

'I do,' she said.

'I am as disgusted by this as you are, but - '

'But?'

He didn't know what to say - but if this is true, there's nothing I can do? Could he say that, because that was the truth. He knew the Party policy towards Jews. Had he simply tried to ignore it?

She crossed the room to a low beechwood sideboard, and from a drawer took out a framed photograph, about the size of a postcard. She passed it to him. It showed a man in the uniform of a colonel of artillery. It was a studio portrait and the man stood stiffly between a low plaster column and a large fern in a brass pot. Behind him you could see a painted sunset. The photograph was of high quality, and Hoffmann could see that the colonel wore the Iron Cross First Class with Oak Leaves.

'I haven't talked much about my family,' said Kara neutrally. 'That is my father.

Hoffmann handed the picture back.

'He was proud of his country, even though he had misgivings about what the Kaiser was doing, taking us into a war we couldn't win. My mother told me he fought bravely. Before the war, he was a civil engineer. That picture was taken in 1917, on his last home leave.'

Hoffmann hesitated. 'Are your parents here?'

'My father died in the war. But my mother was, until recently.' She looked at him steadily.

'And now?'

'She has left. After thirty-five years here, she has gone home to New York.'

'New York?'

'Yes.'

'Then you are half American?'

She looked at him drily. 'Sherlock Holmes has nothing on you. Oh, I am German, born and bred. I don't even speak very good English. But, yes, I am half American.'

'Why did your mother decide to go home now?' Hoffmann could have understood if she had gone back to the States after her husband's death, taking her daughter with her, or during the black days of the early Twenties; but he closed his mind to another reason.

'Because she is Jewish,' Kara said.

46

Hoffmann had driven all day with scarcely a break. The roads were pitted and treacherous, and it was late afternoon by the time he saw the delicate spire of Neuenstein church pointing out of the horizon.

Don't be afraid, Kara, he told her; *I was wrong. I was too late. But I can still make amends.*

Her revelation had come as a shock. The way things were going, though he didn't want to admit it to himself, she'd be in danger if she stayed. He thought of Hartmut Cassirer. He thought, selfishly, of himself. Perhaps nothing would happen after all - perhaps it was exaggerated. There might be a few deportations, but... He knew that he didn't want to lose her. He looked around the room as if he were in a dream: there was suddenly an unreal quality about it, and yet it was the same room, the soft lights, the elegant, modern furniture. Everything seemed so safe, so normal. And out there, beyond the closed curtains, something was loose that he couldn't contain, that he himself was part of.

She was looking at him.

'Nothing to say?'

'I had no idea.'

'That's brilliant.' She picked up the bottle, saw that it was empty, put it down again. 'Well, I don't know about you, but I need another drink.'

'Yes.'

'There's a bottle of Mosel in the icebox. Would you get it?'

Fetching the wine gave him a moment to collect himself, time which he knew she'd granted him deliberately. When he returned she had drawn the curtains back again and was standing at the window, smoking, looking down at the city.

'So what do you think will happen?' she asked as he uncorked the bottle and poured.

'Happen?'

'To us. To the Jews.'

'Nothing.'

'Like nothing's happening to the communists and the social-democrats, and anyone else who stands in your way.'

'Listen, I'm not - '

'Not what, exactly? Not a policeman? Not a Party member?'

'My work isn't political.'

She almost laughed. 'In times like these, everyone's work is political. Do you imagine they haven't got a file on me somewhere? Half-Jewish *and* a former communist?'

He was silent.

'Oh, don't worry. Your lot won't last. I can't see how they can.'

'Then why did your mother go?'

'She was scared.'

Why did Hartmut go? he thought.

'Didn't she want you to go with her?'

He thought he caught a flicker of something in her eye. She didn't reply immediately.

'Yes,' she said, finally.

'Why didn't you?'

She spread her hands. 'I have my work. My work is here.'

He wanted to ask more questions, but instinct made him stop. 'Why am I still here?' he said, instead.

'What do you mean?'

'Why haven't you asked me to leave?'

Then she smiled. 'Because I am used to you, and because I think you are capable of redemption. Let's see if I'm right.'

He didn't have to go home that night, but there was something absent about her, something remote in her lovemaking, which told him more than any words.

47

They didn't meet again for ten days. The death of the child prostitute was hardly worth investigating, and though his recent promotion kept him behind his desk far more than he liked, a breakthrough in another case, the arrest in a brothel in Potsdam of a big drug dealer for rape and murder, took him away from Berlin for a week, his presence resented by the Potsdam cops, who kept assuring him that they could handle it, that there was really no need for someone of his rank and expertise to concern himself with what was an open-and-shut matter. But he was glad to get his hands dirty, to be back at the old work. It focused the mind. It kept the doubts at bay.

But they, already present even before he'd spent that evening with Kara, were now awake and active, and would not go away. He knew he was compromised. He knew - once again the fact was borne in on him - that his beliefs were gone. No matter how hard you tried, life refused to be simple. Life struggled in any net you threw over it, until it escaped.

The day he decided to return to the Werderscher Markt, he received a coded message signed simply, Hans Oster, requesting a meeting, and leaving a telephone number. The name was familiar to Hoffmann, but he couldn't connect it to any police business. The note had simply said, 'when convenient', so he folded it into his wallet and left it until he got back to Berlin.

At his flat, there was another message waiting from him, from Kara, dated three days earlier. She asked him to call as soon as he returned. Written in her neat hand, the message was nothing out of the ordinary, but he noticed that some of the letters were badly formed, as if her hand had been shaking when she penned them.

48

She opened her door as soon as he pressed the doorbell, but the door was on its chain. She released it and let him in. She was breathless. His wanted to take her into his arms, but she backed away as he approached.

'What is it?' he said, frightened for her and for himself.

'I'm so glad you've come. I was going to ring you, only I didn't know where.'

'Sit down. Tell me what's happened.'

She obeyed him like a child - and this was very unlike her - taking comfort in being told what to do.

'Can I get you a drink?'

She looked up and nodded. He was surprised to see tears in her eyes. 'Don't worry,' she said, half-smiling, 'It's relief.'

In the kitchen, fetching the bottle of cognac, he noticed, on the worktop, a vast bouquet, now withered, of red, white and black roses.

He gave her the drink, sat opposite her, and waited. She drank a little whiskey, and looked at him over the glass. The expression in her eyes and the set of her lips had become firmer.

'You noticed the roses?' she said.

'Hard to avoid.'

'Third bouquet since you left.'

'Party colours.' Hoffmann was interested and jealous. 'Not like you to accept things like that.'

'Do they look as if they're appreciated? The others went into the bin. I kept these to show you.'

'Who sent them?'

'Someone who won't take no for an answer.'

'Out of the blue?'

'Not exactly out of the blue.' She paused, put her drink down, stretched uneasily. 'Wolf Hagen.'

He remembered the man who had tried to get off with Kara at Tilli's party, but that was months ago. 'Is this the first time he's been in touch with you?'

'I know you're a bastard too, but you're all the protection I've got, so please don't interrogate me.'

Hoffmann thought fast. After the party, he had researched Hagen. Power and connections, at least in the making. If Hagen had waited until Hoffmann was away to start sending Kara flowers, then he had chosen his moment from *knowledge*. He put the thought aside: it wasn't possible. But Hoffmann couldn't believe in coincidence.

Kara was reaching a decision. She drew in her breath. 'I haven't been open with you, she said. 'Because I wasn't sure I could trust you. Now, I must.' She frowned, looking away from him. 'The first of these Nazi bouquets arrived at Christmas. Anonymously. I threw it away, but another came in January. Then nothing until now. The first two had messages - sentimental stuff, snippets of Schiller, bits of Goethe, you know the kind of thing. I threw them away too.' She'd anticipated his question, but now she broke off, looking at him again, though he could read nothing in her eyes.

'The third bouquet he delivered in person,' she said at last.

'What happened?'

'Nothing. He was tongue-tied. He put the roses on the table. He said that he'd been away, but that he was back now, and that I'd find him a hard man to get rid of. I remember he gave a little laugh when he said that, a sort of titter. Perhaps he was embarrassed.'

'And you?'

'I told him he was wasting his time with me, and that I didn't want his flowers.' She was silent for a moment, got up and paced the room. 'He didn't say anything. He'd had his hat in his hands. Then he put it back on and made for the door. I followed him into the hall. I thought he'd just go, he'd already opened the door, but then he turned back and said, "I won't give up, you know. And if you're wise, you'll come round. The way things are going, people like you are going to need all the help they can get." '

Kara had begun to cry. Hoffmann got up and stood near her, but did no more. He sensed that, once more, she didn't want to be touched.

'No-one's following me, and he doesn't know the truth about you,' he said, as if he were the one who needed reassurance. He took her shoulders in his hands at last and she didn't resist. 'Let me find out for sure.'

'I don't want him to come back.'

'He won't.'

'But he must know about my mother.'

'The Brownshirts don't have access to that information.' Nor would they, he hoped, as long as Hindenburg was alive and still President. He paused before reluctantly asking: 'Have you thought any more about leaving?'

'Running away?'

'You could join your mother.'

138

'Running away on account of that little shit?'

'Why didn't you go with her?'

She wiped her eyes and collected herself, gave him a wry smile. 'You know, I never really got on with my mother. It was a relief for both of us to see the back of each other. Not that we weren't fond of each other, in our way - we just had nothing in common.'

'But you wouldn't have to be with her, once you were there. And there are hospitals in New York, and children, just as needy as the ones you treat here.'

She gave him a look of such bottomless despair that it threw him. 'You think it's that simple, don't you? Tidy me up so you won't have to worry. The kid I told you about died. They'd punctured one of his lungs. We'd missed it.' She drank some brandy. 'I'm not leaving. I'm not giving in to them.'

49

The following morning, Hoffmann sat down with one of his inspectors and gave him orders. The man, reliable and quiet, who suffered from a permanent head cold, made notes and, after their half-hour conference, left. Then Hoffmann picked up the phone and called the Central Office of the *Sturm-Abteilung*. If Hagen held the rank of SA-*Standartenführer* and had the right to wear one of their famous brown uniforms, he'd better do something to earn it. Viktor Lutze was an old acquaintance and, only a handful of months back, had been a close political ally. Now he was Number Two in the SA command, and it was time for Hoffmann to call in a favour. It shouldn't be too hard to arrange for Hagen to be ordered away from Berlin - to Munich, perhaps - for a few months.

He drummed his fingers on his desk as he waited to be put through.

Later, though he'd been acting for more-or-less selfish reasons, he realised that these had been his first acts of subversion. Within twenty-four hours, Lutze rang back to tell him that Hagen had been seconded to command an SA training camp for new NCOs in the Black Forest. He'd be away for the entire summer. Hoffmann was amused: most of the SA were roughnecks and even the officers were toughs; perhaps Hagen, with his genteel pretensions, might be able to give the NCOs a veneer of respectability.

But then he remembered how Veit Adamov had described Hagen's enjoyment - though a senior officer - of beating people up in the Berlin street battles that had preceded Hitler's getting the Chancellorship.

He thought of Kara, not that she was ever far from his thoughts these days. But within another twenty-four hours his inspector, snuffling into his handkerchief, was able to assure Hoffmann that no-one was shadowing either Kara or himself. This didn't surprise him. The Brownshirts were fighters, not spies.

It was the best he could do, for now.

50

Work claimed him after the inspector left - reports to read on cases he'd rather have been working on himself, internal memoranda to plough through and meetings to attend, including one with Rudolph Diels, the director of the new Department 1A of the Prussian State Police. Diels was on a recruiting drive, and wooing away some good men. No-one quite knew what the role of 1A would be, but it had the backing of both Hitler and Heinrich Himmler; great things would be expected of it.

Kara was working nights that week. He'd rung her before she went on shift, at about the time his own day was drawing to a close, to reassure her. Leaving the office, he was about to make his way home for a drink before going out again to his usual restaurant, when he hesitated. He wanted to feel part of the crowd. He wasn't in uniform, so he made his way to the Kurfürstendamm, found a congenial Rathskeller, and ordered a beer with a Bismarck chaser. They tasted fresh and cool. The place was panelled in honey-coloured wood, and the warm light it reflected made the faces round him look more cheerful than they were; but the general mood seemed buoyant anyway. One solitary, bearded man stood at the end of the bar, dressed in a black overcoat and hat, and waited patiently to be served. The room wasn't particularly crowded, waitresses bearing trays loaded with glasses moved from table to table, but the barkeeper refused to meet the man's eye. After ten minutes of this, the man left.

It was none of Hoffmann's business, but the incident, if you could call it that, troubled him obscurely. He reached into his wallet and fished out a bill to pay with, when he discovered the note from Hans Oster. He had forgotten it. He turned it over in his fingers.

Oster... Now he had it; he remembered the file: senior officer on the General Staff; disgraced because of an affair with another officer's wife. That was only last winter. This spring he'd got a job with Göring's so-called Research Department. Still wore his General Staff uniform. What the hell was he after? Hoffmann knew perfectly well what the Research Department was, and wanted as little as possible to do with it.

He ordered another beer-and-schnapps. They'd keep his table at the restaurant.

He'd ring Oster in the morning.

51

Neuenstein had no road-block outside it. Hoffmann supposed the town, little more than a big village, like Teudorf, and lost in a sweep of lush, wooded countryside, didn't merit one. Any newcomer arriving during daylight hours would be noticed immediately. He slowed as he drove through it, wondering if he dared pass the night here. Two-thirds of the way down the main street was a small inn, whose windows spilled dim light onto the road.

There was no-one about. There were no cars parked, only an old van and a couple of carts near the inn. He decided to pull over and stop, at least for a drink and a bite to eat. He'd spend the night somewhere on the road - he could hide in the woods, refill the car's tank, get to Leipzig by this time tomorrow.

He also needed to see a paper, or to catch the news on the radio. The chances were there'd be a radio in the Wirtshaus. Leaving his greatcoat and hat in the car, and locking it, taking only a small bag, which had been stashed in the VW beforehand, and now contained his documents and money, he went in.

There were four or five plain tables in the room, with benches on either side of each. The bar ran along the right wall. Two large kerosene lamps at either end lit it, and three of the tables had similar, smaller lamps at their centre. Four men sat together at one of these, nursing mugs of beer and playing *Skat*. A large, bearded man of about sixty, in a red-and-blue check shirt and dungarees stood behind the bar, or rather, leaned on his belly, which was resting against the counter. The men at the table raised their heads as Hoffmann entered, but no-one was particularly interested in him, and his greeting was barely returned. Only the landlord looked at him with anything approaching warmth.

On a shelf behind the bar, keeping company with an assortment of bottles of schnapps, a radio played dance music.

The landlord was filling a Stein from one of three huge barrels. When he turned, Hoffmann saw that the space between the counter and the barrels was just wide enough to accommodate his paunch.

'Travelling late,' he said, plonking the beer down. 'Try this. Our best. Refreshing and light. Need a bed?'

'No - I'm pushing on.'

The landlord looked at him for a moment, then said, 'No cops here, you know. Just the priest and me - I'm the mayor. Heinz Gebler.'

Hoffmann shook his hand. 'Friedmann, Kurt,' he said.

'Don't mind them,' said Gebler, nodding at the card players. 'No livestock left, and nothing to plant. So - how about that bed?'

'No,' said Hoffmann. 'I need to put away a few more kilometres tonight.'

'You won't get far before the blackout,' said Gebler, 'But suit yourself.'

'You wouldn't have a newspaper? I've been on the road for a few days and I haven't heard anything.'

'What, about our glorious tactical retreats?' Hoffmann was alarmed at the booming laugh that followed this remark. Gebler had no idea who he was. Talk like that could get him killed. 'No, no newspaper. Haven't seen one of those sorry-looking things in weeks myself. Do they still print them?'

'Anything to eat?'

'Bread and sausage. And some hot soup. Sit down and I'll bring it.'

The food was good, and the soup, turnip and smoked ham, tasted like ambrosia. He ate quickly; there were too few people here and, maybe it was just his Berlin paranoia, but this Gebler was too candid.

The dance music ceased, gave way to the Anthem. The conversation of the other men died. A voice, interrupted by static, ran through a brief summary of war news, which it delivered in a tone brittle with optimism. One of the items, however, was what he'd been hoping to hear: 'Police pursuing the traitors responsible for the recent cowardly and misconceived attempt on the Führer's life report the suicide by a lake near Storkow of one of the circle's most notorious leaders, disgraced police chief Hoffmann ... ' There was more, but nothing of any significance, before the voice moved on to cultural news, telling the room about Georg Jacoby's latest film, *Woman Of My Dreams*. Then the Anthem again, before the dance music resumed.

Hoffmann paid his bill and prepared to leave.

'Sure about the bed? We're not exactly full up at the moment and there's nowhere else for an hour at least.'

'I'll take my chances.'

Gebler looked at him shrewdly, and Hoffmann could feel the eyes of the other men fixed on him too.

'You must be quite a bigwig,' said Gebler.

'What makes you say that?'

'All that petrol you must have.'

'Ministry of Aviation.'

Gebler smiled. 'There's a blind bend about two hundred metres down the road. Be careful of it - there's more traffic round here than you'd think.'

'Thank you.'

'Good luck.'

52

Hoffmann drove away. With luck, he'd be in Leipzig tomorrow. He'd lose the car and go to ground. But not for long. There wasn't time. He took the blind bend carefully.

He failed to find a barn or a shed to spend the night in. He passed some ruined farm-buildings which looked deserted, but decided not to risk using them. Just as dusk was settling, he noticed an old track leading into a wood, and took it. It led to a clearing where he turned the car round so that it was facing back to the road, and doused the lights. It was now almost pitch dark; after he'd killed the engine the sounds of the countryside rose around him, rustlings and the occasional cry of a bird or animal punctuating the silence which he, as a city-dweller, found uncanny and unsettling. He hadn't slept in the open for over twenty years, and then it had been wartime, in the trenches, with other men around him. The noises then had been made by the wounded, or by those who moaned in their dreams. The darkness then was not absolute; the infernal glow of the guttering fires in No-Man's-Land had pierced it; but he had not felt as vulnerable then as he did now.

On the following day he would begin to look unkempt and shabby. He would have to find a brook or a lake where he could get water and shave. Shaving was essential. It was hard enough to disguise his looks, but the minute his moustache became apparent, his risks would increase tenfold. But if he couldn't, if he could reach Leipzig, it wouldn't matter so much. The enemy was giving the city such a hammering that half the men in it would look like him.

It was a bad night. He hardly slept, cramped in the car, his gun in his lap. Every time he did fall asleep, he awoke with a start, the slightest sound triggering panic. Once, he found himself wide awake, aware that something else, something large, had wandered into the clearing, and was moving about. But the moon had risen by then, and as he peered out of the window, slipping the safety catch off his gun, he saw that a family of wild boar was rooting around the trees near where he was parked. They sensed his presence, and shuffled off into the darkness of the woods soon afterwards, but without haste, and he found himself thinking he would have liked them to stay longer. Towards dawn, about four in the morning, he fell into a deep, dreamless sleep, from which he awoke two hours later, cramped, but more rested than he'd hoped to be. He got out of the car and stretched, walking up and down and smoking a cigarette.

He heard the sound of running water nearby, and made his way through the trees, finding a stream not ten metres away. He splashed water on his face and drank a little too - the first time he had ever drunk from a stream: it was fresh and clear; but he decided not to shave, it would be too hard to do so using the car's rear-view mirror to guide him, and he didn't want to nick himself and bleed. Despite the good meal of the night before he was hungry, and still cold in the dawn, though already he could sense that it would be a hot day. Only his third day on the road. An eternity had passed since he had closed the door on his flat.

He walked up some way up the track, cautiously. There was no hint that anyone was near. He returned to the car and prepared to leave. He'd take it easy. The slower he went the less petrol he would use, and he didn't want to get to Leipzig until evening. The people he needed were night-owls, and daytime isn't good, even in a city, for a fugitive.

He'd reached the road when he heard, above the engine of the VW, the roar of lorries approaching. He backed into the shadow of the trees and waited. A convoy of three large army trucks, two full of soldiers, the last piled with equipment, thundered past. He stayed where he was until the noise of their engines had died, before moving on.

In half-an-hour, he'd reach the main road south. Soon afterwards, he'd cross the Elbe and then he'd be within striking distance of his goal. How efficient would the checkpoints around Leipzig be?

At least on the main road there was a chance of more traffic. He'd checked his reflection in the car mirror, and he didn't look as dishevelled as he'd feared. And perhaps an official, on the road, on urgent business, at this stage in the war, might be forgiven for looking less spick-and-span than the Führer would have wished. Just as long as he could reach Leipzig.

The road ahead presented him with another blind bend, curving between high banks. He passed it, and saw, not one hundred metres ahead, another military convoy.

This one was smaller. One light truck, an armoured car and, preceding them, an open staff car. There was no getting off the road now, and it was so narrow that they'd all have to slow to a crawl to pass each other safely. It was inconceivable that they wouldn't stop him. Indeed, he could see that already their pace had slowed, and the Mercedes flashed its headlights at him. He slowed and stopped, climbed out of the car, and waited.

53

These were regular army, not SS. The big Mercedes drew almost abreast of him before it came to a halt. The officer in the back climbed out and approached him. He wore field-grey, and his collar insignia were gold oakleaves on a bright red ground. At his throat, a Knight's Cross.

Hoffmann knew him. He'd met him several times before the war, at gatherings organised by Tilli, once at the theatre, and on one occasion officially, when Hoffmann was investigating the murder of a civilian typist at a large barracks on the outskirts of Berlin. Klaus Richter had been a colonel then; but that was a long time ago. Their paths had only crossed briefly in the past four years, at conferences, and each time Hoffmann had been wearing his SS uniform. Another thing Hoffmann recalled: before the war, Richter had served with Hans Oster; they'd shared a love of horses and been great riding companions.

How much did Richter know?

Richter walked over to him, peeling off his gloves. Still early, it was already warm.

'Good morning,' Richter said, with a faint smile.

'Good morning, General.'

'It's been a while, Commissioner.'

'Yes.'

'I'm surprised to see you.' Richter paused. 'I'd heard that you'd shot yourself.'

'The Gestapo think so.' Hoffmann looked past him. The other two men in the staff car, the driver, and a lieutenant who was probably Richter's adjutant, returned his gaze incuriously. Beyond them, the driver of the armoured car and the driver of the lorry stared into space. One of them lit a cigarette.

'You'd better show me you papers,' said Richter.

'Shouldn't your adjutant be doing this?'

'Do you think he cares?' Richter took the document and read it briefly before handing it back. 'Quite a career change,' he said drily.

'Yes.'

The general looked past him, towards the fields beyond them. 'I owe you an apology, Hoffmann. I always thought you were one of the worst of the shits. But now,' he paused. 'Now, your reputation goes before you.'

'If you're not going to arrest me, I must keep going. Forgive me.'

'Of course. I'm in a hurry myself. Ordered back to Berlin to help shore things up, I imagine. Make a change from prowling along the Swiss border.' He paused again. 'Any news of Oster?'

'No.'

'Have they got him?'

'I hope not.'

Richter looked thoughtful. He was a handsome man, about Hoffmann's age, but fitter, and, with his lightly-tanned skin and coppery-blond hair, was close to the Party ideal of the German soldier. All he lacked was a monocle, but that, these days, was a bit *vieux-jeu*. He even had a scar on his left cheek. He told admiring Nazi colleagues that he'd got it duelling, when a student at Heidelberg, with Mertz von Hammerstein; friends knew he'd cut his face badly when he'd fallen off his bicycle, aged eight.

'I've fought hard,' he said, almost to himself, 'But since that bloody ridiculous oath of loyalty we had to take to Hitler in '34, I've fought for Germany, not for him, or his crew. Look where it's got us. We're shamed. I wish I knew where Oster was.'

'Couldn't you have got over the border?'

Richter smiled. 'I thought of it many times. Switzerland. Land of Milk and Honey. But there are some things you have to see to their conclusion.' He looked at his watch. 'Well, I mustn't keep you. I don't suppose we'll meet again, so good luck.' He saluted, turned on his heel, and returned to his car. His driver drove on as soon as he'd taken his seat. He didn't look at Hoffmann again.

54

Hoffmann hadn't rung Oster the morning after his drink in the bar on the Ku'damm. He'd been distracted by work, and then he found himself disinclined to make the call at all. He left it a week; he didn't mention it to anyone else. Not Kara, and not Brandau, whom he'd got to know better. Enough to know that the Gestapo lawyer had divided loyalties too.

In the meantime, Hagen had fallen silent. He had made no more contact with Kara, and there were no more roses. Hoffmann wondered if he'd guessed who had been responsible for his posting, but could imagine no conceivable way in which he could know. Hagen's business interests were allied to those of the Party, but for the moment they were in the hands of a Swedish associate - Hoffmann hadn't found it hard to discover that. Hagen hadn't made a fuss over the Black Forest business because it was valuable to him to ingratiate himself with the politicians.

Hoffmann had also found out, by bending Brandau's ear over lunch, the Swedish iron business now had official approval. The imports were running as smoothly as clockwork, freighters from Göteberg docking almost daily at Kiel.

Hoffmann had stopped trying to persuade Kara to follow her mother to New York. He felt guilty about not insisting, but there was little he could do if she would not go. With Hagen out of the way, he could offer her protection; he arranged that elements in her file should be destroyed. It hadn't been easy, but delay would have been riskier.

He had told her none of this. He hadn't seen her for ten days. Not unusual for them, but not this time because work got between them; because Hoffmann wanted to be doubly sure no-one was watching them. All the time he was unable to rid himself of the story Kara had told him. He could not get the picture of that boy, beaten to death, out of his mind.

Early in the evening of the tenth day after he'd received the message, at last he picked up the phone and dialled the number.

'Oster.' The voice was expressionless. Hoffmann was surprised. He'd expected a secretary or an adjutant.

'Hoffmann,' he said.

The voice relaxed, but not much. 'Took your time.'

'Work.'

'Of course.'

'I also wondered what the Research Department could possibly want with me.'

There was a pause. 'Where are you calling from?'

'Werderscher Markt.'

'It might be better if we met.'

'By all means, but I think first I should have some idea of what it's about.'

'It's perfectly informal. There's some information I'd like to share with you.'

There was a trace of humour in Oster's voice, but there was no doubting the authority, either. Hoffmann's own rank was higher than the last one Oster had held, and Hoffmann hadn't been disgraced for seducing a fellow officer's wife. But he had no idea what sort of clout Oster had now, or if he held any rank in any organisation, military or otherwise, at all. Hoffmann was intrigued, but he didn't want to make waves. The Research Department was Göring's spy network. It wouldn't do to ruffle feathers there.

'Where do you suggest? he said.

'Dahlem,' came the answer, immediately and somewhat hurriedly. 'Fabeckstraße. By the Völker Museum. There's a beer garden, quite quiet, called the *Apfelbaum*, close to the corner of Humboldtstraße. Got that?'

'Yes,' said Hoffmann, a littler angry. The man sounded as if he were giving orders.

'When would be convenient for you?'

Hoffmann looked at his own watch. 'This evening.'

'20.00 hours?'

'Right.'

'One other thing.'

'Yes?'

'Don't come in uniform.'

55

The *Apfelbaum* was certainly quiet, and took some finding too. Its entrance was unmarked and you had to walk down a narrow alley off the street to get to it, where a minute green wooden sign, no bigger than a sheet of paper, hung over a rose-entwined arch. Through it was a courtyard smothered in tall shrubs set in pots, so placed as to separate each of the handful of rustic tables which were dotted about. From somewhere came the sound of a fountain. It was a sunny evening, but here it was shaded. Hoffmann was the only customer. He chose a table with a view of the arch, ordered a Berliner Weize with lemon, lit a cigarette, opened the book he'd brought with him, and waited.

He nursed his beer for half-an-hour, looking up from his book on the three occasions when other people entered the garden, all couples, no-one in uniform, then decided that that was long enough. Failing to signal a waiter, he tossed some money on the table, put on his hat, and left.

He hadn't walked ten metres back towards the museum when two men in trenchcoats emerged from nowhere. He bent down fast and went for his gun, but they were pros too and ahead of him. They grabbed his elbows, and shoved him towards a Mercedes with curtained windows at the back, which drew up a few metres ahead of them. One opened the nearside rear door, and he was bundled in. As the door slammed behind him, the car drove off, picking up speed.

'Good evening,' said the voice from the telephone. 'I'm Oster.'

Hoffmann turned to him. Oster was slightly built, and dressed in a comfortable, expensive tweed suit. His expression was genial, and his intelligent dark eyes were humorous. But he was someone used to being in command.

'Sorry about that, but everyone has to take precautions. And we had to wait too - we didn't know when you'd decide enough was enough. Half-an-hour. You are a pretty patient man.'

'What do you want to talk about?'

Oster twitched back his curtain and glanced out of the window at the trees that lined the street. 'It's a pleasant evening. I thought we'd go for a drive. Whiskey?' He pulled a flask and two cups from a compartment in the back of the seat in front of him.

'Will I need it?'

Oster laughed. 'Not sure.' He poured two drinks and handed one cup to Hoffmann. 'Zum *Wohl*!'

'Prost!'

They drove on in silence. Unable to see out, Hoffmann sensed that they had turned west, and so would be heading away from the centre.

'Nice city. You were born here, weren't you?'

'Yes.'

'I'm from Dresden myself.'

'I saw that on your file.'

Oster smiled broadly. 'Got a file on me have you? Of course you have!' He looked across at Hoffmann. 'Look, I won't beat about the bush. There is a strong element in the High Command which feels, shall we say, uneasy, about the new regime.'

'What do you mean?'

'These people feel that the National Socialists are going to have an adverse effect on Germany if they are allowed to continue in office.'

'They've only been in office four months.'

'And how long do you suppose they will stay there?' There was a pause. 'You're a Party man. Do you suppose that there will ever be elections again?'

Hoffmann shrugged. 'Democracy hasn't done us much good since the last war.'

'I agree. But what we are facing is dictatorship. Dictatorship, and a new war, which we cannot win, and the expulsion of about half a million of us.'

'You're being ridiculous.'

Oster was silent for a moment. 'We think you share our doubts.'

Hoffmann opened the curtain on his side a chink. The road and passing trees told him nothing. 'What do you want to do?'

'Stop him.'

'How?'

'You can help us. It won't be easy.'

'You're talking to a Party member.'

'Don't you think I haven't been through what you are going through? We love our country; we do not love the people running it.'

'What about your oath?'

'That, for many of us, is the hardest thing of all.'

'The army protects. It does not question.'

'Sometimes it is easier not to question.'

Hoffmann reached for the door. 'Tell your driver to stop. I won't listen to any more of this.'

'Of course, if you insist - but it's a long way back, and you won't get a taxi out here.' He looked out of the window again. 'Dark, too. Our dear Führer hasn't yet managed to rid our streets of quite *all* unruly elements, either.'

Hoffmann drank the whiskey. Oster was taking one hell of a risk. Hoffmann could agree to anything and then betray him. But Oster had his own men; and he worked for Göring, who didn't like his henchmen tampered with by anyone. It was tricky.

His thoughts were obviously easy to read. 'Contacting you has been a calculated risk,' said Oster. 'But not taken entirely at a venture. And not as risky for me as you might think.' Oster smiled at him, faintly. 'My job at the Research Department gives me wide powers.'

'Are you going to tell me why you think I am worth approaching for - for whatever it is you have in mind?'

Oster drank his Irish in two swallows, and said, 'I served with Colonel von Wildenbruch in the last war. Became a friend of the family. We fought together at Cambrai, and at Cantigny - the bloody Americans bolloxed us there; and that was where von Wildenbruch died.'

Hoffmann said nothing. He felt a curious emotion: part fury, part relief.

Oster leant forward and said something to the driver. The car turned back in the direction of Berlin.

'Just a chat while we take you back,' said Oster. 'We'll drop you in Pariser Platz, if you don't mind. I must go back to my office. No peace for the wicked!'

56

Kara had taken a risk, Hoffmann thought, as he drove along the main road to Leipzig; but the introduction to Oster, trading on his friendship with her father, had paid the dividend she expected. Oster had been discreet, persuasive. They had talked, in the end, for an hour.

Nevertheless, Hoffmann had rejected his proposal. Oster had let him go, though Hoffmann knew that every move he made would be covered from now on. But something prevented him from denouncing Oster. He let his indecision prey on him for ten days. Then he rang Oster's number again.

Their second meeting was followed by the most restful night's sleep Hoffmann had had in months. He had crossed the Rubicon: there could be no going back now.

But things had not gone as smoothly as hoped. Fewer people had joined the conspiracy than its leaders had expected, and a mixture of ill-luck and disunity meant that what was supposed to take no longer than a year had taken ten, the war had come, the beast had been freed, had become unstoppable. They had gone on trying, doggedly, despairingly, and met only failure as the destruction around them grew monstrous. The irony was that in order to continue the fight, the conspirators had to maintain their positions within the machinery that drew in and pulverised all morality, all ethics and all sense.

Once committed, either to the conspiracy or to the hegemony of the Party, there was no retreat. Hoffmann had to serve both. Though he knew his duties to the second were carried out in the interest of the first, he had for years now no longer known how to square them. He could only limit the evil of the second, and use his position to the greatest effect for the first. But what had it added up to? He felt like Sisyphus; and like that sad king in Hades, doomed to roll the boulder up the hill, but never to get it to the summit, he had gone on trying because, against all reason, he thought that, one day, he might.

For a time there had been the option of escape, and if that option hadn't been destroyed, he would have taken it. Oster had not insisted on any formal commitment, nor had he done more than tell Hoffmann to hold himself in readiness, they would call on him when the time came. He'd never been a hero, and now he was not even an idealist any more. All he could do was go on, following the path he'd condemned himself to, until it came to an end.

The motorised traffic was military, and the few unmarked cars were official. Private cars were a thing of the past, except for Party elite, favourites, and men like Hagen. Hoffmann wasn't challenged. Everyone was bent on his own business. Even at the checkpoints on the bridge over the Elbe, soon after he'd passed through Wittenberg, he was waved through after the guards had merely given his papers a cursory glance. The black Volkswagen and Galen's black trilby lent him authority still. Hoffmann was glad he had not yet abandoned his cover. The guards were tired, overburdened, and he had the impression that they didn't care anymore. Except for the dedicated few, most people were beginning to look over their shoulders. They knew that the enemy, above all the Americans, thousands of well-fed troops, with the latest equipment, were advancing on Paris; and word was beginning to spread that they would reach the city well within the month. In the east, the Russians were at the gates of Warsaw. No-one knew which way to flee, but most were heading west, since the Russians, so rumour ran, took no prisoners. There were stories about the 8th Guards Army and the Mongolian divisions, which chilled the blood.

Along the edges of the road, tattered groups of people trudged, pulling wooden handcarts, a few with horses and larger wagons, a few on bicycles. The wagons were piled with cupboards and chairs, beds and tables. Little children perched in front, behind, and on top of the piles. Old men in hats, shirtsleeves, the remains of suits, led the horses, or plodded between the shafts of the handcarts; women in grey dresses took up the rear. People struggled along alone, manhandling suitcases. Hoffmann saw one man throw his aside into a field. Another put his down and sat on it, his head in his hands, as the others marched by.

The traffic backed up as he approached Leipzig. It was 17.00 hours. At the roadblock here, the guards were SS, and took their duties seriously. But his luck held and he passed without difficulty, maybe because the official in the limousine in front of him gave the guards a bollocking for wasting his time.

It was Sunday, and the streets of the city were empty. Everywhere dust, rubble and ruins. A few women, with wheelbarrows, picks and shovels, worked to clear masonry from one side-street he passed.

He had to find somewhere to stay, and somewhere to put the car where it would not attract attention. People here would want to know his business. He had his letter from the Ministry of Aviation, which gave him a roving brief to inspect 'any temporary structural damage attributable to enemy action', and several hotel dockets. He did not know whether the broadcast announcing his death was a blind or not; he couldn't depend on the search for him having been called off.

57

The old Imperial Hotel was untouched by the war, though buildings twenty metres away had been reduced to rubble. In the spacious entrance hall, flanked by enormous parlour palms, a bored female string quartet ploughed its way through Albinoni's *Adagio*. Elderly waiters moved between tables, serving beer to the handful of guests - all, Hoffmann guessed, there in some official capacity or other - who were occupying the armchairs grouped round tables. Most of the men were in uniform - army officers, a few SS, and one Luftwaffe. There were half-a-dozen women scattered amongst them, elegant creatures on the verge of middle-age, not linked to any of the men by blood or marriage. No-one paid any more than idle attention to him as he made his way to the reception desk.

The clerk looked at him. Hoffmann was aware that his appearance let him down.

'I've left my car outside. Have someone park it for me, will you?' he said, rattling the keys as he placed them on the counter.

'Of course, Herr Friedmann,' said the clerk, without enthusiasm. 'As for your room: with or without bath?'

'With,' said Hoffmann.

The clerk pushed a key across the desk towards him. There followed the usual form-filling. 'Water is available in the rooms from six until eight in the mornings and from seven until ten in the evenings. The dining room is open from six until nine, from twelve until two, and from seven until ten. How long may we expect the pleasure of your company?'

'Two or three days.'

'Very well.' The clerk signalled to a woman of about sixty in a bellhop's uniform, who took his luggage and preceded him towards the broad staircase at the rear, whose carpeting, Hoffmann noticed, was in need of replacing. But the Imperial was doing its best to keep up appearances. He might even get some laundry done. Once he was shaved and changed, even without a fresh suit to wear, he felt he'd be able to cut a convincing figure. Better after all to look smart than shabby, given that he was still able to keep his current persona. The problem with a city was that although it had the advantage of anonymity, there would be more people to take notice. The hotel would be sending his details to the local police the following morning, if not that night. He could only pray that he wouldn't attract attention.

He had to wait for the water to come on. He had a beer and a sandwich sent up, and asked for a newspaper. They eventually arrived, with yesterday's copy of the *Beobachter*, in which there was no news of him at all. It was time to take stock. He knew the city well. That night, he'd wander over to the Grimmaische Straße and have a drink in Auerbach's *Keller*. It was a long shot, but one or two of the old crowd might still be around. If he drew a blank there, he'd try a bar he knew on the Rittergasse, if it was still standing. He had no intention of staying three nights at the Imperial.

At 8.00pm, bathed and changed, he set off. The streets were all but deserted, and reminded him of a film set, they were so quiet. It was a five-minute walk to Auerbach's, and in the time it took him to get there he passed three people, all old men, none of whom greeted him or met his eye. But, though didn't feel safe, he felt better, and for a few precious moments, while walking, the stress, which was his usual companion, left him in peace.

Auerbach's, that dark-brown, underground cathedral of a place, whence Faust, with the Devil's help, once rode a wine-barrel up into the street, was oddly comforting. He wandered through the dining-rooms without seeing anyone he knew, until he came to the *Großes Keller*, which was full, mainly officers and their women companions, some drunk. He waved a waiter away and scanned the room. None of the old gang was here. He hesitated, on the point of leaving, when he sensed someone's eyes on him. Sitting alone at a table which was spread with a cloth as white as it could be, given that there was a war on, and at his ease, a half-finished bottle of Goldkapsel before him, sat Veit Adamov.

58

For an instant, Hoffmann considered flight. He hadn't seen Adamov for a long time, but he knew how he'd survived, and who his friends were. On the other hand, if he left, he'd lose the chance of finding out whose side his old acquaintance was on.

His Walther 9 was in his pocket. He would talk to Adamov. If things turned out badly, he'd kill the man and run.

Adamov raised his glass, and indicated the empty chair opposite him. The table was in a corner; Adamov sat with his back to the wall. Hoffmann didn't like the idea of sitting with his own back to the room, but there was no alternative. He glanced around the diners again: they all seemed to be absorbed with their own company. The room was dimly, cosily lit, candles on the tables, the lamps on the walls heavily shaded. He made his way over.

'I wondered if you were ever going to get here,' said Adamov, grinning. 'Have a drink. A little on the sweet side for our taste, but they talked me into it.'

'What are you doing here?'

Adamov waved to a waiter, who brought another glass, and two menus. 'Me? Bird of passage.' He leant forward, 'And waiting for you, obviously. I'd have sat here all night. Where else would you come to?' He paused, drawing heavily on his cigarette. 'You really come straight to the point, don't you? No small talk, not even after - how long's it been? Four years? Five?'

'Longer than that.'

'I know when it was,' said Adamov, seriously; and Hoffmann remembered, whatever else he might think of the man, that he hadn't been mistaken in trusting him then. Adamov poured wine, and drank, grimacing. 'I've had enough of this. They've got some rough old *Frankenwein* here. What do you say to a *Boxbeutel* of something?'

Hoffmann watched Adamov's face, but, except when he was trying to attract a waiter's attention, his eyes never left Hoffmann. So he wasn't signalling to anyone else in the room. Not that he'd need to. All Judas had to do was plant a kiss. Was Adamov a Judas? No - Adamov was simply a survivor. Hoffmann had learned that by the end of the last decade, when everyone sensed war was just round the corner, and the exodus of dispossessed Jews and dissident artists, writers, teachers, had become a flood, Adamov had seriously considered leaving for Moscow. But he hadn't. He'd told departing friends that he'd decided to stay, to fight the system from within. Few had believed him.

He reinvented himself as a producer-director, of hard-core porn movies, tailored to the tastes of senior SS. It all had to be done without either Hitler's or Himmler's knowledge, but demand had grown as war came, and increased after Stalingrad, when most officers with any *nous* realised that the jig was up. Drink and porn were standard escape routes.

Hoffmann had ordered the Vice Squad to keep an eye on Adamov's studio - a disused button factory in Wilmersdorf - but as no small children, or animals, were involved, at least to their knowledge, he'd taken no action.

He wasn't entirely surprised to see Adamov. People were leaving Berlin, if they could, and Leipzig was the nearest big city. He couldn't imagine Adamov ever existing outside a big city: he wouldn't know what to do with himself. But why had the man been expecting him?

The *Boxbeutel* arrived and Adamov sampled it. Satisfied, he poured two drinks into green-stemmed rummers. 'I'm here because Brandau told me to wait for you.' He held up his hand. 'He didn't know for sure that you'd choose this direction, but he guessed you'd be coming south - no cigars for guessing that!'

Hoffmann thought fast - no-one, apart from Brandau, and Adamov, who'd been close to Kara, could have known where he'd be headed, or why. Even they might not have considered it, but they had, and now he had to play with the cards he'd been dealt.

'How long have you been here?'

'Three days. Berlin's too hot now. The Gestapo's arresting everything that moves.' He spread his hands. 'I was going to give you until tomorrow.'

'Where are you going?'

'You're not a policeman anymore, so I don't have to answer that.'

'How the hell do you know Brandau?'

'We've been in touch, now and then, over the years. I'm surprised you didn't know. War makes strange bedfellows.' Adamov laughed briefly.

'I know how you've been making ends meet.'

'Yes - but your Vice boys were very discreet - thank you for that. I think we'd better order. I'm not the drinker I used to be, this stuff's going to my head, and it'll look better if we eat. My party.'

The menu was old and elaborate, though most of the items on it were struck out. They settled for silverside and potatoes.

'Brandau's train stopped here for forty minutes. Scheduled to take on more passengers. You know what the station here's like, hub of the bloody universe. How the Lancasters have missed it is beyond me. By the grace of God, his train was on time.'

'How much else did he tell you?'

' Just that he'd be on that train.'

'And if he wasn't?'

'To walk away.'

Hoffmann smiled to himself. He'd underestimated Brandau. And Adamov, come to that. 'When did Brandau recruit you?'

Adamov looked surprised. 'Oh dear, it wasn't anything so formal. You know me, always ready to lend a hand.' He propelled a forkful of meat into his large mouth. 'If this is beef, I'm Winston-fucking-Churchill.'

'What are you supposed to do for me?'

'I'm supposed to be of assistance.' Adamov poured more wine. 'Shall we have another bottle? Maybe not. Some schnapps to finish, then. They do a good Himbeergeist.' He speared a potato. 'The problem is, most of the old friends we thought we'd find here have gone. Flown the coop. Buggered off to Frankfurt and Munich. The ones with real money are already in Zurich and Madrid. But I've made a couple of contacts and they're arranging my transport. For a consideration, they'll look after you, too.'

'I've got my contacts. I don't need yours.'

Adamov smiled. 'No you haven't. Not anymore. You may not like it, but you need me.' He let that sink in, then leant forward and said, 'Listen: they'll get rid of the car and they'll get new clothes for you.'

'How much have you told them?'

'They don't have to know anything about you - except your size in suits. Off the peg, that one?'

'Yes.'

'Not what you're used to, but needs must ... ' Adamov smiled. 'You think I talk too much. But you're not the only one to be nervous.' He paused. 'Kara was a good friend.'

'I know.'

They were silent. Neither felt like eating any more. Adamov said, 'Let's have that schnapps.'

'Yes. '

'We must meet tomorrow. Early.' Adamov took out a pen and scribbled on a scrap of paper. 'This is where I'm staying. It's a colleague's flat - he's gone away - perfectly safe. Where are you? In a hotel?'

Yes.'

'Check out tomorrow, you won't need it anymore.' Seeing the doubt in Hoffmann's face he added, 'I'm your best friend now, like it or not. Don't forget how much I know. And I haven't passed a word on to anyone. I don't care if you believe it or not, that I've been working against these fuckers all the time I've been peddling porn to them, but believe this: I'm helping you for Kara's sake.'

He swallowed what was left of his drink.

59

Hoffmann stood at the end of Uferstraße at 08.00 hours on the following morning. The sun pushed through a persistent haze which blurred the outline of the buildings, dappling the cobblestones with light. He waited, watching the handful of people who emerged from doorways on their way to work. After a while the street fell silent. He waited a little longer, as long as he dared, unable to gauge whether he was being watched or not, before setting off down the street. He carried his small black leather bag, and he kept a hand on the gun in his pocket. He had left the car at the hotel: time enough to check out and deal with it after he had seen what Adamov had to offer. He held himself ready in the meantime; but no trap had been set for him in the street. He'd have to brave the apartment. Of course they might be waiting for him there. And yet he could scarcely believe that Adamov had set him up. He'd kept the most important secrets. If he hadn't, Hoffmann wouldn't have left Berlin, let alone got this far.

He approached the house and rang the bell Adamov had indicated. He heard footsteps descending a staircase and moments later the door opened. Adamov stood there in trousers and a vest. But his face was alert.

He led him into the house, the ground floor of which was deserted and run-down.

'Lot of people have left,' said the film director, leading the way up the scruffy wooden staircase. 'Plenty of people dead too. Cholera and typhoid in the suburbs. Not a healthy place to stay long. Hope you didn't drink your tap water.'

They passed the first floor, where the open front doors of flats revealed empty, dirty rooms beyond them. In some, furniture was tumbled about, or pushed aside in disarray.

'Been quite a few arrests too. Everybody's getting very jumpy. I'm the only tenant left here. And after tomorrow, when I'm gone, the rats'll take over. Doing a running battle with the fuckers as it is.'

He pushed open a door on the second floor which revealed a spacious, untidy flat. Adamov was the kind of person who could turn a hotel room into a tip within an hour of his arrival. Books and clothes were scattered about, and in the bed crouched a very young, scared brunette.

'Don't worry. She's Romanian. God knows how she got here. Speaks about three words of German.'

'Are you sure?'

'You really must calm down. She does speak some French, thank God, so we at least communicate. But she's as thick as two short planks.' He dropped his voice slightly. 'She isn't a spy. My friends here lent her to me. And she's more frightened of you than you are of her. She thinks you're a Gestapo raid.'

'What are you going to do with her?'

'When?'

'When you leave.'

'She'll get by. I know a survivor when I see one. Drink? There's some beer, but it's warm. Can't offer you coffee, I'm afraid. Or there's this.'

Hoffmann declined the proffered bottle of Bols. 'Aren't you cutting down?'

'Certainly I am. I only have one of these before breakfast. Now, you've got a car you need to lose. What else?'

Hoffmann almost laughed, it sounded so easy; but the girl worried him. 'Who are your friends?'

'Some of the old Monbijou gang are still here - remember them? They need money to get out of town, because they're not as well bankrolled as the others. They've got clothes, petrol and some equipment. And they'll take the car.'

'What'll they do with it? It's a Volkswagen - you know only officials get them.'

'Only officials get *cars*, end of story. But don't worry. They've got their own contacts. Nothing thrives like the black market when there's panic in the air - that's the time when no-one pays any attention to it.'

'I'll need some other transport,' said Hoffmann, glancing past Adamov to where the girl had got up and was washing herself in a china bowl, perched on a dresser in the bedroom.

'She'd better not use up all the water,' growled Adamov, following his gaze. 'I haven't shaved yet.' He grinned. 'Transport shouldn't be a problem - only it won't be a car. A bike?'

'Anything beats walking.'

'Walking beats getting caught.' He looked at his watch. 'I have to go out now. Make the arrangements.'

'I'll go back to the hotel, get my stuff.'

'Where are you staying?' asked Adamov.

Hoffmann hesitated.

'They'll need to know where to collect the car. You tell the staff there that you're having a mechanic pick it up. There's something wrong with the transmission that needs fixing.'

'What's the deal?'

'The car's worth a lot. Anything else, you and I can settle up later.'

'And if I don't hear from you again?'

Adamov shook his head. 'All the trappings are gone, Max. You've got no backup. I'm *all* you've got. Anyway, why should anyone double-cross you? You've got goods to trade.' He held out his hand. Hoffmann gave him the keys to the VW, and told him the name of the hotel.

'Where shall we meet?' he asked.

'You know the Panorama Tower on the Rosentalhügel? It's gone now - it burned down last December - but the remains are still there. At about - ' he looked at his watch - 'Four. You'll have to take your chances. Anything could happen between now and then.' He stood up to go. 'Give me five minutes. Then go yourself, and watch your back.'

As soon as the door was closed, the girl came away from the vigil she'd been keeping by the bedroom window, glancing at him on her way to the kitchen. She quickly re-emerged, holding a blackened kettle, at which she pointed with a crooked smile which nevertheless transformed her face.

'Thé?'

'Merci,' said Hoffmann. The girl shrugged, smiled again, and returned to the kitchen.

60

As he returned to the hotel, Hoffmann noticed a man on a street-corner selling the *Arbeiter-Zeitung*, and bought one. Glancing through its two sheets, he saw, at the bottom of the front page, an item about him, 'believed to have committed suicide as a result of his crimes being exposed'; but there was a very full description. No photograph, thank God; the few that existed of him were - all but one - old, and grainy. In his work, you didn't publicise your looks. There was his official identity mugshot, of course; but in that he was wearing glasses and still had his moustache. His big frame was a problem, but his regular features, despite his large nose, were commonplace and, he hoped, forgettable. He didn't like that full description, though.

He'd reached the hotel by ten. A different desk-clerk was on duty. The man looked up as Hoffmann approached. Then he inclined his head slightly. There'd been something in his eyes - was it a warning? Or commiseration? Hoffmann didn't like it. A very thin man in a blue suit which hung loosely from his shoulders approached him across the lobby.

'Dr Friedmann?'

'Yes?'

The man flashed a card. 'Security Police. Schmidt. May I have a word?'

'Of course.' Automatically he reached for his papers.

The man raised his hand. 'I don't need to see your ID,' he said. 'Friedmann; Ministry of Aviation. From Berlin. Now here. For how long?'

'Three days.'

'Doing what?'

'Damage assessment.'

'I'd have thought there was enough for you to do at home.'

'Colleagues are taking care of that.'

'Naturally.' The man had small eyes, deeply set in their orbits. The skin surrounding them was grey. His hair and his pencil-line moustache were a dead black. He looked like a skull wearing a wig. 'And what are you doing here *precisely*?'

Hoffmann stood on his dignity, though he wasn't sure the ploy would wash with the Gestapo. 'I make a report, and return with it to headquarters. If it's any of your fucking business. What was your name again?'

The thin man raised a deprecating hand. 'It seems very extravagant. You come all this way by car just to do a job which someone here could do just as easily, and telephone his findings through.' Schmidt was enjoying himself. He thought he had a catch in the net. So he was giving this B-Movie performance. Now, he was even examining his fingernails. Hoffmann looked around the lobby. About a dozen people; one youngish man in a buttoned-up suit pretending to read the *Deutsche Allgemeine*. He might as well have been holding it upside-down. Was that the back-up?

'I'm not just covering Leipzig. Dresden too.'

'But they haven't touched Dresden.' The angular chin came up.

'Yet.'

'So you think they will? Maybe you hope it?'

'What are you talking about?' Hoffmann knew where this was leading. Had Schmidt been tipped off? Adamov? Impossible. Though he would never expose his back to Adamov, he had never questioned his loyalty to Kara, and he was certain that Adamov retained that.

His palms were sweating. Then he saw that the policeman's attention had been distracted. He was aware that the lobby was emptying, and that the desk-clerk was abandoning his post. A low, distant hum came to his ears. He knew what it was, and at the same moment the scream of the sirens confirmed it. He looked at the thin man, who seemed to have shrunken further.

'Well, Dr Friedmann, we must defer the pleasure of this conversation. Do not leave the hotel until we have contacted you again.' He gave Hoffmann what he clearly hoped was a bayonet-sharp stare, before turning on his heel and hurrying as fast as his dignity would let him towards the hotel doors. The hum had developed, more quickly than seemed possible, into a roar.

61

What their targets were, Hoffmann had no idea, but they were close. He threw himself behind the heavy mahogany reception desk as the first bomb hit.

The building shook and the central chandelier trembled, though any fragile sound it made was drowned by the noise of the explosion. At the same moment the shock-wave blew in the main lobby doors and shattered their glass. Behind the desk, Hoffmann could hear the shards flying and smashing into the walls and furniture.

He cowered lower. The next bomb was further away, but its force still made the hotel shudder. One of the tall palms by the orchestra daïs slowly toppled and fell into the debris. There was no sound of anti-aircraft fire, nor of the lighter, faster noise of Luftwaffe fighters; only the relentless crashing, like the footfalls of a malevolent giant, of the bombs. The RAF was doing its work unchallenged.

The raid went on for ten minutes, which seemed like ten hours; but after the second bomb no more fell close enough to do damage to the Imperial. They had come for the railway station.

Hoffmann got to his feet. He smoothed his jacket, brushing off the worst of the plaster dust, took his room key from the rack behind him, and, picking his way through the wrecked lobby, made his way upstairs to his room. He packed the two leather bags, which had always been stashed in the VW, quickly, leaving the old suitcase and his soiled clothes behind. He left the room so that it still looked occupied. Praying that the car had escaped the raid unscathed, he replaced his key on its hook, and made his way out of the hotel just as the all-clear was sounding.

A few staff were beginning to emerge, too dazed and wrapped up in their own fear and relief to pay him any attention. One elderly porter's trousers were stained, and he was ashamed, trying to conceal the wet patch.

The first bomb had struck just beyond the far side of the square in which the hotel stood, and two of the buildings there had tumbled to rubble behind their façades, which still stood, ending in jagged edges towards the roofline. Rubble littered the square as far as the steps of the hotel, and the dead and dying lay scattered amongst it. A near-naked woman, her clothes torn off by the blast, reclined, in a parody of sleep, at the foot of the steps.

Further off, an officer lay supine, clutching at the air with arms reduced to stumps. In the centre, pinioned by a large piece of masonry, was a sack-like shape, the pulverised remains of a man in a blue suit. The body had no head. As he skirted the square towards the wounded officer, Hoffmann found it, face up, and undamaged, the dark eyes open and still carrying the startled expression which was their last.

A lean, skull-like head. Gestapo-man Schmidt had not made it in time. Over all hung a momentary silence, as deep as the silence of snow.

Hoffmann looked up from Schmidt's face. Other people were beginning to emerge from cellars. Two men, the older carrying a doctor's bag, were making their way to the officer, who still groped the air, but uttered no sound. Hoffmann went over to them, and as he drew closer he could see that there were shallow, bloody craters where the officer's eyes had been. The doctor knelt over him, and gently probed the man's torso with strong, long-fingered hands. Then he stood up.

'There's nothing we can do,' he said. 'I'll ring for an ambulance if I can, but...' he let the words hang. 'He probably doesn't know he's lost his arms. He probably doesn't even know he's lost his eyes.' He turned to the younger man. 'Stay with him.' Then he made his way over to the hotel. God knew if the phone lines had survived.

Hoffmann retraced his steps to the alley behind the hotel which led to the hotel car park. It was empty. There'd been no opportunity to tell the hotel staff about the 'mechanic' who'd be along to pick the car up, but as the place was unguarded the Monbijou boys obviously hadn't had any trouble.

They'd worked fast, that was for sure. Hoffmann looked at his watch. It was only an hour since he'd arrived back at the hotel from his meeting with Adamov. Schmidt was dead, but the guy who'd been in the lobby reading the *DAZ* might still be around. There were no other bodies in the square. Hoffmann was without transport, with nowhere to hide, and five hours to kill. The grain of comfort was that, with the car gone, anyone watching the hotel might think he'd made off, frightened by the encounter with the Gestapo - the tousled room he'd left behind wouldn't fool anyone if the car was gone without explanation. But the air-raid would have interrupted surveillance, and there probably hadn't been any before his meeting with Schmidt. Schmidt had been very sure of himself. Hoffmann was certain that, had it not been for the air-raid, he would be under arrest now. He remembered the clerk who'd checked him in. Had *he* put in the report to the Security Police? Above all, was Schmidt working alone or not? Hoffmann was big game: there'd be competition for the honour of bringing him in.

It was a pleasant day, not unbearably hot, for which Hoffmann, with his two bags and his leather coat, was grateful. There was even a cool breeze, but that didn't solve his immediate problem, which was to get his head down somewhere. It occurred to him, also, that either Adamov might have been killed in the raid, or that Adamov might think *him* dead. He'd nothing left to trade, and even if he could contact the Monbijou boys, they might not be impressed, even if he gave them all the money he had left. But he wasn't going to go down yet.

He remembered the bar on the Ritterstraße. He made his way there. His route skirted the track of the air-raid, and he passed tableaux from a landscape in hell. Groups of women were already shifting rubble, indifferent to the scenes of ordinary grief being played out near them as they worked: an old man, the grandfather perhaps, on his knees in the dust, in his shirtsleeves, silently cradling the body of a little boy, maybe three years old, stroking his hair; a woman in a black dress patterned with white flowers, standing on bleeding bare feet, keening to herself; a girl in her *Bund Deutscher Mädchen* uniform, long blonde hair in plaits, in the doorway of a ruined house, smoking a cigarette, rocking a battered pram.

Ritterstraße was untouched by the raid, but every building in it was shut, and the bar he was looking for, the Red Hen, a cellar dive that was once used as a clubhouse by the city's lightweight criminals - forgers, conmen, burglars - didn't have a sign up any more. He descended the iron stairs to its door, and knocked, but the sound echoed within.

He returned to the street. Five hours in the open didn't appeal to him. He thought of Auerbach's again, but it was too likely to be frequented by soldiers and SS. He hefted his bags onto his shoulder and made for the one place where he'd be sure to blend in with the surroundings - the station. There'd be secret police on duty there, of course; but he knew their surveillance methods well enough to handle them, and the crowds would help him.

62

The massive bulk of the station had taken a knock or two but still stood unbowed. Under the huge curve of the roof, he bought himself a paper cup of ersatz coffee and found a seat on a long wooden bench facing the platforms.

There were only three or four trains in, all passenger traffic, the carriages stretching back beyond the giant black locomotives which hissed and growled and occasionally screamed in a shroud of white steam. He was far from alone here, and there were people sitting amidst their bags who looked as if they might have been waiting days for a connection.

Soldiers patrolled in front of the trains, but no-one paid any attention to Hoffmann as he re-read the paper he'd bought earlier that morning, sipped the coffee - far too hot to allow any flavour, good or bad, to register - and began to think about continuing his journey by rail - one of the trains was going to Munich - if it ever left - another, to Nuremberg. The second would be ideal. If he could get a ticket. He still had travel warrants, but the problem was time. Long delays had been posted on the announcement boards in front of each platform. The raid hadn't done much damage to the station, but further up the tracks, rails had been ripped up on several lines.

He made enquiries, and was told that although a warrant would guarantee him a ticket, there was little chance of the Munich train leaving before midnight, and possibly not until the next day.

He was mulling over this news when he saw Adamov again, standing at one of the tall tables by the coffee stand, in conversation with a middle-aged blonde woman whose mouth was a splash of bright-red lipstick. He watched them. After five minutes, they parted, the woman walking towards the exit, Adamov towards a train, joining a large number of other people, who, by some unseen and unheard signal, were heading towards it to board.

But Adamov stopped short, and turned left, making for the next platform, which was empty. Hoffmann made his way towards him. Adamov turned at his approach. 'What the hell are you doing here?' he asked.

'The car's gone.'

'Good. Heini must have arrived just in time. What a raid, huh? I thought they might have got you.'

'Is that why you're leaving? When I got back to the hotel, the Gestapo were waiting for me.'

'Oh, Jesus.'

'It was that girl, wasn't it?'

'She doesn't speak German.'

'So you say.'

'She's at the flat. And the phone lines are down. Christ, if you knew the trouble I've been to - '

'Are you leaving?'

'I was here to meet someone. She's organising the bike.'

'And what are you doing now?'

'Wait.'

A porter, pushing a mountain of baggage on a large trolley, was coming towards them. Reaching them, he stopped, let go of the handles, and, with a brief glance at Adamov, turned his back, lighting a cigarette. In one movement, Adamov swung a small suitcase off the trolley, and started to walk away. Hoffmann followed, still unused to not being in control.

'What's that?'

'Your wardrobe. Trust me, Maxie, I'm a criminal.'

63

They returned to Adamov's flat. Ilena was there, asleep in the bedroom. 'Good,' said Adamov, gently closing the door on her. 'She was rather overwrought about you, so I gave her some gin with a little something in it to calm her down. Seems to have worked.' He put the suitcase down and, kneeling, opened it. In it was a sponge-bag containing several luxuries - a bar of soap, toothpaste and a brush, and a shaving kit. There were three shirts, two ties, three sets of underwear, and a brand-new lightweight suit.

'No water to wash here until this evening - too late for you, I'm afraid - but at least you can get changed when you want,' said Adamov. He looked at his friend. 'If I were you I'd put the suit on now. Sorry we couldn't run to a fresh pair of shoes.' He paused. 'But you can leave that leather coat and your black hat here. I've got you some better stuff. No extra charge.'

'I must owe you something.'

Adamov raised a hand. 'Nothing for now. Well, a couple of hundred, if you insist.'

Hoffmann handed the money over. 'And the bike - if it comes?'

'They're getting a bargain with the car.' He paused. 'Anything else you need? I've got a Colt automatic here, big bugger, and a whole pile of extremely imaginative magazines - I'm an editor now, you know, as well as a film director, though I prefer to see myself more as a writer.'

'I've seen your films. There's nothing original there at all. They're all based on stories from Grimm.'

'The Grimms were much more risqué than I am, and how dare you say I'm not original. Folk tales, fairy stories, they make brilliant material for sex movies, and they have a genuinely Teutonic quality which appeals to my clientèle. Did you see my *Robber Bridegroom*?'

'We should have closed you.'

'What, and put all those poor dear people out of work?' Adamov looked bitter. 'Not that I'm not proud of some of my babies. In time I wouldn't be surprised if they didn't become classics.' He paused. 'Actually, neither of us has anything to be proud of.'

They stood in silence. Hoffmann thought how old Adamov suddenly looked, and wondered if Adamov was thinking the same thing of him. He certainly felt it. 'You did nothing,' said Hoffmann. 'By comparison, nothing. I am a murderer.'

'No-one judges you.' Adamov paused, then looked at his watch. 'Look, to hell with this, there isn't time for it. There's some food. Like some lunch? And perhaps a little wine? Got that too. It's been a busy morning, and the fucking RAF didn't help. But we can't leave until three. They'll deliver the bike near the Rosentalhügel at four, as we hoped. That'll give you time to get out of town and settled somewhere before nightfall.'

Hoffmann was lost in thought. 'Do you think it's been worth it?'

'What?'

'What we've done? Has it been worth the sacrifice?'

'Of what? Of our morality? We have to believe that it has, haven't we?'

'I've done far worse things than you.'

'You had to. Otherwise, how could you have done any good?'

'But what has that amounted to? We've failed.'

'That doesn't matter. The fight mattered. But now it's over.'

No it isn't, Hoffmann thought. He said, 'You only made some movies.'

'Yes, and I played ball with men who are the scum of the earth, men who pushed papers about their desks and sent hundreds of thousands of their fellow-beings to their deaths. They won't last long now, and I wish I could say that I helped bring about their downfall. I tried to. I listened to their drunken indiscretions, I passed information on, I am at least indirectly responsible for a few successful bits of sabotage - oil dumps, armaments factories, supply trains . You too, you've fudged investigations so cleverly that no-one ever knew. You stymied their administration. You've saved innocent lives. It isn't our fault that we failed.'

'How do you know all this? How do you know what I've done?'

Adamov smiled sadly. 'Our paths may not have crossed, but sometimes we served the same masters. Nothing's watertight. The odd crumb fell from the table and I had the advantage of knowing you personally, before all this shit started. You knew about me. But your work didn't cover politics, hard politics: you were a *Kripo* man, not *RSHA*. Internal Intelligence was after us - people like Heinrich Müller. Department IV. There was communist resistance all along. Not big, but it never lost its teeth.'

Hoffmann wondered how much else Adamov knew. Hoffmann had sat down with the same men, he had worked with them, helped them plan, carried out their orders. Did Adamov know the truth about the concentration camps? He hadn't been involved in the serious films - the films that showed the model camp, Theresienstadt, as a haven for the Jews - Christ, they'd even managed to pull the wool over the eyes of the Red Cross! And the other films, the secret ones. Hoffmann had been to the other camps, the ones Jews were taken to from Theresienstadt to be killed. He'd been to Sobibor, he'd been to Auschwitz, he'd seen how it was done, he'd sat down with the men who did the job.

The geese at Sobibor extermination camp - the geese, brought in because their cries drowned the cries of the inmates. He knew that the images burned into his mind would never leave him, that not a day would pass in this life when they would not be before his eyes, and that not a night would come when he would not fear sleep, because of the dreams.

Did Hagen dream? Hagen, who had become rich in the service of the machine? Once the administration had discovered how effective the poison gas *Zyklon-B* was in the annihilation process, Hagen had been quick to see the commercial opportunities and had made himself indispensable as a middleman between the manufacturers and the users.

Hoffmann remembered how Hagen used to joke about the chemist who'd developed *Zyklon-B* as an insecticide. Fritz Haber - winner of the 1918 Nobel Prize for Chemistry, presumably not because of his pioneering work in the field of poison gas, which in turn had led to his wife's suicide - was a Jew who'd left Germany in 1933.

'One good thing the Jews did for us, anyway,' Hagen used to say of his commodity.

Tens of thousands of cans of the stuff, conveniently supplied in a solid form which vaporised when exposed to the air, had been shipped by train to Auschwitz and Majdanek. Quicker than exhaust fumes. Infinitely cheaper than bullets. The process got so fast that the crematoria couldn't cope with the bodies. 'A reliable and cost-effective means of processing the product,' Adolf Eichmann had reported smilingly in his clipped, clerical voice.

And there was this deal going on now to ship thousands more cans to Auschwitz to kill off the Hungarian Jews, a deal Hagen would want to manage, to squeeze the last pfennig out of the system to finance his escape. The only predictable thing about Hagen was his greed.

Had Hagen ever watched children being herded into the so-called shower-halls. It was impossible to fool children. They always knew. They didn't know better than to think the worst of things. Death hung in the air. Working with the Party to work against it, Hoffmann's moral compromise had sucked him dry, and for nothing. He was a shell.

Let me save what's left of my family; and let me settle one debt. Then I will welcome death.

It was a tall order.

'I've killed more people than I've saved,' he said.

'Do I have to remind you that for over ten years we've been living in a country that has turned into Tartaros? The smallest criticism, a chance remark, can kill you,' said Adamov. He poured himself a Bols, but Hoffmann refused the bottle. 'Believe me, my friend, we have at least been brave. Anyone with all their integrity intact is either dead, in the camps, or in exile. We wouldn't be here if we hadn't pawned our souls. We'll get them back when we come out the other side.'

'Do you think it's so simple?'

'I can't afford not to. You want me to shoot myself? Sorry, I'm not built like that. I'll bite a cyanide pill rather than have them torture me to death, but that's it.' Adamov drew breath. 'If you're not drinking gin, and I have to say you're making a sensible decision, I'll get the wine. I'm not going to get you drunk, you still have a long day in front of you. But I am going to drink hard. I only wish it had any effect any more.'

Adamov stood up, stoppered the Bols, and took it to the kitchen. Moments later he was back, nursing a bottle of hock, and two glasses. 'I know you have done terrible things, Max. I have heard. But you must not let them get in the way of why you did them. Whether the result is failure or not, it doesn't matter. It really doesn't, Max. You can't afford to think like that. You fought on the right side.'

'I did too much for the wrong side.'

Adamov laughed, but didn't really know how to counter the remark, or give any comfort. Instead he said, 'I know the feeling. But we can still turn the fucking tables.'

They looked at their watches. Adamov went back to the kitchen. Returning, he brought a tray with plates, knives, bread, cheese and sausage. 'We must eat. There's more. We'll pack some for you to take. Those Monbijou guys may not have enough cash to get out, but meanwhile they've certainly got themselves organised. Look at this: Real *Knackwürste*. Real Emmenthal.'

'Don't you get stuff from them regularly?'

'Mostly, we keep ourselves to ourselves. Safer that way. In any case, I haven't been here long enought to reforge any of the old Berlin relationships.'

Adamov laid the food out on the low table between them.

'Do you ever think about Kara?' Hoffmann asked.

'Of course I do. Less than you, I imagine.'

'That wouldn't be hard.'

'You ought to let her go, too.'

Hoffmann looked at him.

'What are you going to do?' said Adamov.

Hoffmann smiled, shook his head.

'How is Stefan?'

Hoffmann tensed. 'Well, I hope.'

'Is he safe?'

'I hope so.'

'You'll see him?'

'I must.'

'Then you will.' Adamov paused. 'Can you get him out?'

'God willing.'

'He must be – how old? Ten?'

'Yes.'

There was a pause. Neither touched the meal in front of them. 'I could come with you,' said Adamov.

'No. Only I can handle this.'

Adamov nodded. He seemed to be making up his mind to say more. Hoffmann, realising this, waited.

'Hagen has been here. In Leipzig,' said Adamov at last, watching his friend.

Anxiety flooded Hoffmann's mind. 'I'd heard he was heading south. But that was days ago. When was he here?'

'He was here for about a week. He had some business to wind up. Got some money stashed here with someone, I heard.' Adamov hesitated again. 'He left yesterday.'

'D'you know where he's gone?'

Adamov shook his head.

'Oh shit.'

'You don't think he's going after Stefan?'

'He can't possibly know where he is.'

'Could he guess?'

'I've destroyed everything I had that linked me with Stefan. There was one photograph of him. I kept it in a book in the flat in Berlin. I burnt it before I left.'

'Hard.'

'Yes.' Hoffmann wondered if Adamov could begin to imagine how hard. But that was unfair. For all he knew, Adamov might have wanted children himself. He stood up, paced the room like an animal in a cage, unable to stretch, unable to bear the confinement. 'What time is it?'

'We can leave early. It'll be best to walk. It's forty minutes from here on foot.'

'I've got to get going.'

'Patience.' Adamov spread his hands. 'Look. What would he want with Stefan, after all? The only thing he can be interested in is saving his own skin.'

'He's got time. He'd be on a boat to Buenos Aires by now otherwise. The war's not over yet, you know.'

'As good as,' Adamov said.

'Not this year. It'll be months yet, at least, maybe another year. Look at the damage they could do in that time.'

'We have to leave it to our friends the *Ammis* and the Tommies to stop them now. In the meantime, Hagen's not on the run. Loyal servant of the Reich.'

'Loyal servant of himself,' said Hoffmann. 'He's gone to ground and he feels safe. But he's not just interested in the money he can still make. He'll have got that organised anyway; and as long as he thinks no-one's after his skin, he'll indulge himself.' He looked at Adamov. 'He was in love with Kara. Desperately in love with her.'

'He just wanted to own her, Max. He used to come to me, later on. Wanted me to find girls who looked just like her, with the help of a little make-up and a change of hairstyle. Dress them up and film them for him.'

'And did you?'

'No-one got hurt.'

Hoffmann bit his lip. 'Why didn't you kill him then?'

'He was too well protected. You know that as well as I do. He was never without at least a couple of sidekicks.' Adamov paused, 'In any case, the girls never satisfied him. Look like her they might, but they couldn't mimic her mind, her soul.'

'Were you in love with her?'

'With women I've really cared about, I've always preferred the safety of friendship. Why didn't *you* kill him?'

Hoffmann laughed shortly. 'Same reasons. It would have put my work in jeopardy. Hagen was too important to them. And later I could never get close enough either.'

'You could have got somebody else to do the job.'

'You know better than that. Whom could I trust?'

'He'll never go after Stefan.'

'I can't be sure.'

'But why?'

'Do you really need to ask that question?'

Adamov was silent.

'You said he'd indulge himself as long as he thinks no-one's after his skin.'

'Don't take any chances,' said Adamov. 'The RAF saved your neck today. But do you think that Gestapo shit was the only one to know about you?'

'Big coup if he was. Big thing for him to bring me in. He was bloody sure of himself. He might have kept it to himself. As long as Hagen thinks I'm dead...'

'Do you think he's that stupid?'

'He's not stupid. But he is arrogant. And this is the endgame.'

Adamov shrugged. 'Just concentrate on getting Stefan out.' he shoved a plate towards Hoffmann. 'And eat something, for fuck's sake!'

64

The walk calmed him, and by the time they reached the burnt-out remains of the tower on the Rosentalhügel his mind was quiet. Adamov had timed the walk so that they would arrive shortly before they were due. Moments after they'd reached the rendezvous he had arranged, the woman from the station came up to them, climbing the slope with some effort. She was carrying a parcel, which she handed to Adamov.

'All set?' he asked her.

'It's in the Heuweg. Just head north out of the park and you'll get there. It's being watched, but they'll know who you are. You won't see them at all. It's just security. This is a good bike. Hard to replace.' She glanced at Hoffmann, but neither made to shake hands, nor smile.

'Good.'

'Here are the keys.'

The woman looked at Hoffmann again. Her face relaxed fractionally.

'Good luck,' she said, and immediately turned and made her way back down the hill, out of sight. Adamov handed the parcel to Hoffmann.

'Open it.'

It contained a half-length leather coat, and a pair of goggles. Hoffmann looked at him.

'You can put the coat on now.'

They walked out of the park. The Heuweg was a quiet street just beyond it. It seemed deserted. Towards one end there was a cluster of large dustbins. Behind them was a BMW motorbike – an XX750.

Adamov handed him the keys. He looked at Hoffmann wryly. 'What were you expecting - a bicycle?' And then, as an afterthought, 'You do know how to ride one of these things, don't you?'

65

'I'm not impressed.' *Gruppenführer* Heinrich Müller let the file containing Kessler's report drop onto his desk, and looked up from his chair to where the inspector stood at semi-attention, the other side of its littered surface. The only other person in the room was Müller's duty clerk, the same studious-looking young SS-*Obersturmführer* Kessler had seen on his previous visit to the Prinz-Albrecht-Straße.

The clock on the wall said 10.00am. Kessler had just spent the longest fifteen minutes of his life in the room.

'It's the only possible conclusion we can draw, sir. The way we found the car, what it contained, everything –'

Müller stood up himself. 'Come on. You know him better than that. Double-bluff? Remember? Shit, it's only the day before yesterday that we discussed it!'

'That was before I visited the site. He probably wanted to keep us tied up for as long as possible, even though he'd intended to kill himself all along. So that we couldn't relocate our resources immediately. All the circumstances point to suicide, sir.'

'Then where's your fucking body?'

'We're dragging the lake.'

'Another bloody waste of time!' Müller brooded, pacing his cavernous office, picking up one paper or dossier after another before returning it to its clumsy pile. He paused, 'As for your request to stay in Berlin...'

'Sir?'

'It's denied.' Müller sat down and picked up Kessler's report once more. 'Try harder on this. I don't want to see you again until you bring me a body; and if you find him alive, bring him back in one piece.' Müller waved to his clerk as an indication that the interview was at an end. 'You can keep Kleinschmidt with you,' he added as Kessler prepared to depart. 'And get this done fast: it's priority. I'm getting two calls a day from the Führer's office. It won't be my head on the block if we don't get a result soon - and you, Kessler, are eminently expendable; it's no secret how friendly you were with the traitor Hoffmann.'

'Yes, sir.'

'Not that you suspected anything?'

'No, sir.'

'One more thing.'

'Yes?'

Müller shook the sheaf of paper in his hand. 'There *are* one or two things we need to verify in here. Double-check, you know.' He made no attempt to hide the threat in his voice. 'We'll be in touch when we have. Won't take more than a day. In the meantime, report to your office. And don't go further from it than your flat. We'll know if you do. That's all.'

'I thought you said this investigation was urgent.'

Müller looked up. 'We won't hold it up, believe me. Now get out.'

'What about the call from Althof?' Müller's clerk asked him after Kessler had saluted, and left. 'Shouldn't he know about that?'

'Of course,' said Müller. 'And he'll be told this time tomorrow. But for now we need him where we can see him.'

The SS-lieutenant nodded.

'What's next?' said Müller.

'Sturmbannführer Schiffer is here already, sir.'

'Good. Get him.'

The clerk left through a side door, and reappeared moments later with Müller's next visitor.

'Did you hear any of that?' asked Müller, gesturing to a chair.

'Enough.'

'And what do you think?'

'Hoffmann's clearly alive,' said Schiffer.

'What makes you think so?' Müller had made sure that Schiffer hadn't been told anything about the call from Althof.

'He's not the type to kill himself. And my guess is, he's got unfinished business to settle. After that, he'll make for the frontier.'

'Which?'

'I can't tell you that.' Schiffer shifted in his chair, showing slight impatience, which Müller didn't mind at all. 'In the meantime - '

'Yes, yes. What have you found out?'

'We know where his daughter is. We checked all the possible places on file. Just a question of looking at them all and whittling them down.'

'You took your time.'

'Hoffmann had scrambled his files and address cards, destroyed a lot - but we had several duplicates he couldn't have gained access to even if he'd known about them, and he didn't have time to do a thorough job.'

'Where is she?'

'At Inspector Kessler's parents' old house. It belongs to him now.'

Müller didn't look at all surprised.

'I suppose they thought it wouldn't be in our notes any more. Kessler's father's case is a very old one,' Schiffer added. 'And there's no evidence that Kessler uses it much, if at all. It was all shut up until recently. Still looks that way.'

'I imagine so.' Müller paused briefly. 'So, what are you doing, still sitting here?'

'I need you to sign the order. The house is being watched. She can't possibly get away.'

'Rainer?' But the SS-clerk was already approaching with a sheaf of papers. Müller put on his glasses, skimmed them hastily, and signed where he had to, before handing the top two copies to Schiffer.

'Tell your men to handle her with kid gloves.'

'They'll do their best,' Schiffer said.

'She mustn't be alarmed. You must be discreet. Do you think Kessler's involved in this?'

'She would have known about the house. Kessler and Hoffmann were close - I don't need to tell you that. She has keys.'

'How do you know?'

Schiffer made a little gesture with his hands. 'We've been watching the place; and so, of course, have the locals.'

'Weren't she and Kessler friendly, at least at one point? They probably had assignations there, after his parents ... moved away.'

Schiffer shrugged. 'If you say so.'

Müller leant forward. 'Careful, Major. Everyone's edgy at the moment and a word out of place can be very risky. Kessler's working for me now, but he has direct orders from the Führer. No-one can countermand them but the Führer himself.'

Schiffer spread his hands. 'Do you want her brought here first?'

'I don't think so. Get her on a train to Munich as soon as possible. Two men should accompany her - first class seats for all three. They should take her directly to Dachau from the station - get them to phone ahead, the people down there should send a car. Are you remembering all this?'

'Yes, sir.'

'I fucking hope so. You're too cocky, Schiffer. If this goes wrong I'll personally see to it that your arse gets ripped inside out, understand?'

'Sir.'

'They'll put her in the Privileged Prisoners compound.' Müller looked reflective. 'Got a good chance of survival there, unless orders change. Got all that?'

Schiffer stood.

'Report back when it's done. You can telephone Rainer. Or send a man if there's an air-raid.' The *Gruppenführer* looked at his watch. 'She should be in her new lodgings by this time tomorrow.'

'Sir.'

Müller looked at him. 'Don't worry about Kessler,' he said. 'In any case, I may have a new assignment for you when you return. It'll involve a bit of travelling.' He looked at the wall-clock. 'Come back tomorrow at 10.00 hours. I shouldn't have to keep you long.' He stood up and saluted:

'Heil Hitler.'

'Heil Hitler.'

66

It was late afternoon when the telephone rang in Müller's office. The young *Obersturmführer* answered it, and spoke and listened briefly. He rang off and immediately dialled the Hotel Kaiserhof where Müller was attending a meeting of heads-of-department.

Müller was on the line in moments. He listened while his clerk told him that Emma Hoffmann had been apprehended without fuss. She was found to have a small suitcase already packed, so they had evidently been in the nick of time; but it also meant they could leave the house without delay, which they had locked and sealed.

Three of Schiffer's men had driven her directly to the station and two of them had boarded the 17.09 Munich direct express with her. It was expected to arrive at its destination at dawn the following day, and the men would report once they'd handed over their charge at Dachau Concentration Camp.

Müller hung up, pleased with his day's work, and returned to the smoking room where the meeting was in the process of winding up. Stewards were appearing with decanters, coffee, and cakes.

The following morning he would send Kessler and Kleinschmidt to Althof - it was worth the short delay to ensure that Kessler was denied any opportunity of contacting Emma Hoffmann before he himself had been quite sure of arresting her. Of course he might have led them to her, but Müller had few men at his disposal for such a job and every confidence in Schiffer.

In any case, Kessler was still the best man to sniff out Hoffmann, so he had to be kept clean, as it were. But the professorial little inspector had to have an eye kept on him, too. Pity there was nothing Müller could do about the Hitler-Order Kessler carried, but there it was.

He thought about the call from Althof. Some woman who ran a hotel down there. Someone who'd known Hoffmann in Berlin in the old days and who had a score to settle. Hoffmann had run the Vice Squad too successfully not to have made a few enemies. Müller didn't know the details. Rainer had taken the call. But it sounded like a positive identification.

Which meant that friend Hoffmann hadn't shot himself in the woods after all.

Müller wondered how Kessler would react. Of course he'd present the news to the policeman as if it had come in since their meeting. He knew the cop was back at his flat now, probably champing at the bit because he knew he was being watched and wouldn't dare rush out in search of his lady-love. All rather ironic, really.

Müller ordered a large Martell and selected a black cigar from a box on the conference table. Quite convenient, too, that Schiffer and Kessler had been such rivals in the past.

He snipped the end of his cigar, dipped it in the cognac, and placed it in his mouth. He was lighting it when a colleague from Department VI B appeared.

'You're looking very pleased with yourself,' he said.

'Yes,' said Müller. 'I have reason to be.'

67

The bike was heavy, but powerful. The panniers either side of the rear wheel were large enough to accommodate his bags and, counterweighted, a five-litre jerry can of petrol. That, with the full tank, would be enough to see him through.

As a means of transport, the bike had worried Hoffmann at first. It was years since he'd driven a bike and he'd been uncertain if he still could, but after a day on the road, he had mastered it again. Its advantage was speed.

He'd had to drop the Ministry of Aviation cover, but he'd hung on to his Swedish passport, and he was now the proud possessor of another set of travel documents and ID papers in the name of Dieter Weitz, a reporter for the *Völkischer Beobachter*.

It was a riskier cover because it was more controversial, but while it might make things less easy when dealing with officials, it could smooth his path with ordinary people. He had money and ammunition enough to see him through. There was more with Tilli, if he could reach her.

Before he slept, he checked and cleaned the service pistol and the Walther. He should have asked Adamov for another gun. God help him if both the ones he had jammed.

He travelled west out of Leipzig, but as soon as he was able to get onto country roads, he headed southwards. He was beginning to smell his destination. Not long now.

He spent the first night with a farmer and his wife who showed no curiosity about him whatsoever. They were only interested in relieving him of the exorbitant five marks they charged him for a straw bed made up in their lean-to. He'd refused the attic, as there he'd be trapped. There was no telephone or electricity, and the place was remote; but he knew he would still sleep lightly, with his PPK in his hand, and he'd brought the bike into the lean-to with him. In fact he found it hard to sleep at all after the heavy meal – pork and dumplings – which they'd given him; but he was grateful for apparent lack of interest in him.

The lean-to smelled of cow-dung, and he rose before dawn, stripped naked and washed himself vigorously at the pump in the yard, where the chained dog eyed him with suspicion. He drove away before they had risen, satisfying himself with a breakfast of cold water and cigarettes – the last of the Murattis.

He thought of his flat in Berlin. They'd have ransacked it. He had no home, no bank account, not even a sense of belonging, an identity. And how tedious this limbo was, of being on the run. In the course of his career, he had tried to place himself in the minds of the criminals he pursued, and it was a fundamental tactic he'd always taught his students; but he had never sympathised with his quarry until now.

Who was pursuing him? He wished he'd been able to find out more about the Gestapo in Leipzig. Another question: at this stage of the game, where did his pursuers' loyalties lie? And if their loyalties were divided, how much influence would fear have on them?

68

He reached the little wine-growing town of Freyburg without difficulty and managed to find a restaurant in a small hotel overshadowed by the twin towers of the church. Although the state's influence was less evident in so rural a place, he had no intention of staying longer than he had to. A stranger would stand out like a sore thumb, and after his encounter with the Gestapo in Leipzig, he was under no illusions that Berlin would still believe him dead.

His friendly host and hostess served him a late lunch and he hastened through it, as his main reason for stopping here was to use the telephone, which stood at the end of the bar, in a quiet corner. There were two other people eating, an elderly man in country clothes and his wife, who both nodded hello. The man recommended a local Müller-Thurgau, and by the look of him he was a man well experienced in wine-drinking.

Hoffmann bought cigarettes and asked if he could make a call to his office. Would the phone, if it worked at all, be monitored? He doubted it, not here. In any case it was risk he'd have to take.

They were more than happy to let him. Hoffmann noticed that they looked careworn. They'd probably had enough of the war, like everyone else. They were impressed, however, that he was a journalist, and even moved away to the other end of the bar. Unfortunately, they also dropped their voices in deference, as did the elderly couple, who had finished their meal, and were lingering over the rest of their wine.

Hoffmann picked up the receiver and dialled Tilli's number.

She answered immediately.

'Were you sitting by the phone?' he asked.

'Not exactly. Can you talk?'

'Briefly. How is he?'

'Fine. A bit bored. Doing a jigsaw puzzle, but his heart's not in it. Are you coming?'

'Yes.'

'When?'

'I don't know. I'm not far. Two days.'

'Have you got transport?'

'Yes. I may not be able to call again though.'

'Will I recognise you?'

'I hope not. How is he?'

'I've told you,' she said gently.

'I won't know what to say to him.'

'We'll cross that when you get here.'

'Yes.'

'Max.'

'Yes?'

'Are you all right?'

'So far, so good.'

'There's been quite a lot about you on the radio and in the papers. For a moment even I was taken in. Then I told myself that there was no question of your shooting yourself – when you still have things to do.'

'What's the news?'

'The latest – this morning – is that they've sent a team after you to Althof. People have been warned to look out for you. They gave a description, too.'

'On the radio?'

'Yes - it wasn't very good. But be careful.'

'Nothing official from Leipzig?'

'No - should there have been?'

'It doesn't matter.' Hoffmann felt a small sense of relief. Perhaps Schmidt really hadn't tipped any of his colleagues off when he'd got the call from the hotel clerk. But what of the hotel clerk himself? What of Schmidt's assistant – if the man reading the newspaper *was* his assistant – he was certainly clumsy enough to be a Gestapo-man.

'Are things still safe with you?'

'Touch wood.'

'No visits?'

'None.'

'Max.'

'Yes?'

'If you think the risk's too big, don't come. I can look after him.'

He wondered for a moment how she could ask the question. 'I have to see him. How could I not?'

'I only meant –' But Tilli didn't complete her sentence.

Hoffmann sighed, glancing at the people at the other end of the bar. The elderly couple were leaving. He smiled, waved at them. 'I must go.'

'Come quickly, then.'

'As soon as I can.'

He hung up. The Gestapo, luckily, relied so heavily on denunciation and betrayal that they'd never become good investigators; but they still needed watching, especially the careerists. As for the rank-and-file, he could skate around them. He rubbed his eyes. He'd better get going.

'Got a lead?' asked the landlord, as he paid his bill.

'What?' Hoffmann tried to be as friendly as possible. No point in antagonising anyone. But he was under so much strain that he could hardly bring himself to act a part.

'No offence,' said the man. 'I know the form – you people don't reveal your sources. It's just that I heard on the radio, they got a description of this big-shot cop they're looking for. Got a sighting in Althof. Thought you might be on his track.'

Hoffmann managed another smile. 'Maybe. But you know, you're right – I can't tell you anything.'

'Of course, of course. Just wondered, you know. They said he might be making his way in this direction.'

'I wonder what gave them that idea?'

'Althof's more-or-less on the road south of Berlin. I suppose they think he's heading down to the Swiss frontier.'

'He'd be lucky.'

'Right! Big bloke in a black Volkswagen. Shouldn't be hard to catch.'

'Yes.'

'Bastard. Sits in Berlin on his fat arse for years and then it turns out he was working for the enemy all along!'

'There's been a lot of fall-out since the assassination attempt,' Hoffmann said. At least he could catch up on news when he reached Tilli's. All his life he'd lived on information. A fortnight ago, there had been every hope. It did no good to brood on what might have been, but a fortnight ago, only a fortnight, everything was at his command. Now –

'Bloody bastards,' said the landlord. 'I hope they get them all.' Hoffmann noticed with surprise that he was close to tears. 'Excuse me,' the man added, then turned his back and made his way through a curtained doorway at the rear of the bar. Hoffmann watched him go.

'Forgive him,' his wife said. She handed him his change. 'We lost our son on the East Front eight weeks ago.'

'I'm sorry.'

'He was a good boy. Already had a little vineyard over by Neuenburg. Wanted to expand, of course. Hated the interruption. But when his country needed him, he went.'

She was a slightly-built woman of perhaps fifty. Hoffmann was silent, thinking that the boy scarcely had a choice. He realised that the careworn expression, almost apologetic, was truly one of grief.

She fished out a framed photograph from among the bottles on the shelves behind the bar. There was a strip of black ribbon across the top left-hand corner. It showed a dark-haired young man in a check shirt and dungarees, leaning on a hoe and smiling at the camera. Behind him, neat rows of vines.

'I'm sorry,' Hoffmann said again.

'What did he want to go and die for?' said the woman. She wiped her hands on her apron. 'Well, I mustn't keep you.'

69

Hoffmann kept to country roads all that afternoon.

Where was Kessler now? Had he got Emma away? Had he been arrested? That seemed unlikely; Kessler knew how to take care of himself. But Emma? Poor, dear Emma! Kessler couldn't keep her under his protection for long, he didn't have the power, and Hoffmann knew all about the Gestapo policy of arresting the families of men and women who in their eyes had betrayed the state. It had been in Himmler's mind well before the 20 July debacle had thrown Germany into an even lower circle of hell. Just another insane idea of theirs – that a traitor's blood was bad, and so by extension the blood of his kin must be as well. The concept was Himmler's of course, that terrible, bloodless creature who'd been the means by which Hitler's worst ambitions had been realised. Diels' Department 1A, Göring's Research Department, the Police, all had been sucked into one vast organisation – seven Departments, over 180 Sub-Departments, a hideous bureaucracy which was the ponderous but all-reaching machine which Himmler had built for his idol: The Head Office of Reich Security.

A world ruled by a handful of madmen who weren't even that bright. How had it come to this?

And Emma, who could never disguise her feelings, whose dislike of the Party was often dangerously open even when she enjoyed her father's protection, Emma, whose ambition was to be a professional violinist - what could possibly become of her now?

He remembered her sixth birthday, in 1930, when they had given her her first violin. Ursula was already ill. Though neither of them spoke much about it, they knew the cancer which had invaded her body a year earlier would soon claim her. They were both aware this would be the last of Emma's birthdays that Ursula would see. They hid it from the child, but Emma sensed that her mother was going to leave her. It was as if Ursula were standing on a boat, her suitcase at her feet, while her husband and daughter stood on the shore, waiting for the moment when the vessel cast off.

After her death, in the Charité hospital, at seven in the morning on 5 October 1930, a cold, clear day when Berlin was bathed in watery sunshine, Hoffmann resolved to do all he could to realise his wife's dreams for her daughter. Emma was intelligent and musically gifted. She was never conventionally beautiful, but the strength of her character made up for that, and more.

He'd not been a good father; he'd been too absorbed in his work. The way he had to live his life and the nature of his work demanded that Emma be found a more secure environment in which to grow up and she had done so with her aunt, Ursula's older sister, a music teacher at the high school in Nicolassee.

Margaret also taught piano privately, and among her many friends in the musical community was a young violinist, Harry Thalheimer, who undertook Emma's lessons. He'd left Germany for France in 1936, soon after the end of the Berlin Olympics in mid-August, when the Party no longer found it necessary to present a smiling face to the world, and when the previous year's Nuremberg Laws, which made the Party's view of its Jewish countrymen and women more than clear, began to bite seriously.

It had taken a few months for Hoffmann and Margaret to find a successor of equal talent. Margaret adored her niece, and threatened to leave with Emma herself. Hoffmann, already gnawed by doubt, begged her to stay. Now he felt punished for his selfishness and vacillation.

As Emma grew from child to girl to woman, Hoffmann was able to see less of her. He continued to do his work, but it had a double edge now that he had joined the ranks of those who planned to topple the regime, a task made increasingly urgent as official policy led to the leaching away of more and more intellectual and financial talent. He was acutely aware, too, that the precariousness of his life could threaten her safety. But he saw her as often as he could, taking his clarinet with him, and proud of her irritation with him on the occasions that he could not keep up when they played together. Even allowing for the prejudice he knew he had as her father, he was musical enough himself to know that she had more than adequate talent, with luck and a following wind, to launch herself when the time came. He allowed himself foolish daydreams in which he saw her auditioning successfully for one of the great conductors, Furtwängler or Karajan. Hoffmann had even reflected once or twice that he might exert some influence on Karajan, who, like himself, was a Party member.

He and Emma had remained close until latterly, despite the turn his own private life had taken. And hers, for that matter, though of course it wasn't until much later that her heart became involved with someone else's. He laughed inwardly even now at the recollection. She and Kessler thought they'd been so careful to keep it a secret from him. He'd known almost from the outset. It had worried him at first, he didn't think Kessler was right for her, the man was ten years her senior apart from anything else, he thought she was too young and that she should be thinking of her career. He didn't want her sacrificing that to love, throwing her chances away just for the sake of another human being.

No-one kept secrets from him. He had the power to set men to watch anyone he chose. His reputation and his record shielded him as surely as his uniform and his low Party membership number. In the early days, Himmler had wanted him to switch to the Gestapo, to train its officers as well as he trained his own. It was a bad moment. He'd talked to Oster about it, since, even though he felt that his soul was as mortgaged as Faust's, there was a limit to what he would do. By good fortune and careful negotiation, he was able to stay on his side of the fence, though Himmler, testing his loyalty perhaps, had made him pay a cruel price. There was blood on his hands which he hoped his family would never discover.

It was Kara, Kara alive, and Kara dead, who had kept his feelings from freezing over completely. Would he have done what he'd had to do to remain useful in the battle against the Party, if she had lived? He smiled coldly. He'd made no decisions then; Fate had.

70

The bike bounced violently, yanking him back into the present. He'd hit a pothole in the road, luckily small, and was just in time to swerve to avoid a larger one. If he'd hit that he'd have wrecked his front tyre, and he'd have had to walk. He pulled over and stopped, killing the engine. He was shaking. He sat on a grassy mound a few feet from the road - it was more of a lane - which he was driving down. He lit a cigarette.

It was late afternoon now. He'd have to start thinking of somewhere to spend the night. He hadn't passed anywhere since leaving Freyburg.

He took out one of his remaining twists of snow and rubbed the powder on his gums. He'd have to find water somewhere soon. There was no sign of a stream near here. The drowsy sunshine fell on him. He listened to the crickets carolling to infinity, and watched as a breeze rippled the leaves on the trees. He felt rooted to the spot. He had no desire to go on. He had to go on. It was the living who drove him, as much as the dead.

It was mid-May when she told him the news. Night-time. They'd been looking down from the windows of her flat at one of the processions the Brownshirts had begun to stage in Berlin. Hundreds of marching men, carrying flickering torches, singing the *Horst-Wessel Lied*, which had just been proclaimed Germany's new anthem. The brutal aggression of these would-be soldiers and heroes, wrenched from hopelessness and unemployment and easily turned into unthinking zealots, chilled the atmosphere in the room and for a while killed any conversation between them. Each knew what the other was thinking.

She'd broken the silence abruptly with her news, but her voice hadn't risen above a whisper. Was she really that scared of his reaction?

He was pleased and concerned at the same time. His mind was already racing. The consequences of this were still out of range for him. He still had the words of the song the men had been singing in his ears – *Raise high the flag! In serried ranks the Brownshirts march boldly, firmly on...*

'How long have you known?'

'I meant to tell you before, but I wasn't sure –' she broke off. 'God, I sound like someone in a play.'

'When?' He kept his voice gentle, and smiled, encouraging her, though he could not yet smile with his eyes.

'I was worried a month ago, but I've just missed my period a second time, and there are... other signs. I'm afraid it's almost certain.' She fell silent again. He did not speak, not wishing to break her concentration. 'Look, we took precautions. I can't help it.'

Did she think he was blaming her? She was sombre, but not anywhere close to tears. She wasn't appealing to him, either; she was stating facts. She was brave. Did he have the same courage?

'Don't worry,' he said. He was thinking hard and fast.

'What shall we do?'

'Let me get used to the idea first,' he said, and she laughed.

'It's a hell of time to be starting a family,' she said. 'Especially with my pedigree.' She paused for a moment, and he could see that she was sinking back into her former mood. 'I've had more time than you to think about this.'

'Yes.'

'When I said I wasn't sure, I meant – ' She broke off.

'I know. That doesn't matter. I'm grateful to you.'

'I'm sorry. I've been on edge. It's a relief to have told you, whatever we do next.'

71

He was silent. They knew what the alternatives were. That was simple, and at any other time – at least as far as he was concerned, for he did not yet know her mind – the decision would have been easy to make. In the seven months that had passed since he'd met her, he'd acknowledged to himself - though he hadn't yet told her – that this wasn't just the simple affair he'd hoped it would be.

He was in love with her. Perhaps because of the times, perhaps because after grieving for Ursula and being alone for two years, he was ready to need someone again. He didn't know what the reason was, if there was one at all, and he couldn't, didn't even want to analyse it. He did not know if his love was returned. He doubted it. She still saw him as a National Socialist, didn't she? But if that were the case, why was he still here? Why were they still lovers?

His first instinct had been to regret the pregnancy, but it had happened – once or twice he had been too impatient, they had been too impatient, in their lovemaking, but there could have been no breaking that glorious spontaneity, and he could not regret that. Now they both had to accept what had happened.

He also knew that if she decided that she didn't want the child, he would respect that decision. But he knew just as surely – and it surprised him – that he wanted the child to be born.

'This isn't a trap,' Kara said.

'I know.' It was something that hadn't even occurred to him. As a policeman he was losing his grip, he thought fleetingly, to have missed that.

She looked at the floor. 'As if there weren't problems enough.'

'This isn't a problem.'

She looked at him in surprise. 'Really?'

'I mean, it isn't something we can't solve. It depends on what you'd like to do.'

'Doesn't it depend on what both of us want to do?' She was angry. 'Do you ever commit yourself, Max? Has all that police training robbed you of any feeling at all?'

'No.'

'You don't talk like that when we're in bed. You don't stand back from me then.'

'I'm not standing back from you now.'

'Then help me. Give me a clue about what you want to do.'

He was silent. He knew she was right. He had become so used to containing himself that it was hard, even with her, to lower his guard. Was that a weakness? Or did he need that armour to get through, especially now?

'Do you just prefer to see everything from the outside? Don't make me feel alone in this.' She was waiting for an answer, and in the silence he could feel her need. Who was he? A successful state employee, thirty-four years old, a widower, with a nine-year-old daughter. His life with Ursula stayed in his memory but it had taken on an ever more dreamlike quality there. When he saw Emma, he saw traces in her face, her mannerisms, her character, of his late wife. Could he not relax again, and trust the water to carry him if he dived in? Hadn't he already done that? He knew he loved this woman and there could be no disloyalty to Ursula in that. And he had as much as agreed to work with Oster and his organisation against the State he'd served for his entire career, but now accepted as dangerous. He was not used to choices like this.

He hadn't told her about the meetings with Oster. Should he? She was watching him now, waiting. She looked completely alone.

'I love you,' he said. 'And I would like to have this child.'

A new expression had appeared on her face. It wasn't relief, it was too soon for that, but it was perhaps that she felt that she could, very tentatively, begin to trust this man. And perhaps there was another element - that she had no choice but to. Even though she was far from weak, she knew how hard it would be for her to survive alone, even without the baby.

Hoffmann wondered how he could reassure her that her trust would not be misplaced. He had already, on his own behalf, committed one small act of treachery against the state. He had used his influence to gain access to her papers and doctor them sufficiently to remove any trace of her Jewish ancestry. If he'd asked her permission, he knew she would not have given it. It'd been a question of practicality, and he'd had to move fast. He wasn't the only one to have access to files, and anyone with sufficient influence, and with any kind of personal interest in Kara or the von Wildenbruch family, might have looked at them and possibly copied them. He could only hope that he hadn't been too late to prevent that. At least Kara's mother's original papers would still be in some records office or other in the United States - and she had never become a naturalised German. Kara, he knew, had never opted for dual nationality. It would be hard to sort something like that out now.

He went and sat by her, put his arms round her. 'Please tell me what you want.'

'Do you really love me?'

'Yes.'

'Why have you never told me before?'

'I don't know.'

'You're not just saying it now?'

'No. Maybe I wasn't sure before.'

'This isn't something sentimental. I don't want you to think I'm leaning on you. I can do this by myself if I have to.'

'You don't.'

'Well then, I'd like to have the baby too.' She laughed briefly. 'I'm nearly thirty. I may not get another chance!'

'When can we expect him?'

'Him?'

'Or her, of course.'

She smiled, but still carefully. 'If he's on schedule, next January.'

'Should I rush out and get you some oysters and chocolate?'

'No! At least not for another two months! And then I'll probably prefer herrings and strawberries.'

'I'm out of practice.' He had told her all about his marriage, Ursula's death, and about Emma. He remembered Ursula and her sister had managed everything to do with that pregnancy and birth. He had been too busy. Fatherhood had been a remote business for him, and it was likely to remain so. Already he knew he would have to persuade Kara to leave Germany. He would join her later - if he could.

He wanted to say that perhaps by next January the Party would have foundered, that the country would have escaped the fate it had wished on itself; but he knew now, if not from his instinct and the evidence of his eyes, then from the seriousness of the engagement of a man like Oster, that that possibility had disappeared. 1934 would do nothing but confirm the bleakness which 1933 had ushered in, though in the euphoria of the moment, all but a few were cheering the leader who had apparently enabled Germany to hold its head up once again. 'When the sword is unsheathed, all reason is in the trumpet' - the phrase drifted into Hoffmann's mind as the relic of a memory from his seminary days.

Another thought unsettled him: the Party was introducing a new kind of ID which covered a person's racial 'purity'. It was already turning hundreds of thousands of Germans into frantic researchers of their families' pasts, for the Party did not deem a citizen to be a true Aryan if even one of his grandparents had Jewish blood.

Kara nestled against him, but she didn't tell him what he hoped she would. He wanted to kiss her, but unaccountably felt shy of doing so. After a minute, she broke away, tidying her hair, smoothing her dress.

'So what are we going to do about the dear little bastard? We have seven months, and the baby will begin to make its presence pretty obvious in three or four. I'll have to stop work, I suppose. That, or explain the situation. They're very understanding at the Charité, but I can't trust everyone.'

'What about Tilli? She'd help. And she loves children.'

She hesitated. 'I might take Veit into my confidence, you know.'

'Adamov? Why, for God's sake?'

'You don't know him. He's always been a very good friend to me.'

'The fewer people who know, the better. And I can take care of things, take care of you.'

'Yes, but you also have to think about Emma.'

'Emma is fine.'

'How will she react to this?'

'I think she'll be pleased.'

'You mean, you hope she'll be pleased.'

He was thinking. 'We'll talk to Tilli.' Did he dare bring up the idea of her leaving Germany? It could be arranged, but she'd have to agree. It wasn't something he could put off for long. But to take a child with her! How could something be a curse and a blessing at the same time?

She hadn't said she loved him. He wondered again if Hans Oster had told her of their meetings. He doubted it. It would be far better if she were not implicated at all in such matters, even though she had suggested that he contact Hoffmann. Clearly part of her plan of redemption. It was a risk she would have left Oster to weigh, and Oster had taken it.

He felt elated. He could take action. He was always happiest when he could take action. The danger, the doubts, and the horrible choices the various ways ahead offered him, none of them safe, all fell into perspective. But there was a new element: he'd never thought about death before. God knows, he'd seen it often enough; he lost Ursula when she was the same age as Kara was now; but he'd never thought about death coming for him. Why now, when the prospect of a new life was before him?

He thought of Hagen too. Hagen had been silent since his departure for the Black Forest. Kara had not mentioned him again. Hagen must never know about this. Hoffmann had considered the possibility of having Hagen killed. It would be difficult to arrange, he was well protected; but not impossible. But perhaps the danger was past. But perhaps Hagen had got over his passion, forgotten it.

'We should celebrate,' said Kara, standing and walking to the kitchen. 'But I've only got Sekt.'

'You should have warned me,' Hoffmann said. 'I would have brought some champagne.'

'What, from the SS canteen?' She caught his expression and came back, took his hands. 'I'm sorry.'

'Why?'

'I'm sorry.' She went away again, returning with a tray and glasses, the bottle in an ice bucket, a bowlful of snacks. 'As long as we're together in this, anything with bubbles will do,' she said; but the mood was subtly broken, and she knew it.

She filled the glasses and passed him one. It felt cold and pleasant in his hand. He wished he could tell her that he had all but changed sides, but that would have to come later. He'd said yes to Oster, but uncertainties lingered, not least for his own safety, let alone that of those he cared for. But he knew that despite the doubts, and even if he recanted, he would not now betray the men who'd decided to resist the Party.

He shook his head to clear it. For the moment he would concentrate on the problem before him, and solve it. That was what he had always been best at. He liked things to be concrete. He would talk to Tilli. Perhaps she could more easily persuade Kara to leave than he could.

He caught an anxious expression on her face. He raised his glass, then hesitated.

'Well, we have to give the baby a name,' he said, trying to be cheerful in order to ease aside the awkwardness which had arisen between them. 'We can't just toast "it".'

'We don't know what sex - '

'Well, let's choose a name for each.'

'All right,' she smiled more naturally, relieved that he seemed to have forgotten her remark. 'You choose for a girl.'

Hoffmann thought. He really had no idea. 'Helga? Franziska? Luise?'

She wrinkled her nose at all of them. 'Anyway,' she said, 'Franziska's the name of Göring's mother, isn't it?'

He swallowed the joke that was on his lips and said instead, 'And if it's a boy?'

72

Hoffmann shook himself. He hadn't quite slept, but he'd been drifting far enough away not to have noticed time passing. It was close to six. His throat was dry. Around him, nothing had changed. The crickets still sang, and the wind still moved the branches of the trees. He'd go on a little further, find some water, and somewhere to sleep.

The wind refreshed him a little as he drove, but he was tired from the sun and the tension. He'd thought he knew how to control it, but he'd always been the hunter, never the hunted. Now he was both. He wondered if Brandau was in Bern, and pictured him sitting in an armchair in the sun, drinking a glass of *Gewürztraminer* and reading a book – although he'd be far more likely to be at a desk, in an office full of Americans, the only one not in his shirtsleeves. Either way, Hoffmann wished he were with him. He wished it were all over. Well, in a week, either way, it would be.

The dusk was gathering when he saw the village, so low on the horizon and so dug into the hillside it sheltered against that he might have missed it had it not been for the last rays of the sun catching the weathercock on the church spire. He kicked down a gear and slowed, not wanting the roar of the BMW's engine to announce his arrival too soon. How would he explain himself here? It was too small a place to stay in.

There was no sign announcing the name of the village as he approached. He reached the outskirts. Larger than he'd thought. A dirt road with houses on either side and one or two lanes which looked like farm tracks. In the middle of it, the road opened into a square with a huge elm at its centre, the church on one side, some kind of public building, perhaps a market hall, on the other, and next to it the inn. There'd been no telegraph poles along the road for some time, and there weren't any here. No electricity, no telephone.

It must have been a rich place once, for the church and the market hall respectively had grand gothic and baroque façades, which looked out of place now, overtaken by time and changing fortunes. The church porch was raised above the floor of the square, and an ornate, though now dilapidated flight of broad limestone steps led up to it. A large number of saints, angels and kings were crowded around the porch, most of their faces too weather-beaten to have expressions any more, though the ones that had were merely grave, indifferent, cold. The tympanum showed the usual Christ in Majesty and Last Judgement, and as usual the mediaeval masons had enjoyed themselves far more with the images of the Damned than with those of the Saved. Here, stone screams issued from mouths in agonised faces, caricatures of local worthies dressed in the robes of monks, knights, lawyers, moneylenders, and an obligatory pope. Stone flames lapped their bodies as grimacing demons pushed them silently and forever downwards and backwards into hell, plunging pitchforks into their bellies and groins and strangling them with tails that had the heads of serpents. On Christ's right, cosseted by solicitous angels, the Saved held their hands together in prayer, intolerably smug smiles on each of their faces. Across the square, the elegant baroque swirls and swoops of floral stems and branches, topped by two angelic trumpeters (one beheaded by time) flanking a crumbling coat-of-arms, seemed optimistic by contrast, and filled with light.

Below the tympanum, the heavy oak doors of the church were bound with iron, but they stood ajar. Darkness behind them. Hoffmann looked at the doors, and then raised his head and looked again at the Damned. Silently screaming in flames forever. Hoffmann lowered his head again. God, he was tired of the lies. And he wanted his children safe.

He had parked his bike in the shadow of the staircase. He checked his gun, and made sure spare clips were in his pocket. He shouldered the lighter of his two packs, the essential one which contained the money, ammunition, documents and the last few twists of snow, and skirted the sides of the square in the gathering gloom. He was making for the inn, but he was already aware that there was no-one about, no-one had been curious enough to emerge from door or appear in window to take a look at him, and that, beyond the soughing of the wind, silence hung over the village.

The double doors of the market hall were locked, and its windows were too high and dark for him to gain any clue about what was inside. But the low door of the inn opened to his touch. There were no lights inside. He cast an eye back across the square, up at the windows. Nothing stirred except the dust and the first fallen leaves in the wind.

Hoffmann let the door swing open and stood aside for a moment, his gun in his hand by now. Listening for the slightest sound in the dead silence, he entered cautiously, keeping his back to the wall.

He waited again for his eyes to grow accustomed to the gloom, keeping his breathing slow and light. He could see the tables and chairs, the bar, and the bottles and glasses glimmering behind it. There were beer mugs on some of the tables, and one or two dead flies. He could tell that there was no-one here. The silence was too dense, and when it was broken, the furtive rustling could only have been made by rats or mice.

There was little dust on the tables, and mould had only just started to grow on the dregs in the beer mugs. So the village had not been deserted long. He wondered why everyone had gone, and where.

He considered going upstairs, but he didn't want to be anywhere that didn't have a line of escape. He was tempted to take a bottle of schnapps from the bar, but decided against it. He tried the tap over the sink. Water flowed. He was so thirsty he decided he would take the risk. He filled a glass and drank. It tasted cool and clean. The noise the water made seemed deafening, but he poured another glass and was about to drink it when he heard the voices.

73

At first he couldn't be sure that he had heard anything, just a murmur that came from far away and might perhaps have been anything. He had all but closed the inn door behind him, so from a distance it would seem shut. He approached it now, the hairs erect on the back of his neck. He opened the door a centimetre or two, praying that it would not creak, and peered out.

He could see his bike. Three youths in uniform stood a few feet away from it, and they were talking animatedly about it. They had large old rifles slung over their shoulders. The uniforms weren't Regular Army issue, but a kind of ragbag SS, and none of them fitted very well. It was hard to see their faces from this distance. Where the hell had they come from? Well, it was clear that they weren't going to leave the bike alone. If he were going to get it back, he'd have to brazen it out. God, he thought, how much he missed his own uniform and the authority that went with it. He'd have been able to wipe the floor with them. But he was just a journalist now, and even one who worked for the main Party paper wouldn't cut much ice with these guys.

He knew who they must be - something new - they were called 'Werewolves', another bloody stupid fairy-tale macho name dreamt up by the Leadership. Teenagers mainly, poor, dispossessed and unemployed, hard-bitten bastards at eighteen, recruited to form a kind of cross between Home Guard, SS and last-ditch fighters. They were supposed to be fanatics. They certainly weren't funny. Keeping his hand firmly on the PPK in his pocket, he opened the door of the inn loudly, so they'd be forewarned and not shoot in panic. Once outside, he paused and ostentatiously dusted himself down, giving them time to take him in. Then, shoulders back and walking towards them with a firm but unhurried step, he set off across the middle of the square towards them.

They'd unslung their guns, of course. They were long, heavy things, and Hoffmann recognised them as Mauser 98s from the previous war. He knew all about them and made calculations as he walked. 7.92mm bore; five cartridge magazine, easy to reload if they had much ammunition, but no good for rapid fire because they had a bolt action. Three of them. Fifteen shots if every cartridge was full. Good range. Against them, his PPK, seven shots, fast reload, and his little peashooter which could only do real damage at close range and if aimed at the right place - eyes, groin, kneecaps. There were three of them, but

Hoffmann knew they wouldn't have had much training, and he was damn sure he was a better shot.

Hungry faces. Hollow cheeks, sunken eyes. Lank hair under the caps. But strong lads, used to bearing the brunt, now glad to have a whip in their hand. A few months ago they'd've been barefoot in dungarees, maybe. Nothing in the faces, except suspicion and mistrust. No pity and no humour. Fingers far too close to the triggers. He hated nervous children with guns. The caps they wore were old, hand-me-downs; the edges of their peaks were ragged.

He was within three metres of them when one spoke.

'Get 'em up!'

Been reading too much Karl May, thought Hoffmann, but he stopped, and, letting go of the pistol in his pocket, raised his hands casually to shoulder level.

'What the hell's going on?' he said, affably enough, but with an edge which he hoped lent his voice authority.

'Never mind. Who the fuck are you?' The one in the middle was talking, shorter and stockier than the others. They could beat me to death with the butts of those bloody guns, thought Hoffmann. Before I could get a shot off.

'Where is everybody? Can't even get a drink around here,' he answered.

The stocky one took a step forward, the barrel of his gun pointing up at the middle of Hoffmann's face.

'I said, who the fuck are you?'

'Who the fuck are you?'

The boy came forward again - seventeen? Maybe sixteen - and shoved the muzzle of his rifle hard against Hoffmann's right nostril. If Hoffmann hadn't seen it coming and taken a quarter step back, the force would have cracked the nasal bone. Little shit. Probably used to spend his Sundays putting cats in sacks and chucking them in the river. Summoning up as much dignity as he could, and aware that his face had gone white, he pushed the rifle barrel firmly aside with his right arm, and moved one step towards the boy, and smiled.

'You want some kind of identification, farm boy? On whose fucking authority?'

74

The Werewolf suddenly looked uncertain. Shout at a bully and he'll fold, thought Hoffmann, though it was one hell of a risky strategy to adopt right now. From the corner of his eye he could see that the other two, shadows of the first, were wavering. Now he'd cowed them, he'd stroke them a little, bit of sweet-talk, flash the ID, promise them a mention in the *Beobachter* - 'The Werewolves: with a will of iron and nerves of steel, Germany's Youth - fearless guardians of Our Führer's heritage' - and be on his way.

'What do we have here?' Another voice. Hoffmann looked to his left to see a fourth member of the group approach. This one had a proper black uniform, real wool not wood fibre, jodhpurs, boots, *Waffen* SS insignia which didn't however quite match the cap, whose badge was that of the *Totenkopf* Brigades. Modishly battered cap, rakish angle. Tanned face, cold eyes.

Looked like a *Stabsscharführer's* insignia on the jacket. As tall as Hoffmann, confident, maybe nineteen or twenty years old.

The others were quickly recovering their own confidence.

'Found this bike, sir - ' the stocky one began.

'Yours?' The hybrid SS-man said.

'Yes.' Hoffmann produced his papers. 'Weitz. *Völkischer Beobachter*. On assignment.'

'I am Commander Kurtz,' said the SS-man, inflating his rank a little. 'On assignment where, exactly?'

'Nuremberg. Must have taken a wrong turn.'

'A little late for Nuremberg, aren't you?'

'I have an interview there.'

'I see.' Kurtz was taking his time over the ID. He was also taking control of the situation. He spent a good while over the papers before handing them back. Then he strolled over to the BMW.

'Nice bike.'

'Yes.'

'Standard issue to journalists, are they?'

'I'm on assignment.'

'So you said.'

'What's happened to this village?'

'Evacuated.'

'Why?'

Kurtz turned back to him. 'Are you interviewing me?'

'I don't know. Is there something for me to write about here?'

'There is nothing for you to write about.'

'Then what is a Werewolf detachment doing here?'

'You know about us. You are well informed.'

'I am close to people in Berlin.'

'Berlin is a long way away.' Kurtz was eyeing the bike again. he walked over to it, and ran his hand over it, gently, proprietarily. This was his kingdom. He could do anything he liked.

It was almost dark now. The wind had dropped, and a faint chill was in the air, another harbinger of autumn. Kurtz's next words came at Hoffmann out of the night like an arrow. 'I think you are lying, Weitz. I don't know who you are yet but we'll just have to kick the truth out of you.'

'You would be making a grave mistake.'

'Are you threatening me, you shit,' said Kurtz, suddenly savage. 'We'll rip your fucking face off!' He came close. Hoffmann could smell his breath - it smelt of rose cachous. 'You're a fucking spy. No-one knows about this village!'

Hoffmann had had some experience of people like Kurtz. He waited. This self-important little creep would want to talk some more. But handling him would be a dangerous task. Too much rope, or too little, would be fatal. 'Just doing my job,' he said humbly. 'I'm a reporter. Reporters ask questions. Anyway how would I know about your precious sodding village? You haven't got any guards posted. Anyone could wander in here. Where're your officers?' Kurtz looked again at the ID. He was relenting slightly. 'There's obviously something important going on,' Hoffmann continued. 'My paper won't print anything that isn't in the interest of the Party, you know that. But it won't do you any good to mess with me. Anything happens to me, people will ask questions. And people know where I am, and what bike I'm riding.'

Kurtz looked thoughtful. The eyes of his men were on him. He came to a decision. 'I will give you a story.' Still believing himself in command, Kurtz preened. 'This village is now a Werewolf command centre. The villagers were kindly treated. They have been relocated. There was an outbreak of typhus here; the victims are being taken care of, and the place has been sanitised. We are the advance guard of temporary occupation. You can print all this. Only the location must not be revealed. There will soon be a network – '

But Hoffmann had heard enough. Soon the darkness would be working against him, but there was just enough light left for him to turn this thing round and get away. Kurtz was standing close to him. The stocky boy's Mauser was still trained on him. He had to act now.

75

They were half his age and strong, but they were amateurs and they were led by a lunatic. Hoffmann knew he hadn't convinced them, that Kurtz was acting out of vanity and his mood could swing back to aggression just as fast as it had swung away. He couldn't take any risks. The least they'd do would be to detain him until some real soldiers arrived.

He shifted his weight and half turned, seizing the rifle by the barrel and wrenching it out of the stocky boy's hands, hurling it far across the square. The Werewolves, taken aback, watched it arc through the air and in that moment Hoffmann had slipped the safety on the PPK, drawn it, and pumped two bullets into Kurtz's abdomen. They were so close together that the force shoved Kurtz backwards and spun him round as his guts began to spill black blood. The other three were rooted to the spot.

Hoffmann fired twice at them, hitting one, while another let his rifle fall and threw himself to the ground, crouching and whimpering. The third, the stocky one, moved fast to pick up the abandoned gun. Hoffmann fired again, and missed. Now he had to close in fast. He dropped his pistol back in his pocket and lunged at the stocky boy, seizing his right wrist and forearm in both hands and twisting hard, at the same time pulling the boy round, and away from him, dislocating his arm at the shoulder. As the boy reeled away, bellowing in pain, Hoffmann drew his gun again, shooting him as he fell. It was now too dark to tell where he'd hit.

But the others were recovering now. The one Hoffmann had wounded had his rifle up and was firing wildly. His five rounds were soon spent. Hoffmann had one left in his own clip. He fired, hitting the Werewolf in the neck as he was struggling to reload. The fourth stayed on the ground, rolled up, his head on his knees and his hands over his head. His trousers were wet round the crutch. He was keening something, but Hoffmann couldn't make out the words.

He punched in a fresh clip and crouched on the steps of the church, shielded by part of the stone balustrade. In the faint light that remained he looked at the mess. Kurtz lay motionless in the black pool he had shed. The stocky boy sat on the ground near him, in another dark pool of fluid, uttering grunting sounds, and nursing his wrecked arm with his good one.

Hoffmann stood up. He was winded and dusty, but there was no blood on him, as far as he could see. He looked around again. There had been one hell of a noise. If there were more of them, they'd have been here by now. Where had these hidden themselves? In the church?

The church loomed behind him, the door still half open, the darkness beyond it now total. He could not make out the figures on the tympanum any more. They were cast in shadow.

He walked back down the step. He stood over the stocky boy, who raised his head and looked at him, not with hatred, but in bewilderment and pain. Hoffmann looked down at him. He knew that if the tide hadn't turned as it had, not three minutes earlier, he would be lying there now, if not dead already. He knew, too, what reason was telling him to do, but he did not even raise his gun. He walked over to the other boy, who stopped weeping and looked up at him, his eyes glistening with fear.

'Get up,' said Hoffmann, gently, miserably; but the boy stayed where he was. Day had given way to night and the light now was obscure, silvery. The wide sky was scattered with stars, and the sickle moon was halfway up the horizon. 'Look,' said Hoffmann. 'I am not going to kill you. Are there any more of you?'

The boy was silent. He was shuddering.

'I am not going to kill you.'

The boy stayed silent, but his eyes did not leave Hoffmann's face. Hoffmann did not know what he read in them now, but his attention was attracted by a smell which must have been in the air already, but which he had only just noticed. Petrol. He hurried over to the bike. Two of the wild shots from the Mauser had ripped into the lower part of the tank, and petrol was trickling out onto the ground from two gashes. There must have been a cascade at first, for the tank was almost drained. Hoffmann bent to examine the bullet holes, felt them with his fingertips. He had the spare can of fuel, but it would be of no use unless he could repair the tank, and he could see that even if he had the means to do so, it would be a long job. The gashes were too wide and too low down to wad with cloth.

He'd hoped to be in Bayreuth the next day. Now, Christ knew how long it would take him, and as a pedestrian, he'd be that much more vulnerable. He hadn't got shoes fit for long distances, and, with the exertion of walking in the summer sun, his appearance would degenerate fast. He couldn't pass himself off as a *Beobachter* journalist if he looked like a tramp. He kept looking at the bike impotently, wanting to kick it, as if it were a dead mule, as if it had some consciousness of how badly it had let him down; but he soon drove such thoughts from his head. They wouldn't help. He had to adapt to the new situation. He wondered about the boots the boys were wearing. Might any of the pairs fit him? Might they make walking easier, at least until he found some new form of transport, which he'd have to do.

But how far could he go tonight? He thought again of how reduced he'd become by the loss of the bike. Now that he couldn't get far away fast, the mercy he'd hoped to show the two survivors of the little battle would be misplaced. He'd be overtaken in two hours at the most. And he had to sleep and eat - more important now than ever. In that instant he realised that he had dropped his guard badly. Two of the Mausers lay within reach of the surviving Werewolves, and one was still loaded. The stocky boy was in no condition to handle a gun, but the other -

He turned swiftly and dropped low as the first bullet flew past him, close enough to nick the shoulder of his jacket.

'You killed my mates, you fuck!' The whimpering boy was on his feet, his gun veering in his hands as he struggled to calm himself and control it. 'Bastard!' His words came through an angry sob, the kind of noise a thwarted child makes. He fired again but on the third shot the bolt closed on an empty chamber. Not a full magazine. Hoffmann heard the click too late, he had already fired himself, and fired to kill. One bullet smashed the boy's nose, crushing his face and snapping bone and teeth inwards; the second hit the gullet, fountaining blood as the boy staggered about, clutching his neck to dam the flow, stumbling over the rifle which had got entangled with his legs as he let it drop, and then falling to lie on the earth, but not yet still, though dead. The epileptic twitching went on for eight seconds.

Hoffmann was shaking as he pocketed his gun again. Five left in the clip. He walked back to the stocky boy, now sallow, and sweating. Fear in his eyes. His right arm, swollen, swung from his shoulder as he tried to push away from Hoffmann, using his legs, backwards along the ground.

This was the worst of the three, the one who would have led the torture under Kurtz's direction, the one whom Kurtz would have allowed to fire the final bullet. A bullet in the groin, to ensure a slow death. Hoffmann knew the methods, he'd seen people like Kurtz in action, he'd stood in the camps as an official witness, dying inside as he saw the people herded naked into the 'delousing' sheds, snapped at by dogs and slashed with whips. Telling himself that he had to keep his cover intact, that keeping his rank was important for the greater good. Except that the greater good was never reached, and never would be, now. Hoffmann had served evil too well. The good he'd hoped to achieve was valueless. The good had failed.

He'd tried to minimise the damage he was responsible for. It was cold comfort now, and would never banish the horror which gnawed him.

Wearily, he got behind the stocky boy and manoeuvred him, as gently as he could, to the elm, leaning the boy's back against it. The wind had come back now, and it was chilly, it was an autumn night wind. There was nothing to cover the boy with. Hoffmann stripped off Kurtz's messy jacket and placed that over his chest. The boy looked at him but there was nothing in his eyes.

Hoffmann wondered if he would last the night, and strangely found himself hoping that he would.

Christ, what a world.

He bent over Kurtz again and took off his boots. Good quality. Soft leather. Almost new. Where the hell had he got them from?

They fitted Hoffmann perfectly. He sorted out what he could carry in his shoulder bag, abandoned the rest, and, once he'd set fire to the bike, set off.

He'd have to walk through the night.

76

Hoffmann had been wrong about the innkeeper in Althof, but right about her face tugging a memory.

She hadn't spent her life in the factory town, she went there after her brothel, which catered to specialised tastes, was closed down by the Vice Squad in autumn, 1936, when Hoffmann had been ordered to effect a post-Olympics cleanup.

Where their quarry had gone, she couldn't tell them, but the next place to look was Leipzig. Kessler and Kleinschmidt drove there in their police Volkswagen. Kleinschmidt could barely fit his gut behind the wheel, but once ensconced he was a driver of genius, or so it seemed to Kessler, who, not knowing cars himself, had no idea of the risks his sergeant took.

Kessler knew his old boss would take advantage of Leipzig to shed a skin. Despite Müller's threats, he hoped the trail would go cold there. But he also had to reckon with Kleinschmidt, in whose presence Kessler would have to do things by the book. He had considered taking his sergeant into his confidence, sure that the man was riding out the storm, like most others. But he'd learnt caution, and in any case the chances of the trail really disappearing in the city were high.

The local police had nothing at all for him, and the Gestapo were, as always, unwilling to cooperate. That hoop had to be jumped through, and Kessler had a lot of pull, working on a direct Hitler-Order. It even entertained him to see how much clout it gave him.

He was waiting now in a well-lit corridor, along one wall of which was a series of polished oak doors. Kessler was alone, having sent Kleinschmidt to ferret out leads. He sat uncomfortably on a wooden bench under one of the gleaming windows of the corridor - the place was like a merchant bank - and read through his list of questions for the tenth time. Even in a matter like this, he thought, they liked to let you wait a while. Especially if you were from Berlin. How the provincials hated that.

But someone must have telephoned someone, for he didn't have to wait long. Within five minutes, one of the doors opened and a young man in a blue suit stepped out.

'Inspector Kessler, first name Paul?'

Kessler stood up, pushing his glasses to the bridge of his nose. The Gestapo-man was taken aback by his dishevelled appearance. In any other circumstances, Kessler would have been amused.

'Eisenberg, ' said the man by way of introduction. He didn't mention his own rank, and appeared ill at ease. 'Come this way.'

The office was plain and functional. A large desk and two chairs, one on either side of it, the visitor's decidedly less comfortable than the other; a table against one wall piled with papers. A bookcase with legal publications. A map of Germany hung on one wall, and a city plan on another. Eisenberg gestured to the visitor's chair and took the other seat himself. He offered cigarettes, good ones. They both lit up.

'Yes,' he said, as Kessler removed his glasses and polished them on the end of his tie. 'You may take notes, of course,' he added.

Of course I'll take bloody notes, thought Kessler, prepared for half what he was about to hear to be cover-up and lies.

'We had a covert operation going. It was being managed by a team under *Sturmbannführer* Schmidt.' Eisenberg hesitated. He obviously didn't want anything bad to get back to Berlin, to Müller's office, or, worse, to the Führer himself. How he must hate me, thought Kessler. I'm regular police, he outranks me, that's for sure, look at the size of this office, it's even got a carpet, but he's got to pander to me. That must hurt.

'Yes?' he prompted politely.

'Schmidt had him virtually in his grasp,' said Eisenberg. 'The net was closing.'

'How many in the team?'

'Dealing with a man like Hoffmann, who has eyes in the back of his head, one has to be discreet, deploy one's best men. Schmidt and a back-up man.'

'Who was leading the operation?'

'How do you mean?'

'From here.' Kessler leaned forward.

'Uhm - I was ultimately responsible.'

Kessler knew what he meant. This was a cover-up. Schmidt had recognised Hoffmann, or someone had tipped him off, and he'd acted on his own, wanting all the glory of the arrest for himself. The people here had given Eisenberg the can to carry, he was junior enough to be the scapegoat if necessary. But who was the back-up operative?

'What went wrong?'

Eisenberg stood up, clenching and unclenching his hands a little helplessly. 'There was an air-raid. Bloody RAF. Schmidt was killed. No-one saw Hoffmann afterwards. By the time the dust had cleared, it was too late.'

'And the back-up man?'

Eisenberg was silent.

'The *other* man?' Kessler pressed him. 'I am here on a Hitler-Order,' he added.

Eisenberg sighed. 'I'm sorry. Just a journalist. Schmidt, as we later discovered, had him there to witness the arrest. Please don't let this go any further.'

'And was he killed too?'

'That is unfortunately the case.'

But not by bloody Biggles, thought Kessler. The Gestapo were masters at covering their own backs; but in this case it was to Hoffmann's advantage, and Kessler felt relief for his old boss, though at the same time the policeman in him regretted the death of a lead. He considered asking whether they knew anything about Hoffmann's transport, but realised that he'd get nothing out of the Gestapo even if they knew. One of their men had buggered things up for them in a big way by trying to go it alone, and then there had been that unfortunate air-raid. Now, all the Nazis were concerned with was damage-limitation. Eisenberg stood up. Shrugging mentally, Kessler took his leave. No point in hammering one's head against a brick wall.

77

He met Kleinschmidt at Auerbach's *Keller*. His sergeant sat at a table near the door, his back to the wall, in front of him a mug of beer and a pair of *Weißwürste*, and potato salad. He looked up philosophically at his chief.

Kessler joined him and ordered a white wine. 'Anything?' he asked, knowing what the answer would be. Even Kleinschmidt would be taking some kind of action if they had anything remotely resembling a lead.

Kleinschmidt waved his fork expressively. 'Our old master was driving a black VW, just like ours. He and it have vanished into thin air. Officials are hopeless, and I can't root out any of the old under-the-table lot. Waiter here who knows them says most of the old Monbijou people have cleared out. Everyone else has gone to ground.' He cut a slice of sausage and shovelled it into his mouth, swilling some beer after it and wiping his chin with a large napkin. 'I've got one last thing to follow up after lunch. Meeting at two. But it's a long shot, so don't get your hopes up.' He surveyed the table. 'Need some more bread,' he grumbled. 'Can't get decent stuff anymore, even in a place like this.'

'Can you manage this meeting on your own?'

Kleinschmidt winked theatrically. 'Much better, sir. Old grass of mine; gets nervous in company.'

Kessler thought about the car. Kleinschmidt was far from being a fool, though it amused him to appear one; if he said the car was gone, it was gone. Whoever had acquired something as valuable as a VW would have had time by now to change its colour and plates five times over if they'd wanted to, and they'd have moved fast, because if they'd been caught with it they'd have been strung up. His guess was that it would be in Switzerland by now, sold there for solid Swiss francs which would remain in a bank until the vendor could pick them up once Germany had capitulated. The *Reichsmark* would be worth zip soon, though Kessler knew that no-one would let Germany fall into economic chaos, while the *Ammis* and the *Russkis* carved Europe up between them. He wished to Christ he had some Swiss francs himself.

'So what have we got?' He asked himself.

'Fuck all,' answered Kleinschmidt, unbidden, but concisely, through a mouthful. 'Let's go home.'

'We can't do that without a head on a platter.'

'Yeah, I know,' said the sergeant mournfully. 'And we can't conjure one out of thin air, so on we go.'

Kessler watched his colleague slowly but surely clear his plate, then wipe it clean with a slice of bread. 'Who's on *our* tail, do you think?'

Unsurprised by the question, Kleinschmidt said, 'Bound to be someone, make sure we keep picking our feet up.' He sucked his fingers and inspected his nails. 'They've got so jumpy upstairs that I shouldn't be surprised if you didn't have two people on your back - one to watch you, and one to watch him.'

Kessler was following his own thoughts. 'They won't approve of us farting around here.'

Kleinschmidt shrugged. 'A man's got to eat. In any case, I came here to interview that waiter, and you came here to pick up my report. That's work. Want a cognac?'

'We've still got plenty to do.'

'A cognac's never stopped me yet. Anyway, what have we got to do? The trail's gone cold. No-one's fault. Happens all the time.' Kleinschmidt paused. 'Still, be a feather in your cap, wouldn't it?'

'Yes.'

Kleinschmidt called their waiter over and ordered two Asbachs. Then he lit a cigar.

78

He had waited until Kessler and his sidekick had searched Hoffmann's room at the Imperial. The room had been used since Hoffmann's evident departure by other guests, since no authority had issued an order to seal it, so it came as no surprise that they left apparently without having been able to gather any kind of forensic clue about their quarry; and as Kessler and he had been trained by the same master, he was able to second-guess his colleague's train of thought with, he flattered himself, relative accuracy. The local police had been through the stuff Hoffmann had left behind, but it had yielded nothing of any value to the investigation.

As soon as he could, he moved into the room. It had already been reserved for someone else but a wave of his Gestapo card changed all that. Once installed, Ernst Schiffer, now *Obersturmbannführer* Schiffer, conducted his own inspection.

It was of a different kind from Kessler's. Schiffer would spend a night here, sitting in the chair and sleeping in the bed, and try to coax out of the very walls an impression of what had been running in Hoffmann's mind when *he'd* been here, five days earlier. Get inside the quarry's mind, and you have the key to his actions. At the same time, Schiffer hoped that by a stroke of luck or flash of inspiration, he would pick up something Kessler had missed. It was a fantasy, of course; only the purest good fortune would hand him a break like that, for he knew that Kessler, always the favoured pupil, had a flair which he could only envy.

He had been able to put Kessler's girlfriend away. Emma. He'd fancied his chances with her once himself, but she'd made it plain, in the way women do, that she wasn't interested.

Stuck-up little bitch. But her arrest had brought a jump in rank, and this lonely, but responsible assignment - all from Big Cheese Müller himself. Schiffer smiled. His star was on the ascendant. If only it wasn't rising too late. If only Kessler would make a slip, give himself away. That would be the coup for me, Schiffer thought, allowing his fantasy to get the better of him. He was in so far now there was no going back. No retreat. He had to cling to the ship he'd joined, and even if a part of his mind refused to let him forget that it was sinking, he suppressed the thought. he couldn't afford to admit to himself fully that all he was clinging to was wreckage, for if he did, what would there be left for him.

Of course he found nothing in the room, and spending the night there did no more than spook him.

He wondered if he dared fabricate something - some evidence that he could make to look as if it had been overlooked by Kessler. No. Too risky. But if he couldn't bring Hoffmann down, he'd make sure that Kessler fell. And then it struck him. If Kessler found out what had happened to Emma, wouldn't that be enough to dislodge him? Wouldn't that put him off his stroke? Wouldn't that make him desperate to find her, to save her if he could?

Schiffer smiled again. It was perfect. He sat down at the little desk in the hotel room, and started to write a short letter. It didn't take long. When he'd finished it, he sealed it in an envelope and put it in his pocket. Then, to put icing on the cake, he went down to the reception desk and wrote a coded telegram to send to Müller's office in Berlin. In it he said that he was by now convinced that Kessler was deliberately stalling his investigation, but for proof he'd have to keep him under further observation. These days, he knew, the suggestion would be enough to keep them salivating, provided nobody questioned it, and he knew how unlikely it was that anyone would.

He waited for his delivery boy.

79

Kessler walked back to the temporary office which had been set up for them at Police HQ, Kleinschmidt having gone off on his last errand, which Kessler suspected was simply an excuse to sneak in another couple of beers. He himself was convinced they had reached the end of the line, here.

Kessler had drunk his wine and a cognac, but he'd eaten nothing. The alcohol had relaxed him enough for him to feel more relieved than worried. After all, if he'd lost Hoffmann, he'd lost him. He'd done what he could, and by the grace of God it hadn't been necessary to try to obscure any evidence they might have turned up. And what could they do to him? Demote him? Sack him? In fact, they'd probably just tell him to keep looking because no-one would want to have to tell the Führer that the little cat-and-mouse diversion he'd set up had come to naught. Far better to delay until something else came up to distract him, or they could throw him a bigger fish, though everyone knew that Hitler never forgot and never forgave anyone who crossed him, and the waiting game might therefore be a long one.

He might even be able to use this to his advantage. They'd be bound to recall him, and once in Berlin he'd try to find out what had happened to Emma. She must have gone by now. He thought of her with desperation. Would he ever find her again? Where the hell would he look? But at least if he knew that she'd left his parents' place, there was half a chance that she'd be safe somewhere. She was resourceful, he told himself.

He'd barely entered the building before the duty officer picked up the internal telephone. He walked over to the desk as the man hung up.

'Glad you're back. They've sent people out everywhere to look for you.'

'I left word where I'd be.'

'Yes, but this only reached us ten minutes ago. When our man got to Auerbach's they told him he'd just missed you.'

As he spoke, a detective hurried down the stairs which descended to the grey reception hall and came over to him.

'We've got something for you.' He rushed Kessler across the hall and through an entrance which led to a corridor whose grubby cream walls were studded at regular intervals with mud-coloured doors. He pushed Kessler through one of them into a modest office. Going round the desk he picked up the one file on it, which Kessler noticed was sealed, and handed it across.

'This might have something to do with your man.'

'Where?' Kessler's heart sank.

'Name's in the file. I guess. Some village in the middle of nowhere, south-west of Freyburg. The SS took it over a couple of weeks ago, some hush-hush business, but it's on the line where you'd expect the enemy to advance - not that they'll ever get that far, of course.'

Kessler ignored that. 'What happened to the people?'

'What people?'

'The villagers.'

'Oh – relocated.' The cop looked away briefly. 'Anyway, it's in the file.' The detective was a weather-beaten man of perhaps fifty who wouldn't look out of place in a village himself. He indicated a chair, a battered carver which was surprisingly comfortable, and lowered his own bulk into the swivel-chair on his side of the desk. He took out a pack of Roth-Händle and waved it at Kessler, who leaned over and took one, but refused a nip from the bottle of Korn which was also produced and brandished. 'Some kind of fight down there,' the Leipzig cop continued, lighting their cigarettes. 'This kid in a kind-of SS uniform turns up at a little local cop shop down in Memmelstein at about four in the morning, one arm smashed to pieces, state of collapse, been walking for hours. One guy on duty down there, old man, half asleep, sort of hears the story but then can't rouse anyone by telephone for two more hours. Finally they send a squad from Weimar - locate this sodding village, find a massacre down there: three soldiers - some kind of SS – all dead, and a burnt-out motorbike.'

'Where's the survivor?'

'They had to take the arm off. Died under anaesthetic. They managed to get a description of the man who did it out of him before he died, but it's more or less useless, and of course if it was your man he's long gone.' He scratched his head, took a pull from his bottle, lit another cigarette. 'Big cover-up, of course. Gestapo around like flies on meat; but then we get this report cleared for you by Berlin – Prinz-Albrecht-Strasse, no less.'

'Who else has looked at it?'

The cop grinned. 'Oh, no-one, of course. For your eyes only. All I just told you is hearsay I got over the phone from the boys in Weimar.'

'And what's your clearance?'

The cop kept grinning. 'I'm a section chief here. Don't look so surprised, Inspector Kessler, it hurts my feelings.'

When he got back to his own office, Kessler found Kleinschmidt already there, told him the news, and got him to arrange for their things to be brought round from their hotel. 'Get the car round too – full tank, we'll need it.'

'And where am I supposed to get the petrol?'

'Get them to organise some from here, man. You think anyone's going to make difficulties on a thing like this?'

'If they've got any,' grumbled Kleinschmidt, getting up. 'When did all this happen anyway?'

'Two nights ago.'

'And it'll take us –'

'We should be there by this evening. Get them to give you a large-scale road map too.'

'And where do we stay? Want me to organise a tent, as well?'

'Get on with it. I want to be out of here in an hour.'

Kleinschmidt made his way to the door. 'By the way,' he said as he left, 'There's a letter for you. I picked it up from the duty officer.' He jerked his head at an envelope on the desk.

'Did he say when it arrived?'

'No – when you were in your meeting, I guess.'

'All right.'

As Kleinschmidt closed the door behind him, Kessler opened the letter. His name on the envelope was written in neat capitals, as were the contents, which were unsigned. Both envelope and paper were otherwise plain.

YOU WILL BE INTERESTED TO KNOW THAT EMMA HOFFMANN WAS ARRESTED NEAR BERLIN LAST MONDAY AND TAKEN INTO CUSTODY. HER PRESENT WHEREABOUTS ARE UNKNOWN TO US BUT SHE HAS BEEN TAKEN AWAY FROM THE CAPITAL.

THAT WE KNOW YOUR PRESENT WHEREABOUTS SHOULD CONFIRM THE LEGITIMACY OF THIS COMMUNICATION, WHICH YOU SHOULD DESTROY IMMEDIATELY ONCE READ.

Kessler reread the note twice. Then he did as he was told, using his lighter to burn the letter and the envelope, crushing the blackened remains to nothing in the ashtray, all the time glancing towards the door. He lit a cigarette and smoked it hard, so that its smell would cover any that lingered of burned paper. Finally he mixed all the ashes, poured them into a fresh envelope from the desk drawer, crumpled it, and threw it into the wastepaper basket.

80

There was only one way in which they could have got to her so fast: Schiffer had been detailed to make the arrest, and Schiffer must have been thinking more quickly than usual. But Kessler knew that Schiffer had been put on the case. He should have realised that Schiffer would have put two-and-two together.

He should have taken Emma somewhere else, somewhere anonymous. But there hadn't been time. He hadn't had time to think. But he should have thought of that at least... Should have...

Too late! He rubbed his forehead. Three and a half days ago. Oh, Christ! And there was nothing he could do, unless he threw everything up, went on the run himself, but what good would that do her, and without any authority at all, and people almost certainly after him, he'd be as powerless as Hoffmann was now.

He forced himself to breathe evenly. He lit another cigarette, almost the last in the packet, coughing slightly because he was not a heavy smoker. He pushed his glasses up to the bridge of his nose. Where the hell might she be, if she wasn't dead already? But he refused to believe that. He couldn't bring himself to believe that, and in a curious way he knew it wasn't true. Not just because he didn't want it to be true, but because it didn't add up. They'd have shot her there and then, if they'd thought for a minute that she'd been directly involved with the attempt on Hitler's life.

And who were his informants? Was there anyone left in the Resistance organised enough to be able to contact him in this way? He couldn't think straight. For a moment the wild notion crossed his mind that the letter was from Hoffmann himself. Then another thought struck him. It was obvious. He smiled bitterly.

He stubbed the cigarette out and sat upright in his chair, the file about the killings in the village still unopened on his lap. Of course it might be nothing to do with Hoffmann, but if the village was south-west of Freyburg it would be on a route Hoffmann might easily have chosen —country roads. If it was Hoffmann, the trail was hot again. If he got on with it, if he could nail Hoffmann, there'd be nothing they wouldn't let him do, he'd have such cachet. And he'd be free to find Emma. They might even let her go, if she was a prisoner. If –

He stood up, putting the file on the desk. As he did so, he decided to break the seal. Kleinschmidt wouldn't take that long to get things organised, and anyway anyone might come in at any moment. The country cop who'd given him the file, for example. If he had that kind of clearance, who was he really working for? He certainly wasn't a typical Kripo man.

Before he broke the seal, he examined it. He wasn't surprised to see that someone else had in fact opened it already and skilfully – but not quite skilfully enough – re-closed it.

Kessler had to cut a way through the trees. And he'd calmed down enough to know that his momentary impulse was insane. What would Emma think or feel if she found out – as she would – that her freedom had been bought at the cost of her father's betrayal?

He sat down again, took off his glasses, and cleaned them. At last a reasonable and maybe even hopeful possibility occurred to him. He'd heard about an 'Arrest of Kindred' measure that the Gestapo had brought in. The wives, sons and daughters – even the fathers, mothers and cousins – of conspirators against the Party were being jailed, but if there was no immediate need, they were not necessarily also being tortured or killed.

At least that was what he'd heard. There were also rumours that they were being taken to a camp - or more than one - where there were special facilities for them, where they didn't share the same fate as the other prisoners, where they were being kept, as it were, on ice. Quite why, he didn't know, but he had an idea of where: there'd been talk of secret amenities at the concentration camp at Dachau. If they were true, then maybe... But he wasn't sure if he wasn't leaning more on hope than reason.

His shoulders slumped again. She may be alive, even alive and well, but how would he ever find her? And if he found her, how would he reach her? Well, he thought, let's find her first. Dachau was just one possibility. There were plenty of other camps where women were kept, and the one reserved for women was at Ravensbrück – seventy-five kilometres north of Berlin – a world away for Kessler.

His head ached. He lit another cigarette but it didn't make him feel any better. He had to get on. Reluctantly, he opened the file, and began to read. As he did so, his mind gradually but automatically re-engaged with his work, and that was some comfort. But Hoffmann and his daughter would not leave his thoughts, and as he read, planning what he might do when he examined the burnt-out bike, and whatever other evidence he might find that the Gestapo and the local police hadn't already trampled over, he was also thinking, though without much success, about any means by which he might yet be able to snatch at least one of them from the fire.

There was little in the file he hadn't already been told: the description the dying boy had left could have fitted Hoffmann, but it wasn't precise enough. A big man in a leather jacket. And, as the cop who'd given him the file had said, whoever it was would be long gone by now. However, without transport, he couldn't have gone far. But the cop hadn't mentioned the description in detail, he'd just said that it was there.

Was this some kind of test for him – to see if he'd suppress it or act on it? And how the hell could they check? He decided to tell no-one else about what he'd read, and returned the file to the front desk, to be locked in the secure archive.

81

They arrived at the village later than Kessler had hoped, and dirtier, because they'd had a puncture on the way and had to change the tyre, which had plunged Kleinschmidt into a deep gloom - which unfortunately had not resulted in silence, but a long and repetitive diatribe against all things rural. Kleinschmidt, it appeared, would never set foot anywhere again where he could not feel paving stones beneath his feet, and see buildings wherever he looked.

But it was still light when they reached the square. The motorbike rested where it had been left, against the flight of steps which led up to the entrance of the church. The market hall was open and so was the inn next door, both dimly lit, as were the half dozen tents pitched near them. There must have been twenty SS and Gestapo personnel in the village, along with another half dozen regular police, all constables, roped in for auxiliary duties.

They'd barely drawn to a halt when their car was surrounded by a group of men, three of whom carried machine guns at the ready; though it was the other two who stepped forward, one a *Hauptsturmführer*, the other, taller man in civilian clothes.

'Scholz, *Leibstandarte* Adolf Hitler,' the uniformed man said.

Kessler introduced himself, thinking, Christ, they are putting weight behind this. A *Leibstandarte* officer in charge.

'We've been expecting you. They called Memmelstein from Leipzig. They radioed the message through to us from there.' He turned to the other man. 'This is Bauer, *RSHA*.'

The other man nodded coldly. His patch, thought Kessler. National fucking Security. Doesn't like me muscling in.

They walked over to the market hall, where the ground floor had been converted into an operations room. There was a radio transmitter on a table against the wall near the door, and beyond it boards on trestles, on which an assortment of items had been laid out. Among them Kessler recognised the charred remains of a large leather bag. There were also bloodstained uniform fragments, three old-fashioned rifles, and what looked like the contents of people's pockets, rendered pathetic by the deaths of their owners: packets of cigarettes, condoms, handkerchiefs, wallets, keys, loose change.

'They'll take your bags next door,' said Scholz. We've got a couple of rooms fixed up for you. And the water's OK. Where do you want to start?'

'Here. I'll take a look at the bike in the morning, when it's light.' Kessler walked over to the neatly-labelled exhibits and glanced at them.

'How many people have touched this stuff?'

'Just my men,' said Bauer in a frozen voice. 'We're used to handling evidence.'

'Shouldn't have been moved at all before I arrived. Didn't they tell you that?'

'No.' Several degrees lower.

'Well, I'll do what I can. I see there's nothing personal here.'

'Like what?'

'Soldiers usually carry photographs of their loved ones, letters, things like that.'

'These men were on a secret mission,' said Scholz. 'Their identities have been confirmed by local SS-command.'

'And what was their mission?'

Scholz smiled thinly. 'I believe your remit is to trace the traitor Hoffmann.'

'I have a Hitler Order to do so.'

'I am aware of that.'

Kessler suddenly felt less sure of his ground. He was after all talking to a captain in the most elite squad of the *Waffen*-SS, and, for all he knew, Scholz was a member of Hitler's personal bodyguard.

'Of course, we can discuss anything relevant to your investigation,' continued Scholz, who had noticed, as Kessler had, a look of satisfaction creep into Bauer's face. Kessler immediately saw something that he could use to his advantage. Scholz, like him, was an outsider. Also, regular police and *Waffen*-SS officers were not over-fond of the Gestapo, especially local bigwigs like Bauer. Scholz had no intention of putting Kessler down in front of a Gestapo-man, though clearly he was also intent on ensuring that everyone knew who was boss around here.

'Give my sergeant and me five minutes to freshen up and unpack our forensic equipment. Then I will start a thorough examination.'

'By all means,' said Scholz, turning to the aide who stood at his elbow and muttering instructions. 'You have had a long drive.' Scholz, despite his inauspicious surroundings, was as immaculate as if he had been on the parade-ground. Kessler was aware that his shabby appearance was worse than usual after the tyre-changing, and Kleinschmidt had an oil stain on his shirt and mud on his shoes. But Kessler had to keep up his advantage. He turned to Bauer.

'I'll read your preliminary reports when I return,' he said, taking care to keep any trace of condescension out of his voice, but hoping Bauer wouldn't be ready for this. He wasn't.

'I can give you a verbal report,' he replied stiffly. 'The facilities here - '

'In the morning, then,' said Kessler, drawing himself up for once, and adding just enough edge to the kindness in his voice.

'Inspector.'

82

By ten the next day, Kessler had read the five badly-typed pages of Bauer's report. They told him nothing that he didn't already know, except to outline the means by which the uniforms had been detached from the bodies, give the names of the slain, and describe the motorbike. No doubt Hoffmann - if he had been the rider - had picked it up in Leipzig, where, as the Inspector no doubt knew, said the report, investigations were in hand.

Kessler had spent since sunrise looking at the site. There were still dark stains on the soil in the square where the Werewolves had fallen, and the blackened bike was no more than a shell, its panniers gone and its saddle reduced to a metal frame. If anything had been concealed on it or in it, it was gone now, though Kessler had the fuel tank cut open to make sure that it was completely empty, taking care that he was alone except for the oxy-acetylene operator, whose presence there was as much a mystery to him as that of the bulk of the SS-men, who clearly had no part in the investigation, and kept themselves to themselves. Apart from making regular patrols of the village they confined themselves to the vicinity of their tents. Kleinschmidt had tried to interview their NCOs, but this, he reported, had been blocked – with great politeness, but nevertheless blocked – by Scholz's aide.

The inn and the market-hall were both in use - the former as a canteen and officers' billet, and Kessler deduced that the operations being conducted in the latter were not confined to the killings. He also found himself closely accompanied when he wanted to inspect any building beyond the square. What he was permitted to see yielded nothing: simple rooms with wooden furniture, kitchens leading directly into byres. The smell of dung still hung everywhere, though Kessler had no means of knowing when the place had been evacuated and no-one told him. Scholz remained polite, but seemed uninterested in the investigation. Bauer had begun to unwind, and was helpful – had he decided that it might help his career if Kessler looked kindly on him? But it was clear to Kessler that his motivation was also to get the policeman away from there as soon as possible.

There was little to detain him. The church, which he co-opted the local constables to help him search – yielded nothing. Apart from its pews, some of which had evidently been partly broken up for firewood, and some of which had been hauled out of place, the nave was empty. The altar was bare, no brass or silver or any furnishings to be found anywhere, the vestry and the choir equally void. The robing-room wardrobes contained a couple of dusty vestments, which blew out a little cluster of moths when he touched them, the only other sign of life being the bats which nestled, black specks, in the vaulting. If he hadn't noticed their droppings on the floor he might never have been aware of them. A melancholy place, whose emptiness was emphasized by the chill in the atmosphere there.

And there was no evidence of Hoffmann either. Cartridge cases Bauer's men had picked up in the square belonged to the rifles and to a Walther PPK - the weapon the killer had used. The dead NCO's holster contained an old Luger, which had not been fired.

Kessler decided to leave the village the following morning. He'd considered going to Weimar to file a final report, but when he'd radioed Leipzig to confirm, he was told that he should continue following whatever route south he thought Hoffmann might have followed. That meant, roughly, Coburg, Bamberg, Nuremberg. If that was where Hoffmann was headed. Kessler wondered if he shouldn't fabricate a little evidence to put them off, but it was a high-risk consideration, especially as he wasn't working alone. And his mind was still preoccupied with thoughts of Emma.

But he seemed to have a charmed life – he'd half expected to be recalled to Berlin for questioning, if the information in the anonymous letter he'd received was true. Perhaps Hitler's protecting hand was still over him.

In the late afternoon Kessler decided he'd have a last look at the material which was still spread out on the trestle tables. He knew Hoffmann would never have been careless, but if he'd been caught off guard something might have slipped through, and better that he found any lead than anyone else. And something was gnawing at the back of his mind.

The large bag which had been recovered from the bike was high-quality, heavily grained cowhide, and had escaped complete immolation. The bag had several compartments. He'd been through them before, and so had Bauer, but looking at it again, he noticed a side pocket - visible just as a slit on the outside of the bag - which hadn't attracted his attention before. He glanced around. The handful of people in the room were absorbed in paperwork, the radio operator was fiddling with dials on his machine, and cursing under his breath.

Kessler slipped a hand into the pocket. It was deep. It ran right under the bag. Within it his fingers located another, buttoned compartment. He opened it and touched something which crumpled, Paper? Cardboard? And there was something hard as well, wood, or, more likely, metal. He closed his hand round whatever it was and drew it out carefully.

It was a small, brown, oblong cardboard box, but almost smashed to pieces, so that its contents were immediately visible. A silver whistle, not unlike a police whistle, but smaller - an expensive toy. Kessler detached it from the remains of its box and brought it up to his eye. There was a name engraved on it.

At that moment he heard approaching footsteps. He palmed his find and turned to the Gestapo-man.

Bauer smiled at him cautiously. 'We've been over that bag with a fine-tooth comb,' he said defensively.

'You didn't find this.' The pieces of the cardboard box were on the table in front of him.

'What is it?'

'No idea. Remains of a box?'

Bauer looked. 'Could be. Ammunition box?'

'Could be. Too smashed up to tell.'

'Want us to tag it?'

Kessler shrugged. 'No. Not worth it. Let's bin it.'

Bauer was relieved. 'I told you we hadn't missed anything.'

'Quite right. I was clutching at straws. You know how it is.' He slipped the whistle into his pocket as he said, 'Have you seen my sergeant?'

'Next door.'

Kessler nodded and made his way to the inn. Kleinschmidt, a beer in front of him, was busy with his notebook. He looked up as Kessler approached.

'Made the report?' Kessler asked.

'Yes.'

'Orders?'

Kleinschmidt shrugged. 'What do you think? They want us to carry on. Bugger it.'

'Tomorrow. When we get to Coburg, we'll look around there. After that, Bamberg, or Bayreuth.' Kessler spoke reluctantly. This was the route he would have taken if he'd been Hoffmann, but there wasn't much leeway, and he knew his own actions were under scrutiny. He was not the only one to know how Hoffmann's mind worked. There'd been no positive identification of his old boss here; and if Kessler could get the trail to lead to Munich, he might - possibly - manage to trace Emma. Dachau was on the city's outskirts.

'Well,' said Kleinschmidt, interrupting his train of thought. 'The bastard can't get far on foot.'

'If it's him.'

'It'd better be,' said Kleinschmidt. 'For our sakes.'

They had a muted dinner with Scholz and Bauer that evening. The whizz-kid from Berlin had failed to work a miracle. Bauer's men were bagging up the evidence to take back to Weimar, where it'd be archived in case a fresh lead ever came up, but it was more likely that it would gather dust in a storeroom for years. Bauer and his men had nothing left to do here either, and would be leaving soon after Kessler and Kleinschmidt. No-one knew what Scholz's plans were, and he was keeping the talk small, though he was clearly relieved that the police were departing.

Kessler had to stop his hand from going to the whistle in his pocket. It was only after dinner, when he was alone in his room, that he had an opportunity to examine it more thoroughly. He held it close to the oil lamp by his bed, turned it over in his fingers, and brought his face up close to the inscription.

'Stefan…' he said quietly, reading it.

83

Hoffmann had been on the road for two days since the fight. But he had found shelter now.

He was in the living room of a farmworker's abandoned cottage. There was a table and two chairs, and a divan on which he had slept - or tried to sleep - for most of the night. At least there were no bedbugs here: it had been too long since the place had been inhabited for them to have anything to prey on. Not even mosquitoes disturbed him.

After the battle, he'd walked until dawn, keeping to the edge of the road, which had widened as it left the village. He didn't want to run the risk of encountering any more SS, and it had seemed to him that the likelihood of their presence was high. But there had been no-one, and finally he stopped to rest. He knew very little about typhus, but after he'd heard Kurtz mention it, he'd worried that he'd drunk the water at the inn. Was it a water-borne disease? Kurtz had said the place had been sanitised, but had it? Were those boys really living there?

Towards nine in the morning he could go no further - he thought he might have made twenty kilometres - and climbed off the road into a dense copse, where, come what may, he knew he'd have to lie down and rest.

He slept deeply and dreamlessly until late afternoon and for a moment after waking lay calmly and drowsily, the warm sun on him, but an instant later he was alert, aware again of where he was and of his situation. He sat up cautiously, thirsty and conscious of his aching legs. His whole body ached, felt dirty. His shirt collar chafed and the insides of his thighs were sore. He could not become ill. His body could not let him down. He would have to find some means of transport.

He thought about the motorbike and cursed. Then he remembered something else. He searched his pockets in increasing panic, then rummaged through his bag, but all along he knew that he had left Stefan's whistle behind. Fool! He could see it in his mind's eye, hidden in the inner pocket of the pack he'd left in the village. But why had he been stupid enough to bring it at all? Perhaps it had melted? Unlikely. All he could hope was that whoever found it would have no idea of Stefan's identity.

But if they linked the bike to Hoffmann, they'd start foraging in his past. What might they find? What could he have overlooked?

There was nothing he could do. But now he had another, even more pressing reason to keep ahead of the game.

He remained still, listening, but there was no noise. He'd have to find water again, and then food, but water was more important. And he'd have to brace himself for another night's trek. Luckily, there was enough moonlight to guide him, and the road was a solitary one - there were no turn-offs except for cart-tracks, and he had not come across another village. He only had a dozen cigarettes. He'd have to ration them.

He had slogged through another night and by the end of it he thought he was at the limit of his endurance. He had not eaten for nearly two days and what water he had found he had drunk from rivers and streams. He had no idea what effect this might have on him. Close to dawn on the second day he noticed a hamlet some way off the road, a track leading down to it. He'd been tempted to go there but feared a possible trap. He didn't dare take off the boots, which by some miracle remained comfortable, though his feet felt foul. There was a partly-cultivated field at the side of the road and he'd managed to dig out a couple of black radishes, straining his ears for dogs as he did so.

The sun rose roughly behind him and a little to his right, so he guessed the road was still taking him in the right direction, and he stayed with it. There had been three or four other turnings off it by now, but he knew the pursuit would follow every lead.

He'd eaten the radishes with an appetite he wouldn't have believed possible two weeks ago, though his stomach ached afterwards, and later on he had to plunge towards the cover of some bushes, victim of a violent bout of diarrhoea. But it was better afterwards. He cleaned himself with leaves.

Christ, he had to get out of this.

84

He forced himself to keep going the whole of the following day, though he doubted if he'd made more than seven or ten kilometres. Maybe thirty or thirty-five in total, now, since leaving the village. He'd started to look for somewhere to rest when he'd noticed an overgrown path to his left. In desperation he'd taken it, and after one hundred metres or so he saw the low roof ahead of him. He drew his gun and stumbled forward.

A farmhouse.

He could tell from the look of the place that it was empty. Weeds grew everywhere and a vegetable garden near the house had long since turned into a wilderness. Thistles and brambles crowded round the stone walls of the low-slung stone main building, and the wooden barn and sheds wilted, their sides licked by an encroaching green tide. By one of the sheds stood a forlorn cart with a broken wheel.

This farm, like so many, must have been empty for a year or more. Some of the smaller outhouses were falling down, and the yard had been invaded by nettles and dockweed. In the yard there was a rusty pump, which hadn't looked promising, but he'd managed to unstick the lever and after a few minutes' perseverance clean water spouted from the nozzle. He'd drunk deeply, scooping the water up in an earthenware bowl he'd found among other bits and pieces of crockery, some smashed, in a sideboard in the farm's kitchen.

He explored the place quickly but thoroughly. Upstairs the rooms were tiny, two of the three containing beds too broken down to be slept on, and wardrobes which contained farm overalls.

Downstairs, the living room covered most of the floor area; it led off in one direction to a byre, and in the other to a kitchen, with a huge stone sink and a large wooden table. A few kitchen implements hung to one side of the range, but he could find no fuel to fire it up. In any case, he was afraid of drawing attention to his presence by chimney smoke.

The outhouses contained rusting farm equipment, a harrow and a plough, a yoke for oxen and some harness, the leather rotting, the brass green. There was a pitchfork, a couple of rakes, a mattock and a spade, and a long-handled axe. In the barn, bales of hay mouldered.

He took the mattock and used it to dig in the vegetable garden but the ground was choked with weeds, and after a short time he found the effort beyond him. He began to think dangerously that as long as he could rest he would not care if they caught up with him.

He returned to the house, thinking despondently that at least there was water, but hunger clawed at his stomach in a way he had never experienced before. He was neither as fit as he should have been, nor was he used to the country. He had no idea what wild berries or mushrooms he could eat, if there were any; there was a small orchard, but the trees were twisted with neglect and tangled with ivy and mistletoe. Wizened fruits hung on some of the dusty green branches, but the thought of encouraging another bout of diarrhoea prevented him from trying them.

In the living room, he'd noticed a mirror above the chimney-piece, and checked himself in it. He was appalled at what he saw. The transformation was bad. The face was haggard and unshaven. He'd have to let the beard grow now, no choice. Maybe the full untidy growth of hair would take attention away from the moustache.

He went to the kitchen and rummaged through drawers without much hope, and indeed all they yielded was a handful of rusty utensils and cutlery. Then he noticed a larder door. He didn't want to waste ammunition on rats, but there weren't any - there was nothing for them here. On a high shelf he noticed a handful pickle jars. Why had they been abandoned? Forgotten when the owners of this place had left it?

There were gherkins, onions, cherries and eggs. Tentatively, he unclipped the lid of the jar which contained the eggs, and pulled one out, nibbled it. Vinegary, but otherwise... He ate some more. It seemed fine. He finished it.

He knew he'd have to go easy, but he made himself a rudimentary meal, washing it down with plenty of water. Nectar and ambrosia couldn't have tasted better, he thought.

Having feasted, three eggs, three onions, some gherkins and a very few cherries, he dragged one of the chairs over and made a more thorough examination of the upper larder shelves. At the back of one, he found two pots of sausage meat. One revealed nothing but a puffball of mould, but the other looked and smelled fine. He ate a little, then finished the pot.

By now it was late, and darkness had gathered. It had also grown cold. The silence was oppressive, but he was too tired to care, and, flushed with his minor triumph, he lay down to sleep.

But, tired as he was, he failed to enjoy real rest. The boys he'd killed came back to haunt him. And Stefan's whistle blew through his dreams, the ghosts of the kids he'd shot dancing to its blast. What had they known about anything?

Brutalised and conditioned by Party propaganda, weren't they also his responsibility? Hadn't he helped create them?

He'd rehearsed often enough the argument that if he hadn't done what he'd done for the regime, one of his colleagues, not a member of the Resistance, would have worked in his place, and only returned evil for evil. But in the course of his career over the last decade, there had been no escaping the question: hadn't he himself committed worse crimes than those young men, blindly following what they were too ignorant to question, could even dream of?

No matter how often he told himself that the only reason he had had for serving the state was to maintain a position from which he could most effectively work against it, no matter how much he tried to persuade himself that his job had enabled him to obscure and waylay investigations into at least three assassination attempts on Hitler; or reminded himself that he had managed to misroute and delay shipments of poison gas to the camps; that he had secured profoundly confidential information on the administration of the camps and relayed it to Oster and his associates as proof - one day to be presented to the Allies by a surrendering provisional government after a successful coup against Hitler - of the regime's crimes: no matter how frequently he trawled and dredged his mind and his conscience, over and over again, revolving it as long as Ixion ever turned on his wheel, he could not convince himself that the evil he'd done would ever justify the good.

There had been no coup. The Resistance had failed. The good had come to nothing. Only the bad remained. In the eyes of the enemy, who were not the enemy, but the liberators of Germany and of the camps, Hoffmann would still be just another Nazi on the run. How could he convince them of where his heart had been for ten long years and more? And even if he could, he would never escape the memory of the screaming women and children, the terrified infants, at Auschwitz and Sobibor and Treblinka, at the camps he'd had to visit as a member of various efficiency consultancy units, discussing better ways of processing the Produkt; and once hearing and seeing that filthy Alsatian dog - snarl and bark as it chased a naked, fleeing little boy at Treblinka; having to watch what happened when it brought the child down.

And those guards, even the officers, so full of schnapps they could hardly stand, applauding. And the sound of the geese at Sobibor, that flock of geese brought in to cry down the howls of the Jews as they were herded into the death shed, so that the Poles on nearby farmsteads would not hear?

He had to concentrate on his last work now. In the dawn which followed, after his second inspection of his battered features in the mirror, and after checking the perimeter of the farm to make sure he was still undisturbed, he peeled off his clothes and washed as best he could at the pump in the yard. The farm overalls he'd discovered the day before were clean, at least, though musty and damp, and one set was almost big enough for him. Better than the clothes he had been wearing since the gunfight, and though they'd scarcely go with the journalist Dieter Weitz's identity, at least he hoped they'd let him pass unnoticed in a rural environment. He'd taken the boots off at last. He inspected his feet, knowing from experience that when you are up against it, your feet must be cosseted. If your feet can't carry you, you're dead. But Kurtz's boots had treated them well. He slid the boots on again over his dirty socks, which he'd turned inside-out, and flexed his feet. Then he took the sharpest knife he could find from the kitchen and used it to cut pieces out of the other pair of overalls.

There were a few other jobs to do. He wrapped some gherkins, onions and eggs in the bits of cloth, and stuffed them into the pockets of the overalls, filled a discarded bottle with water from the pump, shoved the knife into his pack, ate as much as he dared of the rest of the food. He buried his old clothes under three or four bales of decaying hay in the darkest corner of the barn.

He knew that his instinct not to finish off the stocky Werewolf boy had been sentimental, stupid. But with luck the little bastard would have died anyway. He was messed up enough.

He would have to find transport. Meanwhile, he would make his way to a bigger road. There would be people on the move, on foot and in carts, and the advantages of being one among many, of losing himself in the crowd, outweighed the risk. He might even get a lift, though travelling alone would be preferable.

He slung his bag over his aching shoulder, and set off.

85

He thought, *she didn't say she loved me.* When I told her I'd met Oster; when I was already committed, when I was beginning to pass on what information I could information from the meetings. I shouldn't have told her: perhaps she sensed what I had done anyway. I know part of me regretted ever having taken the step, but things were happening within the Party which... She hugged me and she laughed...

But there was still something hidden in her eyes...

His thoughts trailed off, bringing him back to the present. It was ten o'clock. The road he was on had grown broader and there were more frequent tracks and lanes leading off it. There were clumps of alder and birch, and dark swathes of pine further up the sloping hills. There were villages again, no more than two or three kilometres apart, but the people about, women and children and a few men, most of them over fifty, paid no attention to him. His road came to an end soon afterwards, where it reached a much larger highway running roughly north and south. There was no signpost.

He turned southwards, and as he walked the sun rose, beating on his back and the back of his neck. He worried about his bag, which, though battered now, did not go well with his country clothes. He paused to rub mud from a cart-track onto it, but he need not have been concerned. The occasional cart passed him, and now and then he either overtook, or for a short time fell in with, groups of people moving from village to village. He did what he could to disguise his Berlin accent without attempting to mimic the local dialect, but he found that his fellow travellers were too much taken up with their own concerns to feel any curiosity about him. Some were simply moving from job to job, even from field to field, busy with what harvest there was. People still had to eat. Fields were jealously protected, but the only dogs he saw were trotting along beside the carts they were tied to.

He'd been walking for two hours when he saw a crowd up ahead, though still moving slowly forwards. He got into the lee of a wagon and soon reached the checkpoint, manned by two Home Guard soldiers wearing campaign medals on their tunics and sporting Hindenburg moustaches. They would be easy to kill, but what then? By now he was surrounded by other people. He had no papers which would serve him here. He kept his head down and he kept behind the wagon.

As he approached the two soldiers, he realised with alarm that they knew many of the people passing through the checkpoint personally, nodding and greeting, occasionally putting out a discreet hand to take a proffered piece of fruit or a salami, which they would transfer into the canvas forage sacks slung from their shoulders.

But he needn't have worried. They were waving people through. So no-one had telegraphed ahead to this town - Neuhaus, as he saw from a sign - to alert them. What route, then, did they think he had taken? He couldn't afford to let up. In the pretty little red-roofed main square he found a shop which sold him a canvas bag and two pairs of hiking socks; and another where he bought a loaf of bread, sausage, potato salad and beer, tobacco and cigarette papers. He didn't want to linger, and he needed to husband his money.

He had reached Neuhaus! He had made better progress than he'd expected; but there was still a long way to go, and he wouldn't relax until Tilli's door closed safely behind him. A little country town like this was all right, even ideal: there were plenty of people who looked as scruffy as he did, and he could hide among them. But he would have to avoid any large place from now on.

He went into a church and, in a quiet corner, transferred his belongings to the canvas bag, together with his supply of food, putting his guns, ammunition and money in a separate compartment. The papers which were still usable, the travel documents and the Swedish passport, he stuck in an inner pocket of the overalls with the little Walther pistol. Leaving the church and circling it, he found a crumbling pile of masonry behind it, part of a forgotten restoration project, and buried his leather satchel under it. The now useless ID papers he tore into shreds and discreetly fed into different drains, as he walked through the town, eyes open for any kind of transport. His thighs still chafed from the walking and he needed to make better speed.

There was only one possibility, as things stood. Near the southern outskirts of the town stood a cart piled high with furniture, the modest contents of someone's cottage. A mule stood between the shafts, and sitting up on the driver's box - a plank of wood fixed to the front of the cart, sat a young woman, her arm round a little boy of about six. They were waiting for someone. Both had the blank look that tiredness and travel weariness bring. Tied to the back of the cart, hidden from the front by the bedstead, wardrobe, table, chairs and rugs, was a bicycle.

It would have been easy; but he couldn't take it. In any case, he didn't want to get caught just for stealing a bicycle.

As soon as he was clear of the town he found a place to sit, eat and drink. He thought about Tilli's country house. It was in another world.

86

The truck laboured down the country road, spitting stones, raising dust. It was a 1940 Ford, one of thousands sold to the Party by the Americans before things turned sour. Hoffmann knew all about them, just as he remembered being told by a colleague that Hitler had once had a picture of Henry Ford, whom he admired, displayed in his office.

Though newish, this lorry had come down in the world, from army vehicle to farm workhorse, converted to run on coal. It wouldn't be joining its fellows on the West Front, facing similar vehicles, adorned with white stars instead of black crosses, as the Yankees poured eastwards across France. Hoffmann, travelling in the back, bracing himself against two of the sacks of early-harvest grain which filled the space, grinned sourly at the thought.

He'd been walking along the side of the highway, climbing up onto the verge to be nearer the shelter of the trees as he heard the hammering engine getting louder behind him. When he sensed that the lorry was slowing, he slackened his pace and turned.

The truck stammered to a halt, shrouding itself in fumes, but the motor, though it gave a kind of death-rattle, did not die, deciding instead to tick over, muttering and clanking through a variety of dissonances.

The passenger door, on Hoffmann's side, groaned open - no-one had given this machine more than the bare minimum of love - and the driver, a hairy giant in a tattered check shirt, beckoned to him. On the remains of the passenger seat perched a wooden crate containing several wretched-looking chickens.

'Where're you off to?' the man said.

'Anywhere south.'

'I can see that. Coburg any good to you?'

'Sounds fine. Thanks!'

'Get in the back. Make yourself a chair out of the sacks, and don't throw up over them if you get sick.'

'What's in them?'

'Wheat. I'm going to the Scheidmantel brewery. They're lucky to be getting this much.'

The driver heaved himself out of his cab, lowered the tailgate, and gave a mock bow.

'Whatever happens, there's got to be beer.' The man went and rummaged in the cabin, and produced two dusty bottles. 'Not as cold as they could be. *Prost*!'

'Prost!'

The man stuck out a hand. 'Kirchner,' he said.

'Grosz.' This guy wasn't going to ask for papers, and Weitz the journalist hardly fitted Hoffmann's present *persona*.

'Where're you from?'

Hoffmann hesitated. 'Freyburg.'

'You're a long way from home. And you could do with a bath! Been working on a muckheap, have you?'

Did Hoffmann imagine a flicker of doubt in the man's eyes? He knew his accent was imperfect, but he hoped he'd managed sufficiently to disguise the Berlin in it.

But he wouldn't pass for a labourer - one had only to look at his face, his hands. A couple of days on the road and a bit of grime only stood up to the lightest inspection, despite the fact that he smelled like a midden. What would Brandau have thought?

Had Brandau made it?

If he had sensed anything, the driver let it go.

'Got to make one stop,' he said as he closed the tailgate again. 'Get rid of these birds. We'll have a really cold beer and a natter then.'

He returned to the cab and wrenched the gears around, giving a thumbs up through the tiny rear-window. Hoffmann considered. Garrulous but not too curious. And going to Coburg. The driver might have been sent by God; but Hoffmann knew he couldn't depend on God. He looked up at the sun, then at his watch. They should be there by early evening.

The road wasn't as rough as he'd expected it to be.

His thoughts turned to the past again.

***

The summer had passed quickly. By the end of October, her pregnancy was obvious. She worked among doctors. Some of them were curious. Kara had never mentioned a partner to any of them, but she had a reputation for secrecy that her colleagues - some of them despite themselves - respected. She insisted on working for as long as she could; and there was no objection at the Charité: she was a valued member of staff for one thing, and for another the Party, eager to increase the population after the lean years that had followed the war, encouraged children, in or out of wedlock. They were even offering incentives to people to get married - big loans which would be written off in percentages, according to how many kids the newly-weds went on to produce.

There was something else. Hagen was back in Berlin, and basking in the triumph he'd made of his stint in the Black Forest. His training-programme had been so successful that they'd extended his stay. In getting rid of him, Hoffmann had helped his career.

Now, Hoffmann was no longer confident that he could contain anything Hagen chose to do.

87

Hagen wasn't the only problem. So far Hoffmann had done little more than relay coded copies of the documents that passed across his desk to Oster, but that was more than enough to hang him if he were caught. He was in no position to raise his head above the parapet.

His decision, he knew, was based as much on wanting Kara to see him in a good light, as on any principles of his own.

Whatever happened, there was no going back now; and whatever happened, though there were moments when, being human, he cursed himself for allowing Oster to have persuaded him, there was never a moment when he fundamentally regretted his decision. The Party had betrayed his faith, and the Strasser brothers, the only members to have stuck to socialist ideas, were losing ground fast.

Apart from that, nothing had changed, except the nature of the game. The game itself was the same: problems and solutions. The solutions were increasingly brutal; but Hoffmann was used to living in a cruel world.

His work now lay in trying to make it less cruel. An impossible task to complete, but always interesting.

They had to be cautious. Emma had become their go-between when she was able. Emma was ten years old, and luckily had taken to Kara as strongly as Kara had taken to her.

Hoffmann hadn't seen Kara for well over a week. He walked to her flat. It was an iron-grey day, the light washing the colour from everything, the first day to indicate that autumn was gone now, really gone, and that winter's cold arms would soon cradle the city. As evening approached, a vile drizzle started, which worked its way through his coat. The wind, nagging its way from the Urals and meeting no resistance in all the space that separated those mountains from Berlin, got into his bones and made his shoulders ache.

He passed a *Weinstube*, the orange and yellow light inside, beyond the glass panes which sequestered the interior from the bleak darkness of the street, spilling onto a mahogany bar and its brass fittings. Men and women, hunched over tables or seated on stools drawn up along the bar, smoked and drank and lingered as if they would never be able to bring themselves to leave that temporary comfort for the reality of the lives that lurked beyond it, waiting implacably to go on. Hoffmann slackened his pace to look, but did not stop, did not go in.

He had spoken to Tilli Cassirer, and prepared his ground. Kara was fond of Tilli, trusted her. Tilli still had some powerful friends. She still saw a lot of the actress Emmy Sonnemann, and Emmy, a pretty woman of some talent, who was under no illusions at all, had been seeing a great deal of Hermann Göring. Göring was popular - he'd been a fighter ace during the '14-18 war - and although he was running to fat now, and, rumour had it, taking just a little too much cocaine for his own good - his charisma and his position at the right hand of the Führer, as Hoffmann liked to think of him, made his friendship worth cultivating.

How far he could be trusted, Hoffmann had no idea. He'd been charming on the handful of occasions they'd met, but he was also drunk with his own success. He was building a vast mansion just outside the city. There were rumours that Emmy would soon be mistress of it. As the Führer showed no signs of marrying himself, it was a safe bet that Emmy would soon be the country's first lady.

For Hoffmann, that was an attractive thought. Tilli had told him not to expect too much, but Tilli herself, he argued, still had cachet and she was divorcing her husband, which turned Party faces warmly towards her. Kara would be safe with her until he could make the arrangements necessary for her to leave.

He got to Kara's door at a quarter to seven.

It took her a while to answer. When she did, he could see that her makeup was fresh. She'd been expecting him at seven, she said. Had she been crying? She stood aside to let him pass, unusually quiet, eyes downcast. She had put a bottle of wine and two glasses on the coffee table, and near them an ashtray and a bowl of green olives; the furniture was as it had always been, and the curtains drawn. But there was a coldness about the light which he couldn't understand, so full was his head with what he wanted to say to her.

Then he became aware that the African masks had been taken down, that there were no pictures on the walls, no books on the shelves. And behind the sofa, he noticed a pile of cardboard boxes. Looking towards the kitchen, he could see more packing-cases, and a heap of straw.

'I've been sacked,' she said.

88

Hoffmann said nothing for a moment, but he was not surprised. Women teachers, doctors, lawyers and civil-servants had steadily been losing their jobs to men since the Party had come to power. Kara had often joked when they'd first met that she'd find herself out of work if the birth-rate dropped any lower. The Party had set out to rectify all that. The propaganda machine had even produced a little ditty to encourage women in their new duties:

Grab your kettle, broom and pan,
That's the way to get a man;
Shop and office leave alone -
Your true life's work begins at home.

They'd discussed the idea of leaving before - Kara had no wish to 'donate a child to the Führer', as the saying went. But her work had always defined her. She was proud of it. Like so many people, they had thought that, somehow, by some miracle, the Party would never touch them directly.

'When did they tell you?'

'Soon after we last saw each other.'

'Why didn't you let me know immediately?'

'What was I going to do? Ring you?'

'You could have told Emma.'

'I wasn't sure the place wasn't being watched.'

'It isn't. And no-one knows about your mother.'

'Then let's be grateful for small mercies,' she said angrily. 'Three thousand women doctors in this country, lots of us specialists, not that it matters. One woman professional for every fourteen men - do you know, that was the same as the proportion of female to male deputies in the fucking Reichstag - until recently. Now look what your Party's doing. They're shitting on the country's administration because they want us women all to go off and produce cannon-fodder for that fuckwit in charge, if he lasts long enough to get his war! Christ Almighty, what's happening to this country?'

She knew more than she should, though anyone with half a mind, he reflected, could hazard a guess at the way things were going. He wondered if she had spoken to Oster again. It had crossed his mind that she might have considered leaving without him. Maybe she had. But she was still here.

'And what about all this?' he said, indicating the partially packed-up flat.

She looked at him. 'You get your way. Actually, it works out rather well. You don't have to try to persuade me to leave now. They've done your job for you. "Children, church and kitchen", Christ, and look at the number of women who voted for them!'

'We knew what was coming.'

'Yes.' She calmed down. 'We did. And at least you've seen the error of your ways.' Finally she gave him what passed for a smile. 'I am very angry. And I have been crying, which I don't like, but it's the bloody pregnancy, and – Oh, have some wine, for God's sake.'

He was silent.

'It's my fault,' she went on. 'I wanted to believe that this couldn't happen. I was actually pleased when my mother left. Of course she tried to persuade me. Even after they got power I didn't think they could possibly last. But now ... ' She looked at him. 'You were right.' She patted her belly. 'And for the sake of this.'

'You are sure?'

'What do you think?'

What could he say? His own situation was doubly precarious. To move too fast would be to invite disaster. And there was Hagen. But he'd thought about it all. There was a way through all this, if he could get Kara's agreement. It was risky, and it would require patience; but it was the least dangerous path to take. And, despite the speed with which the Party was operating, he could not extinguish the hope that it would still create enough resentment to bring it down.

89

Perhaps, Hoffmann thought, as the American lorry carried him down the dusty road to Coburg, he had just wanted to hope, without really hoping at all. But hindsight was always easy.

They drank their wine.

'I shouldn't have too much of this,' Kara said. She refilled his glass, glancing at him. He seemed lost in thought, nervous. 'What's on your mind?' she continued.

'Nothing.'

He looked around the room again.

'I was going to put it all into storage,' she said.

He needed to know what her plans were, and how far they were independent of his own.

'Then,' she went on, 'I was going to take a suitcase and go to a hotel. Think things over. I hadn't thought beyond that. Panic, I suppose. I was going to tell you. I've got some savings of course, but without a job, the rent on this place ... ' she trailed off, gazing into space.

'Has Hagen been in touch with you?'

She shuddered, surprised at the question. 'Don't you think I'd have told you if he had?'

'He's becoming quite a big wheel.'

'I don't read the papers much anymore.'

'Not like that; behind the scenes.'

'Then maybe he's got better things to do than chase after poor little physicians! He's probably already set himself up with some government-approved blonde.'

'Perhaps.'

He was silent again, and she looked at him curiously.

'You don't think he's following me?'

'I'd know if he was.' That, at least, Hoffmann was sure of.

'Then what else is there?'

It was something he'd been thinking about for months. He'd even discussed it with Emma's aunt. He didn't want Kara to think that, when he asked the question, it was merely out of expediency; yet the longer he left it, the more it would look like that. Now, events had overtaken him, as they so often overtake us. 'You can't go to a hotel,' he started, badly.

'Well, it isn't the most attractive option, but people do it, and from the point of view of having a kid, I'm not the worst-placed person in the world.'

'Where will you have it?'

'I hadn't thought that far.'

'It's my responsibility too.'

'I know.'

'Will you marry me?'

There. It was done.

She stared at him. She laughed. He couldn't tell what kind of a laugh it was.

'I want you to marry me. I'd want that whatever else was happening. I'd want that if you weren't carrying our child. I'd want that if we lived in a more fortunate country, or at a more fortunate time. I'd want that even if things were ten times more difficult than they are.'

'I'm half-Jewish.'

'No-one knows that,' he said, wishing he could be certain it was true, and at the same time hating himself for saying it - such a thing shouldn't matter: it was lunacy. 'Think. And things can still change!'

'You don't *mind* that I'm half-Jewish?'

He wondered how she could still think that of him. 'Will you accept?'

'Your flat's too small. And we'd have to keep quiet about it. You're too well-known. And your work...'

'We'll go. Leave. Oster can manage without me.'

'And Emma?'

'I'll talk to her. See what she wants to do.' But he wondered if he really would, and for the moment he didn't say that he thought his daughter would be safer staying with her aunt. If they were caught trying to leave, the Party would make them disappear. Had Kara also considered that?

He would make his mind up about Emma later.

Kara lit cigarettes for them both. 'Where would we go?'

Hoffmann had good contacts with the police in Sweden and Switzerland. They were close, and neutral, but they were also within the Party's reach; and the first country was supplying Germany with iron ore, while the other's banks were handling the Party's foreign exchange.

There were further considerations. As long as their own security wasn't affected, he thought, the people across the Atlantic might never even get involved in a European war.

'Why not America?' he said. 'You're half-American. You have family there.'

'If you mean my mother – '

'Think.'

'What would you do?'

'We're not there yet. My English isn't bad, and yours is fluent. Perhaps I could become a private eye. Like Sam Spade.' He paused. 'Will you marry me?' He felt light-headed, almost like laughing. 'It doesn't matter if our marriage is a secret or not. Oster would probably like a man like me to set an example.'

She laughed drily. 'And I'm pregnant. We could collect our thousand-*Mark* payout from the Party and knock off twenty-five per-cent straight away! And think! If it's twins, we'd only have to pay back half!'

'But will you marry me?'

Why was she making light of this? Well, he was frightened too, but that was just something they'd have to deal with.

She smiled, a secret smile, a smile for herself, one that he knew and loved. 'I don't think you leave me with much choice. And in case you think that's a back-handed answer, I agree with you. I'd want the same. All that bullshit about no matter what, no matter where – I'd want the same.'

90

There was a hell of a lot to discuss, a hell of a lot to organise. It was Kara who decided that the marriage should be discreet, and by some miracle, coupled with help from Tilli, they managed to keep it out of the press. Kara's furniture, books, and masks were packed and stored, and she moved into Tilli's large apartment off Wilhelmstrasse, quietly and unremarked, one rebelliously fine night, before November was a week old.

During that time, and for the rest of the month, Hoffmann kept as close a watch over her as he could, and was finally satisfied that no-one except those nearest to them knew anything of what had taken place; and he knew that it would take a while before anyone who wanted to know where she had gone would find out the truth. He had in any case registered a false residency docket in her name with the Hamburg police. If anyone went so far as to check the block given as her address there, and find the trail cold, the assumption would be that she had left the country - not an unreasonable conclusion to draw, since she could no longer practise her profession at home.

Hoffmann hoped that Kara, at least, would soon be leaving the country in fact - but it wasn't easy for him to arrange passage without drawing attention to himself. And it wasn't easy to arrange a smooth exit from the Police Praesidium. Telling Oster the news would be the least of his problems. As he grappled with them, and they frustrated him, time passed.

He watched with increasing uneasiness as Kara became impatient, then nervous, then resigned. She couldn't work, and she had always worked. She had little company, and she had always been surrounded by people. But she bore it. He continued to work, and his visits to the Wilhelmstrasse apartment were as infrequent as he could bear to make them. He scaled down his dispatches to Oster.

The year had been a black one from the start. Soon after the people had swept the Party to power, someone set fire to the Reichstag. Its ashes weren't cold before the Party had claimed that its destruction was the work of the Communists, and within days they'd used that to restrict, in the name of national security, all possible freedom of expression.

By midsummer, unions and opposition parties were outlawed. The more entrenched the Party became, so only the most optimistic saw any hope of its being ousted any more. Jewish civil servants were forced to leave their jobs. The president, 'Papa' Hindenburg, was spending more and more time at home in Neudeck. He was eighty-six. People said he wouldn't live another year. But Hindenburg had become little more than a sideshow anyway since February, and there were those who said that the only reason he couldn't stand Hitler was because of the Austrian's vulgar accent. The lime trees along Unter den Linden had been cut down. At the cinema, Pabst's *Don Quixote* and Lang's *Dr Mabuse* vanished. They were soon replaced by Riefenstahl's *Triumph of Faith*, and Steinhoff's *Hitlerjunge Quex*.

People began to leave.

But you could still go to a cabaret if you knew where to look, and you could still see a nude revue. And a lot of people were looking forward to Christmas, and a lot of people were feeling more prosperous and confident than they had felt in years. And soon there was even talk that the Party, relenting, was planning to plant new saplings in Unter den Linden. Little trees, though, Hoffmann remembered thinking, which wouldn't get in the way of the processions.

Kara seldom left Tilli's flat, and the constraint quickly began to irritate her. Late in November Tilli, irritated herself, decided that one of the few things she could do to offer some distraction was to give a dinner party, of necessity a small one, to which she only invited one guest, Kara's friend Veit Adamov. Hoffmann hadn't liked the idea, but Adamov and Kara were close, and the man knew what was going on.

To compensate for the lack of company, something she herself adored, Tilli had organised the most magnificent meal her resources and contacts could conjure up. The menu was French, the food simple but exquisite, and the meat, against all German reason, barely cooked at all. Kara loved it. Adamov declared that red wine, especially Burgundy, taken in enough quantity, was capable of killing off any microbe known to man. And there was something to celebrate, though this Hoffmann kept back until Adamov had left. Tickets on the *Europa*, sailing in eleven days. It would mean an untidy exit; and it was late in the day for Kara to be travelling, but it was better than no exit at all.

A week before they were due to leave for Hamburg, Kara fell ill. The first morning, it seemed to be nothing more than a cold, and by the evening it had passed; but in the small hours of the following day she became feverish, and as the morning progressed it became clear that she would be in no position to travel soon. Hoffmann, furious, made the calls necessary to cancel.

When he returned to the flat, Tilli met him at the door. She was a tall, slim blonde with sardonic brown eyes which never gave anything away, elegant in an intangibly cold manner which had something to do with her poise: you felt that she was never other than in complete control of herself. But her manner belied her temperament, and now was one of the rare occasions when the mask had slipped.

He'd arrived later than he'd hoped; it was St Nicolas' Day, and the streets were crowded with people celebrating the beginning of Christmas. Tilli would soon be going to parties, but this year she herself was holding only one soirée, and that only because Hoffmann had begged her to, arguing that not to do so would attract attention. But the soirée had been planned for an evening after their departure.

'How is she?' he asked immediately. Tilli was trying to look less worried than she was. She was a good actress, but not that good.

'I don't know - if she wasn't a doctor herself, I'd have sent for one. She wouldn't let me.'

'What's the matter?'

'She's lost blood. Not much, she says, but it shouldn't be happening at all.'

91

He went to her.

Kara told him there was nothing wrong, that there was nothing to worry about, that she was more than likely to encounter a few minor problems. Anyway, she said, there was barely a month to go until full term; they should be in the clear. But this time she did not raise the question of the child's name again, and as it was something she loved to discuss, he noticed. He said nothing. He held her, but she did not relax in his arms, and when he had to leave she did not protest, even playfully. They'd talked of this and that. He'd wanted to bring up the subject of their departure again, but something told him not to. She had enough to think about.

He stayed away, though he couldn't bear to, couldn't think about anything else. And they had to leave. The Party was growing. Soon it would be unstoppable. But the economy rallied, and people smiled in the streets, held their heads up - most of them. They thought they'd been given back their pride.

He felt as if his feet were mired in mud, as if he were trying to run from a monster in one of those dreams where escape is impossible.

Three days after his last visit, Tilli rang him. She sounded agitated, said she had rung three times without an answer, scared already that his line might be tapped.

Kara had called her own doctor. There was no cause for alarm - many children had been born a month early, and Kara was a strong woman. The early contractions she had had were a false alarm. Rest was all that was needed now.

Tilli's Christmas Party was set for the day after tomorrow: should she go ahead or should she cancel? Hoffmann told her on no account to do that, he would come over as soon as possible.

He was there by nine. Kara's bedroom had a bathroom leading from it. It was well away from the main rooms, down a corridor off which two similar guest-rooms led. On the night of the party, no-one else would be staying. Kara held his hand, looked at him, for once vulnerable, lonely, and scared.

'Don't go far away until we're through this.'

He only returned to his flat and his office as often as was necessary. He was there on the night of the party. He wore his Iron Cross.

Among the guests were Veit Adamov and Wolf Hagen. Protectively, Hermann and Emmy would be there, guests of honour, as would Hans Oster and Hans Brandau. Apart from real friends, the rest of the pack would include a smattering of senior Party members. No Jews had been invited.

The huge tree, which reached the ceiling of the entrance-hall, was already in place, heavily decorated, loaded with the new black tinsel, and red and white glass balls - the golden ones had been consigned to the cellar. The little white candles stuck in their silver holders, clipped onto the boughs, shimmered like tiny ghosts.

Tilli had covered every detail. Nazi snobbery and Nazi nationalism had been catered for to the last degree. Food and drink were solidly German, though Tilli knew that wouldn't appeal to Göring much.

The soirée, on Sunday, 17 December 1933, was what the press called a glittering occasion, and was remembered by many, even years later. The apartment overflowed with distinguished guests. The chandeliers gleamed in the candlelight. People gasped at the tree; a mountain of presents in red-and-black parcels, tied with white string, was admired, before they were distributed by elderly, smiling footmen.

Tilli hated the whole thing for the first time in her life. Emmy had to whisper words of encouragement in her ear.

Kara spent the evening in bed, propped up on satin cushions like a dying duchess. She was too hot: when she kicked off the coverlet, she was immediately too cold. She drank cold water and ate dry toast.

'Don't worry. I don't think I am going to die.'

He sat on the edge of the bed and squeezed her hand. She was distracted. 'Go back to the party.'

'They won't miss me.'

'Tilli says Hagen's here.'

Hoffmann didn't like the fear in her voice. 'Along with a load of other bigwigs. He's got a lot of power, now, thanks to me.'

'You got him off my back, and I'll always be grateful.' She paused. 'I wish he could be gone forever.'

Hoffmann wondered if her wish would be granted. Oster's intelligence-gathering showed that the Brownshirts were beginning to lose favour with the Führer. But Hagen was an eel, a survivor. He'd change uniform from brown to black if the wind changed, and he'd do it with more dexterity and a greater chance of success than most, because he had the gift of making himself indispensable, and had the trick of living for himself alone.

The hubbub of the party, coming from far away, was in their ears; in other circumstances it would have been nice.

Another sound then: someone walking down the corridor towards the door. There was a knock. A pause. Then another knock, louder. The person did not go away.

Hoffmann crossed the room, hand on gun, opened the door.

'Hello, my little chicken. Tilli told me where to find you.' Veit Adamov crossed the room, leaned over to kiss her. Hoffmann saw that she rallied, pushing herself to sit up, aware of how she smelt, of the dampness of the sheets. Veit sat down and took her hand. Hoffmann knew what Adamov was up to these days, how he had reinvented himself to survive. So did Tilli. Did Kara also know?

'Tell Uncle Veit all about it.'

Hoffmann watched as they talked, animatedly and intimately. Why was she confiding in him?

'Because I needed to,' she said afterwards. 'Because he's an old friend. Because I trust him.'

'But he's with them, and he drinks too much.'

'He's still one of us. If you'd tried to join in the conversation you'd have understood that.'

'Do you know what he's doing?'

'I've seen harder porn in gynaecology class. He's not hurting anyone. His actors need money. Some of them need it in order to get out of the country.'

'How do you know?'

'I know he'd make good films whatever they were about. And you can be sexy without hurting anyone. And anyway what's wrong with it? Look at us. These days we condemn lovemaking, except as a means of making babies, but a military parade, that's quite another matter. The instruments of life,' she half-quoted, 'have to be covered up, are somehow shameful. But the instruments of death –'

'He's not one of us.'

'You don't know that.'

'And you do?'

'Think.'

She was right. Veit was close to her in a way he couldn't compete with. And was Veit any more compromised than he was? Veit rightly knew nothing of Hoffmann's connection with Oster. If Veit was working for the Resistance too, why should Hoffmann know about it?

'But he knows now,' he said.

'He is my friend and he could be yours. It's best that *you* have a godfather as well. You might need him. I think you will.'

'A godfather *as well*?'

'He will be the child's godfather. Emma will be its godmother.'

So, she had made the choice for them.

He wasn't going to argue the case. He was afraid she was dying.

'You'd better go back,' she said again. 'You'll be missed.'

92

Kara did not die. It was a nervous Christmas, and though Tilli's cook was at her best, most of the goose went uneaten. Emma and her aunt joined them at dinner on Christmas Eve. Emma's concern for Kara, and her happy anticipation of the baby, lightened the mood. She'd bought Kara a garnet necklace, and a recording of Furtwängler conducting Beethoven's Ninth. Kara rallied in Emma's company, and the family stumbled through a handful of sonatas and trios together. They didn't listen to the radio.

Kara would return to her bed after three hours, but the greyness left her cheeks, her eyes cleared, began to sparkle again. Emma put a hand on her belly, marvelling.

1934 arrived and the future was to be glorious. Homosexual men found that the freedom of the Weimar days was over. Gay Party members were disappearing. Jewish holidays no longer appeared on official calendars; non-Aryans were forbidden to adopt Aryan children; Marinus van der Lubbe was executed for starting the Reichstag fire. Shortly before that, on Three Kings, Kara gave birth, quickly and with little pain. Everyone was amazed at how well she did. And afterwards she seemed fine. She was very pale, and there was a little darkness under the eyes, but that was hardly surprising.

The baby was a boy. Someone joked that they should call him Balthasar Caspar Melchior. The godfathers were Ernst Udet and Veit Adamov. They didn't get on. Emma and Tilli were the godmothers.

They called him Stefan Alexander, after their fathers. But he was little, he didn't weigh two kilos, and they had to encourage him to cry after he'd emerged.

'We must leave soon.'

'Not until he's strong enough.'

Hoffmann paced the room. He couldn't bring himself to tell her they had to take the risk. Stefan had a Jewish grandmother - that was enough to condemn him. The Ancestry Document had been introduced. You didn't have to carry one, but if you didn't, you had to have a good reason not to. What might you be hiding? There was no way in which Hoffmann could depend on his falsification of Kara's documents being enough to protect them. They would have copies somewhere, his relationship with her would have been documented.

Stefan stayed small. The doctor pursed his lips, talked of jaundice out of Kara's hearing. Kara breast-fed him, he put on weight slowly. At a month, there was no more talk of jaundice, but he was still small.

'We must go.'

'Not until he's stronger.' She looked at him. 'He mustn't die.'

'We must go.'

'No.'

He consoled himself with the thought that Berlin was hosting the Olympic Games in two years. The Party would behave itself on the world stage until then. Werner March was planning his stadium. They would have to leave before then. Every moment they delayed increased their danger. His son's health worried him. There were moments when he wished Stefan had never been born. Without him, they would be in America by now. He kept his options for sailing tickets warm, but he dared not appear insistent until he could make a positive move, in case he drew unwelcome attention to himself; and Kara remained obdurate.

By the beginning of March, Stefan was making better progress. By then the Party had published a new version of the *Psalms* which cut out all references to Jews. By then the Jewish War Veterans Association had declared its loyalty to Germany, reminding the Party that 12,000 Jews had died fighting for their country in the last war. By then Paul Czinner's film *Catherine the Great* had been banned because its star was a Jew.

93

'We must go.'

'Have you talked to Oster?'

Hoffmann would make a clean break with it all. With his experience and contacts, he'd get a job in the States, somehow. He wasn't 36 years old. He'd like to continue in regular police work, but if that didn't happen, he might really consider becoming a private detective. Somehow.

First things first.

Tickets for the liners weren't easy to organise. There weren't many sailings, and those with money, influence, and intelligence were beginning to queue at the embassies, to get visas, to get out. They were being encouraged to do so. They were allowed to keep whatever they planned to take with them. Some thought they'd be able to return before long, and pick up where they'd left off.

Hoffmann couldn't rest until his family was safe. 'We must go,' he said again.

This time there was compliance in her eyes. But only the ghost. Stefan was smaller than he should have been. No-one knew better than Kara that he was a sickly baby, that until he was stronger, until she was confident of that, he should stay put, despite the risks. Another thought struck her: was the nature of her husband's work making him start at shadows? Surely another couple of months would make no difference?

Hoffmann had to talk to Oster, but there were things to do first.

He'd made up his mind that they'd leave at the end of the month. If loose ends were left behind, too bad. He felt greater relief than he'd felt in months.

He spent a morning in Oranienburg, walking from café to café in the spring air, the pale sunlight barely warming him through his heavy black overcoat. He found the man he was looking for in the third place, drinking his early *Rummer* of white wine. The man wasn't particularly happy to see him, but, after a few words had been exchanged, he relaxed, then became intrigued, then faintly amused.

'I won't pretend we'll be sorry to see you go.'

'I can imagine.'

'You're a pain in the arse.'

'Yes.'

'The man grinned. 'You can't imagine how good it makes me feel just to be able to tell you that.'

'I'll be back.'

'Will you?' The man looked thoughtful. 'Well, you won't find me here. Never mind, I'm sure our paths will cross again - maybe in New York - who knows?'

'It'll be a pleasure.'

'You haven't nailed me here. There's no reason why you should do any better there.'

'Maybe you were just more useful to me on the loose.'

'Don't hurt my feelings.'

'Can you get the tickets?'

'Queue-jumping's expensive.' The man shifted his weight on his stool, drained his wine. 'I'll see what I can do.' He drew a notebook from his pocket, wrote a number on a page, tore it out and gave it to Hoffmann. 'Call me in a couple of days.'

'Thank you.' Hoffmann rose to leave.

The man drained his glass. 'Schnapps before you go?'

'With you?'

'We've got a common enemy now. Makes us friends. We should drink to that. Or did you come to me because you already knew I was a Jew?'

'Do you have any idea of a date for me? I need to do some housekeeping before I leave.'

'End of the month, you said.' The man considered. 'There's a sailing on 24th. Might get you on that.'

Later, Hoffmann sent a note to Oster.

94

The rhythm of the truck had changed. It was slowing. Jolted back to the present, and immediately alert, Hoffmann looked ahead. They had turned off the country road and were bumping down a track at the end of which he could see, half-hidden by the curve of the hill on which its was built, a low farmhouse. It was very old. Its walls were a metre thick, its small windows sunk deep within them.

The truck drew to a halt and the driver got out, waving to him to climb down as he opened the passenger door and heaved out the chickens. The chickens squawked as he dumped the crate on the ground. A black dog chained to a post had begun to bark and strain at the end of its tether. The inside of its mouth was deep red, its teeth yellow. Hoffmann looked away from it to where a door was opening.

A woman in a headscarf, print dress, apron and gumboots came out. She might have been any age between thirty and fifty, her black eyes glittering in her tanned face. She had a strong jaw, large, ivory-coloured teeth, like the dog's. There was something animal about her. When she came close, Hoffmann could smell the soil on her. Two small children stumbled in her wake.

'Uncle Ludo!'

The driver squatted down and held his arms out to hug them, then rose and introduced Hoffmann to the woman as his workmate.

'You can wash under the pump here, get a bit of that stink off of you,' she said to him with a smile that made her pretty. She handed him a sack to use as a towel. The driver followed her into the house. The children stayed to watch. Hoffmann couldn't tell whether the younger one was a boy or a girl. The dog, realising the uselessness of its endeavour, subsided.

He stripped, and sluiced the freezing water over him - it must have come from deep underground. It felt like the best wash he'd had in years, and he enjoyed the rough texture of the sack as he rubbed his skin with it. He stood in the sunshine, smelling the earth and looking at the trees and the sky, and felt free, and even that he might win. But the moment passed as he dressed, and his clothes seemed dirtier than they had before. He made his way towards the house.

He was unsurprised to hear – through an open window – the sound of the driver making love to the woman. A short time later they came out, smiling, the driver with a jug of beer in one hand and in the other two pairs of Knackwurst. The woman brought bread, wooden plates and mustard.

'Forgot the mugs, Branka,' the driver said.

She returned to get them, swinging strong hips.

'Why did you tell her I was your workmate?' Hoffmann rolled them both cigarettes, less skilfully than he'd have liked.

'You know,' said the driver, 'I've always found explanations get people into trouble.' He looked at him evenly. 'Don't worry, I'll see you right in Coburg. And I'm sure you've got a little money stashed away, so you'll give me something in return for the lift.'

Two sacks of cabbages replaced the chickens. Hoffmann continued to ride in the back. He wasn't sorry. He needed his solitude. They wouldn't stop again until they reached Coburg. He'd used up the last of his snow. He hadn't drunk or eaten much, and he was tired. The sun began to weary him. He tried to stop thinking of what might have happened if they had only sailed for New York on that 24 March, a decade ago now.

95

Kara had been furious when he'd told her. Why hadn't he consulted her? Stefan wouldn't be ready to travel by then, did he want to risk the child's life for no reason? What if he caught pneumonia, or influenza, or scarlet fever, or whooping cough? Each was a distinct possibility if he was taken out of the safe environment of Tilli's flat. That it was still safe, Hoffmann was sure; but he didn't want Tilli too closely involved, for her own sake. The sooner they left the better.

The tickets wouldn't be held if they hesitated. What was there to dither about, Kara wanted to know. The fact that getting tickets at all wasn't the easiest job in the world didn't impress her.

It rankled with him that she would not listen to reason, though he knew that concern for Stefan would bear every other consideration before it. Her stubbornness depressed him for other reasons too, which either he could not put his finger on, or would not face.

He let two days go by before ringing the man from the café. During them, he went from resignation to Kara's will, to a bloody-minded decisiveness, determining to take the tickets anyway, drag her onto the ship by force if need be.

He had still not made up his mind when the message came from Oster.

They met at Wannsee. It was a harsh day, a dying day of winter, and a freezing wind ripped at their trousers as they walked along the shore of the lake between the station and the Restaurant Schloss Wannsee, past the ranks of neatly moored yachts and dinghies, their rigging singing and snapping. Oster looked older. The lines between his nose and the corners of his mouth, and across his brow, seemed deeper; but his eyes retained their humour.

'I got your note,' he said.

'It isn't easy.'

Oster spread his hands. 'I understand. You will be missed, but an army cannot depend on one soldier.'

Was there a cutting note there?

'In any case, that isn't the reason I asked you to meet me,' continued the General. He paused and looked out across the lake, his eyes watering in the wind. 'I have a last favour to ask of you. You are free to refuse, but if you accept, you will be giving us a valuable parting gift.'

Hoffmann said nothing, but inclined his head, and they continued their walk.

'We have intelligence that Hitler is planning something against his Party rivals, in particular the Strasser brothers.'

'That doesn't surprise me,' said Hoffmann.

'If he succeeds, nothing will stop him, and it's common knowledge that the position of the Strassers is weakening.' Oster paused and smiled coldly. 'Good principles they may have, but they lack good showmanship.'

'Take them away and you take the socialism away from National Socialism.'

'They're all servants of the devil,' said Oster soberly. 'But the Strassers are pliable. If we can stop him before he stops them, we still have a chance to sort this mess out.'

They walked in silence for a few minutes before Oster spoke again. 'Hitler is preoccupied with these affairs of his at the moment and the Party is in a state of flux. Our intelligence indicates that about the middle of next month, shortly before our glorious leader's birthday, in fact, he is to speak at an informal rally in Potsdam. A lot of the Old Guard will be there, so he'll be relatively relaxed.' Oster paused again. 'We might get a shot at him. But we'll need to know what the police movements are going to be, liaison with the SS, with his bodyguard, that sort of thing. If you could delay leaving until then, if you could get us that information, then I would consider that you had more than done your duty.'

Hoffmann would look back on the moment for the remainder of his life. At the time, however, he did not hesitate. Here was the opportunity to soothe Kara's anxiety and pacify his conscience at one and the same time. There was no right or wrong about his decision: it was opportunistic and profitable - something that would make everyone happy.

The two men shook hands, hurried back to their cars, both of them relieved. Oster knew that most agents had short useful lives in the field, and though he could have done with Hoffmann for longer, at least he felt he was squeezing another few kilometres out of him. And it was good to get out of the wind and into the relative warmth of their cars. Then the short drive, for them both, by separate routes, to Berlin, their offices, and the continuing tension of life.

Hoffmann, with that sense of euphoria that only comes when a particular stress has been lifted from your shoulders, rang his contact to change the sailing dates, shrugged off the man's irritation and the difficulties he made about arranging another booking. He had spoken to Kara, who had thrown her arms round his neck and cried, tasting her own relief, proud of him, and agreeing that the possible new departure date, 28 April, would be fine, they would go then, Stefan was improving by the day, there seemed to be no reason now to fear that he would relapse. But she would not hear of their leaving without Max. So much could go wrong. They might never meet again if once they separated. What would they do if they encountered difficulties, and he was not there to help them? He knew that he did not want to stay behind. It seemed to him that everything was falling into place – that it must be 'meant', as Kara said.

The man from the café sent him a note, and a bill, for the new tickets. They were confirmed. There were instructions about where to collect them. If he had believed in God, as Oster did, Hoffmann might have felt that a divine hand was occupying itself with their tiny destiny.

He'd done his job for Oster. Everything was in place a few days before Hitler's forty-fifth birthday, and the man himself was awaited on the podium, where there was a table spread with a starched white cloth on which only a solitary microphone and a glass of water stood. Below, stretching the length of the beer hall, long trestle tables, with beer mugs and bowls of pretzels arranged along them, and on the benches, the arses of the faithful, three hundred of them, the elite, not, of course, a March Violet among them - those Johnny-Come-Latelys had already been purged from the SS. SS and SA bravos lined the walls, more outside, eyeing each other as suspiciously as anyone in the crowd. But there were two gunmen high in the dark gallery, knowing they would probably die if they got a shot in, but ready to bring the bastard down at the signal.

The moment came. There was a stirring near the podium, and, as a result, of expectancy in the hall itself. A man in a brown uniform stepped up to the microphone, the convenor of the meeting, ready to make the introduction, no doubt.

Instead he said, 'Gentlemen, I must crave your indulgence. Our Leader is unexpectedly indisposed, and unable therefore to be with us today. But I am happy to say that he has sent a high representative, someone close, someone who really needs no introduction from me ... '

The gunmen holstered their weapons and slipped quietly out of the gallery. Hoffmann, near the podium, seated among the guests of honour, cursed silently.

There would be other opportunities.

But he would not change the date of the passage to America again.

96

They spent time packing. It had to be a careful job. Enough to start a new life, all fitted into two suitcases.

He had spoken to Emma's aunt. Only at the last minute would Emma be told. It would be tough, but they could not risk her speaking to anyone before they left.

It had been impossible, working with him as closely as he did, to keep his relationship with Kara a secret from Paul Kessler. There was no reason, apart from his own extreme caution, for him to have done so. He chose not to be too open about it on account of the risk of its ever getting back to Wolf Hagen, or any other potential enemy, as the Party divided against itself. Hoffmann toyed with the idea of telling Kessler the rest, but decided against it. Even if it would be useful to leave someone behind to cover for him, Kessler was too young, and he didn't want to endanger him by giving him knowledge he didn't need to have. As it was, he had to summon up all the skill in dissimulation he had ever learned to get himself through the week. Luckily there was an investigation - a university professor had fallen to his death from the roof of his apartment block - which covered his movements, though in practice he left most of the work to others in his department. It looked like a suicide anyway.

Tilli helped. Tilli was a rock. But there were times in the middle of the night when he found himself - against all reason - mistrusting even her. He spent little time with Kara at the flat. He collected the tickets. He arranged a car, through the same people at the same time, nearly clearing out his current funds, which would take them to Hamburg. What remained of his money he encashed and packed, though leaving some in his bank account to alleviate any possible suspicion.

He missed Kara most at night. He longed to make love to her, and even more, just to lie close to her, to have her in his arms, to feel the kind of safety he never felt anywhere else. But soon it would be all right.

She disappeared forty-eight hours before they were due to leave. She had gone out to buy a new coat for the journey. Had someone been watching the house after all? This could not be a coincidence.

For a day he scoured the city desperately for her, confiding in Kessler at last, not wanting to believe the worst.

Even ten years later, when he thought of it his heart raced unbearably. Then her body was found.

97

It wasn't an untypical crime scene. She'd been discovered by a factory worker taking flowers to his wife's grave, on the bank of the Plötzensee, on the edge of one of the big cemeteries that bordered its northern shores. Kessler hadn't wanted him to see the body before the post-mortem, before they could clean her up, but he'd insisted, scared more by the young man's distress than by the unknown. In his career, he'd seen bodies in states of wreck beyond the imaginations of most. But the people *he'd* loved and lost had departed peacefully. Kara had not been so privileged.

He asked to see the photographs first. Kessler reluctantly handed copies over. He wanted to prepare himself, and perhaps to escape into professionalism. He saw images that were familiar. A young woman's body in a pose too contorted for life, the limbs frozen into positions of unimaginable pain. The face wasn't visible. She still wore her brassiere and shoes. Smudges around her on the dark grey earth she lay on, indistinct in the photographs, must have been her other clothes. There was a large carrier bag from Bister's, the name of the shop extraordinarily clear. The coat she'd already bought. Her body was too white, a cold white made worse by the photographs, and on it he could see dark marks that he did not want to see.

He had thought himself strong. He had thought himself prepared for the sight of the body itself. He was wrong.

What was worst? The simple fact of her vulnerable nakedness on the marble slab? Or that her face was so drawn, her nose so sharp, an old woman's nose? Or was it the bruises? How badly they must have beaten her. And the messy rupturing around her vagina - what had they used on her there?

This was the person he had loved above anyone. She had been alive and in his arms. Those broken hands had caressed him. Those blue lips had been warm on his. Now there was just a broken body, nothing to do with Kara; except that it was Kara. This shattered cold wreck had been vibrant days ago. Where was she now? Where was the spirit?

There were things to be taken care of fast. Somehow, he knew he would cope. Emma had not yet been told anything. She would have to be told about Kara, but she was safe. His concern was for Stefan. He would have to talk to Tilli. He had no idea what else to do. And he would have to talk to Kessler.

He told himself that he shouldn't hate Tilli, shouldn't even be angry. It was natural that Kara would have wanted a last walk in Berlin, and it was perfectly possible that she would have wanted to take it on her own. Why should Tilli have tried to stop her? There had been no reason to expect any evil. But had they been shadowed? Had they been betrayed?

First things first. The shock brought a curious calm. He would function for as long as he had things to do. Only when he was at rest would the vacuum break and the grief tear in. He would have to be prepared for that, too. He had seen enough other people go through this; but always as an observer of violent loss, not as a participant, even in the war. He had kept himself aloof. The thought of his first wife came to him, but Ursula was no more now than an idea, even a dream. Ursula. Ten years with her, and now it seemed as if it had never been. Had he dreamt their time together?

He had to start with Tilli.

'I am so sorry,' she had said. 'We thought it was safe.'

'People play long games. I should have thought of that.'

'What about Stefan?'

'I need your help.'

'Anything. Max, believe me, I am so sorry.'

'It wasn't your fault. You know what she was like. If she wanted to go out, how could you have stopped her?'

'It was to buy a coat for the journey. And to say goodbye.'

'I know.'

'We must think about Stefan. Where are we going to hide him?' Tilli paused. 'Chez *moi. A la campagne?*'

'At your estate?'

She put her arms around his neck. 'I think that would be the safest place.'

Stefan. All that was left of Kara. He had to trust Tilli.

'When will you leave?' he said.

'As soon as possible. I hadn't planned to stay in Berlin anyway. It's not much fun here anymore.' She smiled ruefully, and kissed him. 'And you?'

'I'm staying.'

98

What else was there for him now, but to continue the game? Stefan would be safe with Tilli, though he wondered if it would ever be safe for him to know the truth about himself. Not until all this was over, certainly; and the worst, Hoffmann knew, was yet to come.

He said goodbye to his son. He had no idea when he would see him again. He was uncertain about what he himself would do. But Stefan would be safe. Emma was still with her aunt, and had never known about the plan. She had to know that Kara was dead, but they dressed it up for her as a car accident. It scarcely deadened the blow, for the girl and the woman had been very close. Grief is the price you pay for love, her father tried to tell her, repeating the adage he himself had once been told. In her short life she had now paid that price twice. It was good that she had taken so warmly to Hoffmann's new assistant, and he to her. What's more, the scruffy young man - too young really to be taking on the responsibilities Hoffmann was giving him, for he was only about ten years older than Emma - was turning out to be as intelligent as he was - apparently - loyal.

Grief is the price... Mad with his own pain, he tried to anaesthetise it with work. Within the police, only Kessler knew his personal involvement. Hoffmann needed another professional to help him, and in the short time the men had been working together he knew from experience that a rare thing, a professional friendship, had formed between them. In any case, he would have to trust the young man now, since he wouldn't be allowed to spend all his time on what, from an outsider's point of view, was a routine rape-killing.

His instincts told him to mistrust everyone, but you can't live life like that; completely alone you are more vulnerable. The trick was to let Kessler know only as much as he needed to know. But he found himself telling the young man more than that, about how much he had loved Kara, about what their plans had been.

Hoffmann also needed a focus for his hatred and anger. Kessler, always calm and never asking any more questions than were necessary for his investigation, acted unwittingly as a brake on emotions Hoffmann could not afford to have. They did not know who was responsible for Kara's death. But they made no progress. After a week, it began to look as if an invisible wall had been erected against them. That in itself was significant. Hoffmann began to think that

Kessler's investigation was being led in a certain direction. He decided to let it take its course. This kind of manipulation sometimes revealed the hand of the puppet-master.

He dreaded the nights, his dreams. He stopped drinking almost completely because he knew that if he started to use booze as a comfort he would drown in it, and be left a greater prey to his emotions than ever. His flat seemed unbearably cold and empty. He worked routinely, doggedly.

But he was not alone. He intended to enlist Adamov's help. Adamov's increasingly successful blue film company had begun to earn its founder some strong links with the city's underworld. Hoffmann didn't like him; but he had been Kara's friend. In the event, it was Adamov who got in touch with him, with the same idea in mind.

Hoffmann also rang Oster. The general invited him to dine at his home. 'It's quite safe. This can be an official meeting. No reason why we shouldn't meet openly from time to time, given our mutual professional interests.'

He arrived to find that there were no other guests. Oster greeted him with a formal embrace.

'This has not turned out well,' said the General.

'No.'

'I grieve for you both.'

Hoffmann said nothing.

'I have been doing some investigating on my own account,' Oster continued. 'We, too, have come up with nothing.'

'I know you would have contacted me otherwise.'

'Do you think it could have been a terrible chance occurrence?'

The pain twisted in his heart like a living thing. 'I can't accept that.'

'It's good that you have got Stefan out of the way.'

'What makes you say that?'

'Nothing. I mean, simply, somewhere safe, away from Berlin. I assume that's what you've done.'

Hoffmann looked at him.

'I hadn't contacted you because I knew what you must be going through, and as you guessed, because I had nothing to tell you. But now...' Oster spread his hands awkwardly. 'Now...'

'What is it?'

Oster turned to him. 'Something's afoot. Something big. Have you heard anything?'

'If you want my help, forget it. I have only one job to do now.'

'If you help us, we can help you.'

'I doubt it. This is a criminal investigation. It has nothing to do with espionage or betrayal.'

'It has everything to do with betrayal.'

Hoffmann could hardly bear the pain. It was the kind of pain you cannot get used to, the kind that renews itself every moment of its existence, the kind that only death can silence, only vengeance appease. At its worst, he found himself hating Kara for what they had done to her, for her vulnerability, for making him impotent in the face of her torturers and killers.

'Give me a brandy.'

Oster poured drinks, and sat in the chair next to Hoffmann's. 'Hitler is scared of a coup within the Party. He's going to wipe out the competition before that can happen.'

'So, there'll be a fewer of them. But he'll still be there.'

'We've got to monitor this. We need everyone we can get, everyone in a high position, to watch what is going on. There's going to be a bloodbath.'

'You mean there isn't one already?'

'A purge.'

'Which we can use to our advantage? No,' Hoffmann shook his head. 'The game's over. We must get out or sit it out. He can't last. Germans won't stand for this.'

'They're not only standing for it, they're applauding it.' Oster paused. 'Help us. What have you to lose?'

Hoffmann sneered. 'My life. On a rack. I've done enough. I'm going to find whoever killed Kara, I'm going to kill them, and them I'm getting out. I want to be sure that my children will be safe.'

'Don't you think they're safe enough where they are? And no-one suspects you of anything. You're Max Hoffmann. You've got a low Party number and a high SS rank. Use them, for God's sake!'

Hoffmann hadn't touched his brandy. He looked at the glass on the table in front of him. 'No,' he said.

Oster stood up. 'Then you'd better make your arrangements fast. You might as well take no chances. Who knows if someone isn't preparing to denounce you? A lot of very important people are going to be dead by the beginning of July. If you were among them, you'd scarcely be noticed, and you know Hitler always thinks it's better to be safe than sorry.'

'Are you threatening me?'

'Help us. We need men like you. And don't you think Kara would want you to?'

'She was coming away with me.'

'Circumstances have changed. Do it for her. For her memory. Someone's got to stand up to these shits. Did you see that thing in *Der Stürmer*? About Jews ritually sacrificing Aryan kids? Did you know they're planning to kick all Jews out of the army?' Oster laughed shortly. 'They'll certainly lose any damned war they go in for if they do that.'

'It's a futile battle,' said Hoffmann, but he knew it might be all he had left. 'They get stronger every day. Their information system is already so good that people are frightened of speaking within earshot of anyone they don't know, and even then - '

'You exaggerate. In any case, it's a system that relies on denunciation and betrayal, not on deduction and information. It's a stupid system. It can be worked round.'

'It's effective.'

'Unlike you, not to face a challenge. And you know Stefan and Emma are safe. If there's the slightest sign of danger to them, do you think we haven't the means to get them out? The frontiers aren't closed, you know.' Oster smiled bleakly. 'You haven't touched your drink.'

'I don't need it now.'

99

A month passed. Kessler and Hoffmann were no nearer finding out who Kara's murderers were. Underworld contacts knew nothing, but they were getting jittery themselves, some teaming up with the SS, and others beginning to move away, to Frankfurt, or Munich, to take their chances in rivalry with the resident gangs of those cities, or further afield: New York, London, Zürich. If anyone knew anything, no-one was talking.

Hoffmann had been sceptical about Oster's prediction but he had finally been swung by argument, not threat. And he would find out the truth about Kara's death. No-one could stop him from using his reason, even if they could block his enquiries. And he could be an implacably patient man.

Then it happened, exactly as Oster had described. There hadn't been a ripple to warn anyone of it. The SS and the Gestapo were honing their skills fast. Afterwards, people said it had been a necessary evil. The Brownshirts were beating people up in the streets, smashing shop windows, swaggering around, terrifying everybody. President Hindenburg had warned the Chancellor that he should do something about it.

It happened so fast, too. The whole thing was over in three days, over the last weekend of June. At the end of it, everyone who posed a threat to Hitler among his own ranks was dead, and the Brownshirts were a spent force. On Monday, 2 July, Paul Hindenburg, who'd entered the final month of his life, sent a telegram to the Chancellor, thanking him for saving the German people from a catastrophe.

The door was shut and the bolts shot home.

Adamov had been in touch frequently, but even he had drawn a blank. Now, after the wave of killings, hardened criminals were also watching their backs. No-one was willing to talk about anything. Adamov himself was leaving for the South of France for the summer. He had some business down there. He offered to stay, but Hoffmann let him go. If he'd found nothing in two months, it was unlikely that he'd find anything now.

The coarsest of the Party's propaganda sheets was *Der Stürmer*. It was hard to say who read it apart from uneducated, unemployed men, but it was unmissable because it was displayed everywhere in red cases, behind glass. It concerned itself with hysterical diatribes against the Jews.

Hoffmann remembered Kessler's face as he told him. It must have been a week after the purge. No longer.

'I wouldn't normally have glanced at it, but a series of photographs on one of the pages on view in one of the *Stürmerkästen* caught my eye.'

'Yes?'

'I don't know whether I should be telling you this or not. Look, I bought a copy. You can see for yourself.'

There were four blurred photographs, reproduced at approximately postcard size, and going across a double-page spread. It was a sequence of photographs, in which a group of three or possibly four men in civilian clothes, their faces hidden, were kicking, and stooping to punch a woman lying on the ground. The woman's face too was hidden; but there was no mistaking the clothes she was wearing, nor the shop-name on the carrier bag that lay near her. The headline, which ran across both pages over the photographs, read: 'The Kind of Villainy Jews Perpetrate', and under them was a brief article Hoffmann did not trouble to read. However, he looked very carefully at the photographs. He looked up at Kessler, his face pale.

'There's something there, isn't there?' said Kessler.

'It's hard to make out.'

'They stopped taking photographs before they stripped her.' Kessler, Hoffmann knew, had struggled with himself whether or not to impart this news. He'd done so, finally, Hoffmann also knew, because it was better to advance the investigation than to spare his Chief pain. Now he was trying to mitigate that pain by suggesting the photographer had stopped. But whatever else he'd taken couldn't be worse than what Hoffmann himself had seen. And even *Der Stürmer* wouldn't dare publish more specific pictures than it had - besides, they did its job for it perfectly well.

The worst thing of all was an indistinct detail in the third photograph. Hoffmann didn't want to believe what he thought he saw there.

'We must get proper prints of these,' he said.

'Yes.'

'Copies. No-one must know we've got them.'

'I'll see to it.'

'Be discreet.' Hoffmann hoped he wasn't placing too heavy a load on the young man, but Kessler just smiled faintly, abstractedly almost; seemed confident.

The nature of his own work was becoming increasingly political, involving more and more surveillance and logging of people's movements, more and more paperwork. Investigation was left to junior officers, and Kessler was one of a diminishing number of them who were not Party members.

When Hoffmann returned to his flat each night - he no longer kept alcohol there, he did not trust himself - he stuck to the same routine. He made himself tea, put some Bach on the record-player, for Bach was easier to take in his present mood than Beethoven, Schubert, or even Mozart, and settled down with a book and a packet of cigarettes. A colleague had given him a few little twists of cocaine in brown paper and he was finding that helpful. It kept his mind clear and his spirits up. But he knew nothing could protect him from sleep, from dreams, or from waking in the night imagining he was curled up to her and safe.

He wanted the comfort of Kara, and he would never have that again. She was dead; needlessly, cruelly killed. Her flat was gone, a memory, her things all in storage, where they would probably remain for years, forever. He'd intended to keep one or two of the African masks she'd retained, but he hadn't been able to bear to, and in the end he had kept nothing, not even a book that had belonged to her, not even her fountain pen. It was better that way.

Two days later, Kessler had come to the flat with a stiff brown envelope in his hand.

'That was fast.' said Hoffmann

'You're too high up the chain of command to know all the petty details, but I'm not. Department C has two or three men infiltrated in all *Der Stürmer's* main offices. When I started in the force I was on the beat with one of the guys who's now in the Berlin office.'

'Did you find out who took them?'

Kessler shook his head. 'No. Apparently they were handed in anonymously, together with the editorial. The big boys were delighted, just the sort of stuff they thrive on. Stuck it all in with no questions asked.'

'And no arm-twisting?'

'That I don't know either. But obviously these guys aren't Jews.'

'Obviously. The question is, are these photos any better? Can we –' Hoffmann hesitated. 'Can we... fix anything for sure?' His heart was beating hard. Part of him did not want to know.

'I think we can.' Kessler's face was serious, concerned.

He switched the desk light on, opened the envelope, and from it drew four photographs. Hoffmann produced a magnifying glass and they both pored over the pictures, especially the third.

The left hand of one of Kara's attackers was clearly visible to the right of the picture, though his head and most of his body were outside the frame. The hand was in movement, and the film hadn't been fast enough to arrest this, but the definition was clear enough to show that the ring finger of the hand was nothing more than a stump.

100

The roadblock on the outskirts of Coburg presented no difficulties. Ludo Kirchner and the fat old guards knew each other well, and when Ludo produced a couple of bottles of schnapps from under the driver's seat, the soldiers waved him through. Hoffmann thought it was possible they hadn't even noticed him in the back of the lorry. He wished everyone was that slack.

It was six in the evening and the driver went straight to the brewery.

'Well mate,' he said as he lowered the tailgate for Hoffmann to descend. 'Time to say goodbye.'

Hoffmann had already taken two notes from his wallet - he didn't want Kirchner to see how much he had got altogether - and now he handed them to him.

'Thank you.'

'Thank *you*.' Kirchner took the money, glanced at them, and stowed them in his pocket. 'So, where do you go from here?'

'West.'

Kirchner gave no sign of whether he knew Hoffmann was lying or not. 'Whatever you do, keep clear of Frankfurt. Pass it to the south. They're bombing the shit out of the place.' He looked at Hoffmann. 'Got enough money left for some new clothes?'

'Why should I need them?'

'Because you're no more a farmworker than I'm Max Schmeling. And I want more than this.' He didn't sound quite so friendly now.

It was a pity, Hoffmann thought, that Kirchner had left it so late to be greedy. If he'd made his demand back at the farm, or anywhere where escape might have been harder for Hoffmann, he would have stood a better chance of striking a deal. But now Hoffmann could see too much greed in Kirchner's eyes. He glanced round quickly. The grey walls of the brewery rose above them, and near the lorry a pair of huge green double doors were open, revealing beyond them a nave-like storeroom, in the depths of which men in overalls were moving about. No-one was coming towards them, but this would have to be quick.

Hoffmann raised his arms fast and pressed the points of his index fingers deep into the hollows behind Kirchner's earlobes. He flexed them hard, twice, and the driver went down like a sack. Hoffmann glanced up. No reaction from the

278

brewery workers. Sickened at the necessity, he bent over Kirchner and made quite sure the man was dead. He removed the money he'd given him from his breast pocket, and moved away, not too fast, towards the centre of the town.

He was on his guard. If anyone had guessed his route, they'd have got here before him. The question was, would they know his destination? They might have decided to move on, towards Nuremberg and Munich, or they might have decided to wait. It would be a question of balance. Move on, and risk losing the trail. Wait, and risk wasting time. He remembered an old military dictum – was it Clausewitz? – you can always recover space, but never time. Would they act on that? If anyone was here at all.

He needed to eat and get clean, somewhere to sleep, new clothes - Kirchner had been right about that - and some kind of usable ID. All he had was the Swedish passport, and if anyone found that on him it'd mean more trouble than salvation. He thought about dumping it, decided not to. What he also had was money.

He found a dark doorway and, hiding in it, he drew out his wallet, extracted a few modest and worn notes, stuffed them in a pocket, and then hid the wallet deep in his overalls. He could smell his armpits and crutch. The dousing at the pump hadn't done that much good.

He made his way cautiously into the town centre. On the hill above loomed the vast form of the castle. Few lights were on, and it was already a dark mass against the waning sky. The Ehrenburg looked deserted, and there were few people about. What Hoffmann was looking for was a cheap lodging house. He might have to move on that night, but he needed somewhere to retrench, and he needed somewhere where no-one would comment on him. He wished he were a better actor, able to disguise his accent better.

No-one had seen him. No one knew he was there. At the brewery, they would have discovered Kirchner by this time. Would they know what had happened to him? There'd be no obvious mark on the body. They'd think it'd been a heart-attack, send for a doctor - that'd buy him time.

He calculated that he had maybe four hours. By the time they'd discovered that Kirchner had been murdered, and questioned the road-block guards, if they had noticed Hoffmann at all, the most casual description, the big man, the big nose, would be enough for them, if they were halfway on the ball. Who would they have sent after him? Schiffer? Kessler? Would they trust Kessler?

The first thing to do was acquire an identity card. Hoffmann made his way to a *Wirtshaus* on the Löwenstraße, near the bridge. Just right, Large and crowded, dimly lit.

To be a good cop, you have to know how crooks ply their trade. As a rookie, Hoffmann had learned his pickpocketing skills from a master. He moved across the large, low-ceilinged room, which smelled of fresh beer and cheap tobacco. A lot of women and old men, a few labourers, a few soldiers, some already drunk. One of the drunks stood near the stove, leaning on it, admiring the scenes painted on its tiles. He was younger than Hoffmann, but the same height and build, and his face had the same heaviness. Casting an eye over the room for any possible plainclothes cops, people he'd recognise in an instant, Hoffmann sat down heavily at a table nearby and ordered a Maß.

The bargirls moved quickly through the mob, carrying two or three Steins in each hand, dumping them swiftly in front of the assortment of gloomy men bent over the scrubbed tables, and, swinging their hips through the smoke, made their way back to the bar, to repeat the process. They wore lipstick and fixed smiles. Most of the men gazed into space with dead eyes or talked guardedly, the talk was of beer and the harvest. Hoffmann noticed one man of about his own age who had the Coburg Badge in his lapel. He sat alone over his beer, perhaps thinking of the glory days when the Leader had marched through the town twenty-odd years ago, smashing the Commies in a series of bloody street battles.

Hoffmann sipped his beer - it came from Ludo's brewery - and watched the man at the stove. He was dressed in a cheap suit, his worn white shirt buttoned to the collar. He was hugging the stove as if for warmth, though as it was August he was clearly hugging it for support.

The time came when he summoned the willpower to cast himself off and weave to the lavatory. Hoffmann followed him. Three paces from the door, Hoffmann, likewise weaving, bumped into him, apologised gruffly, and peeled off, the man's wallet in his hand. A few minutes later he was outside, inspecting the ID. It would do, but not for long.

He made his way to a general store which was still open, under grimy paraffin lamps, and found there a suit, shirt and tie which more or less fitted him, and above all comfortable new shoes, telling the unfriendly shopkeeper that he needed them for a wedding. The ready money, counted out slowly in grubby notes, aroused no suspicion. And there was an equally modest hotel down by the Itz, with a room, and a bathroom down the corridor, and no questions asked. They even had packets of smokable cigarettes.

All he needed now was to wash and change. He'd slip out of the hotel as soon as that was done and find some transport and get out of there.

It was nine o'clock and growing dark as he approached the corner of Steintor and Obere Anlage. He saw an untidy young man in a hat standing, his back to him, under a streetlamp. The lamp wasn't lit but he knew who it was. He shrank into the shadow of a church porch.

101

Kessler sensed the movement, for he turned before Hoffmann had time to hide himself completely. The porch was set deep, but there was nowhere else to go now. Hoffmann pressed himself against the carved wall and drew his Walther 9. He could hear Kessler approaching. He slipped off the safety catch. Kessler stopped at the threshold, his shadow fell across it.

'Come out,' he said softly.

Hoffmann stayed where he was.

'I'm alone.'

It's a trap, Hoffmann said to himself. It must be a trap. But then he thought of Emma. His only option other than leaving his hopeless place of concealment was to shoot Kessler, and if Kessler was not alone, then Hoffmann would be dead anyway. He was in check, possibly checkmate. And it had happened so suddenly, so undramatically; and it was not even as if he hadn't been expecting trouble. Perhaps if he hadn't been so tired. If this hadn't come so soon after killing Kirchner. If he hadn't been so preoccupied with getting on to the next stage. All he could now was make the next move and see what happened.

He only needed to walk forward one pace. He did not lower the gun.

***

Kessler seemed embarrassed to have found him. Shyly, he held out his hand. Hoffmann pocketed his gun.

'I congratulate you,' he said. He was furious, and conscious of how dreadful he must look.

'I had a good teacher.'

'It's not over.'

'I can't stay. There's someone on our tail. But he's not here yet.'

'Do you know who it is?'

Kessler hesitated before replying. 'Whoever it is couldn't follow us to that village back there immediately, it was too small, we'd have seen him. So I reckon we've got a day on him. But he'll catch up with us.'

'Is it Schiffer?'

'He had a good teacher too.'

A car approached and drove past. Both men stepped into the deeper shelter of the church doorway.

'I must go.' Kessler looked out across the street. 'I have something for you.'

He took out the whistle and handed it to Hoffmann. 'I hope you manage to give it to Stefan.'

Hoffmann exhaled, covering his fury.

'Emma told me. A long time ago. Don't be angry with her.'

'Where is she? Do you know?'

Kessler hesitated. 'They got her. But she isn't dead, I'm sure of that.'

It took Hoffmann a moment to recover from this. Wasn't Kessler supposed to be looking after her? What had happened? 'How do you know?' was all he said.

'Schiffer. That's what made me wonder about him. It was an anonymous note, but he'd already as good as told me he was on the case.'

'Why did he tell you?'

'He knew what I felt for your daughter. He hated me for it. But what he sent was an official communication. We were working on different aspects of the same investigation.'

Hoffmann was silent.

'I'll find her again. I will.' Kessler's embarrassment had increased. He knew what Hoffmann was thinking. It had been his own first thought, at the news.

'Yes.'

They paused, not knowing what else to say. 'Where will you go?' said Kessler.

'You know better than to ask me that.' Normally, they would both have smiled at that familiar formula.

'I could take our search in another direction,' said Kessler, earnestly.

'They'd notice. They know you're not stupid or they wouldn't have given you the job. You must follow your instinct.'

Kessler hesitated. 'You mean I must follow you?'

'We don't know how much Schiffer knows. Don't flatter yourself. You must continue the chase. Just,' he paused for a moment, 'Just don't be too energetic. This meeting never happened. But you have let me out of checkmate, and I won't forget that.'

'You could have shot me.'

'I still don't know if you are really alone.'

'We thought you would come this way. I found you by accident.'

'Accidents like that are not supposed to happen. When are you leaving?'

'Early tomorrow.'

'Where will you go?'

'I don't know yet.'

Footsteps now, far enough away, but coming closer. Kessler looked at Hoffmann. 'Goodbye, Chief.' And he was gone.

Hoffmann turned and walked swiftly away in the opposite direction. He could not think about what might have happened to his daughter, he could not bear to, he could not afford to. There would be a time for that later. But there was one thing he had to think about. Up until now, his goal and his duty had been clear to him. At the back of his mind, however, the possibility that Emma might be taken had always lurked. Now it had happened. If she wasn't dead, if they had tortured her, if they had tried to wring information out of her which would lead them to him, how much would she tell them? She knew where Stefan was. His only hope was that they would not yet be aware of his existence. Hoffmann had taken every precaution; Stefan had been safe for a decade. Would they know the right questions to ask?

There were still too many holes in the blanket which concealed his son.

Kessler had taken a huge risk. If Schiffer had already got there, and if he had seen the encounter, it would be the end of them. What would become of Emma and Stefan then? How would Kessler himself react to torture?

Hoffmann pushed the thoughts away. The game was not over yet. He needed to leave Coburg quickly. There might be the chance of a train directly to Bamberg, but he didn't want to risk public transport. He felt vulnerable in small towns. Bamberg could wait. Stefan was more important.

102

Tilli's estate lay well on the other side of Bamberg. A car would be too dangerous, draw too much attention, and almost impossible to find. A bicycle would be too slow, though the easiest thing of all to steal.

Another motorbike would be ideal. Motorbikes, Hoffmann thought, fleetingly amused - always motorbikes, like cowboys in Karl May books always have horses: the ideal anonymous fast transport. He'd get out of town, hole up somewhere until dawn, for country roads he didn't know would be too dangerous to negotiate at night, and reach Tilli's district late the following afternoon. Of course they'd be looking for any bike he was lucky enough to steal as soon as its loss was reported, but from their point of view he could have gone in any direction from Coburg, and how many men could a small-town police force spare for an immediate pursuit? But once the Gestapo knew...

He had no means of cutting telegraph lines.

Only important people had access to petrol.

It was late, and there were only a few man and women about. He made his way back to the hotel, and once there wasted no time in washing and changing. By ten he was back on the street. He walked along the river but there was nothing. He doubled back into town, making his way to the station. Here, there was more activity.

Outside the station was a metal rack to which three or four bicycles were chained with heavy padlocks. There were two cars, a Volkswagen and an Adler, and a motorbike, chained to a lamp-post, an old Blucher with a sidecar, its tyres covered with mud, untidily parked in a way that suggested its owner had probably had more than a few beers before he arrived here. But where was he now? There wasn't anyone on the street outside the station, though Hoffmann could see three or four people through the glass doors which led to the station concourse.

The ignition wouldn't be a problem, but starting the thing would make a hell of a noise and he would have to get away immediately. If it took two or three attempts, that would be too long. He'd have to run, and where would he run to? The station square was wide, and he'd be seen before he got to the streets which led into it. The sidecar would be a problem. It made the thing slower and more unwieldy, apart from the fact that the bike itself was unusual, stood out. Could he uncouple it later? Could he afford the time to do so? He had to weigh his chances.

He glanced towards the windows of the station bar, but the blinds were down. He went in. It was busy, full of people, mainly in uniform, but the atmosphere was dull, and the conversation muted. A bunch of morose drunks hunched around the *Stammtisch*. Pity, he could have done with a more raucous crowd. No-one paid him any attention, except the barman, who, irritatingly enough, was immediately attentive, forcing Hoffmann to buy a beer when he would rather have slipped out again without drawing any attention to himself. He drank half of it quickly and left, fearful that the owner of the bike might have returned during his reconnaissance. But outside, all was quiet, and the Blucher still sat there.

One of the men in the bar had to be the owner of the bike. Hoffmann at least knew how to get out of town. But he didn't know how much petrol was in the tank. It wasn't a military bike, but not many people would have access even to such transport as this, these days.

He could wait until the next day, even go back to the hotel. But Kessler and his sergeant would be somewhere in town, and the Gestapo covering them would be here soon, if not already. Hoffmann had made slow progress, and the others would have cars. Staying or fleeing, the risk was as great either way.

He wouldn't get another opportunity. He strode over to the Blucher, stooped as if to tie his shoelace, and deftly picked the padlock holding the chain. After one more glance round, he climbed on, engaging the ignition wires and stamping on the pedal. It fired first time and the engine sounded sweet. What was more, the fuel gauge needlé swung confidently to three-quarters full. Without looking round, he headed out of town.

103

He took a country road south-west towards Schweinfurt, hiding in a wood for most of the night. The following day, he left Bamberg well to the south-west. The roads were mired and going was slow, but there was little traffic. Hoffmann dropped down via Volkach and Dettelbach to Iphofen.

He had one twist of snow left, but he'd keep that until he really needed it, and better not to use it at all, better to keep it as reassurance. He would have to ride out the panic as he rode out this journey, the dangers of which presented themselves to him starkly: anyone within a radius of thirty kilometres of Coburg might recognise this bike. This was an area of small towns, villages, country roads, places in which it would always be hard to take cover. But he'd had no choice, unless to continue on foot, an even greater risk, and he told himself that he was on the home stretch, that he would be with Tilli and Stefan soon, it was vital that he reach them as soon as possible; he would make sure they were safe, and then...

Well, then he would see. He could not plan that far ahead.

He abandoned the bike some way outside Iphofen, concealing it in a copse some way from the road. Iphofen was a tiny place, a large village, but he hoped at least he could buy some food there and then walk the last few miles to Tilli.

He thought about Stefan. Stefan scarcely knew him, but he had accepted him as, vaguely, a godfather. It was important that he shouldn't know there was any blood link between them. Only five people knew the truth. Emma and her aunt were irreproachable, as was Tilli, and, he could only hope, Adamov. He felt easier about Paul Kessler after their recent encounter. Kessler wouldn't have taken that risk without having decided whose side he was on, and besides, even with all his reservations, Hoffmann was beginning to see and accept that Kessler really was bound by his love for Emma. If any other reason was needed, the man was too bright not to see that the Party's sun was setting.

Hoffmann didn't know how much Schiffer knew. He didn't know if Wolf Hagen knew. But if Hagen had known, why had he not acted? He'd had ten years.

They might not have touched Emma. He tried to convince himself of that. It was a slight hope, but it was a real one. Chasing the Party's enemies within the state was one thing, damage limitation in the wake of the defeat which was coming, was another. Brandau had told him an increasing number of so-called privileged prisoners were being held in the camps, dissident politicians, senior army officers who refused to play ball, and their families, whose lives were deemed negotiable. Himmler thought that by these means he could save his own skin when the Führer fell.

There was Brandau too. Brandau had been close enough to him in the old days, and had overheard his phone call to Tilli from Police Headquarters in Berlin only a matter of days - a whole lifetime - ago. If Brandau got through to Switzerland, and if Brandau chose to, he might be helpful. He had contacts, and there were Allied agents in the south now, they all knew that. Had Brandau guessed? But what would he do with the information? And would he - could he - help? He had a more important agenda to attend to than verifying whether or not Hoffmann had another child hidden away somewhere. Yet Hoffmann had to try to guarantee Stefan's safety in every way he could. Stefan no longer had Hoffmann's protection. Tilli knew the score, but Tilli was alone. Stefan was a quarter Jewish. More than enough to condemn him.

The last time he had seen his son was before Christmas, 1943. Tilli had given up the theatre, ceased to visit Berlin, despite invitations from Emmy Göring. She was enjoying her semi-retirement, running her small estate and taking care of Stefan, who had become like a son to her. It was she to whom he was closest, she who organised his education, she who protected him. Officially, he was her nephew. Unofficially, everyone thought they knew he was her love-child by Göring, and everyone respected and indulged that. There had been some trouble about his having a private tutor rather than going to school, but the Görings had supported Tilli's decision, and she had got her way. Neither she nor Hoffmann wanted the boy to be lonely, but better that than to have the kind of education the Party offered in its schools.

Stefan had inherited many of his mother's looks. Her eyes, her cheekbones, but most of all, her manner. Hoffmann had always longed to see more of him; but when he was with him, he had been torn. Sometimes it was like being with Kara's ghost. He'd adopted the role of Stefan's godfather, and didn't use his real name. Stefan treated him, not with suspicion, because he enjoyed the novelty of different company, and the affection and attention, but always with reserve. He was a reserved human being. Hoffmann told himself that was no bad thing.

He was tired. He was edgy, and he decided that now was the time to take his last twist of snow. Once it was gone, it was gone, and he doubted if Tilli would have any, given that he managed to reach her. Perhaps now, at the beginning of the last slope he had to ski down, with the lights of the town almost in view below him, he could do without it until it was all over. he heard his father's voice again: just get down this slope, and you can rest.

He'd need a couple of hours' sleep during the night before continuing, or he would run the risk of making mistakes, and he didn't want to fall at the last fence; but he'd have to get into the countryside to do so. Though this place was small, lost in deep farmland, even here there could be prying eyes. But he needed food too, he'd have to get something.

He'd been fortunate in his stolen documentation: his new identity papers were those of a telephone engineer. As long as he wasn't asked to use skills he didn't have, he'd be all right, since no-one would question his being on the road, though he'd have to be careful if anyone asked how he'd got there. His clothes fitted his profession well, that was something. Could he have hitch-hiked? It didn't sound likely.

He should have thought. He reminded himself that it is always on the home stretch that the fatal mistakes are made. You start to relax. You think you're home before you really are.

104

Dusk had fallen by now. A baker's shop was still open. He could smell it before he saw it. A small place at the corner of a square near the Rödelseer Tor. No-one else about. He must have been the last customer.

She was maybe thirty-five or forty, a strong body and a strong face, dressed in a black cotton print frock which clung to her full breasts, broad hips and buttocks. Dark brown hair curled up over her forehead and fell down over her neck from under a black headscarf streaked with flour. Her eyes were violet blue. In the light from the oil-lamp her skin looked dark and fine.

'You're lucky, I was just about to close,' she said, smiling, though weariness, even sadness, did not leave her eyes.

'On my way to Munich,' said Hoffmann.

'Oh?' She wasn't all that interested. 'I was there once. Before the war. With my husband. What can I do for you? There's not much left.'

'Smells good.'

She smiled again. 'I'm not as good a baker as my husband was, but my Apfelstrudel's not bad. Try some?'

'You'd better wrap it. I've got to get on.'

'No hurry at this time of day, surely. And I'm closed now.' She drew the blinds over the windows and door, and clicked its latch. 'You can leave when you've eaten. There's milk, beer, wine. No tea or coffee. I don't really run a café but there are a couple of tables through there,' she indicated an archway. 'You're going to have to stop to eat. You might as well be comfortable.'

She moved closer to him. He sensed the warmth of her body, and its warm smell mingled with the childhood smell of bread. The lamplight was warm too, and its narrow pool made the interior of the shop seem safe, apart from the world, a sanctuary. Hoffmann was tired. The woman's suggestion made sense, and there was nothing in her manner to rouse his suspicion. She seemed uninterested in him.

'Thank you,' he said. The warmth in the shop was good. For some reason he felt close to tears. He shook his head vigorously and coughed.

'What do you do?' She was just making conversation.

'Why aren't I in uniform, do you mean? I'm a telephone engineer.'

She pursed her lips slightly, shrugged. 'Come on.' She led the way into what turned out to be a tiny dining room. People probably dropped in for a coffee in the old days. Now the place looked neglected, though it was still cosy. She brought the lamp in from the shop, and food and wine.

'My husband's on the East Front somewhere,' she said. 'I haven't heard anything from him for seven months.' Her voice was bleak.

'I'm sorry.'

She paused. 'Do you think there's any hope?'

Dangerous talk, to a stranger. 'I don't know.'

'Eat. Go on. I'm glad you stayed. It's nice to have someone to talk to.' She looked around. 'I'm leaving here when it's over. Go to a big city. Back to Munich perhaps.'

There was suddenly such loneliness in her voice that his tears flowed. He staunched them with the napkin she had given him but they would not stop, and when he tried to apologise, he found he could only sob. This was no good. He couldn't crack now. But she simply laid a hand on his arm and looked at him. The tension flooded through him and out of him, not just the tension of the past days, but of the past years.

He did not know how, but she managed to pull him to his feet and guide him through the shop and to another room, where she placed the oil lamp on a side table and sat next to him on a sofa by a wall. She cradled his head on her bosom and he sank there, letting all his own loneliness and sadness rise to the surface of his mind to be confronted.

She smelt of bread and of fresh grass. The tears ceased, though his head felt heavy, and his chest ached. He knew he should get up and go. He had to leave. Only hours from Tilli's now. A pleasant walk down country lanes edged with birch woods, and over fields. He could be there by lunchtime the following day. If he fell asleep now, this woman could denounce him. He must not fall asleep.

He tried to force his head upward and back, but when she held him, he could not resist. It was too comfortable. He scarcely cared, he found, about the risk he was taking. He had taken so many risks. If they came for him, he had the little Walther in his pocket and he would kill himself before telling them anything, before they could even arrest him. Better than the suicide capsule. More like a gentleman. His head swam. He had eaten and drunk nothing after all. At last he sat up, but he remained by her, and she by him, pressed closely together, their arms about one another, as children might, if lost or threatened, cling to one another for comfort. By turning his head slightly he could feel tears on her cheek, too.

She whispered something to him and stood, a certain insistency about her now. It was forever since he had made love. She led him up a staircase sandwiched between whitewashed walls. Off a small landing one door led to a room almost completely filled by a wardrobe, a dresser and a bed of matching, massive oak. On the bed the huge white eiderdown which covered it was of great softness, and Hoffmann was seduced further by memories of childhood, of his first erotic yearnings in just such a place, wrapped in just such a featherbed.

Hoffmann was well aware what powerful aphrodisiacs comfort, relief and sadness can be. The baker's wife and he cleaved to one another with as much urgency and power as if they were bent on becoming one person. Surely in making love they were preserving themselves against all the horror of the world that had forced itself on their lives and cut them adrift, just two among millions of victims of a handful of greedy men. They hardly paused between each climax, so great was their need, their mouths and hands seeking each other out with something close to desperation, their arms and legs entwined, bruising each other on the wooden bedstead in their passion and not caring, draining each other of every drop of desire.

At last it was spent, and they became all but strangers again. They ate together formally, and when they returned to bed, it was to sleep. But there, as he groaned and muttered, turning, twisting the eiderdown as if he were drowning in it, and once sitting up, eyes open, but not awake, she comforted him, cradled him, wiped his sweating forehead with a towel.

Before dawn she left him to bake her bread. An hour later, washed and shaved, in another set of clean clothes, her husband's, slightly too large - he must have been a huge man - but more comfortable than those he had bought in Coburg, he was ready to leave.

She knew her husband would not return from the East Front. He had tried to comfort her when she spoke of it, but it was then that she excluded him, the only time. She had a new dream to pursue, she would wait out the war and then leave to rebuild her life.

He told her again he was making his way to Munich. She asked no questions, though he knew that she'd sensed he was lying about being a telephone engineer. Would they trace him here? If they came, would they arrest her? Was this another act of selfishness in the long list he burdened himself with? They had given themselves to each other without any thought, but was that excuse enough for him? Should he warn her of the danger he had put her in? He wrote a Munich address on a piece of paper, crumpled it, and left it in the shop where a search would find it quite easily.

They shook hands when they said goodbye.

He headed out of Iphofen towards the rising sun, trying to forget his dreams. The night had left him feeling wounded and cleansed.

105

Even what he could dredge up to his credit, it seemed to him, now looked like attempts to shore up a collapsing building. The Resistance had never had enough cohesion. It was necessary that it should have existed, but where were the brave individuals who had constructed and been part of it? All dead? Few could have escaped the horrific net Hoffmann knew had been cast over the country since Hitler had most recently cheated death.

His thoughts dragged him back to the RAF prisoners who'd haunted his mind only days ago. The business had taken place four months earlier, a lifetime ago.

***

He'd had filing cards with their details inscribed on them stacked on his desk, and after two days of harsh choice he had divided them into two piles, the damned, as he thought bitterly, and the saved. The orders, stemming from the Führer himself, had to go out. He had delayed as long as he could.

But the coded telexes carrying the orders were failing to reach their destinations, the Gestapo offices wherever the recaptured prisoners - only a handful had got clean away - were being held in police custody. Fifty of the airmen were to be executed. The telexes were sent using a simple code, based on prime numbers, which was shifted around every few days. It was unlikely that the enemy had tapped into it. So what was going wrong?

Hoffmann summoned his assistant, Alfons Martens, a young lawyer, who was supposed to be relaying the information without knowing precisely what it implied. When he entered the office, Martens was running his hands through his hair and sweating into his collar.

This wasn't going to be a hard interrogation.

'What's going on, Martens?' Hoffmann asked.

'Sir?'

'The telexes. They're fucked.'

Martens looked even more flustered. 'I'll look into it.'

'You'd better. Müller's breathing down my neck.' Hoffmann leaned forward. 'Sit down.'

'Yes, sir.'

'Worried?'

'No, sir.'

'You do know how to set codes, don't you?'

'Yes, sir.'

'Of course you do. You've been with us three months.'

'Yes, sir.'

'It's your responsibility. What's going wrong?'

Martens hesitated. 'I don't know.'

'I'll ask you again.'

Silence.

Hoffmann remembered that he'd stood up and walked slowly towards the window, drawing a finger along the edge of his desk. There was no way he could take Martens into his confidence, but if Department Four got wind of what Martens was doing - and he was doing it so clumsily that even they would work it out soon - the whole house of cards would come down. If Martens had to be thrown to the lions, so be it.

'Tell me,' he'd said, his back to the room, looking out over the misty city, grey as always, greyer under this March sky.

Martens swallowed. 'I've nothing to say.'

Hoffmann rounded on him. 'Listen, you filthy little arsehole, don't you fucking patronise me. You know who you're talking to? You think I can't tell when some fucking little cunt like you is lying? Tell me!'

Martens looked down, trembling. Good middle-class boy. Not used to language like that. How old was he? Not thirty, certainly.

Hoffmann resumed his seat.

'They haven't got this office wired. Tell me why you are messing up the codes.'

Martens didn't conceal the distaste in his eyes as he gave up. 'It's a barbarous act. It's unworthy of any country, let alone ours. It spits in the face of the Geneva Convention.'

So Martens had found out. Hoffmann didn't blink. 'Atrocities are committed by all sides, in all wars.'

'And that fact justifies them?'

Hoffmann leaned forward. 'Our military situation is critical. These airmen are key personnel. They are already bombing our cities, deep within the country. Haven't you seen the statistics? Tens of thousands of our women and children - not soldiers, *women and children* - are being killed on the orders of that pig-eyed sack of shit, Churchill, and that bloodthirsty fucker, Arthur Harris.' Hoffmann paused. 'They're not even hitting military targets.'

Martens would not look at him.

'Look,' Hoffmann had said. 'Each bomber pilot is an expert. So is his navigator. So is his bomb aimer. Each bomber, each Lancaster, each Wellington, controlled by these three men, has the potential to kill hundreds, maybe more, on each raid. Such men cannot be allowed to get home, and return to murder more of us.'

'I have read the statistics. One per cent of escaped prisoners *ever* make it back. In this case, most of the airmen have been recaptured.'

'That's not the point. The point, in your situation, is whether you would rather be sent to a concentration camp, or hanged right away at Plötzensee. You are a saboteur.'

Hoffmann walked on through the morning, angrily remembering.

'I'm not ashamed,' the young lawyer had said, though his lip was trembling. He knew all about the gallows at Plötzensee.

Hoffmann looked at him. Martens' eyes were staring. He was close to tears. He was looking at his own death, a brutal one, within a day.

Hoffmann considered the situation. No-one else yet knew precisely what was going on. Sometimes despatches were held up, signalling systems broke down. The delay on this one was not yet really suspicious, but it would be well to nip suspicion in the bud. Already Hitler's attention was elsewhere, though it would return; the man never forgot.

'I'm dismissing you,' Hoffmann had said at last. 'You give me no choice. Go home and await orders.'

Martens looked at him angrily, in disbelief, then - almost - in hope. But he wiped that out of his eyes fast. He couldn't bank on being off the hook, even if Hoffmann hadn't ordered his immediate arrest; and his contempt for his superior was boundless.

'You studied criminology as well as jurisprudence, didn't you?'

'Yes.' Martens was ready to bolt, despite himself, just as scared as everyone else.

'At Freiburg, wasn't it?'

'Yes.'

'That's all. Clear your desk on your way out. And Martens - '

'Yes?'

Hoffmann let enough warmth into his voice to give the man hope. 'Don't do anything foolish.'

He followed Martens to the door and watched him cross the outer office, which he shared with the secretary. A woman then, Heidrun Silber. Once Martens had gone - it didn't take him long to scoop his few personal bits and pieces into his briefcase - Hoffmann had Frau Silber place a call to Freiburg University. He returned to his office. After only five minutes she was able to put him through.

He spoke at length. It was fortunate that Professor Pallenberg hadn't left: he was good at wool-pulling too, and he owed Hoffmann a favour. When he had finished, Hoffmann put his head round the door. Frau Silber looked up, her face, as usual, carefully expressionless.

'Frau Silber, Dr Martens is being redeployed to the Department of Criminal Studies at Freiburg. He should leave by the end of this week. Please arrange his travel warrants and send them, and the usual official letter informing him of this change, by special messenger today. And get Dr Palitzsch over here. I'm transferring Martens' duties to him. But, Frau Silber,' he had added, noticing his secretary's mask slip, 'I don't need Dr Palitzsch to change offices. He can stay where he is. He just has to report to me. It's a temporary assignment.'

Frau Silber smiled - just a trace.

Palitzsch was a good Nazi. Someone would have to do the job, and it might as well be him. Besides, if Department Four noticed the appointment of a hard liner, any possible suspicion of Hoffmann might be deflected. But neither he - nor, apparently, Frau Silber - could stand having the man physically near them.

Hoffmann had done his best, all he could - from the filing cards he'd selected the young men with families to be returned to prison camp. As for the other Allied airmen, the Gestapo had received their orders, and the job had been done.

106

It was a fine day, though colder. Summer was losing to autumn.

Was saving Martens all he could think of, saving that handful of airmen, or at least selecting those to be spared who had most need of life - as if he was in any position to judge at all? He had supplied Oster with papers from his department, abetted three attempts on Hitler's life and obscured the investigations which followed them, a hard thing to do if he was to retain his reputation in the Führer's eyes at the same time.

How hard it was to go against the grain, like a musician having to pretend to play badly. For ten years he had gone on like this, little jobs, bigger jobs, never, any of them, culminating in what he was striving for. But he and his colleagues had persevered, some for private reasons, some on principle, some against all their training and learned loyalty to the State, right or wrong. Hitler had been no fool when he'd got the Army to swear an oath of personal loyalty to him.

Hoffmann's own motives had been mixed, but he knew in his heart that the one of them was simple revenge. It had been a long wait, the outcome was still uncertain, and during it he had become a monster.

He remembered the investigation that had followed Kara's death. How their quarry was untouchable. How after months it had dwindled, how he had been obliged to run it down, how his personal interest in it, however well-disguised, had drawn unwelcome attention. Kessler had said nothing, but the work forged a bond between the two men that nothing could break. And meanwhile the killer flourished and his henchmen dispersed, into the SS, into the forces, to disappear in the turmoil of war.

Ten years. Like a dream. Another dream. Wherever it took him, soon it would be finished. Hagen had made a career for himself, iron ore from Sweden, money transfers to the Swiss; he'd even had a hand in selling off the modern art which Hitler loathed for knockdown prices in Lausanne in exchange for the hard currency the Party desperately needed, taking five Picassos for himself. But that had been nothing compared with what had happened after 1942, when he'd been one of the Party's middlemen in the construction and supply of the death camps. He'd creamed off a discreet one per cent of every sales deal he'd made, and on the poison gas shipments alone he had become a millionaire.

But as long as there was money to be made from poison gas, Hagen was probably still in the country. Had he gone to ground in Bamberg, his home town, where he knew the ground and could be confident of protection? American and English bombers were smashing German cities to pulp, but the army was still holding the bastards on the ground. And there was no sign of the death camps closing. In early July, 400,000 Hungarian Jews had been deported to Auschwitz. And the enemy wasn't bombing any of the railway lines to the camps.

Hoffmann cleared his head. Make sure Stefan was safe first. He looked at his watch. The countryside was beginning to look familiar. He'd be there soon.

It was silent. A handful of women working in the fields. It had grown hotter. His clothes were sticking to his back.

He quickened his pace as the road curved over a low hill. From its crest, only a couple of kilometres away to the north east, half-hidden by the dark trees of its driveway, Hoffmann saw at last the yellow walls and red roofs of Tilli's mansion.

107

They were about to leave Coburg when the bike was reported missing.

'It belongs to someone called Zimmermann. Big farmer round here,' said the local cop. 'He's furious.'

'I'm sure,' said Kessler.

'Any idea what direction it's gone?' asked Kleinschmidt.

The local cop shook his head. 'Not yet. We've sent patrols towards Nuremberg, Frankfurt, Bayreuth and Erfurt. But there are no tyre tracks and whoever it was could be anywhere by now.'

It was six o'clock in the morning. Kleinschmidt yawned vastly as they left the police station, and, coughing and hawking, lit a cigar. 'So, what do we do? Hang around until they come up with something?'

'Could take days,' said Kessler, wondering which way Hoffmann had gone, having a fair idea.

'If it's our man, he won't have gone north, so that rules out Erfurt.'

'If it's our man.'

'Well, we've got to do something.'

'Frankfurt?'

'No.' Kleinschmidt considered. 'You said we should check out Bayreuth and Bamberg. Means going south-east and then back west.'

'Why not Frankfurt?'

'Enemy's in that direction. But he'd have to be a born bloody optimist to think he'd get as far as them. They're in north-western France. We'll push 'em back into the fucking sea.'

'Plenty of contacts in Frankfurt.'

Kleinschmidt shrugged. 'You're the boss.'

Kessler had his own plans. He lit a cigarette. 'We'll go south. Forget about Bayreuth. We'll head straight for Nuremberg. Bamberg's on the way. It's not that big, we can talk to the local people there, see if they've picked anything up.'

Kleinschmidt sucked his teeth. 'Long shot. Both those towns are stiff with Nazis. Would he be likely to stick his head in the lion's mouth?' He paused. 'But, like I said, you're the boss.'

'Then let's go.'

'You'd better phone in first. Let Berlin know what you're up to.'

It hadn't slipped Kessler's mind; he was just sorry that Kleinschmidt had reminded him.

108

The Blucher motorbike was still missing twenty-four hours later, when Schiffer arrived in Coburg, tired, dirty, and irritated to have lost so much ground. He'd wasted time in the village too, rooting around for himself, going over the burnt-out BMW and the damaged baggage Hoffmann had abandoned, convinced an overlooked clue would reveal itself. However, there'd been too much trampling over the ground, the bike had been moved, no-one had expected another investigator to turn up, and Bauer resented the presence of another Gestapo man even more than he had the presence of the regular police.

Schiffer had no Hitler-Order either, and had to keep his real job - keeping Kessler under surveillance - quiet. He had no business to be doing any direct investigation at all, though he burned to do so. He longed to steal a march on that cocky little academic, and run Hoffmann to ground himself. But despite his desires, his former colleague hadn't put a foot wrong yet; if he had, he'd concealed it well.

Which was probably why, when he'd rung Berlin from Leipzig to apply for permission to arrest Kessler and take over the job himself, he was sharply turned down and, moreover, rebuked, despite the way he'd described the situation, painting Kessler in the worst possible light. He hadn't liked the rebuke. It had humiliated him; he saw in it the implication that Kessler was the better man.

The rebuke also reminded him of his position. He'd overreached himself, played his hand far too soon, let his ambition rule his reason, maybe even let his promotion go to his head. The fact was, he was still an underling. This was a job carrying a great deal of trust with it, he knew; but he knew why he was there: he was another Hoffmann-trainee. But he was an also-ran. They hadn't given the actual task of *hunting* Hoffmann to him.

Schiffer calculated his position, and with it, his future. After his gaffe, he'd have to work hard to redeem himself. Did Kessler know he was being shadowed? He'd have considered the possibility. Kessler had told Scholtz that he was making his way to Coburg, and he'd told them in the presence of his sergeant, so it was probably true. Schiffer was certain that Kessler would contrive not to corner their old boss. The men were too close, had been for years, Kessler wasn't even in the Party. *He* should have been given the job, *he* knew how Hoffmann's mind worked too. He felt slighted.

Maybe, Schiffer thought again, despite himself, he'd taken the wrong career turn with the Gestapo. At the time, the move seemed a better option than remaining in the police. Quicker promotion, greater standing, more clout, more money. And when he'd worn his uniform on formal occasions, what a tart-trap that had turned out to be.

Not that he cared much. They were all tarts, women. He never seemed to have much luck with them, and, once it was over, he quickly lost interest, hated the sweaty sheets, the smell. He wanted to be with one person, to be true to her. He wanted a family, a quiet life, a future. He wanted so many things. Above all, he wanted his integrity back. He could have wept for its loss, but could not see how he might make his way back.

He wanted to leave. He'd been fighting the niggling thought down for months, it had been that business with the RAF men that had started it off. He'd been detailed to one of the assassination parties. Total bloody cock-up that had been, up near Danzig. They'd driven four of them out into the countryside, one of them Free French, the others Brits, and shot them in a field. Schiffer hadn't recovered from that, but he'd never believed in Party principles anyway, and, although he had no love for the enemy, especially enemy airmen, shooting them in the back and not even making clean kills disgusted him.

What was there left to believe in? Some of them, back in Berlin, still thought that Jews and Communists and Freethinkers were a menace to society, and that cleansing it of them was the only principled thing to do, but they were like people clinging to planks in the sea after a shipwreck, clinging to ideas like that. Was he one of them, only without whatever conviction they had?

He wanted to leave, but he didn't know how to get away. He was trapped in his job; the only way out would be to desert, and that would mean death if he was caught. He'd be lucky if all they did was shoot him. Kessler was the lucky one. Kessler got the girl and what turned out to be the plum job. In an obscure way too, Schiffer realised that Kessler was more of a survivor than he was. But if Kessler wasn't around to taunt him with his success, maybe he'd breathe more easily.

His thoughts churned. He'd made the wrong choices. He was a loser. He didn't like facing these ideas, but during his time on the road alone they came to him thick and fast. He struggled against self-pity; it was hard late at night when he lay in bed, vulnerable as the child he could hardly believe he'd once been, but still feeling like a frightened eight-year old. It was hard, too, when he woke before dawn, eyes gritty with sleep, longing to return to it, beset by thoughts which would not let him go.

There was one ray of light. One line of escape that might be available to him if he chose to take it. It was not one his better self would have chosen, but he was so mired now that his better self was half-forgotten; and the door was open, and the light that came from beyond it seemed warm and welcoming. In the meantime, he had his job to do.

He decided he would hang around in Coburg until early afternoon, in case news of the stolen bike came in, though he hadn't much hope. He needed to rest, and he needed to talk to his Gestapo colleagues. From the outset he had decided to avoid unnecessary contact with the regular police, for fear they'd let news of his presence slip to Kessler. No point in giving the bastard any rope, he was too clever as it was.

He'd get him yet. Perhaps that was the only thing to do, Schiffer thought. Keep an eye on the simple goals. get on with it, wherever it led, and worry about the consequences later. In a hard world you had to be hard. He'd put his doubts behind him and keep gambling on the numbers he'd backed: as if he had a choice.

109

Early in the afternoon, bone weary, Schiffer set off towards Nuremberg. He flexed his cramped hands on the wheel of his car and glared at the postcard-pretty countryside through his fly-spattered windscreen. Soon after he had left, the Coburg police got a phone call: the old Blucher had been found in a wood, well covered with cut fir branches, a couple of kilometres from the little town of Iphofen. It hadn't been damaged in any way. This was good news, as Zimmermann carried a lot of weight in the district.

Kessler and Kleinschmidt drew a blank in Bamberg, though they split up to save time. When they reconvened Kleinschmidt smelled strongly of *Rauchbier* and Kessler guessed that any snooping his sergeant had done was well within range of *Zum Schlenkerla*. The Nuremberg road was closed owing to an accident - the local cops said a lorry had hit an ox-cart, killing one of the beasts, and overturning, blocking the way both north and south - so they were forced to spend the night. Kleinschmidt knew the town, and got them rooms at an inn near the centre, *Die Blaue Glocke*, run by some people he knew, Max and Barbara Peßler. They listened to Max playing the zither late into the night. Kleinschimdt probably drank too much *Michelsberger*.

The following morning the road was clear again and they set off early, to Kleinschmidt's disgust. Real city boys are seldom early risers, he complained to Kessler. They were only two reasons for waking early, maintained Kleinschmidt: to make love or to make money. Kleinschmidt didn't look as if he'd ever been successful at either.

They reached Nuremberg late in the morning, passing the wrecked truck, which had been dragged to the side of the road. When they arrived to make their routine check-in at the Police Praesidium, they were surprised to find that they were expected. The police here, in the Party's heartland, where the great rallies had been held, were keen to be associated with the hunt. Coburg had rung ahead.

'When did they find it?' Kessler asked.

'Where the fuck's Iphofen?' Kleinschmidt grumbled.

Kessler thought how unlucky it was that the bike had been discovered so soon. Not due to police efficiency, it turned out, just bad luck. A couple of kids, fourteen-year-olds, a boy and a girl, looking for somewhere to have a quiet snog, had discovered it. They thought the pile of fir branches was an inviting-looking hillock to lie on. The boy had playfully thrown the girl down onto it and she'd cracked two ribs on the sidecar.

Not far away the police had found a colossal old kitchen knife - the thief must have used it to cut down the branches to cover the bike, but in doing so, he'd broken the blade.

As they drove west towards Iphofen, Kessler tried to arrange his thoughts. If he could not get himself taken off the case, or bring it to a conclusion, then he wanted the chase to lead them to Munich. He also knew that not far from Iphofen lay the estate of Tilli Cassirer. That was common knowledge, and it worried him, though fewer people now knew how close she and Hoffmann had been in the past, and he knew that Hoffmann had been careful to play down that friendship, after Tilli had left Berlin and the theatre more-or-less permanently a decade or so ago. But if Hoffmann was making for Tilli's mansion, instead of heading for the frontier, that could only mean one thing.

Kessler had burned his own bridges when he had let Hoffmann go in Coburg. Yet the dark thought crawled into his mind once again that he might still arrest his former chief - even if that meant the betrayal of both Tilli and Stefan - and use the cachet which he would thereby gain to rescue Emma, who need never know - perhaps - the means by which she had been saved. But how could he guarantee that? And how sure was he that he could live with himself in such a case?

Well, he would see what Iphofen held for them. Kleinschmidt was having trouble finding it in the maze of un-signposted, similar-looking country roads. He cursed the landscape and the unhurried attitude of every yokel from whom he asked directions. He even cursed the Party, a dangerous thing to do in anyone's hearing unless they were family, or friends of years' standing, and even then you had to think twice. 'The whole fucking thing's going down the tubes,' he moaned. 'I mean, what do you do with a place where the only efficient thing they can do is keep those trainloads of Jews running to bloody Auschwitz?'

It sat uncomfortably with his earlier patriotic confidence that the Germans would soon push the enemy back into the Atlantic, thought Kessler, and he wondered how Kleinschmidt had come to hear of Auschwitz. But what he said was true enough. They themselves barely had enough resources for important investigations, troop trains for carrying the wounded back from the crumbling East Front were constantly being delayed or cancelled, and yet the railway lines leading to the camps hummed with inexorable traffic.

He thought about the camps, trying to imagine them. He knew that Hoffmann had had something to do with them, and he wondered how the man could live with that. Hard labour camps were what they were supposed to be, though no-one seemed to know much about what kind of hard labour.

'About fucking time,' said Kleinschmidt, driving over a pretty medieval bridge which spanned a clear little river that sparkled in the sunlight, and then past an abandoned or deserted road-block. Beyond it, a neat, red-roofed town huddled in the lee of a low hill. 'Now, where do we start?'

It wasn't the easiest of questions to answer. There was a small police station, but apart from details of the finding of the bike, which added nothing to their knowledge, the lazy official knew no more, and cared less. The mayor's office yielded nothing. It was still relatively early, but a door-to-door of the place would take forever, small as the town was.

'We'll try the shops,' Kessler decided. 'Shopkeepers are the most likely people to have noticed a stranger.'

'If he came here at all, *if* it was him.'

'Better suggestion?'

'Lunch.'

'Later.'

Kessler squared his shoulders, feeling them ache after the long hours in the car, and prayed they'd find nothing. If Hoffmann had been here, he wouldn't have left a trace, not so close to his goal.

110

There weren't many shops, and they drew a blank at most. The butcher thought he might have seen someone pass his shop at the end of the afternoon, but he described a thin, small man in labourer's clothes. The tailor-and-haberdasher seemed frightened of something, but they decided it was just the police presence that scared him. Kleinschmidt leant on him a bit too heavily, but Kessler reined him in - they weren't going to complicate matters by arresting a homosexual who'd been lucky enough to escape the net so far.

The sixth place they tried, nearly the last, was the second baker's, on a corner near the Rödelseer Tor. An attractive woman in early middle age stood behind the counter, serving an elderly couple dressed, for some reason, in their Sunday best. The man had a dark brown pinstripe suit, a silver *edelweiss* in his buttonhole, with a white shirt, collar and cuffs frayed, buttoned up to the neck, but tie-less. He had a white goatee, and wore a brown trilby. His wife, back bent by some rheumatic condition, was in a black dress sprigged with tiny white flowers, and a white hat with a grey ribbon. They had a courtly air about them, and as they left, the man raised his hat to them. Kessler noticed when she looked at them that the wife's eyes had a vacant, anxious, overcast look. They were pale with age. Her lips moved without ceasing. She was repeating Hail Marys, endlessly. The man noticed Kessler's expression, and returned it with one that was defensive and apologetic.

Even Kleinschmidt realised the futility of questioning them, and for once was silent, his eyes straying to the loaves and cakes sparsely ranged in baskets and on shelves. He breathed in appreciatively.

The woman behind the counter was looking at them with a mixture of curiosity and suspicion.

'Police, Criminal Brigade,' said Kessler. 'Don't be alarmed. Just a few questions. We're asking everybody.'

'I see,' the woman smoothed her hands on her apron.

'How much for an *Apfelstrudel*?' asked Kleinschmidt.

'Help yourself.'

'Very generous. Thank you.' He took two, cradling them in his handkerchief and balancing one as he ate the other.

'That couple - who were they?' asked Kessler.

'He used to be the butler at the big house. Looks after his wife now.'

'Have they been somewhere special?'

'They always dress like that. He likes to keep up appearances. I think it helps him.'

'Looks like she's lost her fucking mind,' said Kleinschmidt.

'You were chatting to them,' said Kessler to the woman, and glaring at his sergeant.

'They come in every day.'

'Talking about anything in particular?'

She looked evasive but although the expression was gone in a moment, Kessler had caught it. 'No, the usual things, the weather, the cost of living ... ' she trailed off. 'Would you like anything to eat?'

'I'm fine, thank you. So, nothing out of the ordinary?'

'No.'

'I expect you're wondering why we're here.'

Kleinschmidt had started his second *Apfelstrudel*, but was watching the woman now, and she was aware of that. She waited.

'Did you know they'd found a motorbike just outside town?'

'No.'

'Really? I thought it might have cropped up in conversation. You know how news travels, and everybody comes to the baker's.'

'I don't do as well as Herr Poehlmann.'

'You should do,' put in Kleinschmidt. 'These Strudels are delicious.'

'Thank you.'

'I wish I could take you away and keep you. I might even put on a bit of weight.' Kleinschmidt managed to attach a hint of threat to the compliment, and she looked frightened. Kessler could see what Kleinschmidt was doing, but at the same time was repelled by it. There wasn't any need to lean on the woman so hard. These days, both the cops knew, the slightest suggestion of being taken away by the police, whatever the context, was enough to scare the shit out of most people.

'So, nothing about the bike?'

'No.'

'Are you hesitating?'

'Someone may have mentioned it. I didn't pay much attention. My husband's away at the Front, he'll be home soon, meanwhile I have my hands full with this place.' She rubbed her hands on her apron again, looked beyond them through the shop windows into the deserted street, as if some help might come from there.

'Served any strangers lately?' asked Kleinschmidt idly.

'What?'

'You know, people from out of town.'

'No.' But again, the hesitation.

'Come on, darling,' said Kleinschmidt, his mouth full of the last morsel of apfelstrudel. 'You were seen.'

Sometimes, rarely, it was that easy. But only with people who weren't used to the police, and were terrified of them. Kessler watched her face as it struggled with the decision between betrayal and survival. He didn't want her to have to go through any more of Kleinschmidt's bullying, and he didn't want to have to arrest her. He motioned to Kleinschmidt to shut up.

'Tell us what you know,' he said. 'Then we'll go, and you won't see us again.'

So she told them. When she'd finished, before she'd finished, Kleinschmidt started prodding around the shop. He knew the usual places to look. Wedged between the till and the counter's edge, he found a scrap of paper, on it, an address.

'What's this?'

She shook her head. Kleinschmidt handed the piece of paper to Kessler.

Kessler was delighted. A Munich address. Perfect. Now he was quite certain of what Hoffmann had done. He recognised the handwriting. Perhaps he was meant to.

'Are you sure you know nothing about this?' Kessler asked the woman.

'Certain.'

'How often do you clean this place?'

'The shop? Every day.'

'And this man you've suddenly decided to tell us about left the day before yesterday?'

'Yes.'

'You've got a fucking short memory,' said Kleinschmidt nastily.

The woman looked petrified.

'If we find out that you're lying, we'll be back,' said Kessler.

'Why didn't you arrest her?' said Kleinschmidt as soon as they were outside.

'We got what we wanted. We're not going to waste any more time.'

'We could at least have held her until we've verified the address.'

'If it's false, how would she know?'

'If it's him, why would he be stupid enough to give her an address at all?'

'He didn't give it to her. He just got rid of it.'

'Then why didn't he burn it, instead of stuffing it somewhere it'd be found?'

'He was in a hurry. It wouldn't have meant a thing to anyone but us. A scrap of paper with an address. If it's anything at all to do with him in the first place. At any rate, it's all we've got to go on, it's late, and I don't want to end up having to spend the night here.'

'I'll drink to that.' Kleinschmidt seemed half convinced.

Kessler looked at his watch. 'Can we make it back to Nuremberg tonight?'

'If it kills me,' said Kleinschmidt.

Kessler looked back as they got into the car. Through the window of the shop he could see the woman, leaning over her counter, her head up, staring into space. God alone knew what she was thinking. He wondered how long Hoffmann had spent with her. He wondered what they would have talked about.

'Get us there by seven,' he said to Kleinschmidt, trying to keep the jubilation out of his voice, 'and I'll buy you as much Leberkäse as you can eat and as much Lammsbräu as you can drink.' He didn't want his sergeant to have any second thoughts.

Kleinschmidt roared, and slammed his foot onto the accelerator.

111

Emma Hoffmann looked around her at her fellow-travellers. Men, women and a handful of children, climbed aboard two canvas-topped trucks parked in the mist just outside the high walls of Dachau Concentration Camp. All wore civilian clothes, not the striped pyjamas and cap worn by most of the inmates, but inmates they clearly were, to judge from their weary faces and posture.

Their clothes too, had an air of having been worn too long, of dampness, and of a greyness that matched the lorries they were climbing onto. Each carried a small bag containing personal belongings, Emma, frightened and thin, in a threadbare black coat, still had her violin in its battered case as well.

Some of the faces were drawn, some showed fear, some apprehension; others were still proud, many were blank. They were herded by SS in steel helmets and greatcoats, rifles slung over their shoulders, and the three officers in charge had their service pistols in their hands.

But there were no dogs , no cudgels or whips, and there was none of the shouting, the orders screamed, the brutal pushing and shoving, the rifle butts rammed into the small of the back, the kidneys, the neck. One elderly man stumbled and two soldiers hastened to help him to his feet, quickly bundling him up to join the others seated on the benches that ran along either side of each lorry. There was an escort of four motorbikes.

The operation started at dawn, at about four. An officer and a driver climbed into each cab, and the lorries started up, the noise of their engines sounding muted, covert. Two guards climbed into the back of each truck and sat opposite each other in the last places before the tailgates, which were hauled up and bolted. The canvas flaps at the back were drawn together and buttoned shut.

The trucks rumbled forward, jolting the passengers as they rolled over the rough ground and onto the road. The passengers heard a much louder clatter as the motorbikes started up. They sat silently, allowing their eyes to become accustomed to the gloom, eyes glinting. The soldiers lit up, leant forward, arms on their knees, awkward in their greatcoats, rifles balanced between their arms. They did not talk to each other.

The trucks drove along in silence for perhaps half an hour. Once, the passengers heard the powerful roar of a train passing nearby.

Some of the passengers knew each other. They had exercised together in the sequestered compound they had shared, apart from the main camp. Others had shared a barrack, carved, unlike the main barracks, into private rooms by means of planking walls. No-one knew if conversation was allowed, and for some time no-one spoke.

Emma was aware of a man sitting near her, a cadaverously thin man in a black overcoat and hat, who had a look of great concentration on his face, which intensified each time their lorry changed direction. Some of those close to him were watching him. At last, keeping an eye on the guards, he said, almost to himself:

'East. And now, north.'

Out of Dachau then. And away from Munich. But where to? None of them was sure. To their deaths, some thought, since they all had one thing in common: they, or people close to them, by blood, or friendship, or even just by association, had offended the Party. Most of them were old enough to have grown up in a democracy. To live in a State in which a careless remark could lead to denunciation and death was something which even now, and the thin man had been an inmate eleven years, since the camp's foundation, they found difficult to grasp.

Emma wondered how he knew where they were going, as the twists and turns of the lorry's route would only have confused her, even if she'd known the direction in which they'd departed.

'There are some things you don't forget,' said the thin man to no-one in particular. 'Before I had to give up my job I was the city cartographer. I drew the town plans for 1923, 1927 and 1931.'

'Quiet!' said one of the guards. But he didn't yell the word, or even snap. He sounded almost bored, an automatic reaction. 'We've a long way to go,' he added, almost apologetically. He exchanged a glance with his companion. They checked their cigarette packets, decided they had enough to indulge in another fag now, lit up.

His companion unbuttoned the flap, raised it and looked out. The passengers craned to get a glimpse of a grey road winding behind them through a nondescript landscape of spindly trees and low brick buildings. The outskirts of the town?

Some way behind them, the second lorry strained along. No sign of the bikes. Two would be ahead of the first truck, the other two behind the second.

The thin man said aloud: 'Will you allow us to talk?'

'Strictly forbidden,' said the guard. He was about eighteen.

'You can hear every word we say. Do you know where we're going?'

'Classified.'

311

Probably the only people who did know were the drivers and the officers in the cabs.

'Talk if you must. But keep it down,' said the other soldier, the same age as the first, less scared.

'Heini - ' protested the first.

'What the fuck. Where do they think they're going? Fucking home?'

Those casual words sent a cold bolt through the other passengers. Only the man on Emma's right, a man about her father's age in the uniform of a regular army general, did not stiffen at them. Emma noticed that nothing had been stripped from the uniform, none of the insignia at all.

The general's face was distantly familiar, but he had one of those faces that seemed to hide behind, or go with, such a uniform: tanned skin, grey eyes, grey hair, still a strong jawline for a man of maybe fifty. He sat in the same attitude as the soldiers, bent forward, arms on knees. Emma noticed that the soldiers cast the occasional anxious glance at him, and they did not object when he himself lit up.

'They're not going to kill us,' he said, looking at her with tired kindness.

'How do you know?'

'Why move us? Petrol's scarce. It wouldn't make any sense at all.'

'They might want to keep it quiet.'

He laughed drily. 'Listen: I've spent the last five years protecting this lot. I was recalled to Berlin not even a fortnight ago and they arrested me there. I'm lucky. I hardly know what Dachau's like. But I've learned some things since I've been an inmate. People they execute, they send the family a bill for the bullets. They're good little economists. They're not going to waste petrol on people they're going to kill. And there's another thing.'

'What's that?'

'Do you notice any Jews among us?'

Emma was silent.

112

Remembering himself, the general dug into his pocket and took out his cigarette tin, which he opened. In it were five rolled cigarettes.

'I'm sorry. Would you care for...?'

'No, thank you.' Emma was dying for one, but realised how much more he needed them, and sensed the background reluctance, well concealed though it was, in his polite gesture. What's bred in the bone...

He put the tin back.

The rode on in silence. The General smoked quietly, husbanding his cigarette, the roll-up which sat oddly with the uniform. Though scarcely immaculate, it still carried a tarnished dignity. It looked as if he had just returned in it from battle.

Despite the guards' absolution, few people spoke. Occasionally someone asked the thin man if they'd changed direction, but that must have been merely for the sake of saying something, because for two hours the route remained steady and unvarying. One or two people began to squirm or look embarrassed, and the thin man, who'd been in prison since his guards were children, who was himself a man of sixty, called over to them: 'I think we need to stop.'

One of the guards stumbled between the rows of legs forwards towards the pane of glass separating the cab from the body of the truck, and rapped on it. A few moments later, the convoy drew to a halt.

'Men to the left, women to the right,' ordered the guards, climbing out and unslinging their rifles. One covered the men, the other, the women.

'No-one goes out of sight!'

They were well out of any town now, they'd stopped in a sun-dappled valley. Green meadows sloped up and away from them. Below the road, which curved along the left side of the dale, a slender river wound, glistening like mercury in the sun. A few trees - beeches - dotted around, provided a bit of shelter. One middle-aged woman sought it.

'Not behind the fucking trees!' shouted one of the motorcyclists at her, 'Where we can fucking see you!'

She hastened back into the open, and squatted awkwardly on the sloping hill.

The thin man didn't need to piss. He stood instead and drank in the view. It had, after all, been eleven years since he had seen anything but grey walls and death.

Squatting, Emma worried about her violin. It was still in the lorry.

The passengers found their places again, and a cautious bonhomie crept in as they set off. It was good to be out of Dachau, whatever might happen next. The guards produced a bottle of Himbeergeist, offering it to those nearest them, and a bag of boiled sweets, which were passed round. For half an hour, everyone talked more freely. Then the deadening unrelieved motion of the lorry took over, people became subdued, and finally there was silence.

Emma was relieved that her violin had not disappeared in her absence. No-one had lost anything, in fact. She was young, she had already adapted to her new situation, and she would, she hoped, survive it. Her father, her lover, her friends, even her beloved aunt, had become remote, like people in a dream - how quickly that seemed to have happened.

The rhythm of the lorry's motion made her doze. She dreamt. She was in a field, playing the clarinet to an audience of white geese. There was a long low building at the edge of the field but she could not see what was going on there. Her half-brother was there too. Odd, because she hadn't seen him for two years and he had almost disappeared from her thoughts.

Something sharp was pushing into her cheek. She had let her head fall onto the shoulder of her neighbour. It was the corner of an epaulette pushing against her face that had awakened her.

The general's eyes were closed. Emma had no idea what time of day it was, or of how long she had slept. Was it late afternoon? Surely not. She was hungry.

He woke as she moved. He noticed the red skin on her cheek. He touched it.

'Uniforms make bad pillows.'

'I'm sorry. I fell asleep.'

'So did I. And look around you.'

Most of the passengers were asleep, including the guards - their heads were nodding, lips jutting. They looked much younger, even, than they were.

'Where are we going?'

'I have no idea. But I think we'll be safe.'

'How do you know?'

'It's logical. We are Himmler's bargaining chips. Think. A mother rat in a sewer moves her young to a safer nest when the water starts to rise. That's what he's doing with us.'

'When is this going to end?'

'In the Spring. In the Autumn, next year, at the latest.'

'How do you know?' she said again.

He shrugged, and smiled faintly. 'I'm a general. I know what an army's limits are. The Americans are fresh and well-fed, and they have new and limitless supplies. It was a mistake to assume that, for all their posturing, they would leave England in the lurch. As for the Russians, we have made them suffer so terribly that they will be merciless to us, and they have oil. Our leader made the same mistake that Napoleon made. It's only a matter of time now.'

'And what about us?'

'With luck, we'll ride out the storm. The fools who've destroyed Germany and mortgaged its honour will be replaced - no doubt by other fools, but the next bunch will at least, one hopes, not be criminally insane. How long have you – ?'

'About the same as you. I was in hiding. I was warned that I should leave Berlin but I took my time. I didn't realise they could move so fast.'

'The Gestapo? Nor did I.'

'What did you – ?'

The general glanced in the direction of the guards. 'It doesn't matter now. There was... an idea... some of us had... ' he hesitated. 'We thought we might be able to get rid of him. But we made a balls of it. I was down near the Swiss frontier. They recalled me to Berlin. As soon as I arrived, I was arrested. I thought it'd be a firing squad *instanter*. But here I am.' He paused, took out his tin of cigarettes.

'Go on. Have one.'

'Really?'

'Really.'

Gratefully, she took one.

'What are *you* in for?' He smiled again.

'I don't know... ' It was the girl's turn to hesitate. 'My father... he was in the police... I think he may have been involved in the same business as you.'

'Where is he now?'

'I don't know.'

'What's his name?'

She wondered whether she should tell him, but she told herself that of all possible *plants* - and spies were scattered among the prisoner population, she had been warned - he was the least likely to be one. She also had a vague memory of having met him, somewhere, before. Or maybe it was just because he looked a bit like her dad.

'My name's Emma Hoffmann,' she said.

He sat up. 'Max's daughter?'

'Yes. Who are you?'

'My name's Richter.'

'You know my dad?'

'Well... ' he paused and she knew exactly what he was thinking. One learned fast in the camps. 'Yes. Only in passing. I came to dinner at your house once. It must have been in - when? - 1930?'

'I was six then. Later, I didn't live with my father. I didn't know what he was doing. Did you?'

'No. We kept apart as far as possible. In case anyone was taken.'

'Have you seen him since?'

113

Klaus Richter hesitated again. What harm could it do to tell her, even if she were a spy - which he could scarcely believe - but, he reflected, if he told her he'd met Hoffmann on the road and let him go, and she reported it, his own neck would be on the block. Hating himself, at the same time he decided it was better to be safe than sorry.

'No,' he said. 'I haven't seen him in years.'

She cast her eyes down in disappointment. 'I'm going to nip this cigarette out if you don't mind. Keep the rest for later.'

'I remember you played the violin for us. That one?'

'No. How embarrassing. Did my parents make me? I've only had this one since I was thirteen.'

'How old are you now?'

'Twenty.'

His face sank into sadness. 'I hope you make it.'

'I hope we all make it.'

'Listen,' he said.

'Yes?'

'When they arrested you –'

'Yes?'

'Did they harm you?'

She looked into herself, her eyes darkened. 'They showed me things, gadgets, I don't know, simple things, tools, pliers, a hacksaw, and a candle with barbed wire embedded in the wax - but they didn't use them. They interrogated me. They asked me if I knew where he was. That's all. They brought me to Dachau on a train.'

The general was silent.

'If they'd used any of those things I would have told them anything. But they only asked if I knew where he was. They didn't ask anything about – ' She stopped herself.

'What?'

'Anything else,' she said. 'Not that there was anything else I could have told them. Did they torture you?'

317

He smiled. 'They knew all about me. I'd been denounced in Berlin. God knows how I was lucky enough to escape the gallows. Thank you, Papa Himmler!'

Perhaps she was all right. Perhaps he would tell her he'd seen Max. But not yet.

They were climbing a long hill. It was mid-afternoon. They'd stopped once on the journey apart from the pit-stop, and the guards had given each of the passengers a cup of water. But no food. No food for anyone. Now the trucks came to a halt. The passengers could hear the motorbikes rev before switching off. The engines of the lorries died too. There was silence for a moment, and a kind of peace. No movement any more. The passengers could feel the sun through the canvas.

The guards opened the flaps, lowered the tailgate and jumped down, one standing on each side of the back of each truck to marshal the prisoners off. They found themselves in a huge gravelled yard. They were drawn into ranks. A little above them still, on the crest of the hill they'd been climbing, loomed a fortress.

The two officers stood before them. 'Welcome to Schloß Kupferstein,' one of them said. 'Your new home.'

114

As the trucks that took Emma Hoffmann and General Klaus Richter from Dachau to Kupferstein left town that morning for the north, the train their passengers heard passing them was heading for Munich. It was a night train from Berlin, badly-timed, ahead of schedule, and it drew to a halt in front of the buffers at the *Hauptbahnhof* at a quarter to five in the morning. People unglued themselves from sleep and left the fug of their compartments unwillingly for the gritty morning air and the coal-and-oil smell of the station.

The black locomotive let off steam with a sharp hissing wail, which made a little boy in the crowd jump, which in turn made one of the passengers, a man with a lizard-like face, laugh. He must have been strong, for he was managing two large black cases, and refused any help from a porter.

'Oh, fuck,' gasped Veit Adamov, finally dumping the cases in the station bar and ordering a slivovitz and an ersatz coffee. But he was grinning once he'd drunk them both, and looked around.

'So far, so good,' he said to himself. Leipzig-Berlin-Munich. All by train. More or less on time. He deserved another drink.

He knew where to go. And though he was early, they had a car waiting for him.

'Ulli!' he said to the bulky man in the pearl grey suit and matching borsalino who stood in the middle of the station's main entrance. 'Got a cigarette?'

The man grinned. 'Genuine Lucky Strikes,' he said. 'Let's get this shit in the car.'

They drove through the battered city until they reached a restaurant with its blinds down. They unloaded the cases and went past what looked like abandoned chairs and tables to a spacious room at the back, which contained a number of packing cases. Metal shelving along the walls were stacked with film canisters.

'Are you sure this is safe?' asked Adamov, shoving the larger and heavier of the two cases into a gap Ulli indicated on the shelving.

'No-one else knows this is here. The restaurant's been closed for six months now. I'm the caretaker. Perfectly legit.'

'Hmmn.' Adamov was doubtful. Some of the best fruits of his labours over the past ten years - *Red Riding Hood, Beauty and the Beast, The Robber*

319

Bridegroom, Aschputtel - and what he hoped would be the foundation of his fortune in the new life he planned for himself, were contained in that case.

'Don't worry. None of the others knows about this place.'

'Well, I won't be here long. Thanks, Ulli.'

'No problem - we owe you. The other boys are looking forward to seeing you too. Big George says we're to look after you - anything you want.'

'How are things here?'

Ulli was uncorking a bottle. 'Here we are - real *Fürst Bismarck*. Better than the southern crap they give you here.' He poured two large glasses. 'Mind you, it's not cold. Cheers!'

'Cheers.' Adamov was still tense.

'Big George is sitting it out. No big stuff, just a little snow, a few girls. Only thing to do is keep your head down til the Yanks come. Be rich pickings then.'

'What about the competition?'

'Plenty for everyone!'

'You sure the Ammis'll reach Munich before the Russians?'

'May I never get any more cunt if they don't.' Ulli refilled their glasses.

'So who else is here?' asked Veit, drinking. He hadn't eaten since the previous evening and the coffee, the slivovitz, and now this schnapps were making him light-headed. The Luckies didn't help, either. But he felt good, too, relieved, refreshed. He was on his way. Old friends had stayed loyal. Nothing would stop him now. Why was he still nervous, then? Why did he need to cushion himself with drink? He knew how dangerous that was; but with every fresh shot he felt more comfortable.

'The Monbijous are here,' said Ulli, pouring another. 'What's left of them. Our lot, of course, and the Fat Boys from Köpenick, and the Schlemmer Gang. Most of the others are in Frankfurt, the ones we know of.'

'And?'

'Like I said, we're all keeping our heads down. Except the Fat Boys, of course. They're still in with the regime. They the only ones who think it's got a future.'

'Should I be worried?'

'Nah.' Ulli got up. 'Come on, Toller and Herzfeld want to buy you a drink.'

'One for the road?'

'Why not? That fucking heap drives itself.'

'Doesn't anyone stop you? Wonder where you get the petrol from?'

Ulli gave him a sad look. 'I've got a sticker. Auxiliary ambulance. What you got in that case? Your masterpieces?'

'Nah,' said Adamov. 'Army information films. Sixteen-mill. stuff. You know.' He knew he'd drunk too much, too fast. He was already fuddled, but not enough for a sense of possible threat not to have lodged in his mind. He picked up the other case, the one with his clothes and the three best films in it. 'Where am I staying?'

'Nice little hotel. We can lay on some tottie, too, if you want.'

As Ulli drew away from the kerb, two hundred kilometres north-west, a black car drew up outside the bakery in Iphofen. Three or four passers-by looked surprised as three men got out and rapidly entered the shop, but then lowered their heads and went on their way, quickening their pace as they did so.

Schiffer had made good time from Nuremberg. He'd thought he'd lost the trail and his own contact hadn't been in touch for days, but now at last there was a clear lead and the local cops had confirmed it. He was in no mood to trifle with anyone and he'd brought two Gestapo men from Nuremberg with him to emphasise just how serious he was. Before he left, he'd made one phone call. Now he was confident. Now he was on track again. He wouldn't risk repining any more. He was a man of iron.

As soon as they were inside, one of the men drew the blinds. Schiffer grabbed the woman by the arm and dragged her into the centre of the floor before she had time to react to their presence. He let her go and immediately hit her, a close-fisted blow to the side of the head as near as he could get to her left eye and cheekbone. He hurt his hand, and cursed, but he'd knocked her to the floor, where one of the other men kicked her, not too hard, in the kidneys. Then they pulled her to her feet and put her on a chair.

Schiffer brought his face close.

'Where is he?' he said.

There was no-one in the street when, fifteen minutes later, the three men emerged again, two of them half-carrying the woman. They'd put a flour sack over her head and upper body. They shoved her into the car and drove off, back in the direction of Nuremberg.

115

He'd approached the house carefully, seen no sign of any Gestapo, and, thank God, Tilli's dogs remembered him. She greeted him at the door, leaning against the jamb, arms folded, smiling drily as always. She was thinner, wore a sensible country tweed skirt, white blouse and Loden jacket. A brooch at the neck.

Not her style at all, really, but a very good costume, and absolutely in character for the role she'd cast herself in. She done her job almost too well: she looked like a country matriarch, but she'd have killed anyone who'd suggested that there was a real resemblance.

'Welcome,' she said. 'I didn't think you'd make it.'

'Everything all right?' He had seen at once that she was troubled.

'Sure,' she said. 'Come in. What the hell do you look like? You need to wash and change, you stink, but first you must have a drink.' Three years earlier, Hoffmann had left some clothes and shoes at Tilli's, concealed among others belonging to her husband. He looked forward to wearing his own stuff again. It marked a small milestone. He had got this far.

'Where's Stefan?'

'Studying geography,' she said, as she led him through the hall to a small sitting room with a view down the drive. 'For what it's worth, these days. He'll be pleased to see you.'

'I hope so.'

She gave Hoffmann a glance. 'Are you going to tell him, at last?'

'Tell him what?'

'That you're his father.' She was exasperated.

'When it's all over, I will.'

'That moment may never come, Max.'

'It will'

She pursed her lips, but said nothing. It was his decision. 'He's lonely. A new face will do him good.'

'Will he remember me?'

'Yes. He asks after Emma as well, and it's two years since he saw her.'

'I hope he doesn't do that when you have visitors.'

'No. And visitors are few and far between.'

'I want to see him.'

'Drink first. And a cigarette? Or a little snow? Perk you up?'

'Yes to the drink and the cigarette. Whiskey.'

She took him into the morning room, fetched ice from a bucket and clunked it into two big tumblers, splashed in Jameson's, and passed him one, followed up with a Du Maurier from a red lacquer case.

'I didn't know what to tell him.' Tilli hesitated, then said, 'I have news too - good news, I think. But we need to talk. See Stefan first. When you've eaten, when you've changed, we must sit down together.'

'Give me the gist. Then I must see him.' Hoffmann was trembling. He couldn't control it. Tilli had no children. Could she understand his urgency?

Sensing his mood, she spoke quickly. 'We've had a visitor. Your friend Brandau sent him from Bern. And I've made preparations. But it's complicated. It can wait until after you've seen Stefan.'

He was suddenly tired, but this wasn't journey's end, and he could not afford to think that it was; nor, despite the familiar, comfortable surroundings, that any one of them was safe. It was bizarre to be here, where nothing seemed to have changed, and where everything had.

'Give me the details after I've seen Stefan.'

'After we've eaten,' decided Tilli, firmly. 'You'll need your strength for this, and we need to decide what to do. I'll get Stefan now.'

'From Brandau, you say?'

'Yes. Don't worry. It's not any kind of trap.' She was gone.

So Brandau had made it. But he didn't find it hard to put thinking about that away. The most important thing was to see Stefan.

The few minutes' waiting for his son was hard. Hoffmann smoked his cigarette and drank his drink. He was more nervous than he'd expected to be. He was awkward with Stefan, always found himself wanting to say more than he could, to hug him harder than he dared, remembering how the little body became tense when he did so, and how the boy hardly responded, though he was always polite, and never unfriendly. But he was not a demonstrative child, except towards Tilli, and even then he was guarded.

Hoffmann had not been able to allow himself to think about his children too deeply. Now, safe for a few moments, able to breathe, lulled despite himself by his surroundings, he had to give in to a pressing need. He ached for Emma, and he yearned for Stefan, who was still a child, and who bore the extra vulnerability that his mother's race had bequeathed him. He yearned to play with him, to teach him, to watch him grow, and above all, to protect him. But his case was no worse than that of many other people; indeed, he was in a much happier position than many others. He could still see his son. His son was still alive. And in his son, though the thought had never fully formed in his mind, lay a sense of what he could leave in the world, that which, of Kara and himself, might survive and flourish, that which united them, that which might even redeem him, that which would carry forward what was left of the good in him.

He rolled the whistle Kessler had given him round in his hands. He hadn't been able to wrap it. Children liked presents they could unwrap. He had, as a boy. He polished the thing on his sleeve.

The door opened to admit Tilli, and preceding her, a dark child with large eyes in a pale, serious face. He was dressed in rust-brown corduroy shorts and a light, sleeveless pullover over a white open-necked shirt. Hoffmann held out his hand and Stefan shook it.

'Hello, Stefan.'

'Hello, sir.'

'It's been a while. Do you remember me?'

116

'Of course I do.' The boy smiled. 'I've been doing geography. Canada. Do you know, there can be up to fifty thousand caribou in a herd?'

'Really?'

'A big stag can weigh up to three hundred kilogrammes, and they can run at eighty kilometres an hour.'

'Amazing.'

'I wouldn't mind being a caribou. Only you've got to watch out for the wolves.'

'I've got something for you.' Hoffmann produced the whistle and handed it over. 'Hope you like it.'

'It's great,' said Stefan, turning it over in his hands, but Hoffmann could see that his interest was no more than polite. 'It's got my name on it. Is it a police whistle?'

'Sort of.'

'Is that what you do?'

'I used to have something to do with them.'

'I'll leave you for a bit,' said Tilli. 'Chase up lunch. Help yourself,' she added, nodding at the decanter and the cigarette case.

Left alone together, they found it harder to talk. Hoffmann poured himself more whiskey, lit another delicious English cigarette, and learned a little more about Canada; but he didn't know enough about the place to ask the kind of question which would have kept the conversation going, and Stefan scorned any talk of reindeer and Santa Claus.

For his own safety, Hoffmann told himself, he must not know who I am yet. Just the godfather. Just the family friend. Tilli's ward. His mother dead when he was still a baby. Emma his half-sister. His father - absent. That was all he needed to know. He didn't know Hoffmann's real name. Hoffmann ached to tell him, fought down the thought that he himself might die before he could tell his son the truth.

He wondered what effect that would have on Stefan, if he ever did get the chance to tell him. Would he understand why the deception had been necessary? Would he forgive him?

It was a relief to them both when Tilli returned.

They ate in the breakfast room, Hoffmann ravenously, ashamed of his appetite, though his mind was more on Tilli's news than on what he was putting into his mouth. It was a quiet meal. Stefan said little, smiled shyly when Hoffmann spoke to him - how he reminded him of Kara - and soon after he had finished, asked to be excused. Frau Ziegler, who'd looked after the place with her husband for thirty years, had served potatoes and cold beef. God alone knew where she'd got that from, but Tilli, even after ten years' absence from the stage, still had her admirers.

The Zieglers were safe, there was nothing to fear from them. The couple had a large flat within the mansion, and they were well paid. Tilli's influence had ensured that both their sons retained desk jobs far from the Front. All Utz and Adi Ziegler risked were air-raids; and air-raids were a risk no-one could guard against.

Now, the meal over, clean, shaved, dressed in some of his own clothes, a fresh cigarette in his hand, and a glass of very cold Sylvaner at his elbow, Hoffmann sat in a damask-covered armchair in a long, well-lit drawing-room whose tall windows looked out over a terrace, beyond which a lawn sloped down to a lake fringed with trees. Even the inner wounds hurt less, for now.

The colours of the room were blue, cream and green. Outside, the late afternoon sunshine bathed the garden in golden light and produced deep shadows where it hit the trees. He remembered sitting in this chair, in this house, years ago. Now, he was waiting for Tilli to join him. She'd gone to her study to fetch a letter he had to see. She seemed increasingly excited, and he knew her well enough also to know that she couldn't resist the drama of the moment.

How was he going to look after Stefan and Tilli? They had identity papers, but even though Stefan was registered in Tilli's family name, Hoffmann wasn't sure that they would be sufficient to get them across any border without signed and dated travel documents, and even then the risk would be great. The nature of those documents was constantly changing, or he would have organised them himself.

He hardly dared hope that what Tilli had to tell him would provide a way out of the maze.

117

When he'd left his clothes, he'd also left identity papers for himself, identifying him as a personnel officer for a chemical plant associated with I.G. Farben. He also had the Swedish passport. He couldn't use the two sets of documents in conjunction, but he was loath to let the passport go in case he managed to get out of the country. It was too risky to hang onto the telephone engineer's papers any longer. His own clothes, though they hung a little looser on him than they had in 1941, made him feel more like himself again than he had done almost since leaving Berlin.

He stood up and paced the room. He still had work to do in Germany, but he had to get the others out if he could. He was increasingly uncertain that he could bank on their being able to sit the war out in safety where they were.

Tilli had been right. They needed to have a serious conversation.

She placed the letter on his lap, and drew up a chair near him while he read.

'This is too good to be true,' he said at last.

'But it is true. Your friend is a good friend.'

'Yes,' said Hoffmann. He had underestimated Brandau. Brandau had picked up the signals, and he had acted on them. But suspicions still remained. 'Who was the messenger?'

'A man of about sixty, I'd say. Portly, bearded, grey eyes, grey hair, might have been handsome once. He spoke perfect German - maybe a hint of a Schwabian accent, I don't know.'

'Credentials?'

'He just gave me this. I know, I shouldn't have kept it. I was going to wait until Sunday. Then I was going to burn it. Brandau knew all about your escape, something about a faked suicide - does that make sense?'

'Yes.' Had Brandau really made it, or had they caught him and tortured it all out of him? Was the visitor an American agent, or a Gestapo spy? Hoffmann looked hard at the letter. It promised three travel documents. Only the dates, and the names of the travellers, would need to be filled in. The same man who'd brought the letter would return with them as soon as they were ready.

Brandau must have set this up the minute he'd got to Bern, and relied on some inspired guesswork, though he knew where Tilli lived, and the only option open to him would have been to make contact through her. So not such a long shot, though it made Hoffmann realise how much better the lawyer had read him than he had imagined.

'Burn it now,' said Tilli.

He read the letter again. It was designed to reassure whoever received it that it wasn't bait for a trap. He recognised Brandau's handwriting and signature. They weren't fakes and the writing showed no abnormal sign of stress - the first thing he looked for.

He reminded himself that the Gestapo would never go to the trouble of setting a trap as elaborate as this - his imagination was running away with him. They simply weren't that sophisticated, they had no need to be. If they had been suspicious, they would simply have set a watch on the house, and pounced when they were ready.

He took the letter to the empty fireplace, drew the summer screen aside, stooped, held a match to the letter and when it had burnt out, crushed the carbonised pieces to dust in his hand and pushed them through the grate to join what remained of last winter's ashes. He wiped his hands on his handkerchief, accepted another cigarette, finished his glass of wine, and sat down again.

'Did he say when the travel passes would come?'

Tilli leant forward in her chair. 'In two or three days.'

Hoffmann closed his eyes. So, enemy agents were crossing and recrossing the border with Switzerland almost as easily, it seemed, as if it were peacetime again. The ghost of a part of him was annoyed. What had happened to security? How could his country have decayed so much? For a brief moment he had to remind himself that his own country had become the enemy.

'And he delivered this when?' he asked.

'Two days ago. Don't worry about transport. The car's still OK in the garage, and Ziegler's been stockpiling petrol since 1940. I've got five ten-litre cans full in the boot. Enough to get us to America, let alone Switzerland!'

Hoffmann smiled. 'Then we're up and running. If your man makes it back.'

'He didn't seem to think there'd be any difficulty.'

'Tell me what the news is.'

'You mean on the wireless? In the papers? All enemies of the Party have either been arrested, or they're on the run. You are dead, a cowardly suicide to avoid justice. They've arrested thousands of people, more have disappeared, but it doesn't make a ripple.' She frowned. 'Some of my best friends are dead, my marriage is destroyed, but look at me - I live in this oasis and they tell me that even my flat in Berlin has been spared the enemy's bombs. And I never had children, so I don't even have that to worry about. I am supremely lucky. But, do you know, Max, I am getting a little bored with this country life, it's taking it out of me, I'm forty-two years old, my best decade as an actor has been totally fucked, I haven't had sex since I can't remember when, except with myself of course, so I need some adventure.'

'You've cared for Stefan.'

'Kara was my friend. Have you noticed how much he looks like her when he smiles?'

'Yes.'

'He looks even more like her when he's angry. Not that he's angry often. I sometimes wish he was a bit more volatile.'

'That might be dangerous.'

'Who cares? Long live danger! I've been cooped up here so long, playing safe, that I've created my own prison.'

'I never expected you to make such a sacrifice.'

She smiled. 'Please, Max, let me just play my part, let me have my little scene. I'm still here, I may just survive. I'm the luckiest girl alive, and when this is over, I am going to come out of retirement and I am going to give them my *Mother Courage*! And now, if you don't mind, I think we could both do with another drink.'

Hoffmann stopped her. He said: 'If the papers arrive, you'll get your adventure. I'm not coming with you. You've guarded Stefan this long. You'll get him to safety.'

She stopped in her tracks. 'Of course you're coming with us.'

'No. I will stay to make sure you get away safely. And I will keep one of the travel documents Hans has promised us. But I have something to do before I leave. Stefan was the most important thing for me. If I know he's safe, and I pray that fate has been kind and he will be, and you, too; then I can finish the job I'm working on.'

'And that is?'

Hoffmann smiled. 'I've always disliked Wagner, so it seems a miserable thing to cast myself as one of his heroes. But I'm a kind of small-time Siegfried, and I have a small-time dragon to kill.'

She laid a hand on his arm. 'Don't be daft, Max. Help me look after your son.'

'I have to do this. Perhaps I have to do it for Stefan, too.'

'Why?'

'It's the only way - ' he found it difficult to explain - 'It's the only way to find peace.'

118

As Kessler had guessed, the Munich address was a decoy. The old man who answered the door was frightened, but it was obvious that he knew nothing about Hoffmann. He showed them a handful of campaign medals from the last war, swore five or six times he had never wavered in his loyalty, and begged them not to arrest him. His wife was bedridden, he explained, and had no-one else to depend on but him. Unfortunately for him, his wife put in an appearance before they left, a strapping, moon-faced woman twenty years his junior, laden with net bags full of turnips. His confusion was so complete at being caught out that he had an asthma attack. His wife explained that he'd been gassed in the war, at Loos. She'd been his nurse.

Kessler left them alone. He would find an excuse to stay in Munich. That would give him time to get to Dachau, to find out if he could what had happened to Emma. But first he'd have to lose Kleinschmidt. For the moment at least he could send his sergeant off to the Praesidium to announce their arrival, and file a progress report to Berlin. Kleinschmidt didn't like it much, but Kessler sent him on his way. It was not yet noon, and he had no doubt that Kleinschmidt would soon be consoling himself with a *Weißes* and some *Weißwurst* for his second breakfast somewhere on the way to police HQ. Kleinschmidt always seemed to have an uncanny ability to find food when no-one else could.

Paul Kessler had his contacts in the underworld, and he knew which gangs had decamped here from Berlin. Their networks were far more sophisticated than anything the authorities had, and they were designed to continue to function in adversity. The problem for him was making contact, in a strange city, where he couldn't trust the local police. But he did know the places to look, and the right districts, no problem there, always close to the main station; and he struck lucky in a beer garden on the Arnulfstraße. Naturally, the dour man unseasonably dressed in black refused to look at him at first, but this was an old contact of Hoffmann's, a big gun in the Schlemmer Outfit, and Kessler was confident of winning him round. But the man had smelt cop immediately, drained his beer, and started for the door.

Kessler blocked him. 'Hanno, isn't it?'

'What?'

'Hanno Heyme?' Kessler made the name up, not even that, fixing instead on the first name that'd come into his mind, the name of an uncle of his who'd always given him ten marks at Christmas, wrapped in red tissue, when he was a boy. He used to find it hanging on the tree on Christmas Eve. One of his best presents. He always left it until after dinner to open, opulent as it was in its red wrapper against the deep green boughs. During the inflation, he remembered the ten marks becoming ten thousand, ten million, but his family had weathered it somehow, luckily, and so had Uncle Hanno.

No need to embarrass this little crook by using his real name in public.

'You've made a mistake,' said the man.

'But I'm sure you must remember - back in the old days, you and me and Maxie Hoffmann?'

'Fuck off, mate.'

Kessler checked him. One or two heads had turned, mildly interested. The man relaxed slightly. 'Look,' said Kessler. 'If you're going to get through this and stay in business afterwards, it mightn't be a bad bit of insurance to help me now.'

'Think I'm staying?'

'Have a drink at least. You know who I am. Your memory can't be that bad. And I remember you well. All about you.' Kessler didn't add that he knew the man was Jewish.

'All right.' The man subsided. 'Call me sentimental, but we're not far off from kicking these shits in the pants, and I'm not scared anymore.' He looked Kessler in the eye. 'And in case you're thinking it, no, I don't have any family in the camps.'

Kessler lowered his eyes. 'I only want to know if anyone knows where Hoffmann is.'

'Last I heard of him was in Berlin, he wanted to buy steamer tickets for New York. I arranged them. He didn't take them. His girl was killed. Years ago. After the war, if we meet again, he'll get his money back, full whack. Least I can do.' The man looked at Kessler. 'We know what he tried to do. He fucked up, but he did his best. And we know about you, too.'

Kessler took his chance. 'Where can I reach you?'

'I'm still with the Schlemmers.'

'What about the others?'

'Look, there isn't time. People are beginning to pay attention. Bar in Kleingasse, the Aurora, most evenings after eleven. Just ask for Hanno Heyme.' He gave Kessler an arid grin, and was gone.

Kessler pondered his next move.

119

Adamov thought, thank God I kept the best films in my own case. Thank God I switched hotels as soon as Ulli left me. What instinct had preserved him thus far, he didn't know, but it wouldn't be much good unless he got out of this place alive.

He'd played along. He'd told them about the restaurant and the case full of porn films. His anus and his balls felt as if they'd been set on fire; they still thought he was lying, and they were right; but he'd hoped he was a better actor than that. That fucker Schiffer, thought he was a psychologist, thought no-one deserved to second-guess him. The bastard must have gone mad.

Oh, God, how it hurt, how he longed to be able at least to stretch his legs, bent double now for twenty hours. Well, he'd hinted at such things in his films: the simplest tortures are the most effective. What a mind Man has, he thought. He pressed his lips together and tried to focus on what he'd do if he got out of here. No-one knew where his important suitcase was, no-one knew in what little hotel near the Ludwigsbrücke he had a room. They hadn't got that out of him. They hadn't even asked. They were too confident. He tried to cling to that thought.

Ulli and Big George. How could he have taken them on trust? And Moritz? How could he have been so naive? Well, too late now. Allegiances shifted. So Big George thought it was OK to keep in with the Fat Boys and the Gestapo, well, fuck him. If he got out of this, and the Americans came, and the war ended, he'd see their guts torn out and he'd fucking well film it.

Oh, how it hurt. They'd used a poker and a blowtorch. Always the simplest things. And he'd been so close to getting the papers when they'd nabbed him. Trust no-one! But you have to, you have to if you're going to make any progress at all.

The pain was making his mind whirl. He shook his head, gently, otherwise it swam in agony, to try to clear it. The Jews were the best forgers, and he hadn't expected to be betrayed by a Jew. But Moritz had a family to protect, was working for the Party anyway, probably, who knew? So close. Marseilles, Lisbon, Rio de-fucking-Janeiro. This instead. He tried not to think of the other Veit Adamov, already on the boat, on the Atlantic, cocktail in hand, slinky woman opposite, the Old World festering in blood and dust behind him.

Christ. He couldn't sit and he couldn't stand. But Schiffer knew Hoffmann, and Schiffer wanted specific information. Adamov wasn't sure how much more pain he could stand. If they let him go, if they really let him go, if he gave them what they wanted, then he'd collect his case, follow his dream and get out. He thought vaguely of a city in South America, full of tall girls and Spanish churches. He'd never been there. He'd find the right people. His three best films would speak for him, especially *Young Love, Old Lust.* And he would come to an accommodation with his conscience. Better a live dog than a dead lion.

He hadn't told them anything yet. How much did they think he knew? But would they kill him if he gave them nothing? Would they kill him anyway? He thought it likely. He still had a brackish taste in his mouth from the last bottle of schnapps, but it was better than the taste of the blood which had mingled with it. He could do with a drink now. The beating they'd given him had shocked him into sobriety. His tongue was swollen from when they'd hit him, and he noticed that one of his molars had worked loose. It made him feel like crying. He listened in dread for the sound of approaching footsteps.

They came for him again, dragged him out of the cell and down the corridor to the tiled room with its metal desk in one corner. There was a high window, barred, which let in bright yellow sunlight. The floor of the room was plain cement, and there were stains on it and on the walls. Apart from the desk and a few chairs scattered around the room, some with uniform jackets hanging on them, the only other piece of furniture was a heavy wooden stool.

Schiffer sat at the desk, in his shirtsleeves. Five or six burly men stood around the walls, also in shirtsleeves. They looked at Adamov coldly as the two guards who had brought him in stripped him, tied his legs to the stool, and his arms behind his back. Adamov couldn't help it: he wet himself. This had the effect of making some of the men laugh. The guards, their job done, retreated.

'Now then,' said Schiffer, as soon as they were gone. 'Are you going to be sensible?'

'I've told you everything I know.'

'We think you contacted Hoffmann in Leipzig.'

'Yes, I may have seen him there; but that doesn't mean I know where he is now.'

Schiffer looked at his gang and nodded. Two of them moved in on Adamov with rubber truncheons and hit him in the small of the back and in the stomach. They went on hitting him for three minutes, then Schiffer told them to stop.

'Well?'

'I don't know what you want.'

'We know he's been seen near Iphofen - do you know anything about that?'

Adamov was suddenly alert and hoped that it didn't show in his eyes. The location of Tilli's country estate was known, but she hadn't been in the headlines for years. Was it possible that Schiffer didn't know about it? Was it possible that he hadn't checked with his colleagues?

He decided to risk it. 'I don't know where Iphofen is. I've never heard of it.'

Schiffer picked up a paperknife and studied it. 'I don't want to use this on you, Veit, I really don't; but if you won't play ball...' Taking his time, he walked over to where Adamov sat. He took one of his hands almost gently, then tightened his grip as he rammed the blade of the paperknife under the nail of Adamov's ring finger, and twisted it. Adamov jerked his hand away with a roar, the nail tearing off as he did so, throwing himself off balance and toppling over on the stool.

Schiffer withdrew to his desk, then nodded, and watched as his men righted the stool, then kicked and punched Adamov for three more minutes, knocking the stool over again and him with it, flailing him with lengths of wire. Blood spewed out of him, arching across the room to splatter the walls. Then they sent him back to his cell.

Schiffer had got nothing out of the baker's wife, and had finally been convinced that she knew nothing. He'd let her go, she'd be all right, a few bruises, a couple of teeth, nothing much. But he'd reached a dead end again, and Berlin was getting impatient. He didn't want to be taken off the case. He was scared. He needed to nail Kessler. And then fate had dropped this little package in his lap. Veit Adamov. Hoffmann's old crony, old commie, last noticed by the Gestapo in Leipzig. Well worth a shot, when you had as little to go on as Schiffer had. Small world, but not really a surprise; most of the rats had been jumping ship for Munich. Just as well Big George wanted the porn for himself.

At the next session, under the blows, Adamov screamed and cried. He was covered with blood and slime, and finally he vomited. They forced him to clear up his own mess with his hands before he fainted. They threw buckets of ice-cold water over him and let him lie. One or two produced bottles of schnapps and sandwiches and passed them around. Thirsty work. One of them complained that he'd sprained his wrist. The wire lashes had cut the palms of some of the men wielding them. They improvised handles from rags or newspaper. They poured schnapps on his feet and set fire to it.

120

Adamov regained consciousness and crouched on the ground, on his knees, the stool, tied to him, digging into his buttocks and the backs of his legs. He tried to think but all he could feel was a burning pain that shredded his whole body. The molar had worked itself looser, he couldn't help worrying at it with his tongue, and at last it fell out. The loss of the tooth shocked him. He could feel his flesh swelling, his left eye was closed. From far away he heard Schiffer's voice. Did he only imagine a note of panic in it?

'Look, all this can stop. You're not dead yet and you're not past recovery. That won't be the case much longer. We'll cripple you permanently. Now, tell me what you know or I'll have you killed in a way you have never dreamt of.'

What could Adamov say? He could tell him where Tilli lived, and that would be enough. It would be a betrayal of the people who were dearest to him, and it would a betrayal of Kara's son. But he wasn't sure that he could withstand any more pain like this. Death would be better, and death would come more quickly, more mercifully, if he co-operated.

Then suddenly, someone was thrusting a bottle at him. They pulled the stool upright, pulled his head back, and poured schnapps into his mouth. He was drowning in it, he felt small hard bits of matter in his mouth wash down his throat. He fought the bottle, pushed and gagged, but three of them were holding him.

'He's lost a tooth,' said one of the men, in mock sympathy.

'Tell me,' Schiffer said to Adamov.

Adamov couldn't have spoken if he'd wanted to.

'Even him up,' said Schiffer.

They took a pair of pliers and wrenched a tooth out of Adamov's gums on the other side. Then they let him go back to his cell.

They roused him at two in the morning for the next session.

'I've had enough of this,' said Schiffer, and his voice sounded as if it came from the far end of a long tunnel, though at the same time it was crystal clear. Adamov felt his heart pounding, his head was still swimming with the drink, he was flooded with panic. He tasted the blood and the stale alcohol in his mouth.

'Give him a shock. Sober him up, the bastard.'

Two men held his head and neck in a firm grip while a third, after wiping his sweaty hands on a rag, stepped up to Adamov and grunting with the effort, started to tear the hair from his head. Adamov screamed and fainted again. When he came to, and it can only have been minutes later, seconds perhaps, someone held a mirror up. His good right eye sent a picture of a gargoyle to his brain. He started to sob, and could not stop for some time, no matter how hard they clubbed his arms and hands. He felt fingers break.

'Try wanking over your filth now, you cuntarse.' Someone punched him in the right eye. Christ, don't let them blind me, he thought, don't let this go on in darkness.

They threw water at him again. Schiffer came over and brought his face close. Adamov could smell his cologne. It was a scent Adamov had once used himself.

'All right,' said Schiffer. 'Do you know what this is?' he held up, so that Adamov could see it, swimming in blood, an odd home-made contraption consisting of two short lengths of wood connected by wires. 'I'll show you how it works.' He handed it to one of his men, who looped it round Adamov's leg just under the knee, inserting a third stick through the wires, which he then began to twist. As they tightened, blood fountained from Adamov's leg and he felt his flesh tear to the bone. His head exploded with pain, pain to set him beyond screaming, beyond pain itself. The whole world shrank to one dark agony.

He heard himself talking, babbling, hurriedly, getting it out, out of the way, anything for this to stop, even death, he couldn't stand any more of this. Somehow he'd make it all right, he'd outwit them, only he had to get out of here, somewhere safe, recover, fight another day, but first this had to stop. Christ, he'd never walk again, he thought, and hatred mingled with his fear. He tried to cling to the hatred, but the fear won, fear and shame.

They gave him more schnapps, forced it into him, burning his stomach. Then they untied him. He fell on the floor in a messy heap, as if they'd removed his bones from his body, as if he'd been a puppet whose strings they'd cut. They hauled him up, pulled some clothes onto him, just trousers and a jacket, to cover him. Then he was bundled out into the open.

It was night. There was a faint breeze which had cooled the air. He tried to breathe in deeply, but his lungs wouldn't expand properly, he couldn't even cough. They were manhandling him down an alleyway, tall grey walls on either side. At the end, a canal, or something. Dirty water a couple of metres below, anyway, and a muddy bank. They stood him face against a wall and threw a noose round his neck, tightened it and pulled on it until he all but blacked out. His body collapsed again, and this time it wouldn't respond no matter what they did. They kicked him where he lay but although his mind acknowledged what they were doing, there was no pain any more, this sack of flesh and bone wasn't him anymore.

'The fucker's dead,' he heard one of them say.

'Cunt. Chuck him in.' He felt them heave him up, he fell through the air, onto dirty mud. Water lapped at his cheek and lips. He heard their voices recede as they walked away. He couldn't believe his luck, but a part of him wished they'd done their job properly.

He lay in the mud, it cooled him, it cooled the burning. The water caressed his face. He didn't know if this was by the sea, by a lake, where he was. He thought he could hear the wind in the trees. He was standing at the edge of a cliff in the darkness. He thought he had wings, huge dark wings operated by a vast new set of muscles in his back. They felt strange. He could fly. He threw himself out into the night.

121

Schiffer, showered and in a fresh suit and shirt, sat at his desk making phone calls. The ones which resulted in successful connections infuriated him. He had the address, he had the name. What he was not getting was any authorisation to act on them. He bit his nails. He wondered if he could risk it alone. He thought hard. Then he picked up the receiver again, hesitated for a moment, and asked the switchboard for a number. Miraculously, he heard the ringing tone within a minute. But then he frowned and hung up. Why shouldn't he have all the glory for once? He thought again. He'd need a team, and he'd need transport, but without authorisation, that might not be so easy. It would take time; and he didn't have much of that to spare.

He'd try Berlin again, but he knew how much protection Tilli Cassirer enjoyed, and he knew that Göring was losing no sleep at all over any failure to arrest the conspirators against Hitler. He knew, too, that to challenge Göring's authority would be suicide.

But he also knew that he could not let this chance go. If he pulled this off, he'd be promoted. He'd be more powerful, and he'd have more powerful contacts. He had resisted thinking of South America, up to a point, but he had dug out one or two old maps, and pored over them, dreaming, at night.

***

Kessler was woken by a discreet but insistent knocking at his hotel room door. He picked up his watch from the bedside table and squinted at it. Six in the morning. He crossed the room and opened the door to the man he'd called Hanno Heyme.

'Do you want to tell me what I should really call you?' he asked after they'd greeted each other. 'And I assume this isn't just my wake-up call.'

'Hanno's good enough for me, and for you,' said the man in black. 'In fact, I rather like it. And this isn't a social call. I think we've caught you a fish.'

'What?'

'There's a certain amount of adjustment going on in the gangs just now,' said Hanno, 'and there are casualties. We keep an eye on Gestapo HQ and we've got a couple of men in there, just to gather information. Of course they have to play along, but what can you do? - all news is useful news, and we want a few bodies to chuck to the Ammis when they finally arrive - good will, that kind of thing.'

'Yes?'

'There's a lot of flotsam and jetsam drifting down from Berlin,' continued Hanno. 'Some of it gets caught in our nets. The boys in black have been busy interrogating a handful of politicals recently, and they like to get rid of the rubbish when they've finished with it, don't want anything to stick to their hands, so they tend to throw it out in the middle of the night when no-one's looking. But they're nervous, they're in a hurry, they're not all, let's face it, very bright, so they make mistakes now and then. I think from your point of view, this time they've made a lulu.'

'What have you got?'

'Bloke dumped by the canal. Obviously thought they'd killed him. Smashed to pieces but he'll pull through, probably. He's conscious but not very lucid. They broke him. You need to talk to him fast.'

'Do I know him?'

'Veit Adamov, the film director,' Hanno curled his lip as he described the job.

'Where is he now?'

'I'll take you.'

122

Adamov was at Schlemmer's brothel on the Fischerweg, the one the Gestapo left alone because it was patronised by senior SS officers. They'd got him in a room on the top floor, a garret, really, but it had a large bed and he lay on it, propped up by a variety of cushions and covered with an eiderdown. He was in a white nightshirt, and the girls had cleaned him up as best they could, but Kessler wouldn't have recognised him. The face was distorted with swellings, and when Adamov opened his mouth, Kessler could see tears in the gums where teeth had been broken or ripped out. He'd need stitches in a huge gash on his left temple, and his scalp was raw and bloody. His hands were like claws; they'd have to get someone to set those fingers soon, or he'd never be able to use them again.

'We're getting him a doctor. One of ours,' said Hanno. 'Poor sod. But he's lucky we found him.'

'Why did you pick him up? Why didn't you just leave him?'

Hanno smiled, 'Because we're soft-hearted. Because we thought he might just be an investment. Not many people get out of there alive, unless they're being shipped to the camps.' He moved closer to the bed, standing so that Adamov could see him, and spoke more loudly. 'Brought you someone.' Turning again to Kessler he said, 'Hope you can make sense of what he's talking about. We couldn't. But if it helps, well, remember your promise.'

He left them, and Kessler took up his position in Adamov's line of vision. Only one eye was open and that glittered deep within a mound of purple bruises, but Kessler thought he sensed a change of expression. The voice when it came was a kind of slurred mumble as the swollen tongue struggled to articulate sounds.

'Paul... is that you?'

'You remember me?'

'Friend of Maxie's.'

'Colleague. Assistant.'

'Friend. Shit, the way he used to talk about you. Come closer.'

Kessler approached the bed. There was a smell of disinfectant, covering a stale odour of decay. Adamov would be lucky if he made it, Kessler thought.

'I've got to talk to you, fast,' said Adamov. It was hard to hear him and Kessler had to lean in closer than he wanted to. 'God must have sent you.'

'Tell me what you can.'

Adamov said, 'I couldn't take it. I told them what they wanted to know, and then they tried to kill me. I should have put up with more pain. I was beyond pain anyway by then.'

'You don't know what they would have done to you next. You don't know what else they could do.'

'I couldn't stand it,' Adamov repeated, and though he did not sob, tears rolled down his cheeks. 'I couldn't help it.'

'Who questioned you?'

'Schiffer. Remember him?'

'What did you tell him?'

'Where they are. He's been to Iphofen. He had an idea. He kept at me until I broke.'

Kessler took his wrist and squeezed it gently. 'Perhaps you're right. Perhaps God did organise this meeting.'

He left hastily, without another word.

123

Waiting is the worst thing, thought Hoffmann. You can't concentrate on anything but the arrival, and a point can come in the waiting, towards the end, when your sixth sense tells you that you're waiting in vain.

He was beginning to feel like that in the late afternoon of the second day. Brandau's emissary wasn't going to get there. Two days wasted, and they were increasingly vulnerable. He'd seen his son, his son was all right, it would be placing him in greater danger if Hoffmann continued to stay, though the fact that Stefan was safe seemed proof that Hagen didn't know about him.

He'd recovered, and for two days he'd been able to eat well, wash, change his clothes, and rest. He played a few games of chess with Stefan, who usually beat him; he tried to talk to Stefan about dinosaurs and cowboys; he walked in the gardens and talked with Tilli about Kara, about the old days, about Tilli's husband, and whether she would ever see him again. Years of separation change people.

Hagen never strayed from his thoughts. Hagen wouldn't leave for South America while there was still profit in the Party. The enemy might have established a bridgehead in France a couple of months ago, but the transports to the camps went on, and supplies of Zyklon-B for the gas chambers continued to roll eastwards. As long as there was money to be made, Hagen would go on taking their commission on the shipments. The question was only whether greed or safety played the higher card in Hagen's mind. Hoffmann knew that Hagen would have his escape route planned. After so many years, he knew his man. A prior move to the relative safety of Bamberg or Nuremberg, somewhere in the Nazi heartland, would be prudent and logical.

These thoughts gave Hoffmann some relief. But he still had to track his quarry down. The man who had killed his love, and who in doing so had killed his ability to feel anything but a desire for death himself. But Hagen floated like a cork on a stream. He flourished, he never looked back. He had taken his vengeance for his own thwarted love, and enjoyed it. Now he was making a fortune out of death. He had to be brought down. Otherwise the entire fight would end without any meaning at all.

'We're not travelling without you – are you mad? What do you mean?' Tilli ground her cigarette out irritably, and took another sip of her martini.

'You've got to go, papers or not. They're after me, and sooner or later they'll find me. I can go in any direction I like, but if they track me down here, and find you and Stefan, they'll take you both.'

'I don't think Emmy and Hermann would let that happen.'

'They might not hear about it until it was too late. And if they did, do you really think they could do anything about it? The game's nearly over. The last time I saw Hermann he was so coked up he could barely cross a room; and Emmy only has power through him. We are on our own. Brandau tried to help us, but his man hasn't got through. What if they've tortured him? Got his destination out of him?'

Tilli paced the room, poured more gin for both of them.

'We must *all* leave,' Hoffmann continued. 'I don't think I've led them here, but I needed to know that Stefan was safe. You say the car is ready to go, and you have enough fuel for the frontier. Go fast, a car like yours would draw attention at the best of times, let alone now, but at least around here they'll know whose it is and let it go.' He paused. 'You must try to get to Switzerland, or at least somewhere where you can sit autumn and winter out - and spring. It will be over before next summer. It's a simple question of matériel. We haven't got enough supplies left. Germany is finished.'

'We're not going without you.'

'I'll follow if I can'

Tilli let her shoulders fall, elegant shoulders in a loose cocktail dress she'd put on, because, she'd no idea why, really, she would have liked to seduce this embattled man. Strange, they'd been friends for so long without her ever having felt like this about him before. Now, she wanted to be with him, even, mad as it sounded, to protect him, as she had protected Stefan. But she put the thought back. It may just have been, she supposed, because she'd been without a man for so long.

'What about travel papers?' she said. 'How am I going to cross any border without them?'

Hoffmann said, 'You must try.'

'He might still get here. Brandau said two or three days.'

'No.'

'I *can't* leave without you.'

'You must.'

'Give him another day.'

'The longer we leave it –'

She couldn't bear it. She walked over to him. 'Please hold me, once.'

124

The stay at Schloß Kupferstein didn't last long. Even in the last hot days of summer, the unpleasant medieval pile perched on its rock above a valley was forbidding, and though they were treated with a kind of distant consideration, none of the fifty or so prisoners who'd been plucked out of Dachau for this lost castle could think that their Calvary had come to an end. Whether there were other prisoners here or not, Emma never discovered. She never saw anyone other than her travelling companions, and during that time the men were sequestered from the women.

Ten days after their arrival, Emma and the others were reunited and gathered in the great hall, where they were confronted by a jittery SS officer, who hectored them for several minutes in a thick Schwabian accent before announcing that they had a quarter of an hour to pack. When they were ready, he said, they should report to him in the principal courtyard. Once there, they were arranged in a column, five abreast, and marched out of the castle into the weak sunshine of an autumnal day. It had rained during the night, and the leaves hung heavily on the trees, spilling raindrops onto them as they marched down the long drive which led to the road. Emma walked with General Richter. She was glad to see him again. In the ten days, none of the prisoners who had travelled here had disappeared or died.

'South-west,' said the thin man after a while, but only those in his line heard him, and, away from his home turf, he wasn't entirely sure himself.

They stopped for lunch at a *Wirtshaus* by a river, a large party over which their SS guards hovered nervously. The sun shone more brightly now, the trees by the wayside quivered in a light breeze, and the countryside spread itself, wide and green, all around. Lunch was a simple affair, black bread and elderly cheese, gherkins, water and beer. They sat at wooden tables, on benches in the open air. They exhausted the resources of the place, and the two women who served them were scared, but otherwise it might have been a works outing. A camaraderie had developed between the prisoners, and when, in a moment of irony, someone stared singing *In diesen Heilig'n Hallen*, all those who knew it, including two SS-men, joined in. They laughed and clapped when it was over.

It was late when they reached the village where they were to spend the night. The SS escort corralled them in the square, nervous because they hadn't bargained on finding a detachment of regular army soldiers billeted in the same place.

'What's going on here?' Emma sensed their guards' mood change.

'They don't like the army,' General Richter said, and added, with a little more feeling, 'and the army doesn't like them.'

'One or two of our guards don't seem too unhappy about it, though.'

'I've noticed that. Probably they're men who've been forcibly conscripted into the SS.' He paused. 'It happens. Good people, usually, paratroopers, commandos, tank crew, soldiers like that. Not that putting them into black uniforms turns them into model SS-men, much as Himmler would like to think so.'

'I see.' Emma hesitated. 'Will there be trouble?'

'It's unlikely; but it's a situation worth watching.' Richter sounded thoughtful. 'We might even be able to use it. I'm sure Sun-tzu has something to say about it somewhere.'

'Who?'

Richter smiled. 'A general from years ago. Worth a read, if ever you have an idle moment.'

The regular soldiers, curious, wandered round the encampment, eyeballing the SS, offering cigarettes to the captives, tobacco-and-acorn blend, exchanging jokes, not giving a damn really. They weren't happy to see one of their generals among the prisoners.

It was a well-equipped unit, one hundred men, three trucks, two motorbikes, three jeeps, a half-track, five or six NCOs, two lieutenants, all led by a captain. General Richter recognised one of the lieutenants, who saluted him. They'd fought together somewhere - where? Maybe it'd come back to him. He made a decision, and, politely waving aside the SS-*Obersturmführer* who made a hesitant motion of objection, he walked over and exchanged a few words with the captain. The SS-officer watched. He didn't know what to do. He was outnumbered and outgunned, and he didn't know whose loyalty he could trust, even among his own men.

The next morning at dawn, following a night during which only the few children in the company slept at all, Richter asked the army captain and the SS-officer to join him. The general smoked, the SS-officer stood to attention, and they talked, coming to an agreement. The SS-officer kept glancing round. The regular soldiers had his men surrounded. There were five times as many of them as there were SS, so the bargain wasn't very hard to drive. It barely took half-an-hour. The four SS-men who'd been conscripted from other units embraced their old comrades and joined them. They'd have to be found different uniforms, but the quartermaster thought he could organise something. The other SS fled,

345

shedding their firearms and their uniform jackets, leaving their officer impotent. He hesitated, bowed to Richter and the army captain, begged to be allowed to keep his service pistol. Granted this, he too fled, northwards.

'Will he shoot himself?' the captain wondered.

'He'd like us to think so,' replied Richter. 'He certainly can't go back to his unit. I think he'll try to get home. Have to lose that uniform somewhere, though.'

They turned to the crowd of prisoners, who stood about, relieved and bewildered, waiting to be told what to do.

'What are we to do with them?' said the captain to the general. 'We can't look after them, we're fucked - we'll be prisoners ourselves soon.'

'Then we'd better tell them how things stand,' said Richter, and turned to address his former fellow-prisoners. Emma watched the man becoming a general again before her eyes, as if he had ever been anything else. Richter looked at the crowd of anxious faces gathered around him and raised his voice a notch.

'We are liberated,' he said, 'but we are also alone. The army can't protect us, so we must rely on our own resources.' He paused. 'Try to head west, towards the Americans. If you want to make your way home, take indirect routes. The danger is far from past.'

'What about safe-conducts?' someone asked.

The general turned to the captain, who said, 'We can patch something together. But each one'll have to be handwritten on what paper we've got. It'll take time.'

'Do it. I'll sign them,' said Richter.

'The quartermaster has a rubber stamp and a date stamp.'

'Excellent.' Richter grinned. 'Efficiency like that, it's a wonder we didn't win.'

'They won't guarantee anything,' said the captain.

Richter looked at him. 'I know. And most of them won't have a clue how to get anywhere. But at least they're free, and no-one will come looking for them. The bit of paper will give them confidence.'

By mid-afternoon only the army detachment remained, with Richter and Emma.

'We must move on, sir,' said the captain. 'We need to put a bit of distance between us and the scene of the crime.'

'Good luck,' said Richter.

'What will you do?'

Richter spread his hands. 'Make for safety. Himmler will want me dead when he hears about this.'

The captain looked thoughtful. His troops were climbing aboard their trucks. 'You can hardly walk to Switzerland,' he said.

'What do you suggest?'

The captain excused himself, and went to talk to his lieutenants. Quickly he was back. 'We're moving out now, sir. And we're leaving you a little present. Lieutenant von Hammerstein served with you in Libya.'

'I remember now,' said Richter, saluting von Hammerstein again. 'What are you leaving me?'

'Something you have commandeered from us, sir. Officially.' He nodded to his right. Richter followed with his eyes and grinned.

The captain stood back a pace, saluted, and climbed into the lead jeep. The two lieutenants climbed into a second jeep, the NCOs and the remainder of the troops not already in the trucks clambered into the half-track, and the motorcyclists mounted and started their machines. The noise of the engines battered the silence of the countryside as they moved off, trailing exhaust fumes and dust.

Richter and Emma watched the column out of sight. Then the quiet returned, and there was nothing but the sound of the wind in the trees, and, from somewhere, the insistent, repetitive song of a yellowhammer.

'A little bit of bread and no cheese,' murmured Emma to herself, her eyes far away, remembering a distant English lesson.

Five metres away sat the third jeep, with two jerry cans of water and one of petrol, and a half-full tank.

'We'd better get going,' said Richter. 'Coming?'

125

Bureaucracy having guaranteed that communication between the Gestapo and the regular police, never good, was now virtually non-existent, Schiffer spent a long time on the telephone and throwing his weight around in offices before he was grudgingly signed over a car and three men.

He'd lost valuable time, but now he was on the road. It was a roomy car, big enough to take his prisoner back securely, and he tried to settle himself for the journey, looking at the outskirts of Munich as they gave way to scrappy countryside. He'd had no news of Kessler, for his contact with his tracker had been broken off for a crucial day; but he couldn't indulge the hope that the man was nowhere near. For the seventh time in five minutes, he looked at his watch. He couldn't sit back for long, he preferred to sit upright, lean forward even, willing the car on, though it was already going as fast as the road would allow. Would they have already left? Would he find Hoffmann there? If he did, it would be the coup of his life. Why then, in a remote corner of his mind, lurked the hope that he would not?

But it was too late for that.

They got lost once, and consulted the map. That was the only time anyone spoke. The men had their orders, were experienced, knew the drill. The additional waste of time irritated Schiffer more, he knew, than was reasonable. The last thing he wanted to do was to antagonise his crew, men he did not know. But at last they saw the trees and the broad red roofs.

'This must be it,' said the driver, slowing.

'Watch for the turn-off. The drive must be on the right just about now,' Schiffer replied, checking his pistol, as the others did. Tension in the car mounted at once.

They drove fast up the avenue which led to the house. The driver gunned the motor before killing it. The aggression in the men was pounding as they piled out, slamming the doors. Two of them peeled off and ran round to the back of the house. Schiffer and the driver went to the front door and the driver pounded on it. Dogs started to bark inside. Schiffer stood back and looked up. It was a huge place. How the hell could he search it all with only three men?

The door was opened by an elderly man in a long apron. Somewhere well behind him in the house, the dogs continued to bark, but the noise came no nearer. Schiffer could tell they were confined.

Schiffer pushed the man into the house and stood for a moment in the large, deserted hall. They heard a door bang open and shut some distance away, then running feet. The two other Gestapo-men coming in, or someone getting out? How many escape routes were there? But then their colleagues joined them, sweating in their suits, guns high in their hands.

'Anything?' he asked them

'Nothing we could see. We came straight in.'

Schiffer faced the servant. 'Where are they?'

The man babbled, 'In the drawing room.'

'Where?'

The man pointed to a door in the far corner of the hall.

'Why the hell haven't they come out?' Schiffer turned to the driver. 'Go with him. Make sure those dogs are kept locked up, wherever they are.'

He crossed the hall, wrenched the door open and crouched, gun up, scanning the interior.

He was awed by it. It was the room of his dreams. For a split second he imagined himself there, the man he'd like to be, dressed in hunting clothes, his wife and two daughters sitting near him, cigar in hand and a cognac on the table beside his armchair. An armchair and a table stood near the fireplace. Someone was sitting in the chair, his face obscured by its wings. The person stood up and faced him.

126

Schiffer felt a surge of dismay and delight. He looked at his old boss. Thinner, his clothes looser on him, but not without the cold elegance Schiffer had always admired. He nodded to his men to stay by the door. He lowered his gun. All the excitement drained from him, and he felt no triumph at all.

'You are under arrest,' he said.

'I know.'

'Are you armed?'

Hoffmann pointed to the service pistol which lay on the table by him.

'Who else is here?'

Hoffmann's shoulders dropped. 'I want to ask two favours of you, Ernst.'

Schiffer was taken aback. Hoffmann had never called him by his Christian name before. Schiffer thought, it's check-mate. I'm too clever for you this time.

'Tell me who else is here first,' he said, keeping his voice even.

'You know whose house this is.'

'Of course.'

'And you know about her connections.'

'Nevertheless, in harbouring you –'

'No-one else knows what she's done.'

'That can change.'

'What evidence do you have?'

'Your presence here.'

'I might have coerced her. You wouldn't dare torture her.'

Schiffer was silent, then said, 'People know you were friends in the old days.'

'A lot of people were friends in the old days.' Hoffmann paused. 'Don't arrest her. She is upstairs, with her nephew, Stefan. He is ten years old. I ask you to spare them.' He prayed that Schiffer had no real knowledge of Stefan; the secret had been well buried.

'And the second favour?'

Hoffmann glanced at the Walther. 'Surely you know what that is.'

Schiffer, himself again, thought, he's played into my hands. I have all the power at last. His head swam with the thought. That fuck Adamov, I should raise a fucking monument to him when this is all over.

He imagined the Reich triumphing at the eleventh hour, defying fate, and himself elevated to the High Table, Hitler's chosen son; and Emma, forgiving and repentant, his adoring bride. He knew what to do.

'This is the deal I'll offer you,' he said, coming a little closer, but not too close, still wary of Hoffmann. But Schiffer wasn't in awe any more: he was in control.

'What?' said Hoffmann.

Schiffer couldn't let him retake the ground. He squared up. He was well aware of Tilli Cassirer's connections. If he let her go, it might even help him further. 'I will pretend they are not here,' he said, and picked up the Walther, pocketing it. 'But you must come with me.'

Hoffmann closed his eyes briefly. 'If that is the condition.'

Why did Schiffer suddenly feel cheap? It made him angry. In his mind, he was tearing at the faces of prisoners, ripping the whips out of his minions' hands and slashing at their backs himself, rubber truncheon to the lower spine, enough of that, never walk again, bastards, taking his anger at himself out on them.

But he could not shut out the knowledge of what he was condemning Hoffmann to, by taking him back alive.

'Orders,' he said, and hated the apologetic tone in his voice.

The driver came into the room to report. 'I found an old woman, sir, wife of the bloke who opened the door. Servants here. Locked them up in the kitchen with the dogs. Only setters. Nervous not nasty. Didn't think them worth the bullets.'

'Good. Deal with them later. Got all the keys? No way out from the kitchen?'

'All sealed sir.'

'Bullet in your balls otherwise.' All the men grinned at that. Schiffer, the successful, charismatic, humorous leader. 'Now, search the prisoner, empty his pockets, everything.'

The driver did so, but, as Schiffer had expected, there was nothing except a wallet and some change. No papers, no concealed gun, nothing.

He found himself looking into Hoffmann's eyes, and dropped his own. He could not meet those eyes. Why hadn't he had the courage to join the Resistance? But then, no-one had asked him to. He couldn't hate Hoffmann as much as he hated himself; but, as he told himself again, he had nowhere to go any more, and no choice but to continue running with the pack he had joined. As for Hoffmann, he knew part of what the man had been through, but he also knew he could no longer afford to think of it with any compassion. Schiffer didn't even realise that he'd long ago sacrificed compassion to ambition.

He looked round the room, its size daunting him. He ought to search the whole house, but it was more important to get Hoffmann away fast. Back in Munich, among what were now his own people, his worries would be over.

'We're pulling out,' he said to his men.

They looked at each other. 'Just him?' one of them ventured.

'What else?'

'What about –?'

'Leave it. We've got what we came for. Now,' he said, turning to Hoffmann. 'Where are your papers? You can't have got this far without them. I haven't got time to search this whole place, so if you don't cooperate I'll have to take shortcuts.' He picked up a thin metal paperknife from the large bureau by the windows.

He was interrupted by the sound of a car arriving.

127

Despite his Hitler-Order, Inspector Kessler had also experienced difficulty in arranging transport, but it had still happened quickly. Schiffer watched him climb out of the black Mercedes, knowing that the hours he'd had to waste organising his own mission in Munich had all but lost him his advantage. Even now he couldn't understand what had happened; but there was no time to reflect on that. Kessler had the official mandate to arrest Hoffmann. Everything was about to be snatched from him. He watched as his enemy ran up the front steps, recognised, with a catch at his throat, Kleinschmidt lagging behind. Three other detectives accompanied Kessler and his sergeant.

'Who is it?' said one of the Gestapo-men.

Schiffer's mind raced. 'No idea. Might be a rescue.' He drew his own gun, and took out Hoffmann's Walther as well. 'Looks like we're going to have to fight over our bone.'

'Worth fighting over such a big one,' said one of the men. Each of them knew whom they'd netted.

They've seen our car, Schiffer thought; we're not going to be able to jump them. Conflicting impulses cluttered his brain; but he told himself that if he could bring Kessler down, he'd be able to explain what'd happened afterwards: tragic misunderstanding, friendly fire in the confusion. His men would back him up. And if he couldn't...

'Handcuff him and watch him,' he said to one of his men, indicating Hoffmann, whom he pushed down into the armchair. He glanced again at the windows. There were only three men at the door. Kessler, as he had done, had sent a couple of police round to the back. Deep inside the house, the dogs had started barking again. He cursed himself for not getting hold of Tilli and the boy, but there was no time now.

'You two, come with me.'

He returned to the hall; but there was no cover there. The only pieces of furniture were ranged along the walls, and they were massive, couldn't be moved. They'd have to start shooting as soon as the others came through the door. It was the only moment of advantage they'd have. He made rapid calculations. Kessler had one man more; he himself had to keep back a man to guard Hoffmann. Hoffmann couldn't be left alone, even handcuffed. So it would be three men against five. And his men only had automatics. Hadn't he seen one of Kessler's carrying an MP 38? They'd be lost against even that one machine gun, and Kessler would use the gun to shoot his way through the door. He was hammering on it already.

'Get ready.' Schiffer crossed swiftly to the door and opened it, standing back immediately. His men stood ready either side of it, close to the walls, covering the entrance.

Kessler came into the hall, followed by the cop with the machine gun. Kleinschmidt stayed on the threshold, gun out, but looking back to the cars. Schiffer looked at him but he didn't turn round.

A hubbub at the back of the house indicated that the two other cops had located the elderly couple and the dogs. It didn't sound as if the dogs were pleased to see them. Good, Schiffer thought, that might keep their hands tied for just long enough. But he'd have to act fast. No shooting yet.

'Kessler,' he said.

'Schiffer.' Kessler took a step forward. 'Is he here?'

'I have placed him under arrest.'

'Hand him over. I have direct authority to escort him back to Berlin.'

It was now or never, Schiffer thought, focusing the hatred and envy he had been storing for so long. Lose the glory, lose the initiative, sink back into the shadows again, no.

'I cannot do that,' he said, raising his right-hand pistol and shooting the policeman with the machine gun.

128

Kessler and Kleinschmidt pulled out their pistols and threw themselves down as the other two Gestapo-men opened fire, but in the panic and confusion, one of them shot the other in the knee.

The driver rushed out of the drawing-room, gun up. From his position on the floor, Kessler put a bullet in the man's chest before rolling over and struggling to get up, tripping as he did so and stumbling forwards. Schiffer turned his gun onto Kessler before the other man had a chance to get any further, but at that moment the door which led to the back of the house opened. Kessler's other men appeared, and they were ready.

The wounded Gestapo-man, howling in agony, had dropped his pistol. The other turned to face the newcomers; but the newcomers were experienced. They took in the situation and assessed it. They picked their targets. One fired at the able Gestapo-man and dropped him with a bullet which, as much by accident as good marksmanship, given the situation and the range, went through the man's left eye and out through the back of his skull, neatly, but leaving a mess on the wall. The other shot Schiffer through the back of the neck as he pointed his own guns at Kessler. He was screaming something before he went down. But the screaming stopped the moment the bullet hit him, and Schiffer's heavy body crashed into Kessler as it fell, knocking him down again. The noise of his voice continued to ring in Kessler's ears. What had it sounded like? Had he been shouting 'Fatherland'?

That was the word Stauffenberg cried out at his death, or so he'd heard.

There was more smoke and blood and yelling, and then another shot, after which the wounded Gestapo-man stopped howling. No-one knew who'd fired that. By the time everyone had calmed down, a few seconds, they found Kleinschmidt had reached the drawing-room and was keeping a gun on Hoffmann, still in his chair. The only Gestapo operative left alive was the driver, and they did what they could for him, which wasn't much; he died within minutes.

'Sweet fucking Mother of fucking Christ,' said one of the Munich cops. Wiping his hands and face with his handkerchief and trying to control his trembling. 'Who were those guys?'

'Bodyguards,' said Kessler, speaking without thinking.

'Something we'll have to find out,' said Kleinschmidt.

Kessler glanced at his sergeant, went to talk to Hoffmann. At first he couldn't control his voice. He looked back at his crew. Only Kleinschmidt wasn't shaking. Kleinschmidt had found a decanter of brandy and some glasses.

'This is the last thing we should be drinking after something like that,' he said, pouring liberal shots.

Kessler pulled himself together, looked at Hoffmann. 'You'd better have one as well.'

'How will I drink it?' said Hoffmann quietly, no tone at all in his voice.

Kessler turned to one of the Munich cops. 'Find the keys to these handcuffs. Search the pockets.' He nodded his head at Schiffer. 'Try that one first.'

The detective looked uncertain, but located the keys in Schiffer's jacket pocket, unlocked and relocked them with Hoffmann's wrists in front of him, put a glass of brandy in his hands. Everyone drank, someone passed round cigarettes.

'Anyone else in the house?' asked Kessler, taking Hoffmann's glass away. Hoffmann hadn't touched the drink. He seemed to have shrunk in the chair, drawn into himself.

'Old couple. Servants. Couple of gundogs. Left them locked in the kitchen where we found them.'

'Christ, what are we doing to do about this fucking mess?' said a Munich cop.

'We clear it up,' said Kleinschmidt .

'There's blood all over the wall out there.'

'As best we can.'

'There'll be questions when we get back.'

'We'll take care of it.' Kleinschmidt caught Kessler looking at him and added, 'It'll come out, but it'll be all right, sir, don't worry. In any case, we've got what we came for.' He glanced over at Schiffer. 'Whoever he was, that gentleman went rather beyond his brief I'd say, wouldn't you?'

Kessler switched his gaze to Hoffmann, but Hoffmann didn't meet his eye. He still seemed to be looking inward, waiting for something, perhaps even listening for something.

'There's a car round the back,' said the policeman who'd killed Schiffer. 'Big bugger, hidden behind a hedge. Might easily have missed it.'

Kessler was thinking fast. 'Calm yourself down, then go and take a look at it, soon as you're ready. He was still shaking himself, though less badly now. He had a pretty good idea about the car.

'Better search the bloody house too,' suggested Kleinschmidt, 'I suppose.'

'Yes,' Kessler agreed, wishing his sergeant hadn't chosen a moment like this to be conscientious. He turned to the other cop, 'Go upstairs, see if there's anyone else.'

'On my own?'

'Take the machine gun.' Kessler paused, looking at the two policemen. 'Christ,' he said, 'Let's all have another brandy first.' Luckily, no-one was eager to make a move, so there was still time, or so, at least, he hoped. It was all he could do.

Kleinschmidt looked at him, then shrugged his shoulders, grabbed the decanter. Five minutes later, unable to hold them any longer, Kessler nodded at his colleagues. One set off towards the back of the house. The other, more reluctantly, made for the main staircase, pausing to pick up the MP 38 from where it had fallen.

129

'We'll just leave it,' Kleinschmidt said, once they were alone. He got up heavily and drew Kessler aside. 'They started it. They're not in uniform - and you're right, how were we to know they weren't here to protect our friend?' He paused. 'And no-one's going to say anything about how you and Schiffer know each other.' He nodded his head in the direction of the dead policeman. 'Schreiner was the only one to hear you, and he's dead. The others were round the back. I'm not going to say anything - why should I?'

Kessler was silent. What Kleinschmidt was saying made sense.

'Let's see what the *Obersturmbannführer's* got on him,' Kleinschmidt continued. 'Bet he hasn't official papers for this. This was our arrest.'

'Go and keep an eye on Hoffmann,' said Kessler. 'I'll go through their pockets.' This was a job he needed to do himself.

'Take everything they've got, if you want,' said Kleinschmidt; 'No-one in the world's going to bring this back on us.'

Kessler had pulled a leg muscle badly at some point during the mêlée, and limped back to the hall. He knelt by Schiffer, lowering himself painfully to his knees, and rolled him onto his back. He tried not to look at the face, but couldn't help it, noticing the expression of angry surprise in the clouding blue eyes. Schiffer's skin was blotchy, and blood had seeped over the white collar of the shirt and the knot of his dark blue tie.

The trouser pockets yielded the expected keys, handkerchief, loose change. In the jacket, Schiffer's ID, cigarettes and a lighter, and his wallet, full of notes, bulging, and notes on scraps of paper. Two or three addresses among them. One of these Kessler caught Kessler's eye and he pocketed it after glancing swiftly round. Just a street name and number, but it rang a distant bell. Then he moved to the other dead Gestapo-men.

He was getting to his feet when the cop who'd gone to check the back of the house came running. 'The car! The car's gone.'

'Well, who the hell was in it? The old couple?' asked Kessler.

'No, they're still locked up.'

'Jesus. Did you at least check what kind of a car it was?'

'Yes,' The cop looked a little less panicky. He could be exact. 'A Maybach, SW 42.'

'Not many of them on the road. Get its number?'

'Other things to think about when I saw it first.'

Kessler looked towards the drawing room. Kleinschmidt was sitting in a chair near Hoffmann, his gun in his lap. Kessler didn't think either of them could have heard.

'Weigel's still upstairs. Go up and assist. Back here in ten minutes. And let him know it's you coming. He's got the MP 38 and he's nervous.'

'Sir.'

Kessler watched him go. He let out his breath noisily. He knew whose car it was.

He returned to the drawing room, the contents of Schiffer's pockets in his hands. He placed them on the table by the brandy decanter.

'Nothing,' he said to Kleinschmidt. 'Nothing of any significance, anyway.'

'Why don't you let me take care of it, sir?'

'No. I'll put most of it back. Look odd if he was found with nothing on him.'

'We could take the bodies out in the grounds and burn them.'

Kessler looked at him curiously.

'Make identification difficult,' Kleinschmidt explained.

'I don't think so. Someone'll know where he is. We'll have to make some kind of report. Dress it up.'

Kleinschmidt considered. 'You're the one with the Hitler-Order, sir. And you've got your man. Schiffer was a maverick anyway. No-one's going to blame you.' Kleinschmidt paused. 'What are the others doing?'

'Searching the other floors. I want you to go and watch the cars. Christ help us if they had backup.'

Kleinschmidt shook his head. 'They won't have. I'd better stay with you.'

'I'd feel safer if someone kept an eye on the cars. You can do it from the front steps. The columns will give you cover.'

'If you say so.' Kleinschmidt rose and made his way out of the room. Kessler wondered how much brandy he had drunk, but the decanter was still almost half-full.

Left alone, he and Hoffmann looked at each other at last.

130

'Well,' said Hoffmann.

'Well.'

Hoffmann let out his breath. 'Thank you for giving Tilli that break.'

'I don't know what you're talking about,' said Kessler. He knew what he was going to do. 'There isn't much time. Where are your papers?'

'In the bureau drawer. There's a panel at the back. Hidden compartment. Good workmanship in those days.'

There was a large Biedermeier desk between the windows that overlooked the garden. Kessler went over to it and found the Swedish passport, the Farben papers, the telephone engineer's papers, which Hoffmann had not destroyed, and the Walther 9. He glanced out of the window and could just see Kleinschmidt leaning on one of the columns that flanked the front porch, smoking a cigar, his gun in his hand. He looked like an American gangster, thought Kessler.

He returned to his prisoner.

'Schiffer took the other gun,' said Hoffmann. 'I hope to Christ they're going to be all right.'

'My man identified the car exactly. Even with the start they've got, they'll be lucky to get far in a car that, and I'm going to have to get the local police to look for it.'

'The car will command respect at the local road-blocks at least. I just want Stefan safe.'

'You did what you could.'

'I've put him in danger all his life.'

'I'm going to have to keep some of these papers,' said Kessler. 'What can you spare?' He was listening for the cops returning from upstairs.

'Take the telephone engineer's. He'll be glad to get them back.'

'Fine.'

'And find Emma,' said Hoffmann.

'I will.'

Kessler looked at the table near Hoffmann. He put the remaining stuff from the drawer and the handcuff keys on it. Next to them he placed the slip of paper with the address he'd taken from Schiffer's wallet.

They could both hear the other two policemen clattering hurriedly back down the central staircase.

Kessler went to the door, speaking fast. 'I've got to collect my sergeant, put this stuff back in Schiffer's pockets, find a telephone and call the locals about that Maybach.' He looked towards the windows at the far end of the room, which overlooked a summerhouse nestling in a copse about a hundred metres to the rear of the main building. He looked at Hoffmann again. Kessler thought, I'll never see him again. I'll probably never see any of them again. 'I'll find Stefan too,' he said, leaving the room, closing the door, and locking it carefully behind him, in time for the two Munich cops to see him do it. Kleinschmidt, too, had returned to the entrance hall. He took his time returning Schiffer's property to his body. Then he stood up.

'What do we do now?' said Kleinschmidt.

'Go and get those servants, find out where the telephone is and see if it works. Get on to the local cops if it does.' Kessler turned to the other two. 'One of you, take the car and drive to Iphofen. Tell the cops there what's happened. That way someone'll be here as soon as possible.' Weigel nodded and made for the door. Kleinschmidt lingered for a moment.

'Yes?'

'What about him?'

'He's locked in and he's handcuffed. Who do you think he is, Houdini? Get on with it.'

Kleinschmidt nodded and made his way, quickly for him, towards the back of the house. Kessler turned to the remaining cop, hoping to God that he had allowed enough time.

'Let's see how he's doing,' he said. 'Can't leave him alone for long.'

'Like you said, he isn't Houdini.' The cop grinned.

Kessler gave him the key. 'Watch him. I'm going to see how Kleinschmidt's getting on with that phone.' He hurried away before the cop had time to unlock the door.

361

131

The local police treated everyone with suspicion, but cleared up the mess, took the bodies away, and released the Zieglers and the dogs. The old couple were scared to death. Herr Ziegler worried about the dogs' welfare, neither he nor his wife had any idea where their mistress and her nephew had gone, or why. The local cops took them away anyway. Kessler had to give them something. His Hitler-Order had taken care of the rest. And there was no fingerprinting. It'd be pointless in the circumstances, and there wasn't any time to waste.

Kessler's crew split into two teams and used the two remaining cars to scour the area, spent the rest of the day and part of the next at it, going as far as their petrol supply would allow, bullying a few more litres out of the local police, without any success at all. Kessler then telephoned Munich, asked if they should continue the pursuit, but they were angrily recalled. A new team was coming out, a big one. Forty men. All Gestapo this time. It was already on its way. They would take charge. Schiffer's car should be left for their use. It wasn't going to be Kessler's business any more.

Kleinschmidt had been the last to leave the house, emerging from the back carrying a heavy bag which he placed between his feet as he took his seat in the car. The local police watched them drive off.

They'd worked out their story: they'd arrived in the middle of a gun battle between Hoffmann, two henchmen, and the Gestapo. Schreiner had been shot as they hastened to help their secret police colleagues - the last part a little suspect, but they were evidently on the same mission, let the Gestapo in Munich confirm or deny that Schiffer had gone beyond his brief. In the confusion, Hoffmann and his men had escaped in the Maybach.

The car smelt stale. Everyone was smoking.

'He'll find a blacksmith somewhere who won't talk,' said the cop who'd shot Schiffer. 'Get those cuffs off, no problem.'

'He hasn't got any money,' said Kleinschmidt. 'Has he?'

'He might not need it. Some of these bastards don't have any faith left,' grumbled Weigel. 'People are turning against us.'

'I just hope nobody starts digging,' said the cop who'd shot Schiffer.

'He won't get far.'

'What if he talks?'

'Who'll believe him?'

'I'll take the flak,' said Kessler.

'Should never have switched his handcuffs to the front, sir,' said Kleinschmidt.

'We don't talk about that, though, do we?' said Weigel. 'He was never arrested at all. His people shot our people, and he got clean away.'

'If they capture him and he's still got handcuffs on - ' said Kleinschmidt, and let the sentence hang. 'But what I'd like to know is, what happened to the keys?'

'Maybe the Gestapo dropped them,' said Weigel incautiously as his colleague shot him a warning glance: Kessler and Kleinschmidt were outsiders, after all. 'They should have let us carry on after him,' he continued, but more hesitantly. 'Take the new team hours to get here.'

'Out of our hands,' said Kleinschmidt. 'Just as well.' He turned to Kessler. 'Hard lines for you though, sir; would have been a feather in your cap, like I said.'

Kessler was thinking of Emma.

Kleinschmidt rummaged in his bag, producing bread and sausage, and four large bottles of beer. 'Bloody well-stocked kitchen there,' he said. He also brought out a packet of real cigarettes, and passed them round. Kessler recognised them as the ones he'd replaced in Schiffer's pocket.

The men ate and drank, refining their story. Kleinschmidt kept coming back to the point that Hoffmann got away so easily.

They fell silent after that. The drive back was a long one.

132

Once in Munich, Kessler gave the men orders to report to Police Headquarters the next morning at eight for debriefing. He was too tired to start thinking of the contingency plans which he'd have to make if he came in for a serious bollocking, or if he were recalled. But their story seemed pretty watertight, if they all stuck to it. He'd run the man down, after all; and now, with such a horde of secret police on his heels, the Gestapo would imagine - not knowing Hoffmann as Kessler did - that his capture could only be a question of time.

He went to his room, took off his jacket and shoes, loosened his tie, lay on the bed. It wasn't yet ten. He took off his glasses and placed them on the bedside table.

He must have slept without knowing it, for the next thing he knew was being awoken by a thunderous hammering on the door, punctuated by angry, hysterical shouting. He was up in moments, seizing his spectacles and pulling on his shoes. But his room was five storeys up, and the window gave onto a sheer drop. No escape. The ledge was narrow, and the next ledge too far away to reach. There were no footholds anywhere. Kessler was taking stock of this when the door burst open.

The cell had no windows. It was lit by three bulbs which hung high in the ceiling. A new metal desk and chair stood near the centre, and, across from them, a wooden stool, whose seat had holes bored into it to allow ropes to be passed through. Such rooms were familiar to Kessler. He was tied to the stool, and his ankles were bound. He couldn't believe they'd left him his glasses, though they were slipping down his nose and there was nothing he could do about it. Maybe they wanted him to see clearly.

He looked at the dark stains on the walls. The walls themselves were painted two different shades of grey, a darker giving way to a lighter about a third of the way up them. Kessler tried not to think of the physical pain, of broken bones, lost teeth, an eye put out, a punctured eardrum, a ruptured kidney; but he knew what went on, and he'd seen what they'd done to Adamov.

Footsteps at last, and a key turned in the lock. Metal door swinging open and a figure silhouetted in the glare from the corridor behind him. Stout and familiar, it approached and sat behind the desk as the door swung shut, leaving them alone in the baleful, chthonic lamplight.

'I've arrested the others, too,' said Kleinschimdt, having looking at him coldly for a minute. 'I don't yet know what to do with them. I can't return them to duty. But they've cooperated fully, and I'm convinced they know nothing. Just cops doing their job, as far as I can see. But perhaps it'll be better to be safe than sorry in the long run.'

'Who are you?' asked Kessler, trying to remember how long they had worked together. Eighteen months? As long as that? More?

'I don't owe you any explanation, Kessler.' Kleinschmidt took out one of his cigars, looked at it, decided against it, and replaced it in its box. 'You were a bit of a mystery to us. You weren't a Party member, yet you didn't seem to have anything to do with the conspiracy. Of course you enjoyed Hoffmann's protection. We had to keep an eye on you.'

'I thought Schiffer was doing that.'

'Yes, Schiffer.' Kleinschmidt fiddled with the cigar box on the table. What a good actor he'd been, thought Kessler. Took me in completely. He couldn't believe the change in the eyes.

'Schiffer was our backup,' continued Kleinschmidt. 'I was against his appointment. Too ambitious. Too much out for himself. But Müller overruled me. I had everything well in hand. Then the bloody fool went and fucked everything up.' The anger in his face was startling.

'He answered to you?'

'He thought it was the other way round. I didn't reveal my full hand to him, ever. I'm a *Standartenführer*.' He smiled thinly at Kessler's reaction. 'Thought that would surprise you. It's because I'm good at my job.' He clenched his fists gently, staring into the air. 'And now this. I had Hoffmann in my grasp. I would have wished a slower death on Schiffer.' He sighed. 'Well, we must do what we can to limit the damage.'

'But what were you doing at the house? Why didn't you join forces with him then?'

Kleinschmidt looked at him. 'It's odd, Inspector, but that's why I've grown almost fond of you. You do have to ask questions.' He smiled and the room grew colder. 'Schiffer cocked things up. He moved too fast, went quite outside his remit.' He stood up and walked around the room. 'He wanted all the glory for himself, and he thought he had it in his hands. Do you think, if things had gone his way, he would have hesitated to shoot me? His superior officer? He could have passed it off to our masters as an accident, or blamed it on one of the regular cops, and none of them, including you, would have left the villa alive.'

He moved back to the desk and sat at it. 'I kept my eye on you. I half suspected what was in your mind. Perhaps I should have shot you then, and the other two.' He sighed. 'But there were other factors. I might have been outgunned. The other two might have taken your side against me. There wouldn't have been time to explain things. Ah well, it's too late now.'

'I didn't think your interests went further than food and booze.'

'You have a lot to learn. I want to know why you let him go?'

'Because he's a good man. Because of what he did.'

'You could hang in Plötzensee just for saying that. If we bother to take you back. But you might just be enough of a sop to throw to the Führer. Buy us time.'

'Save your neck.'

'That's my principal concern, yes.' Kleinschmidt paused. 'We will get him, you know, despite this.'

'I think you underestimate him.'

'What I don't know, I'll get out of you,' said Kleinschmidt.

'I don't know where he is.'

'I think you do.' Kleinschmidt stood up. 'I'm not going to throw you to the wolves yet. I'm going to keep you for myself. But I'm going to have to work fast, if my boys don't run your man to ground in the next day or two. And you don't seem to think they will.'

That was why they'd reacted so quickly, thought Kessler. Kleinschmidt must have rung Munich from Tilli's house before they left. Tilli's telephone worked efficiently, given the friends she had.

'I'll leave you to think things over; but I'll see you again soon.' Kleinschmidt finally lit a cigar, went to the door, and hit it hard twice with the flat of his hand. It opened immediately. Kessler saw no-one behind it. Kleinschmidt walked unhurriedly through it, into the glaring corridor, said something in a soft voice to someone, then his footsteps receded.

133

They moved Kessler up some stairs to a small cell on the ground floor. It had a high, barred window, a bunk bed, table and chair, washstand and bucket. Kessler saw little of the building, and didn't recognise any of what he did see, but in the short time he was hurried down corridors he noticed plenty of activity. Men were piling papers into boxes, closing down offices, and in one room he glimpsed an officer feeding documents into a stove that roared like a furnace. They gave him some salt herring, some turnip, and a flagon of water, and they left him. He could hear men and women constantly on the move outside in the corridor, but he imagined the cell overlooked an inner courtyard, for there was no sound from outside. He stood on the chair to reach the window, but it was set too high, and deep in the thick wall.

Twice only in the next forty-eight hours, towards noon, as he judged, a jailer came to feed him, and escort him to where the bucket was emptied. He doubted if he were he the only prisoner here, but at times he wondered. There were air-raids during the night, one bomb fell close; the light in his cell flickered and finally went out; it did not go on again.

Late in the afternoon of the second day his cell door opened to admit Kleinschmidt. He looked less confident.

'We're moving you,' he said.

'When?'

'Coupla days.'

'What's going on?'

'None of your business.'

'Have you found him?'

'If we'd found him, you'd be dead,' said Kleinschmidt. 'As it is, you and I will talk soon.'

Left alone again, Kessler noticed how quickly silence fell throughout the building. He wondered if he were the only person left there. He drank the water in the flagon. It tasted of tin. In the distance, he heard the rumble of bombers again.

He thought he wouldn't sleep, but he did, at first fitfully, then deeply. He dreamt that he was in a wood. He recognised it, it was in a place he'd visited three or four times on holiday with his parents when he was a small child. He was six years old in the dream. There was a pool in the wood, in a small clearing. He would go to its bank and sit on some flat stones overgrown with moss, warm in the late afternoon sunshine, and, feet dangling, stir the dark blue water with a long stick, watching the ripples glitter. He had never felt such peace, though he knew he was in the wrong; his mother had forbidden him to go down there alone. Then - gunfire. A hunting party after boar? He stood up too quickly, slipped, and fell in. The water was soothing, like a friend. It covered him.

Kessler awoke abruptly. Shouting, and shots somewhere down the corridor outside. Then, running feet. Stopping outside his door.

'Kessler?'

'Yes?'

'Get away from the door. Well away.'

Numbly, he obeyed, going to one side, under the window.

'Done?'

'Yes.'

Gunfire again. Someone was shooting at the lock. The wood splintered around it. Whoever it was kicked hard from the outside. More wood splintered, and the lock fell away, allowing the door to swing open. Standing in the aperture were Hanno Heyme and two large men. All were dressed in overalls.

'Good morning,' he said. 'Welcome back.'

134

Hoffmann knew the surrounding countryside fairly well and made his way across it, skirting farms, for farms meant dogs.

He tripped over a root and sprawled, fearful in the moment of falling that he might have sprained his ankle. He must go slowly.

Had Tilli and Stefan managed to get away? The Maybach was well-known locally, but it was still a stupid, ostentatious car. She would have to have the devil's luck to get to the border in it now. Or maybe that wasn't the plan. Tilli was very far from being a fool.

There was nothing he could do now. He took comfort in the thought that Kessler, at least, was still in a position of command. He'd be able to control things. And Schiffer was dead. He could breathe a more easily in the knowledge that both his most promising protégés had been neutralised as threats.

There were roads he had to cross. On some of them a few people straggled, locals, going about their business as best they could. And a few outsiders, pushing bicycles, pulling handcarts, overloaded with suitcases and furniture, chairs, tables, curtains even, looking vulnerable and ridiculous in the open air. The master race on the run.

Climbing a bank on the side of such a road, he saw a spire he recognised in the distance. Scheinfeld. He was off course, after all.

***

They were driving through a battered and confused city. It had been another good raid for the enemy. Kessler saw people huddled in front of piles of rubble. Some were alive but, in passive panic, unable to move. Some twisted in the dust, trying to get rid of the pain of their wounds. Others, bunched up, did not move at all. Under the sun, the colours were vivid.

They'd bundled him fast out of the building and into the car. Two men in plain clothes had lain dead in the reception hall of an anonymous building that might once have been an unassuming hotel. The driver was skilful, avoiding obstacles with ease, and they reached the suburbs in ten minutes.

The first leaves were falling. A short driveway, and a solid, limestone merchant's house. Pillared portico. High double doors. They stopped at the back, hastened inside. Kessler had noticed an oldish NSU army motorbike following them, uniformed rider. But he'd stuck close, no-one had bothered about him, and before they'd entered the house, he'd pulled up behind the car and switched off. Fake outrider, give them a dash of officialdom, sensible, thought Kessler. The outrider followed them into the house, tossing the bike's keys into a bowl on a table by the back door.

A large room. Heavy furniture, stuffy, relieved by the sunlight through the net curtains. Honey-coloured wooden floors and Turkish carpets. Kessler collapsed on a sofa.

'Too early for a drink?' asked Heyme.

'Not today.'

'Guessed as much.'

Kessler took the schnapps and downed it in one, letting its heat hug him. He had another, took a cigarette, inhaled deeply.

'What the hell is going on?' he said.

Hanno leaned forward in his seat. 'You're lucky. You've got the same guardian angel as Adamov, and believe me when this is over, he's going to call in his debts.' He smiled. 'They've evacuated the place. The raids. Getting too hot for them. Taken the other prisoners God knows where. Your friend Kleinschmidt was working himself into quite a lather about it all. His masters were getting impatient and he didn't have time to take you somewhere safer to beat the truth out of you.'

'So what's happened?'

'They sent a big bunch of secret police out into the wilds a couple of days ago - '

'I heard. Did they find anything?'

'They found an abandoned car. Happens all the time. A Maybach. Big bugger. Suitcase in it, full of men's clothes and some books. Nothing else.'

Kessler thought, *clever* Tilli. 'Is the Gestapo still on the case?'

'Put ten more men on it and they're fanning out, south-west and south-east of Iphofen.'

'You are well informed.'

'Three of them are in our outfit.'

'Doesn't sound like you'll *need* me after all this is over.'

'Serious crooks are always well organised.' Hanno laughed. 'Look at the fucking Russians. But you can never have too much insurance.'

'Where's Kleinschmidt now?' he asked again.

'Alas,' said Hanno. He pushed a copy of the *VB* across the table:

BRUTAL MURDER OF WELL-LOVED PARTY LOYALIST AND SECURITY CHIEF

Standartenführer KLEINSCHMIDT, A., was found in the early hours of the morning in the Isar, where his body had washed up against a wharf. He had been brutally murdered, and the callous killers had stripped him and rammed 30cm lengths of sausage - allegedly salami - into his mouth and a lower orifice prior to strangling him. This disgraceful crime will be investigated and swiftly solved, and its perpetrators punished with the full vigour of the law!!!

His death will be deeply regretted by the Party, of which he had been a loyal servant since 1940, and his mother and sister, who survive him in his home town of Köpenick, Berlin. Funeral with full Police and Military Honours to be held on Tuesday, 15 August.

'There will be reprisals,' said Kessler.

'Not a chance. Who're they going to hang it on?'

'Why do that to him anyway?'

'You didn't know him that well.' Hanno smiled.

'I've another question.'

'Yes?'

'Do you know what's going on inside Dachau?'

'No. Who're we talking about?'

'A friend. A friend who's been compromised.'

'A Jew?'

'A Political.'

'Oh.'

'That is – a relative of a Political.'

'What?'

'Someone arrested under the Associative Guilt Programme.'

'Just when you thought they couldn't get any crazier, eh?' Hanno smiled again, but not with his eyes. 'Something to eat?'

'I'd better get going. They'll be after me.'

'But you must be hungry. Where're you going anyway? Dachau? Leave here unprotected and you'll end up there quicker than you can fart.'

There was something in Hanno's voice which Kessler didn't like.

'I've got to –'

'Find your friend. Who is she?'

'What?'

'Come on. It's how you asked the question. I haven't just fallen off the Christmas tree, you know.'

Kessler was silent.

'Look,' Hanno said. 'You'll have to trust me a little. Otherwise what progress will you make? Think about it. You are in my power and in my debt. Look at the balance sheet. Have I let you down? Did I let dear old Maxie Hottmann down?'

'What else did you take out of that Gestapo place?' asked Kessler. 'You obviously knew there were only a couple of guys guarding it. Any files left that might have been useful?'

'You know what, Inspector, if you want help, you shouldn't ask so many questions. You should be a little more grateful. And you shouldn't be so transparent. The only major *Political* you're connected to is Hoffmann. You've been with him for a decade. As far as we know, the only relative he's got left is his daughter. Doesn't take a Wernher von Braun to figure out that she might very easily have been arrested under the *Sippenhaft* laws.' Heyme uncorked the schnapps and poured two more, offered cigarettes.

Kessler accepted both, but he felt outgunned and cornered. 'You're right,' he said.

'Better!' beamed Hanno. 'Now, food! We've got suckling pig, dumplings, *Bratkartoffeln*, salad, real coffee. Slightly heavy breakfast, but you've been through a lot. And you shouldn't be drinking on an empty stomach.'

Kessler drank anyway, inhaled his cigarette, and felt better, and then immediately worse. He retched.

'It's not drugged; it's just that you're feeling weak,' said Hanno, reading his thought. 'But we'll see you right.' He went to the door, opened it and shouted, 'Kleist!'

A minute later, one of the two men from earlier that morning - already an age ago - came into the room. Dressed in a suit and tie now, he looked even bulkier than he had in overalls. How had these guys avoided military service?

'Get them to fix our friend a meal.'

Kleist nodded and left.

'Now,' said Hanno. 'We know that some of the prisoners have been moved out, but not the ones in striped pyjamas. Special treatment types. Don't know who, or why, or where, but it's likely that Emma Hoffmann was one of them.'

'Emma?'

'I've worked on this side of the fence all my life. Thirty years. Since I was thirteen. I can remember what it was like during the first show. And the Twenties. Good times. Good pickings. But we always knew how to survive, and we stayed fat. How? Organisation and information.'

'You should be in charge.'

'We are in charge.' He stretched, yawned. 'And you're one of us now, like it or not. Stray, and you're dead. Don't think you can outwit us.'

Kessler knew he had no choice but to play along - tomorrow things might be different, and the world had never been more uncertain than it was at present. He wondered how soon he could get away. He calculated the time he'd been out of action. He needed to find Emma, somehow; but he had no lead yet. Maybe there was another priority. 'Can you help me with transport?'

'What do you want - blood? You're going to have to lay low. Food and sleep first. Decide what to do next tomorrow. Anyway, there's things I need to discuss with you - you might as well start paying us back right away.'

'Where's Adamov now?'

'Why do you want to know?'

'Where is he?'

'He's gone. Soon as he could walk. All Adamov had was stuff we already knew. You are much bigger game. When you've eaten and rested, you and I are going to have a long conversation.'

'What about?'

'What the *Kriminalpolizei* is up to. Everything you know.'

'No. Later. Now I've got to get away.'

Heyme leant forward again. 'You aren't going anywhere. You're staying with us. When the dust settles, we'll get you reinstated. They'll need bright young cops with experience, and they won't ask questions.' He sat back. 'We've been running quite a little recruitment drive here in Munich.'

135

Kessler knew that the drink was affecting him. He took off his glasses and polished them on his shirt. He still had no tie, belt or shoes. He settled the glasses back on his nose. He looked at the door. Where was Kleist? Where were the others?

'I've got to find Emma, ' he said.

'No-one knows where she is.'

Kessler looked round the room. It was another prison. 'I think I need some air,' he said, smiling, and getting to his feet.

Heyme started to get up too, but before he could, Kessler seized the half-full bottle of *Doornkaat* and hit him hard on the side of the head with it. It was a good blow. Heyme fell back down on the sofa, didn't even make a sound.

Fighting to keep his breathing steady, and straining his ears for the slightest sound, Kessler took off Heyme's shoes and put them on - too big, but manageable. He bent over and rummaged in his jacket for his pistol, found it, and slipped it into his own pocket. Kessler had no money and no papers. He took Heyme's wallet as well. He hoped that Heyme's papers would cover him somehow. The risk was huge. But what mattered most was to get away.

He went to the door and listened.

Not a sound. He opened it. The hall was deserted, the heavy woodwork frowned down on him. Stairs led up to a galleried first floor, and down to a half-basement where the kitchen probably was. From beyond a closed door opposite, men's voices, subdued, and the occasional shout. Playing cards. He crossed the hall, his feet slipping about in Heyme's shoes. Reaching the back door, he looked into the bowl. Several sets of keys. Two clearly belonged to doors; but the other two looked more promising. He took both. Then he froze. He could hear footsteps coming up the stairs from below. He could smell food. It smelt delicious. He couldn't believe how hungry he was. He put his hand on the knob of the back door and turned. It gave. As swiftly and as silently as he could he opened the door and slipped through.

The morning air was keen still. He made his way to the bike. The first set of keys didn't work. From the house he heard a yell. He tried the second, forcing himself not to jab the key at the lock. Finally he got it in. Turned it. Kicked the engine alive.

He got moving just as they started shooting from the house.

136

There was a drab-looking house in Bern, off the Bundesgasse, not far from the Käfigturm; but its interior was anything but drab. It was larger than it looked from the outside, and it was one of the main bureaux of the Office of Strategic Services in the city. Thin, fraught young Americans moved through long rooms lined with desks laden with typewriters, telephones and teleprinters, under the aegis of their foul-mouthed, genial boss, Allen Welsh Dulles, whose own office, to their relief, was elsewhere in the city.

In a large, net-curtained room on the second floor three people sat round a low table, leaning forward in their armchairs, their tea, neglected, growing cold as they talked. They had reached the end of a long road.

General Richter, tired after a heavy debriefing, had let Emma tell most of the story. He had to admit to himself that, in retrospect, the worst part of the whole adventure had been the interrogations at the hands of the eager young Americans, one of whom was sitting discreetly in a corner, pad and pencil on her lap. That one, he knew, spoke fluent German, French and Italian. Russian too, probably, for all he knew. These American spies were pros, he'd give them that.

He and Emma had had an easier drive to the Swiss frontier than they'd deserved. People had given up. Road-blocks were ill-kept, if they were kept at all. The only real dread was of SS patrols, but they'd been fortunate. Richter's uniform answered most questions, the girl was his niece, under his protection, they were driving back to his country house near Badenweiler, where he would leave her before ending his leave and resuming his frontier patrol duties. The fact that he had indeed been on frontier patrol for a time and had papers to prove it forestalled any other enquiries; and in the short time he had spent as a prisoner, no-one had inspected his uniform closely, so no-one had found the thousand dollars in tens, fives and ones that had also been sewn into its jacket lining. Transferred to a wallet, those bills had smoothed the rough passages, and the jeep had enough fuel for the journey.

He'd thought that the frontier might be a problem, but the guards who manned it were so used to their SS colleagues crossing with despatches, that a well-heeled and generous regular army general presented them with no problems.

Clearly no word had reached them of his escape, but that didn't surprise him. He reckoned the news would take another twenty-four hours to reach them.

Safe in Switzerland, Richter felt obscurely disappointed. He knew, of course, that they'd keep him here far longer than they'd keep Emma. He knew that more interrogations lay ahead of him, and that in the meantime he'd be kept under hotel-arrest; but that was nothing. He didn't have to lie any more. Whether they chose to believe him or not was out of his hands.

Emma told her part of the story well. She didn't embellish. She was serious and concentrated, even if, for her, it had been far more of an adventure. But she would not be parted from her violin. The violin meant everything to her.

The American girl - how old was she? - twenty-five? Americans always looked younger than they were - took notes occasionally. Hans Brandau, the third person at the table, bent forward, forearms on knees, immaculate white cuffs exposed an exact centimetre beyond his dark jacket sleeve, watched Emma as she talked.

No-one had news of Hoffmann. No-one knew anything about Tilli or Stefan. The courier taking the travel permits to Tilli's mansion had, they learned, been detained by the police at Würzburg. He'd been lucky that it was regular police who'd picked him up. He was Swiss, but able to disguise his Swiss-German accent completely, even able to put on a convincing Freiburg burr. His own papers were in order - a clerk to the Freiburg Judiciary - and they let him go, after questioning, and double-checking with the phone number he gave them. A Doctor Martens answered, vouched for him, seemed impatient. They apologised and hung up. But their investigation had taken time. When the courier finally arrived at Tilli's mansion, it was deserted. He had destroyed the documents and returned to base.

After the meeting, Brandau left them and made his way to an office in another part of the building. He took his place at a desk opposite a burly man in his fifties, harassed behind a battery of red files.

'Well, Hans?' said the man, in English.

'No reason why she shouldn't go, I think. We've arranged an affidavit with Kara von Wildenbruch's mother in New York. Frau von Wildenbruch knows the situation - we sent someone to talk to her personally, and it seems by some miracle she had a letter from Kara all those years ago. And we've checked her own background, just in case. No problem there.'

'Did you tell her about her daughter?'

'What was there to tell? She's heard nothing for a decade. She wasn't surprised.' He paused. 'Of course I didn't tell her everything.'

The man reached for a pad and scribbled on it. 'I'll sort out the details.'

'General Richter stays, of course.'

'We'll keep him here until it's over. I want him under our eye just in case. After that, we'll turn him loose, with a pardon, if he's clean. He'll probably lose his army pension, though.'

Both men laughed drily.

'He'll get a directorate somewhere,' said Brandau. 'They're going to need people like him to run the country.'

'And people like you?'

Brandau smiled. 'I'm not that clean. I'd have to keep my back to the wall all the time. I'll stay here, or go to France.'

'Or come to us. You've been a great help.'

'We'll talk about that later.'

The man tore the top sheet off his pad and placed it in his out-tray. 'That'll be processed by the end of the week. Then we'll get her on a ship out of Lisbon for New York.'

137

Emma didn't see any more of General Richter. The OSS moved him somewhere in the suburbs and broke off contact between them. They left her alone, more or less, though she had to check into the office once a day at ten. Otherwise, she idled about the hotel and the town, not quite able to believe that she was in a place that functioned normally, out of war, where things she'd half-forgotten were freely available. Real coffee. Real tea. Stockings, and shoes that weren't sensible. Brightly-lit cafés, the smell of cigars in the open air. But she remained in Germany in her heart. She thought of her family. She thought of Paul Kessler. She didn't think she would ever see him again.

She sat in a café, gleaming chrome, boxwood and neon, sipping a hot chocolate and wondering what would happen next. She had had nothing but hints from the OSS officers, and imagined she was being kept in the dark deliberately, as a security measure. Departure for the USA had been Richter's idea, and the Americans had gone along with it once they'd located Kara's mother. The arrival, in Emma, of a grandchild of sorts was welcome, and Kara's mother could know nothing of Stefan.

Emma decided she would tell her what she could of the truth, if they did let her go; and, although she was undecided herself, there was nothing she could do now to influence the decisions made on her behalf. She knew no-one in Switzerland, and her family was dispersed or dead. She was lucky that Kara's mother was willing to stand by her.

And, she told herself, she could come back one day, if there was anything to come back for. Brandau would tell her if any hope arose; and he'd promised to pass news of her on to anyone she knew who might turn up in Bern looking for her; so it was not an irrevocable step that she was taking.

But it was a big one. She looked down at her violin, in its case at her feet.

'Hello, sweetheart.'

A voice like a gravel pit, old, a voice whose owner over years had smoked too many cigarettes and drunk too much gin. But it was also familiar, sober and sad. Emma looked up.

'Remember me?'

She did, but it was the voice she recognised. She tried hard to conceal her shock when she saw him. He was smartly dressed, pinstripe suit and bow-tie, though he was the kind of person who makes any clothes somehow look shabby. But his face... A clobbered-looking face, heavy and lizard-like, was looking down at her from under what was a very obvious wig. One eye was gone, leaving a puckered flap of skin where it had been. His mouth could not smile properly, though he tried to make it, and when he opened it she could see the wreckage of his teeth. He leaned on a black walking-stick and when he moved it was with a heavy limp. His left leg bent at the knee at an unnatural angle. His other hand held a suitcase. He must have been in a terrible accident, whoever he was, for now she couldn't be sure she knew who he was after all.

'I know I look worse than Boris Karloff, but they tell me that in a few months and with a handful of nips and tucks I'll be Johnny Weissmüller again.'

He sat down carefully, placing the case between his feet, wincing; looked around for a waiter, failed to find one, looked at her instead.

'You don't remember me at all, do you?'

138

Emma looked at him hard, but there was nothing. 'Not very well,' she lied.

'That's what I like! A diplomat!' He waved vainly at an elderly waiter scurrying past, gave it up, turned to her again.

'I suppose I should have introduced myself before I sat down. Veit Adamov.' he paused, searching her face, and now she could see sadness and pain in his. She wanted to know him, but her memory wouldn't obey her. 'Uncle Veit? Friend of your dad's?'

Emma felt a rush of relief, and, equally, horror. What had happened to him? Had he been in a fire? 'Of course I know you!' she said. 'You were Kara's friend, too.'

'I had that honour,' said Veit, quite seriously. His back hurt badly. Where the hell was a waiter? He needed a brandy. He turned on a smile. 'I expect you're wondering what brings me to the Land of Milk and *Hallau*?'

'How long have you been here?'

He looked at his watch. 'Twenty-four hours. Enough to make contact. get a change of clothes and so on. Sorry I can't make a better impression than I do.'

She couldn't bring herself - didn't dare - to ask him what had happened. She hoped he would tell her himself when he wanted to. 'How did you get here?' she said instead.

'Lorry. Hitched a lift. I'm a travelling salesman these days. In canvas. That's what the papers they gave me in Munich say.'

Emma looked at the suitcase. 'You can't have much canvas in there.'

'That's film-footage of the canvas-making process,' said Adamov. 'In there.' He gave the case a protective nudge with his foot. A waiter finally appeared.

'Cognac,' said Adamov. 'Bring the bottle. And whatever the lady wants.'

'Cognac will do fine,' she said.

He took out his wallet and reviewed its contents anxiously as the waiter withdrew. 'You might have to sub me,' he said. 'I've splashed out on clothes and makeup.'

She looked at him. 'Does anyone know you're here?'

'Christ, I hope not!'

'What are you going to do with the film?'

'Take it with me.'

'Where?'

Adamov grinned as the waiter arrived with the brandy. 'The USA.'

She wondered what was coming. 'How are you going to get there?'

Adamov spread his hands. 'I read somewhere that the Americans have a presence in this town.'

'It's possible.'

'I imagine, with your father's contacts... '

'No.'

'No?'

'I can't. I'd like to help you, Uncle Veit, but I can't just – I mean, I don't have any...'

Adamov poured their brandy and took a gulp of his without waiting. He'd have liked to drain the glass, but he had to make the thing last. He didn't even know how much they were going to charge him for it, and the girl hadn't agreed to sub him yet. 'It's because I'm a Communist, *n'est-ce pas*?' He pointed at his face. 'I daresay you've noticed what they did to me, back in the Fatherland.'

He was ashamed of his outburst, and he didn't want to embarrass the girl, still less antagonise her.

'Go to the police here,' said Emma, after a pause. A thought struck her. 'Do you know someone called Hans Brandau?'

'Heard of him.'

'He has an office of his own. He's a lawyer. He's a friend of my father's too.'

'So Brandau got away? The old rogue. And your dad?'

'I don't know.'

Adamov hesitated, then reached across, squeezed her hand. 'You dad's like me. Indestructible.'

Emma looked anxious. 'Maybe you should see Brandau.'

Adamov nodded, but he was worried, his mind immediately back on his own affairs. He tapped his suitcase. 'This needs to go in a diplomatic bag. It's important stuff. Classified.'

'Show it to Brandau.' She hesitated. 'He has contacts.'

'Got his address?'

'Yes.'

Veit polished off his cognac. What the hell? He was feeling better already. 'Do they run a tab in this place?' he asked.

Ten days later, Emma, feeling more lonely and more nervous than she ever had, sat on a bunk in a shared cabin in a ship slowly churning its way out of Lisbon harbour. At the same time General Richter, dressed now in a dark suit, wearily presented himself for another round of questions in a nondescript room in the suburbs of Bern. At the same time Adamov, clutching his suitcase, was leaving Brandau's office for the last time after a series of interviews, smiling broadly. And at the same time Brandau, having written a memo to arrange Adamov's transport to New York, 'in order for my representative to demonstrate to the relevant authorities the full extent of Nazi sexual degeneracy at high levels', picked up a telephone and addressed himself once more to the more important problem of organising the collection of Hitler's aerospace designers before the Russians could get them.

It was the morning of the third day. Hoffmann, footsore, completed a broad curve round the foot of a hill and saw on its crag the lonely, red-roofed tower of the Altenburg, a thin pillar interrupting the easy slouch of the wooded hills on the horizon. Below the little fortress, and just visible, were the four green spires of Bamberg cathedral.

139

Rain fell as Hoffmann made his way the last few kilometres towards the town. Despite two nights of sleeping rough again, and two days of slogging through the countryside avoiding roadblocks and routine police checkpoints, he felt good. He'd recovered his strength at Tilli's, he knew this countryside; and he was experienced in roughing it - a lifetime after driving out of Berlin with Brandau. This was the endgame. He was calm. He felt as if he were watching an actor in a film, playing his part.

The rain ceased at last, and the clouds dispersed, as if by a theatrical trick, to reveal a warm sun. Hoffmann's shoes, damp and on his feet for two days, were beginning to pinch. He'd have to change them soon. He shared the preoccupation of every pursuer and every fugitive – take care of your feet; never risk being immobile. But then, he thought wryly, perhaps it would not after all be necessary to change his shoes again, ever.

As the town came increasingly into view – the delicate green spires of the cathedral, the two black needles of the Michelskirche – his resolve strengthened. He'd done what he could for his family. He'd got this far. Now he had his own account to settle.

After Stegaurach he walked over the fields to Wildensorg, passing the Altenburg on his right, crossing the Michelsberg and descending to the river, to the foot of the Markusbrücke. There, he passed Paul Krauss' greengrocery, now selling nothing but black radishes, but even before he reached it, he could smell Dels' leatherworks from the courtyard of 14, Untere Sandstraße.

He went down to the river and turned right along the heavy cobbles of Am Leinritt, glancing at the wooden fishing boats on his left, moored in the reeds, and looking across the river at the pretty collection of medieval houses on the opposite bank known for some dotty reason or other as Klein Venedig.

The river flowed slowly and easily here, a gentle river, and he followed it as far as the yellow prison, where he turned right again and away from it, back to more populated streets. He passed the house where a Jewish tailor worked, protected by a discreet Gestapo guard outside. Groceries and laundry were regularly collected and delivered, Hoffmann knew all about it. The tailor had been spared because he was good; he'd spent years making uniforms for the local SS.

Bamberg had been a Nazi hotspot; but it was also the town in which Count von Stauffenberg had made his home, and married. His large flat was empty now. Countess Nina had been arrested, of course, after her husband's coup failed - the failure which had brought all of them down.

But Adamov had been right - it had been worth making the attempt. Hoffmann was finally proud. It was all that had made sense of his life over the past decade.

As he walked, he kept his eyes open. The people in the streets didn't look twice at this large man in country clothes; but Bamberg wasn't a large enough town for strangers to pass un-noted. He'd passed the checkpoint into town without any of the problems he'd anticipated, knowing that a net would have been spread for him since his escape from Tilli's. But no-one had challenged him, or questioned his papers. The good clothes and his physical stature gave him an aura few provincial Nazis would question, and perhaps Kessler had succeeded in throwing them off the scent - perhaps they were concentrating their search southwards. His papers were still good, though Hoffmann knew that he didn't have long, and that when any net they cast to the south yielded no fish, it would be cast again elsewhere. He had no idea who Hagen could be in touch with, or how much clout Hagen still had - if the man were here at all. But he *knew* he was. He *knew* this was inevitable. He had to do his work fast.

The centre of Bamberg, though it is steeply hilly on the cathedral-side of the Regnitz, is small. Hoffmann didn't have far to go. Towards the Concordia mansion, near what used, before the war, to be called the Judenstraße, was an elegant little street, Kunigundagasse. Its Baroque town houses were jewels. Tourists before the war came here to photograph their sandstone exteriors, their ornate little *porte-cochères*.

Hoffmann had long since memorised the address Kessler had given him, destroyed the piece of paper it'd been written on. He glanced at house numbers, keeping to the side where the house he was looking for would be - he didn't want to be seen from a window across the street. He slowed. There was a *Wirtshaus* halfway down - *Zum Sankt Georg*. Three doors beyond it was the house. He touched the door, craned as he looked up. The place seemed, felt, deserted.

As the sun began to set, he walked on, making the circuit of a long block. His feet were tired. He had to stay alert. He made his way back to the river, crossing it by the Town Hall Bridge, finding a large bar on the Obstmarkt. He went in and ordered a *Stein* of beer, enough to cover the time he intended to spend, but he would scarcely touch it. He would give it an hour. He'd go back when it was dark. If there were a chink of light behind the blinds somewhere among the windows facing the street, he would chance it.

He looked around the room. It was a humdrum sort of place. A few local bigwigs seated at the *Stammtisch*, talking loudly about nothing - the hunting season, the unseasonable showers. A handful of men in uniform, bent over their beers and not too talkative at all. A couple of farmers working their way through a mound of sauerkraut garnished with sad little sausages fifty-per-cent made of acorn. Moving between the groups in the dim yellow light, two bargirls with their hair in braids and dirndls on.

The One-Thousand-Year Reich, as 1944 began to creep to its end. Eleven years since it began. Ten years of fighting, for Hoffmann. He lit a cigarette and sipped his beer. Cold and good. A Michelsberger from the Peßler brewery. He watched as the windows beyond the net curtains grew dark.

He thought of Kara. He thought of his children. And he thought, vaguely, of all the people he knew, tried to imagine what they were doing, at this moment, wherever they were. They existed, they had their preoccupations. Were they eating, working, fucking, sleeping, reading, shopping, walking, gazing into space?

What a daft thought: as daft as contemplating eternity or the universe.

But how strange, now and then, in the midst of one's day-to-day tasks, to imagine your friends, even your distant acquaintances, calling you to mind: for *you* to be there, involved in imagined occupations, in another person's head?

And did it work as telepathy? There had been some top-level research on this: Hitler took a keen interest in the supernatural. But there was a scientific basis. Serious papers had been written. Might Hagen *know* he was coming?

What bollocks.

Some time later, the landlady closed the shutters. Hoffmann looked at his watch. His hour had passed. He smoked one more cigarette. He paid for his beer, got up stiffly, and made his way out into the gathering gloom.

140

He took his time. He didn't want to be disappointed. He'd come so far. Suddenly he felt very tired. But when he reached the corner of Kunigundagasse again, he saw dim light through the shutters of the first floor of the house three doors down from the *Sankt Georg*. As he drew closer, he saw a shadow move across the room beyond the windows, coming and going, bulky; bending and turning; deliberate, busy movements. Someone packing.

Hoffmann checked his Walther 9, drew in his breath, knocked firmly on the door.

A pause. Silence. Then footsteps. Another hesitation. Any kind of trap could be set. Then the door swung wide. Warm light behind it, pale yellow walls and wood, bookcases, landscapes in golden frames.

'Hoffmann, here you are at last. I suppose you'd better come in.' Wolf Hagen stood aside. Blue business suit, striped shirt, polka-dot bow tie, like Churchill's. Heavy cufflinks. Weapon? Possibly.

Hagen didn't seem surprised, though his eyes were busy. There was dust on his jacket. Hagen's eyes were trying to smile now, but they stayed hard.

'Expecting me?'

'Well, you got through the net. I thought, either you'd go south of the border, or you'd want to settle accounts first.' Hagen sucked at his cigar. 'Pity. For me. Twelve hours later and you'd've missed me. Still, one has to see the positive side of everything. Despite that idiot Schiffer. I expected more of him, given that you trained him.'

They'd reached the drawing-room, a large space with dark walls and o lot of reproductions of Greek statuary. There were Louis XV chairs, fragile side-tables, two settees in crimson and white, and oriental carpets on the parquet.

'Drink?' asked Hagen.

'Brandy.'

Hagen poured from a heavy decanter into cut-glass balloons. 'We both need one of those. But no toasts. I don't suppose you're in the mood.'

'No.'

'Let's sit down, at least. And let me reassure you, on whatever honour I have left, that I am alone. I don't have a gun either. There's no ambush.'

'But you *were* expecting me?'

Hagen spread his hands. 'You must have known that I would be. Not that I particularly wanted this meeting. I suppose I hoped they'd get you before you reached me. I should have been in more of a hurry, but I've always liked to see whatever work I've had to do... *finished*.' Hagen looked at him. 'I do have you at an advantage. You are on the run. I am not. Officially, I am still respectable. And valued. That's why they let you through the town checkpoint. I didn't want those idiots to arrest you and then have you slip through their fingers. No.' Hagen smiled. 'I wanted you to myself. To be sure of you. And to have a last little chat.'

Hoffmann looked at Hagen's left hand ring finger. Hagen followed his gaze.

'Of course I know why you're here,' he said. The photographs.'

'Not just because of them. But I am curious. Why did you do it?'

Hagen sat on the arm of one of the armchairs. His eyes flickered once towards the door behind Hoffmann's left shoulder. Hoffmann didn't sit down. He moved to the shuttered window.

Hagen sipped, placed his balloon on the miniature table beside him. 'I am sorry we could never be friends,' he said. 'We were after all on the same side, and no-one outside this wreck of a country is going to believe you if you tell them it is otherwise.'

Hoffmann was silent for a moment, then he said: 'I'm curious now - why didn't you have a crack at me long before this?'

'We tried, as you know perfectly well.' Hoffmann kept his voice even. His thoughts were nowhere but here in this room. 'Why else were you always so careful to keep as far away from me as possible? And you had better protection than Eichmann. But I knew I'd get you in time, and I had other work to do.'

Hagen smiled. 'My dear Max, do you think what you did for the enemy ever outweighed what you did for us? You were never anything more than a bunch of pathetic do-gooders, and now you've paid the price.'

'The whole thing's finished. For you, too.'

'Is it? I have money in Switzerland and a ticket for Buenos Aires. What have you got?'

'Nothing. But I did have Kara.'

141

Hagen looked at the floor. His cigar, neglected, had gone out in its heavy crystal ashtray. 'So it's just personal?'

'Don't make yourself ridiculous, Wolf.'

Hoffmann watched Hagen carefully. The man was getting angry. His brow and his palms were wet with sweat. His act was wearing thin. He started to clench his fists, but controlled himself, stood up, poured himself more brandy.

'You mentioned the photographs,' said Hoffmann. 'You must have known they'd lead me to you.'

Hagen didn't look at him. He took out a handkerchief and mopped his forehead, his upper lip. 'I am beginning to regret waiting for you,' he said.

'No you aren't. You're after one last little bit of satisfaction before you run.'

'You were just lucky - if that's the word.'

'Shut up,' said Hoffmann harshly.

Hagen ducked as if he'd been hit.

'You're a clever man,' continued Hoffmann. 'Why did the photographs get into *Der Stürmer*? You must have known. Why court the danger? Or did you really think you were safe enough to send me that kind of signal?'

Hagen spread his hands again. 'You won't believe this, but I loved her too.'

Hoffmann laughed.

'Don't laugh at me,' said Hagen. 'I don't like being shat on.'

'You've taken it from your masters long enough.'

'No-one ever shat on me!' Hagen controlled himself. 'With the Nazis, it was only ever business. I didn't care about their stupid ideas. I loved Kara and she treated me as if I'd crawled from under a stone.'

'You knew she had Jewish blood.'

'She would have been safe with me. She could have gone on working, if she'd wanted to. You took her away. You are as guilty as I am, but you can't see it.'

'The only thing that hurts you is your vanity.'

'How dare you tell me what my feelings are.'

Hoffmann let it go, looked past him into the room. On a sofa against the far wall was an open suitcase, black leather, full of neatly-stacked clothes. Next to it was a briefcase full of American bank notes and what looked like legal documents.

'Look,' said Hagen, drinking and refilling again, changing tack. 'We are brothers, in a sense, aren't we, after all? We even look like brothers!' He stood, walked about the room, glass in hand, cigar forgotten. 'Can't we get over the past? I know what you've done, but with my help, you could get out of here too. Left alone, who is ever going to believe you were on the side of the angels? Whoever picks you up, you're dead.'

'Why would you help me?'

'Because here are still hurdles you could help *me* over.'

Hoffmann knew this was rubbish, and put his hand on the gun in his pocket. Hagen was playing for time. 'Where? In Bern? You said twice no-one outside Germany would believe me. Or aren't you sure?' Hoffmann wondered where the flight to Buenos Aires was leaving from. If Hagen's ticket existed. Hagen was silent, put his glass down, faced him.

There was the sound of a motorbike in the street.

'Why did you authorise the photographs?' Hoffmann asked.

Hagen sat again. 'I really thought the pictures were too blurred to give anything away, and I never noticed that my stump of a finger registered. Foolish, eh?' Hagen looked at Hoffmann. Then his expression hardened. 'But you are right - I decided to take the risk. I knew how clever you were, you and that little shit of a sidekick you have.' He paused, looked up with hard eyes. 'Of course I wanted you to know.'

'Yes.'

'You bastard. You took her away from me.'

'She was never yours.'

'She chose you!'

'Did killing her change that?'

Hagen looked at him. 'You could have been over the border by now. Why are you still here?'

'To kill you.'

'And make sure your little bastard was safe? Another thing Schiffer fucked up for me. I hadn't known about him. That was clever.' Hagen reached for his glass again. 'Your bloody love-child. But they'll get him for me now, whatever happens here. Fucking Jewish brat. They found the car, you know? They'll find him and they'll fucking kill him, the little shit, they'll rip his fucking heart out. Then that'll be every trace of dear little Kara gone.'

Hoffmann took out his gun and pointed it at Hagen. He'd had enough. What was the point of listening to anymore?

Hagen looked at the little Walther. He drank some more. He was agitated; the liquid ran down his chin. 'No. Not with that pop-gun. Most you could do is wound me, even at this range.' He made an attempt to pull himself together. 'You and I are brothers, Max. I made money out of this shitpile, and you helped it more than you harmed it. Time to face facts, my friend. I think I got the better deal.'

Hagen glanced for the second time towards the door. Hoffmann turned in its direction just as a slim young man with a revolver in his hand appeared in it.

Hoffmann, moving fast, fired first, and the man staggered, but recovered enough to get two shots of his own off before falling. One of the bullets hit Hoffmann squarely in the chest, but he kept on his feet and turned back to face Hagen.

'You didn't seriously think I was alone, did you?' said Hagen, smiling.

142

Hoffmann still had his hand on his own gun. Hagen came very close.

He thought he had won. Hoffmann's legs were weakening. He only had seconds. He brought the Walther up and shot Hagen between the eyes, at a range of ten centimetres. Blood fountained over him as Hagen fell backwards, his hands, already dead, jerking upwards in response to the last message sent by the brain to protect what could no longer be protected.

Hoffmann's gave way and as he went down he felt another bullet hammer into his back, not far from the first.

But the job was done. Through the blurred lens of one eye, he could see Hagen crumpled against the skirting board, hands halfway up to a face that wasn't a face at all anymore.

He let his body lie down. He heard feet pummelling upstairs, then other gunshots.

Then, someone cradling him, someone lifting his head from the floor.

'I'm too late,' said Kessler. Was he crying?

Hoffmann recognised the voice. 'You have a knack of cropping up when you're needed,' he said. 'But you need to work on your timing. Who was it?'

'Bodyguard.'

'Didn't finish him. What a fool I am.'

'Why did you let them take you?' Kessler was sobbing, no doubt about it. Was he angry with him, Hoffmann thought. Why?

'It doesn't matter,' he said. 'How did you know I'd be here?'

'You know that.'

Hoffmann realised that it was getting harder and harder for him to breathe properly. He clutched Kessler's sleeve, tried to look up. 'Find them for me.'

'We'll do it together.'

Cradling Hoffmann's head, Kessler reached for a cushion and pressed it hard against Hoffmann's chest wound to staunch it, but the blood would not stop pumping out with every slowing heartbeat, and Kessler could do nothing about the wound in Hoffmann's back. He thought desperately that he might be able to get his boss to the sofa, make him comfortable, ring a doctor, something...

'Don't do anything,' said Hoffmann. 'If you do, they'll get you too. Get away, now. Or you won't be able to help me.'

Kessler breathed hard. 'I'll find them for you,' he said.

'Thank you,' said Hoffmann, holding Kessler's wrist with his right hand. 'Now go. Now.'

He was still conscious, but only enough to know that his senses were drifting. He saw Kara before him, standing in the room, in her coat, with their suitcase ready, smiling, ready to leave with him; but he knew she was not there, not there really, not ever again. There was nothing he could do about it. There was nothing he could do about anything anymore, but if he felt anything as the moments darkened, it was relief. The laughter and tears, the hope and tension, and the horror, too, were leaving him, letting him go, into silence. And all the time his little boy's arms held him tight.

143

Tilli had known she'd have to abandon the Maybach fast.

She'd always known what to do. Ten kilometres from her estate was a farm owned and run by a childhood friend and her husband.

She had to stay inside the house for nine months. It nearly drove her mad, but there were plenty of books. It was easier for Stefan, once the Gestapo searches had swept over and past the farm. In the confusion of the collapse of the One Thousand Year Reich, the presence of one little boy, more or less, passed the notice of anyone in the countryside. The fact is, no-one cared any more, and Stefan, who was not naturally a country boy, seldom strayed further than the farmyard.

They celebrated Christmas 1944 together. Tilli took Stefan to the edge of the farm, among birch-trees glistening their branches in the wind, on Christmas Eve, to listen for Santa Claus' reindeer as they rode through the sky. Their sledge was made of clouds, she told him. He thought she was quite crazy but he didn't have the heart to tell her that.

Spring came, and they looked at the buds stubbornly pushing their way out of what had looked like dead twigs.

Tilli heard the news first, on the wireless. There had been an unconditional surrender.

She was relieved. She wondered what to do next. She wondered if Stefan was ready to be told the truth. She wondered whether to leave Germany, or stay.

THE END

AUTHOR'S NOTE

Max Hoffmann has nothing to do with his First World War namesake; but he is loosely based on Arthur Nebe (1894 - ?1945).

Nebe was an early member of the Nazi Party and a member of the SS. He was a career policeman who rose to be head of the Criminal Investigation Department; and he was active in the Resistance against Hitler from 1934. On the run after the failure of the Stauffenberg Plot in 1944, he was arrested in January 1945 and hanged in March, after two months of torture and interrogation. It is a mystery why he did not leave Germany for Sweden or Switzerland, though the fact that was married with a daughter may have played a role. Some sources maintain that he escaped execution, and there have been reports of sightings of him in, among other places, Dublin and Milan, in the 1950s and early 1960s. A not necessarily reliable biography by his friend Hans Bernd Gisevius, *WO IST NEBE?* was published by Fackel in 1966. It has not, to my knowledge, been translated into English.

In my handling of historical background in this novel, some events, notably the 20 July bombing described in the Prologue, have been either simplified or streamlined without detriment to the essential truth of what is being described.

ABOUT THE AUTHOR

Anton Gill was born and brought up in London but spent some of his early life in his father's home town of Bamberg, Germany. He was educated at Chigwell School and Clare College, Cambridge, where he read English, and later worked for the English Stage Company at the Royal Court, the Arts Council, the BBC and TV-am before becoming a full-time writer in 1984.

Since then he has published over thirty books, mainly in the field of contemporary history, including the award-winning *THE JOURNEY BACK FROM HELL*, a study of the lives of survivors of the Nazi concentration camps; *A DANCE BETWEEN FLAMES*, telling the story of Berlin, 1919-1939; and *AN HONOURABLE DEFEAT*, which discusses the Resistance within Germany to Hitler, 1933-1944.

He is also the author of a series of thrillers set in Ancient Egypt, which have been published in a dozen languages since their original appearance, and which have been re-issued by Felony and Mayhem in the USA.

More recent work includes two thrillers for Penguin, *THE SACRED SCROLL* and *CITY OF GOLD*, and a horror story set in Nero's Rome, *THE ACCURSED*, for Piatkus. For more information, see: www.antongill.com

15800490R00220

Printed in Great Britain
by Amazon